when
you were
mine

BOOKS BY KATE HEWITT

A Mother's Goodbye
Secrets We Keep
Not My Daughter
No Time to Say Goodbye
A Hope for Emily
Into the Darkest Day

THE FAR HORIZONS TRILOGY
The Heart Goes On
Her Rebel Heart
This Fragile Heart

when you were mine

KATE HEWITT

Bookouture

Published by Bookouture in 2020

An imprint of Storyfire Ltd.
Carmelite House
50 Victoria Embankment
London EC4Y 0DZ

www.bookouture.com

ISBN: 978-1-83888-650-9
eBook ISBN: 978-1-83888-649-3

Dedicated to my sister Susie, who is a wonderful example and inspiration of motherhood, and also kindly answered many of my questions about foster care. Thank you! Love you, Suse!

PROLOGUE

"All rise."

As the judge comes into the courtroom—a rather grand name for a space the size of a classroom, fitted out with Formica tables and plastic chairs—my palms dampen. My heart races. For a second, I see stars and I think I might pass out. Finally this day is here, and I have no idea how to feel about it.

The judge, a woman with hair the color of steel and an expression to match, surveys the room, her gaze resting briefly and impassively on me, before she refers to her notes.

"This is the first hearing to review current custody arrangements for Dylan McBride." The words fall into the stillness, and then she clears her throat as she looks down at the case file with all its notes and documentations, accusations and commendations, blame and praise.

I take a deep breath and glance at Lisa, the court-appointed lawyer standing next to me, a woman I've only met twice. So much hangs on her, on this moment, and of course on me. *Me.* I can't pretend this isn't all about me, and whether I am good enough. Strong enough. Mother enough.

I feel someone else's eyes on me, a steady gaze I never expected, and I turn. And then we begin.

CHAPTER ONE

BETH

I'm about to lose my son over a pack of Twizzlers. Of course, that's not the whole story. It can't be. But in the moment when Susan, a kindly-looking woman I've learned not to trust, took Dylan away as he kicked and screamed for me, that's how it felt. A lousy pack of Twizzlers.

But this is how it really happened—I was in the system, and once you're in the system, with calls logged and visits made, with notes in the margins about how messy your house is or how tired you look, you're screwed. That's the unfortunate truth.

So when Dylan lost it in the middle of a CVS because I wouldn't buy him a second pack of Twizzlers, and a woman in the next aisle poked her head around all suspiciously, eyes narrowed as she watched Dylan throw himself onto the floor and start banging his head against it—I realized this was going to be bad.

I've tried not to take Dylan out very much, for exactly this reason. We make do with the places he knows and loves—the park, the library, Whole Foods when it's not busy. When he does melt down, and that happens fairly often, I try to get him out of the situation as quickly and safely as possible. I try, and sometimes I fail, and the guilt I feel is the worst part of it all. No one feels as bad about losing my temper as I do.

So that's what happened in CVS. I told Dylan he couldn't have the Twizzlers because I'd come out with a five-dollar bill and

I'd already spent it. We'd been having a tough morning already, because Dylan woke up at three and didn't go back to sleep till seven, and the only reason I was at CVS at all was because I needed tampons.

So there I was—tired, crampy, emotional, and wishing Dylan hadn't seen the Twizzlers. He doesn't even eat them, he just likes to play with them like they're pipe cleaners or bendy straws, and he makes some pretty awesome creations out of them.

But today I didn't have the money for two packs, and after promising him we could get them later—a concept that, at only just seven years old, he doesn't fully appreciate—I lost my cool when he started screaming—a high-pitched, single-note shriek that I know people think is weird, and makes me feel anxious—that people are staring, that he won't stop, that I can't control this situation.

I shouldn't have lost my temper. I *know* that. Of course I know that. But I did, just a little bit—even though all I did was shout his name, and grab his arm to pull him up from the floor, and then, before I knew it, there was a woman calling the hotline for DCF. That's Connecticut's Department of Children and Families, if you don't know. I do.

Of course, nothing happens the minute someone makes that call. It took the store manager getting involved, and then the police had to come, and we ended up being taken by police car to the station on Raymond Road, with a paunchy officer telling everyone to calm down, although the only one who was upset was Dylan, and he wasn't listening to the policeman's advice.

I had my arm around my son, and he was both punching me and burrowing into me at the same time, and I stayed silent because I know by now saying anything in this type of situation is not a good idea. I just wanted to sit through the inevitable questions and comments, give the right answers and then go home, with DCF off my back, because that's what happened before.

But this time it didn't.

It didn't because I was already on DCF's radar, which I know sounds suspect. Even the most laid-back liberal person starts to look a little prim when they hear that DCF is involved. Their eyes narrow and their mouths purse and they say, *well, what really happened?* in a tone that suggests anything you say won't be reason enough for someone's child to be taken away, because only monsters have that happen to them.

So here it is: the first time DCF was called, it was by Dylan's father, Marco. Dylan was two years old and he'd started to demonstrate symptoms—of what, we didn't know and still don't. Back then he was too young for most diagnoses—autism, ADHD, the nebulous PDD, or pervasive development disorder, when they can't decide what's wrong. The pediatrician, when I took Dylan at eighteen months old, told us to wait and see, and I was happy to do that, relieved to kick that particular can further down the road. But Marco had had enough of the sleepless nights, the tantrums that started for no good reason and sometimes didn't end for hours, the terror of many household things that led to the aforementioned shrieking, the constant clinging to me—and one night, in boozed-up desperation, he called DCF and said he wanted to commit "voluntary relinquishment." He'd looked it up on the internet; it's basically where you give up your own child.

Fortunately, because I certainly didn't want to give him up, and in any case, thankfully, it doesn't actually work like that, no one took Dylan away. Still, DCF had a duty to get involved, and so we received a couple of visits. Our home, a shabby little duplex in Elmwood, was inspected, and we were referred to a pediatric psychiatrist all the way in Middletown, because none of the ones near us in West Hartford who accepted HUSKY—Connecticut's Medicaid program for children—had room on their waiting lists.

I went to that first appointment, even though I was dreading it. Dylan didn't do well on the bus—Marco said he had to take

the car to work, even though he'd known about the appointment—and then the hour-long wait, even with all the toys
and books available, strung us both out even more until Dylan
was clinging to me like a monkey and burying his head in my
shoulder. By the time we arrived in the examining room, he was
about two minutes away from a meltdown.

And that's just what he did, flinging himself on the floor while
the psychiatrist, a stern-looking woman with permed hair and
deep frown lines, looked on and wrote notes; the scratch of her
pen made my own anxiety skyrocket. What was she writing—
about what a terrible mother I was?

"I don't think this is going to work," I said, as I both tried to
catch Dylan's arms to keep him from hurting himself and sound
reasonable.

"This isn't about Dylan being on his best behavior," she told
me in a teacherish voice. She leaned forward, her expression
intent as she spoke calmly. "Dylan, I see that you're upset and
tired. Maybe you're frightened because of this new situation. But
you cannot kick and hurt people, even when you feel that way."

Dylan didn't listen to a word she said, not that he would have
understood, at just two and a half years old. It was undoubtedly
all straight out of a parenting manual, or Psychology 101, and
basically useless when it comes to the actual moment, such as
it was.

I didn't go back. DCF called and asked why I'd missed the next
appointment, and then they visited us at home, and fortunately
Dylan was having a good day, so they finally left us alone. For
a while.

The second and last time we came onto DCF's radar was
when Dylan was five. By that time we were completely off the
grid when it came to parenting—the playgroups, the story times,
the Mommy and Me sessions that most parents seemed to go to,
their worlds revolving around each other and their kids—cut-up

carrot sticks, picnics in the park, wine o'clock for the mommies. I saw it from a distance, but we passed it all by, existing in our solitary bubble, because that was what worked.

I'd stopped with the yearly well checks at the pediatrician's too, because they were too difficult, and Dylan had managed only two mornings of preschool, with me sitting next to him the whole time, talking to him quietly, before I realized that wasn't going to work, either.

Marco had left us when Dylan was three, making do with sporadic visits that tapered off to basically nothing within a year, and Dylan and I didn't go out at all, except for the library and the park, the occasional necessary shopping, and basically it sometimes felt as if, to the rest of the world, we had simply ceased to exist.

Which was why it was a surprise when DCF called eighteen months ago, because I hadn't registered Dylan for kindergarten. Those two mornings at preschool had left enough of a footprint for them to check up on us, presumably since we were already written up in their notes somewhere.

I was annoyed, and afraid, and frankly totally fed up. I mean, you read about these cases of kids being killed by their parents, locked in cupboards or chained to a table, covered in cigarette burns and bruises, and somehow DCF leaves *them* alone but comes after me, when anyone can see I am trying my best. They come after me, and instead of actually *helping* me, they just pretend to, tsk-tsking under their breath while they smile and ask their questions.

That was the first time I met Susan and her kindly smile. She came to my door and she looked so compassionate and I felt so alone in that moment that I let my guard down. She made me a cup of tea while I sat at my kitchen table and sobbed. I hadn't meant to; I hadn't even realized I needed to. I thought, for the most part, that I was fine. Dylan and I both were.

But she asked me how I was doing in a way that made me think she cared about my answer, and then she murmured soothing things about how hard it had to be, and somehow it all came spilling out. Marco leaving. Trying to work from home because childcare simply wasn't an option. Dylan's needs—mainly his need for me, the way he always clung, the way he worried about everything, the fears he had that knit us together as if we were fused at the bone. And while I couldn't have imagined it any other way and I'm not even sure I would have even *wanted* it any other way, sometimes, only once in a while, it felt too hard.

"It just never ends," I remember saying, trying to hiccup back my sobs. "There's never any *break*."

Susan asked gentle questions about support, and I had to confess I didn't have any. My mother lives in New Hampshire with her second husband, who runs some kind of organic farm shop, and has no time for me, never mind Dylan. My father still lives in the house I grew up in, in Bloomfield, but isn't interested and never will be. Friends? I lost them a long time ago, what ones I had. Work colleagues? I make cheap jewelry and sell it on Shopify, squeezing in my hours when Dylan is occupied or asleep. I don't have any work colleagues.

"What about neighbors?" Susan asked with her oh-so-sympathetic smile. I live in a duplex that has been divided into three apartments; Dylan and I are on the ground floor. I told Susan about Angela, the well-meaning elderly lady upstairs who has Alzheimer's. She's invited us in once or twice over the years, but her apartment is full of fussy little knickknacks and I don't want Dylan to break anything by accident.

My neighbor on the top floor is a man who drinks a lot of beer, judging from the recycling bin full of cans on our shared drive, and plays a lot of violent video games, judging from the noise that filters down through the ceiling. I don't know what else he does, if anything.

So, I explained to Susan, there was basically no one, and I know most everyone has trouble understanding that, how absolutely alone you can be when there are people all around you, when most normal people have parents and siblings, relatives and friends, a whole spiderweb of support that has been completely and utterly beyond me. But really that's how it was, how it's always been, at least since I was eighteen. No one.

So Susan comforted me and then she told me she thought I needed some support, and she suggested a group that met at the community center in Elmwood, for parents and caregivers of autistic children. Except Dylan wasn't autistic; I knew he wasn't. I'd looked up the symptoms and they definitely weren't his. He made eye contact; he didn't have "sensory sensitivity"; he didn't engage in soothing, repetitive activity, unless I counted building with Lego or doing jigsaws. Although he was often silent, it wasn't from lack of ability. He could speak, but he chose not to.

Still, I knew, to the average observer, he could *seem* autistic, just because he was different, and shy, and a bit high-strung. I was sure Susan meant well, even if she didn't understand us at all.

I couldn't take Dylan to a support group, not even one with people who would be understanding, with lots of soft toys and a soothing atmosphere and all the rest of it. Dylan gets nervous in crowds; he sticks to me like glue at the best of times, even when we're alone. We only go to the park or library when they're virtually empty, which means showing up right at opening or right before closing.

Neither could I go to a support group without him, because nobody has taken care of him besides me since Marco left. Marco stopped visiting years ago, even though he also lives in Bloomfield, the next town over. Susan asked about that arrangement too, and I told her that Marco wasn't involved beyond visits once or twice a year, although he did put some money in my bank account once in a while.

So, for the last four years it has been Dylan and me for every single minute of every single day—and mostly, that's fine. I like his company. He likes mine. Most of the time, we're very happy together. I love my son, and I've figured out a routine that works for us both. Mostly.

So when Susan gave all her well-meaning and totally improbable suggestions, I just smiled and murmured something vaguely affirmative, all the while knowing she wasn't going to be able to help me at all.

And she didn't. She just put us back on the hamster wheel of appointments with therapists and psychologists that were impossible to get to. I tried once, at least. I took Dylan to the pediatrician for a well visit, since he hadn't been since he was two. He was seen by a junior associate who had never met him before, which could have been horrendous but actually wasn't.

The doctor was young and friendly, and fortunately seemed unfazed by Dylan's behavior—sitting on my lap the whole time, not saying a word, and burrowing his head in my chest whenever the doctor tried to talk to him.

But, amazingly, Dylan still passed all the usual checks—his hearing and eyesight were perfect, he could point to an object or arrange things in order, and in the end the doctor said he didn't see any cause for concern regarding developmental delay—code word for autism—and he sent us on our way with some ridiculous but well-meant advice on children developing at different rates in terms of social behavior.

It was enough, thank goodness, for Susan to leave us alone, saying she'd check up on us in six months.

Sure enough, she came back six months later, when Dylan had just turned six.

I hadn't taken him to any other appointments, of course, which she already knew, and she walked around the apartment and made little notes and ticks on her clipboard which made me want to scream. What did she see? What was so *wrong*?

"You share a bedroom?" she asked in a neutral tone that didn't feel neutral at all.

"There's only one bedroom in the apartment." I didn't think it was as weird as it might have seemed—the only way Dylan went to sleep is if I was lying next to him. So yes, we slept in the same bed. It's easier. And anyway, what about all those people in the Middle Ages who slept, like, six to a bed? That wasn't weird, was it?

Susan came into the kitchen, which was messy, I knew. I usually saved doing the dishes till the end of the day, when Dylan was asleep. I cringed at the way she looked at everything—the dirty dishes piled in the sink, the spilled cereal on the table. All of it made me feel so *guilty*, but surely I wasn't the only mom in the world whose kitchen wasn't sparkling?

"How is your work going?" she asked in a kindly voice, and I said it was fine, even though it was hard to find the time to make beaded bangles and whatnot when Dylan so often needed my attention.

"And you're homeschooling Dylan?" she continued in that same neutral tone as she came back into the living room, which was also messy. Dylan had got a puzzle out and was putting it together by himself, which I hoped counted for something. He loved puzzles, and fortunately I could usually pick them up for cheap at tag sales.

"Yes, I am." Which I thought she must already know, because I'd filed an intent to homeschool with the education authority right after her last visit. Not that I actually *was* homeschooling. Dylan was only six and I figured puzzles and books were enough to occupy him at that age. He knew some letters, and he could write his name. I read him stories and sometimes we colored pictures together. What more did a little boy need?

Susan nodded slowly. She talked a bit about the missed appointments, and encouraged me to go to that support group, and then she smiled at Dylan and said that, despite some challenges, he seemed happy. And then, thank goodness, she left.

That was a year ago. And now I'm sitting in a stale-smelling little room at the police station, the kind of room reserved for suspected criminals, with Dylan asleep on my lap because this whole situation has completely exhausted him. At least he's not screaming anymore. I've seen the side-eye the desk sergeant gave me, that silent, judgmental look which I have become so used to. Usually I get it when Dylan melts down in public, and people assume I'm some lame, lax parent who has no sense of discipline, but getting it from a police officer in the station feels a whole lot worse.

He gave me a look like he thought I beat my child, or neglected him in some awful way, when nothing could be further from the truth. My entire life revolves around Dylan. Whether that's a good or bad thing might be up for debate, but the truth is I'd do anything for my son, and I've sacrificed my whole life for his happiness—gladly.

Because, actually, I wasn't always like this. A lifetime ago—well, about ten years—I was your normal teenaged girl, from a middle-class family—well, almost—planning to go to Connecticut State, working weekends at the Gap in West Farms Mall, being all cute and chirpy as I folded sweaters. I was a quiet girl, not as shy as Dylan, but definitely not the life of any party, but I had a few friends, and a family, and life felt normal.

How I got from that to this is another story, a pointless one since it happened and some of it was my fault and there is nothing I can do about it now.

Now I just want to get through this and go home with Dylan. I want to curl up on the sofa with him, his head on my shoulder, my arm around him, and read *Dinosaurs Before Dark* to him three times in a row. And the longer I wait here, the more I'm afraid that isn't going to happen, at least not anytime soon.

I've been waiting in the room for about half an hour when Susan comes in, with her kindly smile and a cup of tea for me. She even remembers how I like it, milky and sweet. I tense automatically, because this all feels just a little too sympathetic, like she's bringing bad news.

"So, Beth," she says, and her voice is full of compassionate sorrow.

Oh, no.

I don't reply, because I feel like anything I say could and would be used against me, but as it turns out, I don't need to reply, because Susan just shakes her head and says, "As I'm sure you realize, this isn't working."

And I don't ask what she means, because of course I know it already. She means me. Me and Dylan. *We're* not working, and for the first time, it seems like DCF is going to actually *do* something, and I can't stand the thought, even as I feel a treacherous little flicker of relief. *Finally, finally someone is going to help me.*

Little did I know.

CHAPTER TWO

ALLY

Three weeks after we finish our training to become foster parents, the checks and references finally complete, we get our first call.

I am standing at the kitchen island, gazing out at the backyard, which is full of burgeoning autumn color—russets and scarlets and gold. It is a beautiful, crisp fall day in mid-October, the kind of day where the air looks crystalline and feels drinkable. I spent the morning working from home, and then I had lunch with a friend, and in twenty minutes I am due to pick Josh up from cross-country practice. I'm feeling benevolent and contented, even though I am missing Emma, who started college in Boston just six weeks ago. Her absence continues to give me a certain, melancholy restlessness.

This is a similar feeling—in fact, I was standing in the exact same place—to when I first broached the idea of becoming foster parents to Nick, back in April. He was on the sofa, kicking back with a glass of wine, and Josh and Emma were upstairs in their rooms, working or socializing via their phones, probably both. They had the uncanny ability to simultaneously write an essay and take a Snapchat selfie approximately every three seconds. It boggled my mind, but I couldn't complain, because they were both straight-A students and Emma had just been accepted to Harvard, something that Nick and I were absolutely thrilled about but felt we had to downplay. You can't go running around to your neighbors boasting about your kid being accepted to the best college in the country, at least not in West Hartford, where everyone is politely cutthroat about college admissions. We'd been saying she was going to Boston for college instead, but weighing the word *Boston* with a mysteriously significant emphasis. Sometimes people asked, sometimes they just looked a bit miffed, because they already knew.

Perhaps it was because I knew Emma would be leaving soon, and at sixteen Josh didn't seem to need us at all, except to drive him places, that I thought of fostering in the first place. I'd seen a documentary on my laptop, a few minutes of a clip on Facebook about the foster care crisis in America, and I listened to how there are almost half a million children in care in the United States, many of them waiting for placements or adoption.

It was the kind of thing that was meant to tug at your heartstrings, with traumatized, teary-eyed children looking straight at the camera, and it worked. I looked around our house, with the gleaming granite kitchen we'd renovated and expanded a couple of years ago, a pottery jug of tulips unfurling their blossoms in the middle of the island, the photos on the walls of our happy family hiking in the Berkshires, taking the inevitable trip to Orlando, in front of the Eiffel Tower, the Grand Canyon, and of course the ubiquitous portrait of us all in white T-shirts and jeans, goofing around self-consciously for the camera.

We were so lucky. *Hashtag blessed*, and I didn't even mean it ironically. I knew it, and I thanked something—God, maybe, or perhaps a more comfortably nebulous idea of fate—for how much we had. Wasn't it time to pay it forward? Wouldn't that be a good use of my extra time, now that Emma was leaving home, and I was only working twenty hours a week?

I was only forty-six, young for an almost empty-nester, at least in this part of Connecticut. Most of my friends with children Emma's age were well into their fifties. I *felt* young, and Emma's leaving felt like a new chapter not just for her, but for all of us. I wanted to do something different and meaningful with my life.

So I broached the idea to Nick, who looked startled and a bit nonplussed, which was understandable since I'd never once mentioned it before in our twenty-two years of marriage.

"*Foster*? But we're finally getting our lives back." He spoke jokingly, but I knew he was serious, at least somewhat.

"We've had our lives back for years," I returned lightly. "It's not as if Josh and Emma are toddlers." They'd not been needing us since they were thirteen, more or less, except as a taxi service and a listening ear for the occasional emotional outburst from Emma.

"Yeah, but… with Emma gone, and Josh sixteen… we could go away on our own." He waggled his eyebrows enticingly. "A romantic weekend in New York…"

"I can't really see us leaving Josh at home." I trusted him, but not quite that much. "And the placements don't last forever."

"I don't know, Ally…" Nick's gaze flickered towards the television, which he'd muted when I first spoke.

"All I'm asking is that you think about it, Nick. We have so much, and there are kids out there who are in desperate situations." My throat closed a little at the memory of some of the harrowing stories I'd seen on that clip. Kids who had nothing but Twinkies for breakfast or wore clothes three sizes too small, never mind the truly horrific cases of abuse that I couldn't bear to think about.

"Yes, but…" He paused, his wine glass halfway to his lips. "They're all really difficult, aren't they?"

I drew back a little at that; I didn't think he meant to sound so selfish. "You'd be difficult too if you'd grown up the way those kids did." Admittedly, it might have seemed as if I'd positioned myself as an expert after watching something on Facebook for five minutes, but actually I'd done some more research than that. The ad had led me to the website for Connecticut's Department of

Children and Families, and I'd read numerous articles on fostering, the training you did, the references you needed, how rewarding it all was. I didn't know much, not yet, but I knew *something*.

"I know, I know," Nick assured me. "That's what I'm saying. They all have issues. And I don't really think we're equipped to deal with that sort of thing."

"Equipped? How are we not equipped?" I looked pointedly around our spacious kitchen, the French windows we'd had put in a couple of years ago leading out to a cedarwood deck with a huge, gleaming grill. Our house wasn't enormous, but it worked, and I loved it for all it represented, all the memories it had promised and then contained.

A couple of years ago, Nick had floated the idea of moving to one of those big brick monstrosities on Mountain Road, but I couldn't stomach the idea. We'd bought our 1920s four-bedroom house off Farmington Avenue fifteen years ago, and then done it up slowly until we'd got it exactly the way we liked. We'd fallen in love with the street, which looked like something out of a Norman Rockwell painting or an episode of *Leave it to Beaver*—porches with window boxes and rocking chairs, kids riding bikes down the sidewalk or playing kick-the-can on summer nights as the fireflies come out like low-lying stars. It was exactly the sort of childhood I'd wanted for my kids, and we gave it to them. Why not offer it to someone else, even if just for a short time, if we could?

"We're plenty equipped," I said when Nick seemed as if he wasn't going to answer me. "We've raised two children successfully"—Emma's Harvard admission seemed to hover purposefully in the air—"and I work from home part-time. So do you, some of the time." Last year, he'd redone the bonus room over the garage as a home office, complete with skylight and Nespresso machine. "We could do this." But not if Nick wasn't as committed as I was, although I was sure he could be, given time and a little carefully applied pressure.

"Where did this even come from?" he asked. "Because this is the first I've ever heard about it. You're talking as if this is the tenth time we've had this discussion. What's going on, Ally?"

I ducked my head, a bit abashed, because it *was* out of the blue. Last week, I'd been talking about renting a house in Provence for the summer, after seeing a magazine spread of fields of lavender and sunflowers, the sea an azure sparkle in the distance.

I'm a bit like that—I get seized by an idea and then I can't help but run away with it, at least in my mind. Nick tethers me to earth, grounds me in reality. Sometimes it feels like a wet blanket, and other times it's a relief.

Yet right then, watching him sip his wine and glance at the baseball game on TV, just as he did every other night, thinking how *easy* our lives had become, it didn't feel like either. It felt like a disappointment. I wanted him to want it. I wanted his eyes to light up as he leaned forward, the Red Sox forgotten for a second, and say, *You know what, Al? That sounds like a wonderful idea. In fact, I've been thinking along the same lines...*

"I know we haven't discussed this before," I said. "But can't we think about it now? I want to do something more with my life. Something that matters." I heard the throb of feeling in my voice and it surprised me a little, because I hadn't realized just how much I felt that way. This might have started as an idea to run away with, but now it felt real.

"What?" The single word was gently scoffing. "You're, like, PTA queen. You volunteer for everything..."

"That's different." I had done my time on a variety of PTAs, from elementary school class parties and gift-wrap fundraisers, where you're fending off all the overeager parents, to the barren tundra of the middle and high school PTA, where no parent is interested in joining, and you have to do everything yourself. "I want to do something more," I told Nick. "Something that isn't just *ameliorating* our lives."

"Ameliorating?" He raised his eyebrows, giving me that lopsided, rakish grin I loved. "Now you're using fancy words."

I folded my arms and tried to give him a stern look, but I ended up laughing, as I always did, and Nick held up his hands in surrender.

"Fine, fine. I'll look into it. What should I watch? The Facebook ad that got you going?"

"*Nick.*" I shook my head, but I was still laughing. He knew me so well. "Look up some statistics on foster care in the US, or even just in Connecticut." After seeing the clip, I'd done that much, at least. I'd gone on several websites that had given faces and voices to those soulless stats—photos of children, interviews with them.

It had been both heart-breaking and horrible, to scroll through photos of these kids with their bite-sized captions—*There is nothing Jenny wants more than a family. Juan would do better in a home without any other children. Drew needs a patient family who can help guide his choices.*

It reminded me of when we'd been looking for a dog on the SPCA website—we never got one—only this was so much worse. These were people, *children*, and they wanted families. Safe homes where people loved them and tucked them in at night. Where they didn't need to cringe or cower or feel afraid.

My heart ached for every single one of those kids, and I was sure if Nick went on that page, or any page like it, he'd feel the same.

"I know it's out of the blue," I said, "but give it a chance. Give a child a chance."

"I'll put that on a T-shirt, or maybe a mug." I knew Nick was making light of it on purpose, because it was his default setting when it came to talking about anything emotionally serious. It occurred to me for the first time then, although it should have earlier, that this might have been all a bit too close to home for Nick.

I didn't actually know that much about his upbringing, because he didn't like to talk about it, except in broad strokes, and even then with great reluctance. What I knew was that he'd grown up poor in upstate New York, and that his father had disappeared when he was still a child and his mother had, more or less, been a semi-functioning drunk.

I met her once, when we got engaged at the end of our last year at Cornell, two optimistic math majors who felt we had the whole world shimmering before us. We'd been dating for two years but I'd never met his family; he'd always shrugged them off, said I wouldn't want to meet them, and I hadn't minded much because we'd spent time with my family—my mom and dad and sister in New Jersey. I'd been quietly proud to return to my hometown as the new and improved version of myself—the math geek of Moorestown High coming back with a new haircut, a new style, and best of all, a new boyfriend.

When Nick had proposed to me in New York City, spring of our senior year, he decided it was time for me to meet his mom. That one visit had been deeply uncomfortable for both of us—a snapshot into Nick's childhood that made me pity him, and of course he hated that.

Nick's mother Arlene had been living in a squalid little apartment in Albany that reeked of cigarette smoke and despair. She'd had a smoker's voice, low and throaty, and the hacking cough to go along with it. She'd wished us well, but we might have been acquaintances whose names she'd forgotten for all the interest and care she'd shown. She'd kept the TV on the entire time we were there, on an ear-splitting episode of *Cops*.

Afterwards, we drove back to Ithaca in near-silence, Nick's hands clenched on the wheel, his expression grim. I hadn't known what to say, so I said nothing, and after an hour or two, he simply stated, "I had to do that. We won't see her again."

"Ever?" I couldn't help but be startled, despite how difficult the visit had been. "Nick, she's your mother—"

"No," he said flatly. "She isn't. Hasn't been for a long time." I knew he'd been living with his best friend Steve and his family since he was sixteen; Steve was the best man at our wedding. But I didn't know what had precipitated that move, and I never asked. And we never saw Arlene again. She called around the time of our wedding, tearful and tipsy, and I sent her a Christmas card every year out of duty, without telling Nick. She died of lung cancer when Emma was six months old, and in the years since then Nick has never talked about her willingly.

There, standing in our lovely kitchen, watching Nick making light of something so serious, I wondered if he was doing it because the whole concept of foster care reminded him of his own troubled childhood.

I knew I wouldn't ask, at least not right then. Every marriage has a few no-go areas, and Nick's upbringing was definitely one of ours. We talked about it so rarely, and it felt so impossibly distant, that I often forgot about it all and just thought of him as the man he was now, confident, genial, successful.

"Please do look it up," I said, and he dropped the light tone to give me a warm, serious look.

"I will."

And he did. The next afternoon, he came down from his office over the garage—as a financial analyst for one of the large insurance companies in Hartford, he was able to work from home once or twice a week—while I was just finishing my own work as part-time bookkeeper for a couple of local independent boutiques. His expression was so serious and troubled, I thought something terrible must have happened.

"What—"

"I'll do it," he said, and I blinked, not knowing what he was talking about.

"Do what?"

"The foster care thing. I'll do it." He shook his head, as if that were an end to the subject. "We have to go on some course?"

"Yes, for ten weeks. Three hours on Wednesday evenings." I said it like a warning, because I knew it was a big time commitment for him, with his often demanding hours of work, and I was hesitant to get carried away. His about-face was so sudden, I wasn't sure I should believe it yet.

"Okay," Nick said, and I goggled a bit, not expecting this immediate capitulation, and yet cautiously delighted by it.

"Are you sure? Because last night—"

"I'll do it, Ally. I said I'll do it." There was a slight rise to his voice that signaled irritation, and he raked a hand through his hair, agitated. I wanted to press him, or maybe comfort him, but I didn't do either. "I'll do it," he said again, and then he went back up to his office, leaving me staring.

We should have talked about it more, of course, worked through the reasons why we had decided to go ahead with not just the training, but the fostering itself, but in the moment it felt like enough that we'd both said yes. Besides, the state of Connecticut was desperate for foster carers.

We started the course in the middle of June, a group of nine of us in a stale-smelling room at the community center in Elmwood, listening night after night, week after week, to a comfortable but straight-talking social worker, Monica, telling us how unbearably tough it was all going to be. Every week, I wondered why she was trying to scare us off so much; by the end of the course there were only five of us left. Nick and I didn't talk much about what we learned in those three hours; afterwards we sometimes went out for a drink, both of us a little shell-shocked by some of the case studies we'd been told, sipping our Pinot Grigio with vacant looks, occasionally offering a vague comment about something Monica had said.

"Do *all* foster kids have issues around food?"

"You can't even give them time-outs…"

Once, I broached the subject of Nick's childhood. "Do you think all of this affects you more," I asked cautiously, "because of your childhood?"

He'd given me a look of blank incomprehension. "My childhood?"

"I just mean… you know… because it was so tough."

Nick drew back as if I'd said something offensive. Perhaps I had. "Ally, my childhood was nothing like what we've been hearing about. *Nothing.*" There was such a vehement note in his voice that I felt I had to drop it.

And now I'm here, standing in the same place as I was all those months ago, on the phone with Monica, who is telling me she has a placement for us. This is really happening.

"A boy, aged seven, who is from West Hartford, as well. I don't know much more about the situation, only that this is his first placement and that it's likely to be short-term with reunification with his mother the most likely and desired outcome, hopefully within months or even weeks."

"Okay…" My mind is spinning. Somehow, even after ten weeks of preparing for this moment, I don't feel ready. We are going to have a *child* in our home. A stranger. "When would this begin?"

"As soon as possible. I can drop him off this afternoon, ideally."

"This afternoon…" *So soon?* I swallow the words down, because they don't feel fair to say. But I have to pick Josh up in twenty minutes, and I haven't gone grocery shopping in several days, and the guest bedroom isn't actually made up for a child yet because none of it had ever felt truly real. Now it does.

"Is that a problem for you?" Monica speaks matter-of-factly, but I sense a faint coolness in her tone, as if she is expecting me to say it is, and I imagine how many times she's had to deal with disappointment and endless excuses. *Sorry, we're not in a good place right now… maybe next time… we're really more interested in children under the age of one, but not crack babies.*

I heard it all during the course, and I don't want to be one of *those* people, who only wants something easy.

"No, it's not a problem," I say, my voice just a tiny bit wooden. "Of course not." Yet I really should talk to Nick, and Josh too. He'd been nonplussed about the whole thing when we told him we were going on the course, but we get little more than grunts out of him these days, anyway, so I'm not sure what reaction was reasonable to expect.

"Perhaps you should talk to Nick?" Monica suggests patiently, echoing my thoughts. "We need both foster parents to be on board with a potential placement before we proceed."

"Oh, yes, of—of course."

"Why don't you call me back after you've spoken to him? Preferably in the next hour?"

"Yes, will do."

Monica ends the call, and I stare into space for a moment, my mind racing with things I need to do. Clean sheets on the guest bedroom. Empty the dresser drawers of Nick's summer clothes. Grocery shop, because I don't think I have anything in the fridge for dinner.

But first I call Nick, who is at the office today.

"Already?" He sounds as surprised as I was. "It's only been a couple of weeks…"

"I know, and I don't think it will be for that long. This is his first placement and Monica said it will be short-term."

Nick is silent, so I can hear him breathing over the phone. I wait, not sure what I want him to say. Now that the moment has arrived, I feel apprehensive. Unprepared.

"What do you think?" I ask, because I realize I want him to make the decision.

Another beat passes before Nick replies. "I say we do it," he states firmly. "This is what we did the course for, isn't it? So we could actually *be* foster parents. There's no real reason to turn down our very first placement."

"No, there isn't," I agree. Some part of me still feels reluctant, or maybe just nervous.

"So you'll call Monica back?"

"Yes, I guess so."

"I'll try to come home from work early."

"Josh needs to be picked up—"

"I'll do it."

Nick is springing into action, but I feel strangely numb. "Okay," I say. "Then I can whip around Whole Foods before Monica brings him here." I realize I don't even know this child's name. "We're doing this," I say, and Nick sounds almost cheerful as he answers.

"Yes, we are."

CHAPTER THREE

BETH

So they take Dylan away from me. Susan, with her sympathetic smile, gently suggests that I need a break, just as I said a year earlier. She makes it sound like she is giving me a Snickers or booking me a spa day, not taking away my only child.

I sit in that stuffy little room, with Dylan warm and heavy on my lap, and stare at her in disbelief.

"I never meant it like *that*." My voice is shaking.

Susan is placid, her hands folded on the table in front of her, her smile so very sympathetic, and yet I hear a matter-of-fact flintiness in her tone that fills me with a surreal terror. *This can't be happening. All I did was shout and grab his wrist. I love him!*

"I'm recommending this course of action for your benefit as much as Dylan's," Susan says. "You need support, Beth. Support you're not able to access while you remain Dylan's primary caregiver."

"I'm his *mother*." My voice trembles.

Susan nods in agreement, still unruffled. "We want you to be the best mother you can be to Dylan, and we also need to make sure Dylan is safe and well, with his needs attended to—"

"Of course he's safe and well!" He is asleep on my *lap*.

Susan cocks her head as she gives me one of her sorrowful smiles. "You know this isn't the first call to the Department of Children and Families that has been made on Dylan's behalf."

"Yes, the other one was made by Dylan's father," I practically spit. Indignation feels like a stronger response than cringing fear. "Against my wishes. He's not even in the picture anymore, as you already know, so—"

"And another by the elementary school, where Dylan should currently be attending."

"I'm allowed to homeschool."

"Yes, you are." Susan lets out a little sigh before resuming. "Over the course of my association with you and Dylan," she says, choosing each word with irritating care, "I've spoken to various people, and they have registered some concerns."

"People? What people?" This is the first I've heard of any such people and their *concerns*, and I quiver with anger and outrage—as well as fear. Who could possibly know about my life? Who is ratting on me? "My neighbors, I suppose," I state flatly, because who else could it be? It's not like I have friends.

"I'm not at liberty to disclose who has made the complaints, but I have heard about some incidents of shouting."

"I'm not allowed to shout?" I demand, although perhaps I should have denied the shouting altogether. It's not as if I shout that often, and every parent loses her temper once in a while. "You do realize one of my neighbors has Alzheimer's and the other one drinks his body weight in beer on a daily basis? These are your witnesses to my so-called shouting?" Each word quivers with emotion, but at least I got it all out with some semblance of calm.

"We're building a whole picture here, Beth," Susan says in a soothing voice I decide I hate. She holds her hands palm-up as if I'm aggressive and need to be placated. She's also using her "patient" voice, and saying my name too much. I'm sure someone teaches all that as part of how to be a social worker, and I loathe every bit of it. "A whole picture of you and Dylan, and your life together. And I'm afraid that the picture I'm seeing raises some definite concerns about his well-being."

I thrust my chin out, determined to be defiant, even though I know that attitude doesn't work. It will only hurt me, make Susan judge me even more, tick some box on her form. *Mother displayed worrying signs of aggression.* "Like what?"

"Like the fact that you have not taken Dylan to any of his medical appointments or psychological assessments in the last eighteen months."

"I took him to the pediatrician, and *he* said he was fine."

"Yes, that was one opinion."

"And that's not enough? How many doctors do I have to take him to before you're satisfied?"

Susan ignores my question. "It has become clear to me," she says in that same, calm voice, "after speaking with both you and Dylan, and observing your life together, that you love each other very much."

"Yet you want to take him away from me." I speak bitterly, trying to keep the tears from springing to my eyes. I don't want to cry. I can't be that weak. My arms tighten around my son.

Susan's expression remains blandly sympathetic as she continues, "Over time, it has also become apparent that Dylan does not have any peers, or friends, or any social interaction outside of the home. He doesn't speak or interact with anyone but you. That's not healthy, Beth. It's not good for Dylan's social or intellectual development, and, as I'm sure you realize, it will become even more detrimental to his development as he matures."

I am silent, because I know it's true, but what am I supposed to do? And what is so important about *peers,* anyway? As for friends, I don't have any, either, and I'm fine. I don't say any of that, though, because I know it would somehow all count against me.

I also know that my life—Dylan's life—isn't normal. I'm not so far down the wretched rabbit hole of my reality that I don't realize that, that I don't think it every single day—while I'm crouching next to Dylan in the supermarket, praying he'll get up off the floor. When I'm in the library, reading the same book to him, twenty times in a row while the librarian looks on, bemused. When I lie in bed at night, almost afraid to breathe, because I might wake him up.

Most people don't live like this, and there's a reason why. It's hard. It's lonely. Sometimes it's boring, and when it's not, it's worse. But it *works*. What we have works. And I know Susan will never understand or accept that. There's no point in me even trying to explain it, because if I can't tick the boxes on whatever sheet she has, I'm a problem that has to be solved, and the only solution she sees is taking Dylan away from me. But she *can't*. I can't let her.

"Beth, I want you to try not to see me as the enemy," Susan says gently. "I know it's hard, but please, please try to understand that what I am recommending now is not just for Dylan's benefit, but for yours. I want you to be the best mother you can be to Dylan, and I want the two of you to thrive as a family. I am getting involved in a more direct way to help you achieve those goals."

I don't reply, because I am trying not to cry, and the truth is, some desperate part of me *wants* to believe her. If someone can help me, *really* help me, give Dylan and me a chance at a more normal, integrated life, then I want that. Who wouldn't?

Yet not like this. Never like this.

"Beth." Susan reaches over and puts her hand on mine. It is warm and soft, like a grandmother's hand, not that I'd even know. My grandparents died before I was born. But it's a human touch and even though my instinct had been to pull away, I realize I appreciate it, especially as I suspect it's against all those safeguarding rules. "Let me help you," Susan says and I stare at her, my eyes swimming with tears, my boy's head resting against my shoulder. He's still asleep; he must have been really exhausted, or maybe this situation is so overwhelming for him that his body has simply turned off, shut down. I wrap my arms around him, savoring his warmth, the slightly salty boy smell that is so familiar to me. How on earth could I ever let him go?

"He's never been without me," I say, my voice wobbling all over the place. "How could living with strangers help him? He won't be able to stand it." Just saying the words out loud makes my stomach hollow out. Dylan can't deal with strangers. He's still terrified of our mailman, and he's been coming to our apartment every day for four years. Dylan has never been a *single day* without me. He can't start now. I won't let them take him.

"You'd be surprised," Susan says gently, "how children adjust."

But Dylan won't adjust. He never adjusts to anything, which is why our life is the way it is. He views just about everything as a threat or a danger. He's scared of the slide, of hardback books, of broccoli and clothing tags. Each one, unless avoided or carefully managed, can send him spinning into a terrified tantrum.

But I know Susan won't believe me if I try to make her understand, just as I know, with a sickening lurch of realization, I have no real choice in this matter, the most important one in my life. That's been clear from the beginning of this conversation, no matter how Susan tries to couch it in language about supporting me. She's already decided, and there is nothing I can do.

"Why aren't you out catching all the child killers?" I demand in a shaky voice as I yank my hand from under hers. "Or dealing with the pimps and the child prostitutes on the Berlin Turnpike? Aren't they more pressing cases than my son?"

Susan says nothing, but something flickers across her face that makes me think she's heard this a thousand times before. I know I said as much myself, a year ago, but I mean it so much more now, when my life is about to be ripped open, torn apart. *Why me, and not them?*

"Well?" My voices rises querulously. "Why aren't you?"

"The Department of Children and Families deals with many different cases," Susan answers in a quiet, steady voice that suggests she has said this exact phrase many times before. "Some are more severe than others. No one is comparing you to anyone else, Beth. No one is saying you are a bad mother."

"Oh, right. Because good mothers get their kids taken away from them." I let out a huff of laughter that sounds too much like a sob. I know I am close to breaking down, and I really don't want to do that. I want to be strong, for my son.

"Let us work *with* you," Susan persists. "Together we can build a care plan for Dylan that you're happy with, working to ensure that he is back with you as soon as possible."

I shake my head slowly, but already I feel myself weakening. It's so hard to fight when it's only me, and what's the point of fighting, anyway? They'll take him away no matter how much I resist. They have that power.

And more than any of that, deep down I know I need help, no matter how scared I am to accept it. I know I can't go on like this, day after day, year after year, exhausted and overwhelmed and alone. All along I've known that, even as I've done my best not to think about it, even as I hope that somehow, miraculously, things will get better on their own.

But I'm afraid if I let Susan take Dylan away from me, things will change forever. I'll never get him back, or, if I do, he'll hate me. He'll resent me for having given him up. And what if I have DCF breathing down my neck for the rest of my life because of this one slip? Once in the system…

"I'm scared," I whisper, hating that I can't keep myself from saying it.

"I know." Susan nods in sympathy. "You feel powerless. I understand that, Beth, I really do. But you will continue to be involved in Dylan's life, and all the decisions regarding his care. You can see the house where he is placed, and meet his foster carers. You can be involved in every step of the way."

I nod, gulping back tears, trying to hold it together. Am I actually thinking of agreeing to this? What choice do I have? Against me, Dylan lets out a breathy sigh and nestles closer. I feel a physical pain, a tearing in my chest. Am I having a heart attack? I try not to gasp out loud.

"You can do this whether I agree or not," I manage to get out. "Can't you?"

Susan pauses before she replies. "I have made arrangements for an emergency hold," she admits finally. "It lasts for ninety-six hours. After that, we'd have to go to court, unless you agree to a voluntary placement for Dylan, which is what I think would be best in this situation."

And which was exactly what Marco wanted to do, all those years ago. Just give our son away like a raffle prize. But how can I do it now? It feels like such a betrayal of Dylan.

"We want to help you, Beth," Susan says yet again. "Truly, we do. And you have time to think. I can come to your home tomorrow, and go over everything with you."

Tomorrow, when Dylan might be gone. I sniff loudly, trying not to cry.

"Why don't I drive you back to your apartment," Susan suggests. "You can pack a bag for Dylan and explain to him what is going to happen. There will be some paperwork to sign, and then we can take him together to his placement. It's already been arranged. There's a very nice family waiting and ready to take care of him."

It's already been arranged. A sound escapes me, a sort of tortured gasp. My vision blurs and I don't know whether it's from the tears filming my eyes or the shock that this is happening. And, in the midst of it all, I feel myself nodding.

Susan sets everything in motion with quick assurance; she takes me home in her car, with Dylan buckled in a booster seat next to me. He's woken up and he is alert now, his eyes wide with alarm, the only thing keeping him from melting down my hand in his, my thumb stroking his palm the way I know he likes. I can't imagine telling him, telling him very soon, that he is going to leave me. That I will be abandoning him. How can I possibly explain any of this?

Back in my apartment, it feels like a lifetime has passed, and yet everything is still the same. Dylan's cereal bowl, the milk chocolate-colored, is still on the kitchen table. A half-completed puzzle litters the living-room floor. Our bed is unmade, the duvet rumpled, the sheets creased. I'm conscious of the mess, yet I realize it doesn't matter anymore. The worst has already happened. I hardly need to impress Susan with my housekeeping skills now.

Numbly, my mind a blur, I go into the bedroom and start to pack a bag for Dylan. He stands next to me, watching as I take his small *Cars* backpack from the closet. It's the only thing I have, and it strikes me as somehow both pathetic and absurd, that I don't own a single suitcase. Not even a duffel bag.

I bought this bag for preschool, when I had hopes that he might actually attend. We picked it out together, at the CVS where we just were this morning. He kept stroking it like a dog, cradling it like a baby. He was in love with that little backpack.

We've used it since—not for preschool, but for picnics in the park, or to hold the bag of stale bread we sometimes feed the ducks. For library books or a spare change of clothes when we go to the sprinkler park in the summer. Now I'm packing his things in it, so he can be taken away. I can't bear it, and still I start packing, reaching for a pair of his socks, Dylan so silent and trusting next to me. He has no idea what is happening.

It only takes me about five seconds to realize his little *Cars* backpack is not going to be big enough for his clothes, his favorite rabbit toy, never mind the storybooks that he loves to have read to him every night. Will these anonymous foster carers read him stories? Will they know which ones he likes? How will they cope with his screaming, his fears? They won't even know what scares him. What if they're impatient, indifferent, or worse? What if they're cruel?

As I stand there with the backpack dangling from my fingers, a single pair of his underpants chucked into the bottom, Dylan tugs on my sleeve. His wide eyes ask a silent question. *What are you doing?*

I take a breath, and then the impossibility of it all slams into my chest. I *can't* let him leave. He will never understand. And wherever he goes, the people there won't know that he's afraid of crowds, or open doors, or grapes. I mean, what kid is afraid of *grapes?* They'll never understand that, and yet I do.

Dylan tugs on my sleeve again and shakes his head, which just about shatters my already cracked-open heart. I can't do this to him. I *can't.*

And yet I have to. From my living room, Susan clears her throat, a purposeful sound.

I need to get a move on.

How?

I can't bear to look Dylan in the eye as I find another backpack, this one a plain navy canvas one I used to use back in high school. I pack his clothes in that one, and a few of his books, toys, and the worn, lop-eared rabbit he sleeps with in the other. All the while, Dylan watches and shakes his head, faster and faster, as he realizes what is happening. He must be starting to feel dizzy.

Dylan is what is known as selectively mute, and has been since he was about three. At least, that's what I diagnosed from what I'd read on the internet. He can talk, but he rarely does. A word here or there, given like a gift—*duck* when we're at the pond, *Mama* when he's falling asleep. Each one is unbearably precious.

I've learned to get by with his hand gestures and head movements, the occasional word. As much as I'd love him for him to speak, I've chosen not to let it bother me. Still, I know most people would find it odd, and even now, when he must know something is seriously wrong, he doesn't speak.

It's as I'm putting his bunny in the backpack, that Dylan breaks. He lets out that single, ongoing high-note shriek that people find so disconcerting.

I turn to him, forcing myself to look into his face even though it hurts—his eyes are wide and panicked. "Dylan..."

He shakes his head and keeps shrieking as he grabs the ear of his bunny.

"Dylan, don't, you'll rip it—"

Too late, the bunny's right ear tears off, and several wads of cotton stuffing fall to the ground gently, like snow. Dylan stops shrieking for a single second as he stares at the terrible destruction we've both caused and then he flings himself on the floor.

When Susan comes in, he is banging his head against the floor and we are right back where we were this morning in CVS, and I struggle not to sob out loud.

"Dylan." I kneel down next to him, knowing not to touch him when he's like this because he hates that. I have to wait till he's calmed down, and then he wants the best and biggest cuddle in the world, but will he this time? When will I hug him again, and be able never to let go?

I push the thoughts away as I try to take control of the situation. I won't grab his arm, either, the way I did this morning. I'm going to show Susan what a gentle, caring, consistent parent I really am.

Except I can't, because Dylan won't stop and this is all so awful, and I can't help but feel he's right to cry. I want to cry.

In fact, I *am* crying, tears streaming down my face, my voice too garbled now to get the words out that might comfort him, and of course my reaction just makes everything worse.

"I think," Susan says in a quiet, firm voice, "it might be better if I take Dylan to his placement now."

"What?" I stare at her blearily, my face covered in snot and tears, strange hiccuppy sounds coming from me. "*No.* I need to explain first."

"I think it's too late for that, Beth. Sometimes a quick, clean break is easier."

A quick, clean break? She's talking about my *child.* "No," I say again, but I can barely get the word out because I am crying so hard, and I realize then Susan might be right. I'm no help to Dylan when I'm like this, and I'm too far gone to pull myself together.

Besides, I'm not sure I even want to see where he's going just yet. Not when I'm like this, so raw and broken and obviously deficient. I don't want to see the bigger house, the better people he'll be with. Or, if it's not like that, if it's something else, something worse—I can't bear to see that, either. Not yet.

"Take him," I manage to choke out. I am gasping and sobbing, my arms wrapped around my waist as if I have to hold myself together. "Just take him."

Susan moves with such brisk efficiency, I know she's done this many, many times before. She speaks in a low, firm voice, telling Dylan exactly what she's doing, as she scoops him up in a secure hold so he can't kick or hit her.

"The backpacks," she instructs me, and numbly, still crying, I pick them up. I take the rabbit Dylan has hurled onto the floor and try to put its ear back together, but it's useless. I stuff some of the wadding back in and then I put it on top of the other stuff in the *Cars* backpack before zipping it up. I can't believe I'm doing this. I am now complicit.

I am still weeping as I follow Susan and Dylan out to the car. Susan is speaking to Dylan the whole time, heedless of his shrieks, telling him what she is doing as she opens the back door and buckles him into the booster seat. And, amazingly, as she puts him in the car, Dylan suddenly stops fighting.

I watch in shock as he goes limp and his expression turns vacant, all the fight drained out of him, his body seeming soft and boneless. And although I know it must be easier for Susan, it feels worse than if he kept fighting. He's either given up or he's in shock.

"Dylan…" I croak, but my little boy doesn't even look at me. "Dylan," I say again, my voice breaking now, and Susan gives me a reproving look. I'm not helping, but I don't care. "Dylan."

She closes the door before I can reach him, and I end up banging my fists against the window, hard enough to hurt. I *want* them to hurt.

"*Dylan!*" I scream his name this time, a roar that tears at my throat. It feels primal, a maternal instinct that is absolutely necessary in this moment.

Susan gives me a quelling look, worse than the one before. "Beth, stop, please. I know you're upset, but this isn't helping."

She's opened the door on the driver's side. She's going to leave.

I pound the window again. "Dylan!"

Finally Dylan turns to look at me. His face is pale and ghost-like from behind the window; the glass is smeared from my hands. His expression is blank, as if he can't even see me, as if he's gone somewhere else in his head because this reality is too much for him to deal with.

"I'll be in touch soon, I promise," Susan says. "We'll talk, and I'll explain everything that is going on."

I drop my bruised and stinging hands and step back, utterly defeated, as Susan closes the car door and starts the engine. My gaze stays locked with my son's as she pulls away from the curb and drives away, taking my very life with her.

CHAPTER FOUR

ALLY

Every sense is on high alert as I stand by the front door, waiting, too jumped up to do something useful like start dinner or tidy up. Since I returned Monica's call an hour and a half ago, I've been flying around like a demented bird, first cleaning the guest room, then putting fresh sheets on the bed and emptying the drawers. Why didn't we have the room ready?

It's a very nice room—spacious, with a closet and a view of the backyard and trees and houses beyond—but as I got everything ready I couldn't help but think it looked a little bland, even sterile, like a room in the Holiday Inn. I could have bought some toys or books or stuffed animals to make it more age-appropriate, but as we had no idea what age or gender children we might eventually be getting, it seemed like a potential waste. Still, some homey touch would have been nice. Anything.

After I cleaned the room, I dashed out to Whole Foods, throwing things in my shopping cart with wild abandon—ready-made meals and organic yogurt and bags of carrot sticks and bunches of grapes. I threw in some pediatric natural medicine too—Rescue Remedy and some essential oils and some homeopathic stuff I would normally never even look at.

It was only as I was paying for it all that I remembered I might not even be able to give it to him, not without the parent's permission.

Him. I don't even know his name. All I know is he's seven years old, and he's just been removed from his mother—why? I have no idea.

All these thoughts are flashing through my mind as I stand by the door, waiting for this anonymous little boy to show up.

Nick texted to say he'd be late, stuck in traffic on the south side of town with Josh, after picking him up from practice. I'm doing this first bit on my own, and I feel both excited and terrified, everything I learned in that ten-week course seeming to fall right out of my head. I thought I'd been paying attention, but right now I can't remember a single relevant detail.

A few tense and endless minutes later, a beat-up Ford Focus cruises slowly down the street before pulling into our driveway. Monica is driving and there is a woman I don't recognize in the passenger seat, a fiftyish grandmotherly type with a neat bob and a kind, tired face. I can't see anyone in the back, but he—this little boy—must be seated there.

I catch my breath audibly, unsure if I should open the door now or if that would be too exuberant, too much. I want to be natural and friendly, but both feel beyond me right now; I feel like a robot, awkward and mechanical.

Taking another deep breath, I open the door and smile. Monica is already getting out of the car.

"Ally," she calls. "Hi. Thanks for being able to do this on such short notice."

"Of course, it's no problem."

Monica nods to the other woman who is now opening the back door of the car. "This is Susan, Dylan's caseworker."

"Nice to meet you."

She flashes me a quick, weary smile before she reaches into the car, presumably to unbuckle Dylan from his car seat. *Dylan.* I wait for him to appear, having no idea what to expect.

Monica opens the other back door and takes out two battered-looking backpacks. Is that all he has? I keep my expression friendly and interested, trying not to show what I think of his lack of possessions. I remember how, in the course, Monica said foster kids often come to a placement with a few clothes held in a trash bag, sometimes nothing at all.

"These are his things," she says now, and I take the backpacks.

Susan has helped Dylan out of the car, and she leads him by the hand towards me.

The first thing I think is how small he is—such a slight boy, with a mop of dark hair that hangs in front of his eyes. His head is lowered so I can't see his face, and he is walking so close to Susan he's in danger of tripping her up. He's wearing a dirty T-shirt and a pair of cargo shorts that are ripped. Again, indignation burns through me at the sight of those raggedy clothes, a self-righteous fire I do my best to dampen. Now is not the time for those kinds of thoughts. I know that much.

"Hey, Dylan." Thankfully, my voice comes out friendly and normal, pitched right, without that manic, patronizing cheerfulness that is so easy to adopt with children you don't know. "I'm Ally. I'm so pleased to meet you."

No response, but I wasn't really expecting one.

I open the screen door to the house; it's still warm for October, and Nick hasn't changed the screens to storms yet.

Monica flashes me a reassuring smile as she and Susan, still holding Dylan by the hand, walk inside.

Back when we were approved for foster care, we had our home assessed and approved, and yet I feel nervous now, as if something must be out of line, and Monica or Susan will point their finger to the crystal vase on the living room mantelpiece, or the PlayStation in the family room, and say *Sorry, that's against regulations.*

They don't, though. Of course they don't. Monica murmurs something about what a nice home it is, and I lead them back into the kitchen, with its two steps down to the big family room that we extended about ten years ago. It's all nice and neat, because I'd just tidied up, but I don't know whether it's actually welcoming. There are no toys.

"So, Dylan," Susan says. "This is where you're going to be staying for a little while."

Dylan doesn't respond; I'm not sure he can even take it in.

"Should I show him his bedroom?" I ask, and then feel guilty for talking about him like he's not there. Why does this feel so fraught?

"Maybe in a few minutes," Susan says. "Perhaps I'll show Dylan outside while Monica briefs you on the situation?" She gives Monica a significant look, and she nods.

"Oh, okay. Sure." I practically leap to the French windows. "I'll just unlock them," I mutter, fumbling with the key and finally opening the doors. I step aside as Susan takes Dylan out onto the deck. It's late afternoon, the sunlight like liquid gold, and the air still holds the warmth of a forgotten summer.

I watch them for a moment, noting how Susan keeps up a steady, cheerful patter while Dylan remains silent and unresisting, almost like a little zombie as they walk around our fenced-in yard, a few fallen leaves caught in the grass like discarded jewels—crimson, ochre, gold.

I turn to Monica. "Can I get you a coffee, or…?"

"I'm fine," she says easily. She gestures to the table by the windows. "Why don't we sit down and I can get you up to speed?"

"All right." I feel like a student about to take an exam. Why am I so nervous? I *wanted* to do this. "So, Dylan," I say. "He seems nice." I bite my lip at that inanity. "Quiet."

"Yes, he's what is known as selectively mute." I blink. "He can speak," Monica explains, "but he often chooses not to."

"I see."

"He was removed from his mother's care this afternoon, after an onlooker called DCF when she lost her temper with him in public."

Lost her temper? Is that code for being abusive? I nod, not sure what to say, trying to absorb it all.

"Dylan's mother, Beth, has been known to DCF for around five years. She's a single mom, and she genuinely loves her son, but obviously there are some concerns with his care that we are looking to address."

"What kind of concerns?"

"I'm afraid I don't know all the details, but Dylan has been very isolated. He hasn't been in school, hasn't attended any doctor or therapist appointments, doesn't have any friends or acquaintances."

I nod, swallow. "Okay."

"The goal here is for him to be able to attend school, attend those necessary appointments, and hopefully get a diagnosis for his behavior—besides the mutism, he has some issues with anxiety. There might be some further concerns, but there's been no medical confirmation yet. We're also hoping that Beth will be able to receive the support she needs. Susan is hoping that this will be a case of voluntary placement, which means the courts won't have to be involved initially, and reunification can happen as soon as it is deemed appropriate, ideally within three months."

Three months. That suddenly seems like a long time.

I nod again. "That all sounds…" I don't manage to finish that sentence.

"We don't know how Dylan will react to this placement," Monica tells me matter-of-factly, "as he's never been away from his mother, but Susan is keen to discover how he behaves when he's not in her presence."

What does *that* mean?

I just nod. Again.

Monica continues in the same brisk, businesslike tone. "So the first thing we want to do is let Dylan settle in with you here, and then you can register him for school, ideally by next week. Susan will give you a list of the appointments made for him when they come through—they should hopefully all be local to the Hartford area. If you have any concerns or questions, any at all, you can call me on my cell or, if you can't get hold of me, call DCF's direct line. Does that all sound good?"

Monica is already rising from her chair, and I can't believe this is it. She's going to leave me with the complete care of a strange child after about five minutes of debriefing? It feels wrong; it feels *criminal*. I don't know what I expected, but surely more than this. Surely there are forms to sign, phone numbers to be given. Shouldn't I have a file of information on Dylan or something, rather than just be told things so casually?

"Yes, thanks," I say, rising too, because what else can I say? "That all sounds good."

The next few moments seem to pass in a blur. Susan comes in with Dylan, who still hasn't spoken or even lifted his head. Monica stands by the front door while Susan explains to Dylan that she's going to leave, but she'll see him in a few days, and his mother will visit then, too. She tells him that I'm really nice and I'm going to take good care of him, and if he's worried about anything, he can always tell me to call her, and she'll talk to him or come visit.

Dylan doesn't say a word to any of this; he doesn't react at all. I wonder if he's in shock, or if he really is that shy. I can't imagine how utterly overwhelming this must be for him, especially if it really is true that he's never been away from his mother. *Beth.*

And then they're gone, with cheery waves and kind smiles, the front door clicking firmly behind them. I am alone with Dylan. I realize I don't even know his last name. Surely, surely there should have been some sort of paperwork to fill out. I feel like

I should have signed a paper, a contract, or that Susan or Monica should have given me a folder of information, *anything*. There's so much I don't know. Does Dylan have allergies? What kind of food does he like? If he's selectively mute, how am I supposed to communicate with him?

He stands in the middle of the kitchen, his head lowered, his shoulders hunched, unable to look me in the eye. As I stare at him, my eyes suddenly fill with tears, because I can't even imagine what he must be feeling, how frightened he must be. He's only seven, and he's just been left—practically *dumped*—with a strange woman in a strange house. I mean, what the *hell*? I feel outraged on his behalf, even though I know I can't blame Susan or Monica or anyone at the Department of Children and Families. They're doing the best they can, with the incredibly stretched and limited resources they have. They wouldn't have left him here if they had any other choice, or if they didn't trust me.

I remind myself that I have training, that I have references, that I can do this. I tell myself that I may be a stranger to this little boy, but I'm kind and I wish him nothing but good. I take a deep breath and begin.

"Hey, Dylan, I know this must seem strange, but I'm sure things will feel normal soon." My tone is friendly, but the words still sound stilted. "How about a snack? Do you like grapes?"

He looks up then, if only a little, his bangs sliding into his eyes, as he gives his head an infinitesimal shake. No grapes, then.

"Okay. How about an apple? Or a banana?" A pause as he considers, still not making eye contact, everything about his posture wary and defensive—shoulders hunched, head lowered, as if he is trying to make himself as small as he can. Invisible, even. Then he gives a tiny nod, and I nearly sag with relief.

"Great."

I spend an inordinate amount of time slicing an apple and banana into appealing, evenly sized pieces. All the while, I chat away, or try to, telling Dylan about Nick and Josh coming home soon, and how I can show him his bedroom, and how we have some games and puzzles he might like. I can dig some out of the attic, and I will definitely be going on Amazon tonight and buying some suitable toys and books.

Throughout all of this, Dylan doesn't say a single word, and I still haven't actually seen his face. His gaze has remained firmly fixed on the floor, his hair hiding his expression.

I bring the bowl of fruit to the table and tell him cheerfully to hop up on a chair. He comes, slowly, carefully, sitting gingerly on the edge of the chair as if he doesn't trust it to hold him.

I stand back, feeling a weirdly euphoric sense of success—he is eating healthy food in my house!—and then I hear the front door open.

"Hello?" Nick calls, and he has a cheerful teacher's voice, a little too loud, like he's just walked on stage in a sitcom.

"We're back here, in the kitchen." I mimic that slightly manic tone, even though I don't mean to. "Come and meet Dylan."

Nick comes into the kitchen, Josh sloping in behind him, looking unenthused and a bit suspicious, his backpack half-falling off one shoulder.

"Hey, guys, this is Dylan," I practically chirp. "And Dylan, this is my husband Nick, and my son Josh. He's a bit bigger than you. Say hi, guys." I really need to stop sounding like a demented playgroup leader.

"Hey, Dylan," Nick says with an easy smile, sounding more relaxed than I do now. "Great to meet you, buddy."

When Nick puts on the charm, he dazzles. It was what drew me to him all those years ago back at Cornell—that effortless, easy way of talking to people, so different from my own shy, stilted attempts at the time—but even so, Dylan doesn't even look at him, and I can tell Nick is a little thrown, although he tries not to show it.

"Josh," I prompt with an expectant look, and he lifts one hand in a wave.

"Hey."

And then we all stand there, smiling like loons, having no idea what to do next.

Dylan picks up a slice of apple and nibbles it.

"How was practice, Josh?" I ask, striving for normalcy.

He shrugs. "It was okay. I finished a 10k in forty-four minutes."

"That's awesome."

He slides towards the doorway, tilting his head towards the stairs as he mouths "Can I go?"

I nod, grateful that he showed that much consideration. Josh is a nice kid, really; it's just he's in that grunting, monosyllabic teenaged-boy stage, or so my friends with older sons tell me. One of my best friends, Julie, who lives down the street and has two sons in their twenties, told me, with a cackle, that it only takes about ten years to grow out of.

"So, Dylan." Nick comes forward with a friendly smile that Dylan doesn't see because his head is still bowed over his bowl. "Do you like baseball? Or soccer? We could toss a ball in the backyard, if you like." Nick places a friendly hand on his shoulder, his smile still wide and easy.

What happens next shocks us both—Dylan goes rigid, his head jerking up, his face pale and terrified. And then he lets out a scream, an unholy shriek of a sound, one single, piercing note that goes on and on and makes me want to clap my hand over my ears as Nick and I stare at each other in horror.

CHAPTER FIVE

BETH

I don't know how long I stand on the sidewalk, staring after Susan's car. It left my street a long time ago, and yet I can't seem to move. My feet feel as if they are stuck in the concrete and tears are still trickling down my face. An old lady from across the street has come onto her stoop and is staring at me suspiciously, her hands planted on her bony hips.

I live on a street of modest duplexes just off Boulevard; some of them have been carved up into apartments, like mine, and others are owned by single families who take pride in their neat yards and full flower boxes. It's a bit of a tense mix, and I feel that now as my neighbor continues to stare. No doubt she witnessed the whole, terrible show of Dylan being taken to the car, me pounding on the window.

Dylan. Grief swamps me, and I couldn't care less about my nosy neighbor. I want my son back. I *need* my son back. I can't live like this, without him. I don't know how. I wrap my arms around my waist as I double over, choking sobs escaping me. Across the street, I hear the slam of a screen door, and I know the woman has gone back inside. I feel as if I could be sick.

Footsteps pound behind me and then come to a stop. Someone touches me gently on the shoulder. "Hey, are you okay?"

Slowly, I straighten to look into the face of a jogger, a trim man in his thirties decked out in Lycra. He frowns at me as he pulls his earbuds out. They dangle from where they are looped around his neck.

"Are you okay?" he asks again.

"Yes," I manage. The last thing I need is more people involved in this. "I just…" I can't think of any explanation, so I shake my head and turn back towards my front door.

The man watches me, still frowning, but as I head inside I hear him jog off. No one cares that much, really.

Inside, I walk around the apartment in a daze. My mind skitters like a pinball in a machine, going nowhere. I can't think; I can barely breathe. How am I going to survive this?

At some point, I stop wandering and start cleaning. It's the only thing I can think to do that is actually useful. My hands shake as I clear the breakfast dishes off the table and then wash them in the sink. Then I strip the sheets off the bed and bundle them into the washer in the kitchen, even though part of me resists even that. They needed a wash, but they'll smell of Tide, and not of Dylan.

When the apartment is clean, I go to my craft table in the corner of the living room, where I make jewelry. I have a couple of orders that need packaging and mailing, and so I work on those, and then I answer two emails inquiring about custom-made pieces. I'm no artistic genius; I twist wire and set small, semi-precious stones. I make necklaces, bracelets, earrings, and rings, but they're all pretty basic and I sell them for really cheap.

I had a dream once, of setting up a craft shop, a place where kids could come and make jewelry, where I'd have bins of colorful beads and flower murals on the wall, and maybe a funky little café in the back, selling coffee and cake. It would be a place for people to hang out and have fun, a creative safe space for the young and old together.

Of course, I never got anywhere with that dream, with everything that I've had to deal with. The closest I've come to it is this: my little page on Shopify, a card table in the corner of my living room and a jewelry-making craft kit that cost forty bucks on Amazon.

After I package up the orders, I decide to head to the UPS store on Boulevard. I can't believe how productive I'm being, but I know if I stop and think, I'll fall apart. It's only as I'm about to leave that I realize it's after six, and the store will be closed.

I stand at the door, my arms full of packages, and feel despair flood me. All the determined focus I'd dredged up over the last few hours drains away, and I am left with nothing. The whole evening stretches ahead of me, empty and endless. I don't think I've ever felt so alone, with nothing left to do to keep my grief at bay.

Normally I'd spend the evening with Dylan. We'd eat dinner together, and then I'd give him a bath, which he loves. I'd kneel by the tub and scoop up soapy water and pour it over his back while he played with his bath toys—a set of plastic farm animals I bought at the dollar store. I forgot to pack them in his backpack, and he plays with them every night. How will he manage without them? Should I call Susan? Am I even allowed? It hits me all over again that Dylan is gone, that I don't know where he is.

I won't give him a bath tonight. We won't curl up on the sofa and read stories until he is sleepy, and I won't sing lullabies as I lie next to him in bed until he finally drops off. None of that will happen now.

Without Dylan, my evening has no shape, no purpose. The hours feel like they're going to stretch on and on and I have no idea how to fill them. I feel like I can't.

Slowly, I walk back to the table and dump the packages on top of it. I'll have to mail them tomorrow, which already feels like a lifetime away.

In the ensuing emptiness, I can't keep from thinking about Dylan. Wondering how he is. It's been a couple of hours already, so he must be in the foster parents' house by now. What is it like?

Is he crying? Screaming? If he's melting down, how will they manage him? *Love him?*

I sink onto the sofa, my head in my hands. I can't bear to think of Dylan in some strange place, sad and scared, with only strangers to comfort him. I imagine two brisk, stern-looking parents who tell him to settle down or ignore him because they think he's just spoiled. How could Susan have taken him? How could she possibly think that kind of scenario is better than him being here with me?

A sob escapes me, like a hiccup. I can't do this. I can't do this for one night, never mind however long Susan thinks Dylan and I both need before we can be together. Before we can *thrive.* Who is she to decide what that even means?

I want to talk to someone, to tell them what has happened, but I don't know who that person would be. My mom? She's the most likely person, but her disinterest is always evident, audible in the tiny sighs she gives, her distracted tone of voice whenever I call her. She left my dad—left me—when I was seventeen, in my last semester of high school. If I felt like it, which I sometimes do, I could blame her for all my problems, or at least the start of them.

Her departure was so abrupt, so absolute, while she explained to me, somewhat tearfully but with a certain sense of purpose, that she needed to find her own happiness before looking to mine. She insisted that I'd be a better person for it, that no child thrived with a miserable mother. She was sure I would understand. I didn't.

I started to do badly in school, and then, the May before I graduated, I received a DUI while driving home from my job at The Gap. How *that* happened is another story, but it led to a whole lot of things that led to me meeting Marco, which of course led to Dylan.

So, really, my mom caused me to have Dylan, and so I don't want to blame her for anything.

But who else could I call? My dad will care even less than my mom; we haven't actually spoken in over a year. During my childhood, he was gruff but there, and after my mom left, our relationship fell apart completely. We never see each other now, and we rarely speak.

As for my friends from high school, or the ones I made while volunteering at the nursing home where I met Marco—the one hundred hours of community service I had to do as part of my sentencing—they have all long gone. I haven't been in touch with any of them for years.

It occurs to me I should call Marco, and let him know what has happened, but he won't care as much as I want him to—he never does—and I can't make that call now, when I am feeling so alone and broken.

So who? The answer, of course, is obvious. Nobody.

With no one to call, and nothing else to do, I warm up some soup because I can't be bothered to make anything else, and although my stomach feels empty, I'm not hungry. Still, I force it down, for form's sake, even though, of course, no one is watching. But already, in my head, I'm making a log of all the ways I can show Susan I'm a fit parent. A good mother. *See, Susan? I made myself some dinner.*

Later, I try to work on some jewelry, but my fingers fumble and I can't concentrate, so I end up watching trash TV for a couple of hours, trying to keep my mind blank, before stumbling to bed.

I know there are a lot of people who would think it is weird for me to sleep with my seven-year-old son, but without Dylan's warmth next to me the bed feels empty and cold.

Surprisingly, though, I sleep, deeply and dreamlessly, which is a blessed relief. When I wake up, I don't feel refreshed, but at least I feel clear-headed. Today is the first day of the rest of my life. A trite phrase, but I want to make things matter. I need to get started on getting Dylan back.

So I shower and dress, force myself to eat breakfast, and then, just after nine, I head out to the UPS store to mail my packages.

It's a beautiful autumn day, crisp and clear, everything in sharp focus, the leaves just starting to turn, as I walk to Boulevard with purposeful steps. The treacherous thought of how easy this is without Dylan slips into my mind, and I push it away. That feels like a such a betrayal of him, and even of who I am, that I won't let myself think it for one second.

The UPS store is little more than a cupboard, and as I step inside, it's empty, save for Mike, the guy who works behind the counter most days.

"Hey, Beth!" He grins at me, then does a comical double take when he sees that I am alone. "Where's my man Dylan?"

I swallow, try to smile. I hadn't anticipated this, although I suppose I should have. Mike is probably the person Dylan and I know best—Mike and also Sue, the main librarian in the children's department of the West Hartford Library, who is patient with him, and even makes sure she has books set aside that she knows he likes.

As for Mike—I've been coming to this store for nearly five years, always with Dylan, and Mike is almost always behind the desk. We've developed a rapport of sorts, little more than chitchat, but Dylan likes him, and Mike is unfazed by his silence and shyness, chatting to him easily even when Dylan is half-hiding behind me, saying nothing.

"He's…" I stop before I've even begun, because I don't want to tell Mike what has happened, and also because I might cry.

Mike's forehead crinkles with concern. "He isn't sick, is he?" he asks, his voice sharpening with alarm. My expression must be stricken. "He isn't hurt?"

"No. At least…" I don't think he is, but the truth is, I don't know. Did he sleep last night? Did he cry? Does he understand any part of this?

"Beth?" Mike looks really worried now. "What's happened?"

"He's been taken by DCF." I see his confusion and I clarify dully, "The Department of Children and Families. He's been put into foster care." It's both a relief and a torment to say this, because I don't want Mike to look at me the way the woman across the street did, the way the doctors always did when I went to those appointments, the way anyone does when you explain that DCF has involved themselves in your child's life. The judgment, so badly masked—the narrowed eyes, the slight lip curl, the prim straightening of the shoulders, all layered over with a cheap patina of sympathy.

But Mike doesn't look that way. He looks only concerned, and then I realize I am crying, tears trickling down my cheeks as I dump my packages on the counter so I can wipe my face.

"I'm sorry…" I choke out.

"You don't need to be sorry. What happened?"

"I lost my temper in CVS and someone called DCF. They said they were taking Dylan away from me."

"What!" Mike swells up with outrage, his chest puffing out. He's about my age, late twenties, with a round, homely face and a slightly chubby but still muscular build. I've always thought he's the sort of person who actually looks kind, and right now he is and I can't bear it. "Surely they can't do that—"

"They can. And, anyway, it's more complicated than it sounds." I don't want him thinking that this was a one-time thing, totally out of the blue, when it wasn't. Even if it felt completely unfair.

"Complicated? How?"

I look behind me, but no one is coming into the store.

Mike props his elbows on the counter. "You can tell me, Beth."

But I don't want to, because I don't want Mike to think badly of me. And yet it would be such a relief to talk to someone, to tell them what has happened. And so it all spills out, in fits and starts, a jumbled mess of fragmented stories—Marco calling DCF, the one trip to that psychiatrist, and then the whole thing about school, how the neighbors must have said stuff, and how Susan thinks she's trying to help.

"She took him yesterday afternoon. He was screaming, and then he just went so *still*…" I cover my mouth to keep the sobs in. I feel as if I could cry and cry and never stop, but I don't want to, and certainly not in the middle of the UPS store.

Mike shakes his head slowly. "This can't be right. I mean, you're a good mom, Beth. I see that every time you come in here with Dylan. He adores you, and you love him. You're a *great* mom."

Different tears prick my eyes, tears of gratitude. It feels so good to have him say this, to have him mean it, after everything that happened yesterday. Until Mike said it, I hadn't realized just how much I'd started to doubt myself. To feel like I really was the failure Susan made me feel.

"I want to get him back as soon as I can," I tell Mike. "I don't even know where he *is*."

"They shouldn't be able to do that." Mike shakes his head again, looking so wonderfully aggrieved on my behalf. "They really shouldn't. Have you talked to a lawyer?"

"No." I wouldn't even know where to begin with that.

"You should. I'm sure you must have that right, before they took him away. They can't just grab him like that. At least, I don't think they can."

"Susan—the case worker—said she'd gotten a court order, but it was only good for ninety-six hours."

"Then you can get him back after that?"

"I—I don't know. She was going to explain everything to me, but then she left so quickly."

"That can't be right, either."

"No, it can't." The realization burns through me and suddenly I am angry, and it feels *so* much better than reeling with devastation did. That *can't* be right. Susan had said there was paperwork to sign, but I didn't sign a single thing. Now that I am thinking about it properly, she didn't explain *anything* to me, not really. She just took my son. "I don't know what to do," I tell Mike, and I watch as he reaches for his phone and swipes the screen.

"Let me look it up. There's got to be some information online."

I wait anxiously, conscious he's on company time, and that if someone comes in, it could be awkward for him. I should have looked this stuff up last night, but I was so numb and blank inside, I couldn't think about anything. Now I can.

What we learn from a legal website is basically what Susan told me—that DCF is able to take Dylan for ninety-six hours without a court order, but after that, unless I agree to the voluntary placement she was suggesting, there has to be a court hearing, and I have to be given an attorney. It's both reassuring and terrifying. I don't want to go to court, but I also don't want to hand over my child like he's some spare change.

"I think you should go to court," Mike says as he slides his phone back in his pocket. "I can be a character witness, if needed. I'd be happy to."

"Thank you." I don't know if they call character witnesses for this type of hearing; I don't know anything at all. I'm scared to talk to a lawyer, to set this all in motion, but what is the alternative? I just roll over and do whatever Susan says, trust everything she tells me?

Another customer comes into the store, cutting short our conversation, and Mike processes my packages. I pay and then I leave, promising I'll update him on the situation as soon as I can.

There is a determined swing to my step as I head back home. I will google lawyers who deal with this type of situation, I think, only to realize that I can't afford a lawyer, *any* lawyer. I'll have to accept whoever DCF gives me. Fine, I think, then I'll do that. I'll call Susan and tell her I'm not just signing over my rights—my child—like she wants me to. What kind of mother does that, anyway?

But as I near my apartment building, I see that I don't need to call her at all, because she's standing in front of my door waiting for me.

"Beth," she says, smiling. "It's good to see you."

I can't exactly say the same, so I say nothing. I stop in front of her, my keys in my hand. "Why are you here?"

"I wanted to go through the paperwork with you that we weren't able to yesterday." She raises her eyebrows, no doubt sensing my hostility. "Is now a good time?"

Does she think I'd say it wasn't, that I needed to do my nails instead? I am so furious, it feels as if I am choking. Yesterday she manipulated me, played on my fears and insecurities. I can see that now, and it is not going to happen today.

"Yes," I say in a level voice as I unlock my door. "Now is a great time."

CHAPTER SIX

ALLY

The scream goes on and on, one piercing, single note, so it feels like a time warp, the same second played over and over again, a needle on a record player stuck in this one awful groove.

Nick is staring at me in shock and dismay, and I am staring back, and Dylan is *screaming*. His mouth is open like the Edvard Munch painting, a dark, yawning hollow in his pale face. And still it goes on, and I feel frozen and terrified and also weirdly out of control myself, even though I am standing still.

"Make him stop," Nick says, and I think how absurd and unfair that is, that this is somehow my responsibility, or even that I could actually accomplish that.

I have no idea what to do. But I try, for Dylan's sake rather than my husband's.

"Dylan." I extend my hand to touch his shoulder, and then think better of it, since that's what set him off in the first place. At least, I think that's what set him off. I actually have no clue. "Dylan," I say again, gentling my voice as much as I'm able, although I'm not sure he can even hear me. His face possesses a terrifying blankness, as if he's caught in some private nightmare. "It's okay, Dylan. No one is going to hurt you. You're safe here. I promise, you're safe. Look, here's another piece of apple." I hold out an apple slice rather desperately. This is all I've got, and if it doesn't work, I really don't know what I'll do.

The seconds pass, each one feeling like an eternity. Josh has come downstairs and lurks in the doorway with an uncertain scowl on his face. Nick is still frozen, as frozen as Dylan, who is *still* screaming.

And then he stops. It's like a tap being turned off, the flick of a switch. The room is plunged into silence, and I let out a shuddery sigh of relief. My whole body is tense and twitching, and there is cold sweat prickling in my armpits and between my shoulder blades.

Dylan takes the apple.

"That's it. There you go." I am laughing a little, nervously, as I swipe my hair away from my face and give Nick a look of both triumph and relief. I'm not actually sure *what* I feel, but I am very glad he has stopped screaming.

Nick takes a step back, his hands in his pockets. "Well," he begins, and then says nothing more. Josh heads back upstairs without having said a word. It feels as if we were all on the edge of an abyss, and we've just taken a teetering step back, but it still looms there, dark and deep and terrifying.

Dylan resumes eating his fruit, almost as if nothing has happened. His head is lowered again so I can't see his face. Nick looks a bit winded, and as he rakes his hand through his hair, he takes another step back, as if he needs to distance himself from Dylan.

I try for some normalcy. "I think I'll start making dinner. And then, Dylan, would you like to see your room?" No response, but I don't let that matter. "Okay, then," I say as if he has answered me.

"I've got a bit of work to do," Nick says with a half-hearted smile of apology. "I'll just head up to my office for a few minutes…" He's already edging towards the door, and I try not to feel annoyed. He's absenting himself *already*? Couldn't he sit down next to Dylan and make an effort?

But then I remember the screaming, and I decide maybe Nick should leave for a little bit, to give Dylan as calm and unstimulated an environment as possible, since it seems that's what he needs, although I really don't know what he needs, because nobody has told me.

Dylan sits docilely at the table while I start dinner. I decided to keep it simple tonight, just chicken strips—the expensive, free-range, organic kind—and chips, which I think most kids like. As I slice tomatoes for a salad, things almost feel normal. Dylan continues to eat his apple, and from Josh's bedroom upstairs, I can hear the low bass thump of his music.

Yet as normal as this seems from the outside, I don't feel normal. I feel tense and brittle, entirely on edge, and I desperately want a glass of wine, but it doesn't seem right to drink in front of Dylan. In fact, I can't remember the rules about alcohol while fostering— am I even allowed? Or is it just with children who come from a background of substance abuse where you're not meant to? In any case, I don't know if Dylan comes from that background or not, so I decide to leave the wine chilling in the fridge.

Perhaps I'll indulge in a glass later when he is asleep, although I can't even imagine that right now. First, we have to have dinner, and then, I suppose, he should have a bath, and some semblance of a bedtime routine—each one feels like a mountain to climb. This evening is going to be endless.

It's as I'm slicing bell peppers and feeling overwhelmed about bath time that it suddenly occurs to me how ridiculous I'm being. Dylan is a *child*. Yes, he's different, and he might have some emotional issues because of his background, but he's still a seven-year-old boy, and I had one of those once.

I brought up two healthy and well-adjusted children with appropriate boundaries and firm rules and lots of love. I can do this.

It's such a relief to realize that, that I almost sag with it. I almost laugh out loud. I can *do* this. Dylan isn't some alien or monster; he's a child. A little boy. I've been blowing everything way out of proportion, because it's all so unfamiliar.

I take a deep breath, nodding to myself as I finish the salad. I can do this.

Then I feel a little hand tugging on my sleeve, and I turn to see Dylan standing next to me, regarding me solemnly. It's the first time I've been able to look him full in the face, and he's beautiful. Huge dark eyes, like liquid chocolate, and a scattering of golden freckles across his nose. He has a bow mouth like a cherub. He looks so serious, and there is a question in his eyes, but I don't know what it is.

"Are you finished with your fruit, Dylan?" I glance at the empty bowl. "That's great. Maybe now you want to see your bedroom?"

He nods, and I realize that's why he must have come to tug on my sleeve. Again, I feel that sunburst of relief bloom inside me; I can do this. I'm already doing it.

I take Dylan's little hand; it is limp in mine, but he lets me hold it as we walk up the stairs. "This is Josh's room," I say, keeping up an instinctive steady patter, the way Susan did earlier, "and this is Emma's room. She's my daughter, Josh's sister. She's a big girl. Eighteen." I smile at him. "She's away at college—do you know about college? It's when you go away for school, when you're bigger. This is Nick's and my room," I continue, "and here is yours."

I push open the door. It still looks a bit sterile, the decor all in different shades of cream and beige, but at least it is welcoming. The double bed is piled high with throw pillows in various satins and silks, and the gauzy curtains are pulled back from the window to frame the view of the backyard, and the houses beyond, Avon Mountain visible in the distance, a dark, rugged fringe on the horizon.

"We could unpack your things now," I suggest, and Dylan hesitates before he nods. "Let me go get your stuff."

I run down stairs and a few seconds later return with the two backpacks.

Dylan holds his hand out and I give him the *Cars* one unthinkingly; it's almost as if we've figured out a new language, words formed in silence.

He unzips the backpack and takes out a worn, well-loved rabbit. One ear has been torn off and he fingers the gaping hole on top of the bunny's head with such a grief-stricken look on his face that my heart feels as if it is twisting and writhing inside me.

"Would you like me to fix that for you?" I ask. I can see the ear is still in the backpack, along with some cotton stuffing, and I can't bear to think too closely about why it's like that just now. Did he and his mother—this Beth—fight over the rabbit? Was he distraught when he was being removed from his home, or was she? Was she the one who put it in the backpack, in hopes that his foster mother—*me*—would sew it back on? "I could sew it," I suggest. "It would almost be as good as new."

Dylan stares at me gravely for a few seconds; I can tell he's deliberating my offer. Then, wordlessly as ever, he holds his rabbit out.

"Okay," I say. "I'll get my sewing kit."

I'm not the world's craftiest person by any means, but my parents made sure I could do the basic things in life—sew a button, change a tire. Now I sit at the kitchen table and sew as if my life depends on it. Dylan stands behind my shoulder and watches every painstaking stitch.

The last of the day's sunlight streams through the window, touching everything in gold. The kitchen is quiet, the only sound the snick of my needle and the soft draw of Dylan's breath. From the oven, I hear the chips sizzle. The moment is so peaceful, so poignant, I want to catch it in my hands, put it in a jar.

Instead, I keep sewing the rabbit's ear back onto its head, stitch after careful stitch, in and out of its worn softness while Dylan watches.

"There." I tie the seam off with a bulky knot, the best I can do. The ear flops forward a little, but at least it's attached. The rabbit is whole again.

I hand it to Dylan and he takes it silently, clutching it to its chest.

"What's your rabbit's name?" I ask, but I get no answer.

Still, I'm feeling fragilely optimistic as I get dinner on the table. Dylan stands by the big granite island and watches, and once again I keep up a cheerful patter. It feels easier now, almost natural.

"Do you like chips? What about ketchup? Emma loves chips, but hates ketchup. Josh has ketchup with everything, even peanut butter and jelly sandwiches." I make a face to show how disgusting I think that is, but Dylan's expression is opaque and unchanging. "To be fair," I allow, bringing the salad to the table, "he stopped dipping his PB and J's in ketchup a while back."

"Yeah, like when I was six." Josh stands in the kitchen doorway, looking more uncertain than I've ever seen him as he aims a smile in Dylan's direction. My heart expands with love.

"I think it was more like seven," I say. "Dylan's age!" I look between them both, but as some sort of bonding moment, it passes them right by. "Josh, can you get Dad from his office?"

By the time Nick arrives in the kitchen, we've all sat down and, as he joins us, I say grace. I always said grace as a child, and when the kids were little, we did every night, a family ritual, a cozy encircling of hands, a reminder of gratitude.

In the last five years or so, with kids coming in late from sports practice, our family life hectic and disparate, it has fallen by the wayside, except at Thanksgiving and Christmas. Yet for some reason tonight, with a child in the house again, I revert to it automatically.

"Thank you for the food we eat. Thank you for the friends we meet. Thank you for the birds that sing, thank you, God, for everything! Amen." I sound like a kindergarten Sunday School teacher.

Josh looks bored, Nick baffled.

"We haven't done that in a while," he says as helps himself to some chicken.

"Well, no reason not to," I say brightly. I'm heading into manic mode again, and I check myself. "Dylan, would you like some chicken? How about some chips?"

Wordlessly he takes a single chip from the bowl and puts it on his plate.

Dinner passes uneventfully enough, although Dylan doesn't eat very much and says even less. In fact, he says nothing, and as Josh helps me scrape plates into the garbage disposal, he asks in a loud whisper, "Does he even speak? Is he, like, mute?"

"Selectively mute," I say a bit stiffly, trying to keep my voice pitched low. "He can talk, but he chooses not to."

"Weird," Josh mutters as he shakes his head, and while I can't blame him for thinking that, I wish he hadn't said it out loud. Dylan might be selectively mute, but he's not selectively deaf. He can hear everything we say, and I have the distinct impression he is taking in every single word.

After dinner, Nick tries to slip back to work, but I won't let him.

"You don't really need to work now, surely," I insist. "Why don't you spend a few moments with Dylan? You could give him a bath."

"A bath?" Nick looks almost appalled by the suggestion, but then he quickly masks it with a smile. "I mean, yeah, sure. We're allowed…?"

"Of course we're allowed. He's only seven." But as I say the words, I realize I don't actually know. There were so many rules, and they are now all jumbled up in my head. Were we allowed to give foster kids baths, or was it just you couldn't give unrelated children baths together? "Anyway, I'm sure he'll enjoy it." Although who knows? Maybe Dylan has issues with baths or water or something. Maybe his mother tried to drown him, or left him in too long, or maybe she was obsessive about baths and washed him till his skin was chafed bright red. I have no idea.

"Dylan, would you like a bath?" I ask, and his whole face lights up. It's the first time I've seen him smile. He nods, and I glance pointedly at Nick.

"Great, buddy," Nick says, doing his best to sound jolly. "We've got an awesome tub. It even has jets. Come on up and see."

As Dylan follows Nick upstairs, I let out a pent-up breath I didn't even realize I was holding. My shoulders are knotted with tension and I feel exhausted just by routine living.

It almost feels like a luxury, to clean the kitchen by myself, the downstairs blissfully quiet as twilight descends softly outside, a violet blanket draped over the yards and houses, shadows pooling on the ground. From upstairs, I can hear Nick's voice and a few splashing sounds, and I'm relieved that it all seems to be going okay, despite that one awful episode earlier.

When the kitchen is clean, since Nick and Dylan still seem to be enjoying themselves, I pour myself a sneaky glass of wine and take it to my study, which is a boxy little room off the kitchen.

It occurred to me as we were eating that there had be tons of support for foster parents online. Monica gave us a printout of groups and websites at the end of our course, but I filed the paper away somewhere and didn't give it any more thought, because at that point it wasn't needed or relevant.

Now, however, I type *foster care support* in the search bar and breathe a sigh of relief as link after link comes up, websites and message boards and Facebook groups, all for people like me. I spend a few minutes clicking through, and find all sorts of advice. I even discover a thread about the whole bath issue, and discover that I was right—baths are allowed, just not with unrelated children.

More importantly, I discover how relatively relaxed it all seems. The system is overburdened, the caseworkers stretched to the max, and foster parents do what they have to do to get by, without informing anyone of anything that doesn't seem important. Maybe I don't have to tiptoe around so much, after all. The rules can be relaxed, if not actually broken.

I am still feeling relieved from this discovery, and mellow from the glass of wine, when my cell phone rings. It's Monica.

"Just checking that everything's going all right," she says after I answer. "Sorry we had to leave so abruptly—we had another situation. Anyway, how is Dylan?"

"He's great," I practically chirp. "Really great."

"That's wonderful," Monica says after what feels like a slightly startled pause. "Susan will be so pleased. She was worried, but she also wondered if he might do better away from his mother. Anyway. So there are no problems?"

I think of the screaming, but decide it's not worth mentioning. We got over it, after all. "No, no problems. Like you said, he's very quiet, but he's fine. We're figuring out what he needs, and he listens really well. We've had dinner and he's having a bath now and it's all good." I sound as if I am brimming with benevolence, and right now I feel as if I am. What on earth was I so scared about? This is easy. This is *fun*.

"That's terrific, Ally," Monica says. "That will be a big relief to Susan especially, and of course to Beth. I'll be in touch in a day or two about Beth's visit. Is that okay?"

"That's great." I couldn't sound more thrilled if I tried. I've got this.

After I finish the call, I drink the last of my wine, smiling to myself, imagining going upstairs and seeing Dylan all freshly washed and in his pajamas, smelling of baby shampoo and soap, ready for a bedtime story.

Then, as I take my wine glass to the sink, I hear that scream again.

CHAPTER SEVEN

BETH

As I lead Susan up to my apartment, my resolve hardens to steel. I am not going to give up my son without a fight. A big one.

Susan must sense what I'm feeling, because she looks friendly but cautious as she puts her bag down on a kitchen chair, and then pulls out another one to sit in. She gives a quick glance around the kitchen, and I'm pretty sure she's taking in how clean it is, but she doesn't comment on it.

I stand in the doorway, my arms folded, trying not to fidget.

"So, Beth," she says with one of her smiles, "how are you feeling today?"

"I'm feeling like I want my son back." I didn't mean to come out swinging quite so much, but I can't help it. Mike's words are ringing in my ears, and right now I can't believe I just *let* Susan take Dylan the way I did. I'm sure if I talked to a lawyer, he or she would tell me how I'd been coerced and manipulated. Something about what happened yesterday felt not just wrong, but illegal, and part of me wants Susan to know that I know that now, even as another part of me shies away from such a confrontation. It never goes well for someone in my situation. Susan can use anything and everything against me, when the time comes, and no matter how sympathetic she seems now, I'm sure she will.

"I want that too, Beth," she answers carefully, keeping her smile in place. "And that's why I'm here. To talk about how we can make that happen."

"And why do we have to do anything to make that happen?" I demand. I can't keep the aggression from my voice, or my fists from clenching. "I thought I was supposed to sign some paperwork yesterday. I didn't even see whatever order you were meant to have so you could take Dylan from me, and surely I should have. And now you're going to tell me what hoops I have to jump through just so I can get my own child back, when maybe you didn't have the right to take him in the first place?"

All the while I'm ranting, Susan gazes at me steadily, her hands folded on the table in front of her. She looks unfazed but still sympathetic, and I wonder if this is a look social workers have to learn to perfect, no matter what the situation.

"I can see you're frustrated, Beth, and I understand that."

"Frustrated?" I repeat incredulously. "I'm a lot more than frustrated, *Susan*. I'm angry. What happened yesterday was wrong."

"What happened yesterday was unfortunate," Susan corrects me carefully. "As I'm sure you remember, I had to leave abruptly, due to Dylan's extreme reaction, which is why I'm here today, so we can go over the paperwork you mentioned, as well as address any questions or concerns you might have. And I'm sure you're curious as to how Dylan is getting on."

I stare at her in disbelief, filled with sudden, vehement loathing for this woman who keeps pretending to be on my side. "*Curious?*"

She nods, a flicker of apology in her eyes. "I'm sorry. That was the wrong word. I'm sure you're very concerned about Dylan's well-being, and how he has adjusted to his placement."

Susan maintains eye contact, that calm, unflappable look still on her face despite her lapse, and suddenly I can't steam ahead anymore, buoyed by self-righteous rage. She's sympathetic, she's so very understanding, and yet, at the end of the day, she still wants my son to be with someone other than me, and she has the power to make sure that happens. Being angry about it accomplishes nothing.

I pull out a kitchen chair and sink into it. "How is he?"

"He's doing really well, Beth. Ally—that's one of his foster carers—was very encouraging and enthusiastic when Monica, her social worker, spoke to her last night. She said he'd settled in really well, had a bath and was ready for bed." She smiles at me as tears fill my eyes.

I know I should feel relieved, and I *am*, of course I am, but at the same time, I fight a sweeping sense of hurt, even grief. How could Dylan settle in with someone else so quickly? What if I really am that crap a mother, that the second he's with someone else he adjusts? Or what if Susan is lying? Or Monica, or Ally is? Maybe this Ally has him locked in a basement, chained to a chair. How the hell am I supposed to know?

I drag my hand across my damp eyes. "What now?" I ask in a clogged voice.

"Now I can explain to you what happens next." Susan speaks gently, but even so, I think I hear a thrum of satisfaction, maybe even triumph, in her voice, like an expensive engine purring in the background. She thinks she has me submissive and docile now, and maybe she does in this moment, but I'm not signing anything yet.

"So what happens, then?"

Susan settles more comfortably in her chair. "What we talked about yesterday is you agreeing to a voluntary placement for Dylan. What this means is that you would agree for DCF to have custody of Dylan and continue the placement with this family. You would still keep your parental rights, and you would be able to decide any important issues for him—about religion, or school, or medication, for example."

"But if I can decide all that, why does he have to be taken away from me?" I stare Susan full in the face for a moment and for the first time I see her look discomfited, a flicker of uncertainty in her eyes like a shadow. She masks it quickly, smiling again, shifting once more in her chair, but I wonder what she is thinking. What I am missing. I realize I need to always be on my guard. No matter how sympathetic Susan seems, I can't trust this woman. Ever.

"We talked yesterday about you getting the support you need," she says after a second's pause. "And Dylan as well. Both are paramount."

"What support do I need?" I am curious to hear the answer, even as I resent having to ask the question. Why should Susan decide what I need? I know what I need, and it's my child back.

"I'd like you to take part in the Positive Parenting Program, as a start."

I stare at her with blank suspicion. "The what?"

"It's a course for parents who are involved with DCF, although others can take part in it, too. I think it would assist you in developing some helpful strategies with Dylan, so you are able to parent him more effectively without getting burned out or frustrated."

So she does think I'm a crap mother. "Anything else?"

"I'd like to see you take advantage of some counseling," Susan suggests, her gaze steady on my face.

"Counseling?" I practically growl the word. "Why do I need counseling?"

"Just about everyone can benefit from some form of counseling, Beth, and I believe you've been dealing with a stressful situation for some time. Counseling could help you be a better mother. I've had some, you know. Many people have. There's no shame in it at all. It's just one more effective tool in dealing with a difficult situation."

I drop my head into my hands, because I'm not sure I can take any more. This conversation feels like a minefield. I need someone to interpret everything Susan says, and that reminds me of what Mike said.

I lift my head. "I want a lawyer."

Susan blinks once, before she nods, reluctant but acquiescing. "If you decide to contest the order of temporary custody, then the court will assign you an attorney for the preliminary hearing. But I am really hoping we can come to an agreement without all that." She leans forward, her eyes crinkled with compassion. "Beth, nothing has changed. I'm still on your side. We don't need to take this to court."

The thought of lawyers and courts frightens me, because it's so unknown. I picture a stony-faced judge and a tribe of suited lawyers, a courtroom full of rustling, whispering spectators. I don't know if it will be like that, I doubt it will, but the point is, I don't *know*. All I have to go on is *Judge Judy* and *Law & Order*.

"So, if I agree to this voluntary placement," I ask, "when would I get Dylan back?"

Susan pauses, seeming to choose her words with care. "Since this would be voluntary, you can have Dylan returned to you at any time—"

I lurch forward. "*What*?" After all the legal mumbo jumbo, I can't believe she just drops this bombshell on me. I can just say I want Dylan back, and then I have him? "Why didn't you tell me that before?"

"Unless," Susan continues intractably, her expression still so calm, "DCF determines that such a course of action would not be in Dylan's best interest, and takes legal action."

I flinch at that, although I try not to. "And would you?"

Susan purses her lips. "I cannot make that judgment at this time. But a voluntary placement is for a maximum of ninety days, and you would get a date for a court hearing after thirty days. It's my professional opinion that a minimum of six weeks' placement would be most beneficial for both you and Dylan." She draws a breath before continuing, "The important thing to remember, Beth, is that everyone wants him back with you as soon as possible. Everyone." Susan looks at me earnestly, and I think she believes she's telling the truth. I just don't know if she really is.

"So, if I sign this thing, Dylan has to be in placement for at least six weeks, or else you'll take legal action against me." I speak flatly. "Right?"

Another one of those tiny, telling pauses. "I think you need to give this course of action a chance. Yanking him in and out of care is certainly not in his best interest."

"I don't want to *yank* him anywhere. I want him to stay with me. If anyone's been yanking my son…" I pause, not wanting to be too aggressive, but the implication hangs there between us.

Susan doesn't reply, but I have all the answer I need. No one is going to just let me take my child back, now that they've got him. It's so unfair, I want to scream and rage, even as I struggle not to burst into tears. I'm so alone in this. I mean, who really is on my side—Mike from the UPS store? It's so ridiculous, it hurts.

"What would be best," Susan says, "is if we agreed on a length of time in the voluntary placement contract. Then we both know where we are."

A *contract*? It's the first I've heard of that. "So I do need a lawyer, then."

Susan lets out a little sigh. "If you'd like to use the services of a lawyer to negotiate the voluntary placement contract, then yes, but that will not be provided by DCF or the court. I can recommend a volunteer legal service, but they don't always have someone available immediately. And I want to reiterate, Beth, that I'm on your side, and I'm happy to explain everything to you, and make sure you understand it completely, before you even think about signing anything."

My head hurts and I press my hands against my temples. I can't take any more of this. I really can't. "I don't know," I half-mumble. "I don't *know*."

"This is hard," Susan murmurs, "I know it is."

But she doesn't really, not like I do. She might have had this conversation a thousand times before, but she's never been on this side of the table. I still can't believe *I'm* on this side of the table.

I want to go back twenty-four hours—*just twenty-four hours!*—and still be in that aisle at CVS. Dylan is melting down about Twizzlers, and this time I don't shout, I don't grab his wrist, and, best of all, there's no incontinent do-gooder calling the DCF hotline. *If only...*

But it's pointless to think like that. It just hurts, and I need to focus on the here and now. I can't waste time on regrets, not when so much is at stake.

"Perhaps it would help if I showed you a blank contract?" Susan suggests.

Without waiting for my answer, she takes a sheaf of papers from her bag. She lays them on the table and the small print swims before my eyes. I can barely make sense of even the simplest sentences. I'm too tired and overwhelmed, and I know I'll make a mistake somewhere in all this fine print. A costly mistake.

"I want a lawyer before I look at this," I say as I push the papers towards her. "I know you say you mean well, Susan, but I don't actually trust you, and I'm not ready to sign my child's life away without professional advice." I am proud of that reasoned speech, even though my voice trembles as I give it.

Susan stares at me for a moment, her expression opaque. Her smile has finally slipped and she just looks weary. The sunshine streaming through the windows highlights the gray in her neat bob, the lines scored deeply from nose to mouth. It occurs to me that she must have a very difficult job, but I can't afford to feel sympathy for her now.

"Very well," she says after a moment. "I'll give you the name of the legal service I mentioned before." She fishes in her bag before she finds a card and pushes it across to me.

"Thank you."

Susan puts the papers back in her bag. "I'll be in touch after you've been able to speak to a lawyer. Shall I call you tomorrow?"

I nod. Tomorrow it will be forty-eight hours since she took Dylan, and Susan has only ninety-six before DCF has to give Dylan back. At least, I think that's how it works, but the truth is, I don't really know. Maybe they can pull some other order or summons out of their horrible magic hat, and keep him for longer. Forever.

"Do you have children, Susan?" I ask suddenly, and she pauses before she answers. I wonder if there is some rule about case workers sharing personal details. She must deal with some real psychos, but I'm not one of them.

"Yes, I do," she says. "I have a daughter. She's twenty-one years old. I adopted her when she was four."

"Oh." I don't know how to feel about that. What happened to her daughter's birth mother? Did Susan adopt a child like Dylan, who'd been sucked into the system? Just the possibility fills me with terror. I am not going to lose Dylan, not for a few weeks, and certainly not forever.

As I say goodbye to Susan, I am filled with renewed purpose. I'm going to fight.

When I call the legal aid service Susan recommended, though, there isn't anyone available to speak to me until next week, which fills me with frustration.

"That's too late," I tell the monotone-voiced receptionist on the line. "DCF has my child for just ninety-six hours. I need someone now."

"After ninety-six hours, DCF will have to file a motion for an order of temporary custody," she drones.

"I *know*, that's what I want to avoid—"

"At which point you will be granted a lawyer through the court."

"I know," I say again, frustration audible in my voice. My fingers ache from clenching my phone so tightly. "I want a lawyer to look over a voluntary placement contract before we have to go to court—"

"There will be someone available to contact you next week."

I end up slamming the phone down, and then I wonder if someone somewhere is making a note about that. *Defendant ended call in a hostile manner.* I don't know if I'm being paranoid or naïve, and the uncertainty is tearing me apart. I am second-guessing everything I do, suspicious of everyone around me. It's impossible to live this way without cracking up.

I decide to go for a walk, to clear my head. I walk towards the town center, and it feels strange to be on my own, arms swinging at my sides, instead of with Dylan's hand in mine, his shadow trotting darkly next to mine.

West Hartford's town center is full of pedestrians on a Wednesday morning, doing errands or having a coffee, or just window-shopping among the trendy shops and independent boutiques. West Hartford has a wonderful, historical feel to it, with a huge white spire of a Presbyterian church right in the middle, and a wide grassy verge bisecting Main Street. The sidewalks are wide, the shops often with friendly awnings, the cafés with tables outside, even in October, as it's still warm.

Usually, when I walk into town with Dylan, we do our loop of the library, the supermarket, and then, if the weather is nice, the half-mile trek to Fernridge Park, to see the ducks and go on the swings.

But alone I'm not sure what to do. I wander up Main Street and turn left onto Farmington Avenue. Everything is familiar but without Dylan I feel lost, less than, as if I'm missing a limb or even a lung.

I decide to go into a café, simply because I can. Dylan won't usually let me—they're too small, with too many people, and the whole experience scares him. I order an iced coffee and take it outside to a little table. I sit and sip and watch the world go by, and I feel tense and unhappy the whole time.

It's incredibly pleasant—the almost balmy air, the sunshine that spills onto the sidewalk like a stream of honey, the delicious coffee—I wouldn't normally splurge four bucks on a cup of coffee in any circumstance—the leaves of the trees lining the street that are just starting to turn to russet and gold. It's glorious and yet I can't appreciate any of it. My stomach is churning and I still don't know what to do.

Do I call Susan and tell her I wasn't able to speak to a lawyer? Maybe she'll offer to wait on the placement contract until I've been able to look it over. She'd have to, wouldn't she? I mean, it's voluntary, after all. But if she does, what happens to Dylan? Do we just stay in this wretched stasis until I finally bend to Susan's will?

I can't escape the sense of a bomb ticking away, of it being about to explode right on my lap. I'm afraid some unspoken deadline will pass and I'll have missed my only opportunity. I can already picture Susan shaking her head sorrowfully.

I'm sorry, Beth, but you had to sign this paper by nine a.m. this morning, otherwise Dylan becomes a ward of the state. It's too late.

I'm sure it wouldn't happen like that, and yet maybe it would. I know so little, and everything online is so confusing, full of legal jargon, a thousand laws that seem only to sometimes apply.

I take my phone and pull up the search engine just in case I'm able to stumble upon some magical solution.

What I find is a website created by a family lawyer in Waterbury called CONNspiracy, and it doesn't take me long to realize it's a website made for people like me. It offers advice—*tons* of advice—for parents whose children have been taken by the state of Connecticut's DCF, or who are being threatened with an investigation.

As I read, I am filled with both hope and fury. I learn that I didn't have to agree to *anything*. I didn't have to accompany the police yesterday from CVS, and I've never even had to let Susan into my apartment, not once—something she never mentioned to me during her impromptu visits.

In any state in America, you have to have a search warrant to enter a person's home. DCF, the website tells me, gets around this with their so-called emergency orders, but you should always request to see the actual order before you allow anyone inside. I haven't seen *anything*.

The website goes on to say how caseworkers wheedle and trick and basically *lie* to get you to do what they want. They'll worm their way into your home and ask your kids condemning questions and all the while state that they are trying to be helpful. *Just as Susan did.* But what they really want is to take your kids away from you, to be in control.

I'm not so naïve that I don't realize this guy has a serious axe to grind, but *still*. There's a lot Susan should have done that she didn't, and that fires me with purpose. Forget the lawyers, I have a case. I have a *right*.

Reckless yet filled with determination, I call Susan's cell right then and there. She answers on the second ring.

"Beth?"

"Susan." My voice comes out as hostile as it was this morning, maybe even more so. "I wanted to let you know that I will not be signing any voluntary placement contract." I think of how many times she's shouldered her way into my home, without even informing me that she needed my permission, and for a second I can't speak for the sense of rage and violation I feel. And she said she was on my side.

"I'm sorry to hear that, Beth." Susan sounds quiet, a bit resigned, as if she was expecting this.

"I'm sure you are," I choke out. There are so many things I want to say, but I don't, because I'm going to save them for my day in court. I'll be my own damned lawyer, if I have to. "Are you going to file for an order of temporary custody?" I try to sound as if I really know what I'm talking about, but a few minutes scrolling various websites hardly makes me an expert. I don't actually know what happens next.

"I believe that is what will happen, yes. If you don't agree to the voluntary placement, there will be a preliminary court hearing within ten days."

"Ten days!" I practically yelp the words, my ignorance revealing me. "I thought you were only allowed to hold him for ninety-six hours."

"After that period of time, we have to file for the order. He remains in custody until it is resolved by the court."

I swallow hard, absorbing this. Ten days isn't six weeks, but it still feels way too long. Why can't he come back to me until it's resolved by the court? Why does DCF have all the power and I, his *mother*, have none?

"Beth, you really don't have to do this," Susan says. She sounds weary rather than earnest now. "Remember, with the voluntary placement, you can take Dylan back whenever you—"

"No, I *can't*, because you told me DCF can take legal action to keep me from it."

"Yes, but—"

"Why should I believe anything you say?" I practically spit. "You've lied to me all along."

"I haven't lied," Susan replies with dignity, and I am so filled with rage at this that I am shaking with it.

"Yes, you *have*. All along. What about not informing me that you had no right to come into my home?"

"I always asked if I could come in, Beth." Susan sounds tense, and I wonder if she's worried I'll make a legal complaint. Perhaps there will be an investigation—not into my parenting, but into her professionalism. The thought is intensely satisfying.

"You never told me that you couldn't unless I let you," I tell her coldly. "I am *not* just rolling over and taking this, Susan. I contest the ninety-six-hour hold, *and* the order of temporary custody, and whatever else you throw at me." For a second I am flooded with power and triumph; I am dizzy with it. "I'll see you in court," I declare, and then I disconnect the call.

CHAPTER EIGHT

ALLY

"So how *is* it?"

My neighbor and best friend Julie's eyes are wide over the rim of her wineglass as I take a sip from my own and relax into her sofa. It's been three days since Dylan came to live with us, and while nothing terrible has happened, they've felt somewhat endless. I am grateful to be somewhere other than home, watching Dylan and walking on eggshells.

"It's been okay," I say, because in truth it has. Mostly.

When I heard Dylan scream again that first evening, I raced upstairs. Nick and Dylan were in the guest bedroom, Dylan wrapped only in a towel that fell to the floor as I wrenched open the door and he continued to scream.

Nick's eyes were nearly as wild as Dylan's. "Hey. *Hey*," he said shakily, a weak attempt at calming him down. "It's okay, Dylan…"

I picked up the towel and wrapped it around him more firmly. "Let's find your jammies, Dylan. Do you know where they are?"

I glanced at Nick, who shrugged helplessly and spread his hands.

"It was all going fine," he said. "He had a bath. He loved it. Then we came in here and he just *went*—"

"That's enough." I knew it was hard not to talk as if Dylan wasn't here, especially when he didn't speak, but I also knew we needed to talk *to* Dylan, not about him. I reached for the backpack we'd ended up not unpacking because of the bunny detour. "Let's find your jammies, Dylan," I said again.

Fortunately he stopped screaming as I fished a raggedy pair of *Blues Clues* pajamas out of the backpack—they were far too small, but I helped him into them, mentally adding pajamas to the shopping list I'd been composing in my head.

The rest of the evening went okayish; I read Dylan a story and tucked him into bed. Nick had disappeared again, back to his office, and it occurred to me what an escape hatch it was turning out to be, since I had to go outside to the garage to fetch him back. He was probably banking on me not wanting to make the effort, or leave Dylan alone.

"What do you think is wrong with him?" Nick asked, *sotto voce*, as we got ready for bed three hours later. Josh had stayed holed up in his room, and thankfully Dylan had stayed asleep.

"There's nothing *wrong* with him." I sounded irritable, and I wasn't sure why. I couldn't decide how much I resented Nick going to the office and leaving me to deal with Dylan alone. In some ways it was easier, but it still felt unfair.

"I mean the—What did you call it? Selectively dumb."

"Selectively *mute*."

Nick rolled his eyes. "Please don't be PC with me. Save it for the social workers."

"Words matter, Nick." I sounded prissy even to myself, but I couldn't help it. Even after several productive and calming hours of tidying up and shopping for some toys and games on Amazon, I still felt edgy about everything. I had no idea what tomorrow would hold.

"Why do you think he's *selectively mute*, then?" Nick asked, putting unnecessary emphasis on the words I'd told him to say.

"I don't know. A coping strategy, maybe."

"Do you think he's been abused?" Nick gave me a frank look. "I looked him over when he was in the tub, and I didn't see any bruises or burns or anything like that."

"That's good, I guess." I shook my head. I was exhausted, and I wanted to read my book and not think about Dylan for a little while. "Hopefully we'll learn more from Monica when she visits in a couple of days."

Nick seemed content not to continue the conversation, and we did our usual twenty minutes of reading in bed, although for Nick that was swiping through news articles on his phone. I was trying to get into this month's book-club selection, a rather pretentious tome with a lot of overblown language, but my mind kept skimming away.

I was tired but I couldn't sleep; Nick dropped off almost right away, but I lay in bed, rigid yet trying to relax, straining my ears for any noise. I heard Josh open his door and then, a few minutes later, the flush of the toilet. It was after midnight and he should have been in bed over an hour ago, but I'd forgotten to remind him, or to check if he'd done his homework. I would have to do better tomorrow, and the day after that, and the day after. Right then, the days marched ahead, each one feeling impossible to fathom, never mind get through.

Another hour and I dozed in and out of sleep, my eyes gritty every time I opened them. And then, almost as if I'd been waiting for it, and I think I probably was, Dylan started screaming again, that piercing note splitting the still night air.

Nick lurched up in bed, hair standing on end, eyes wild. "What the—"

"I'll deal with it."

I ran into Dylan's room, tripping over a backpack, and ending up half-sprawled on the bed. "It's okay, Dylan, it's okay," I kept saying, as I reached sightlessly for him in the darkness. When I connected with his shoulder, he flinched away. "It's okay, it's okay." I was dazed as I righted myself and sat on the edge of the bed, willing him to calm down, or at least to stop screaming.

The hours of that night blurred together; I can't remember what happened when, or how, only that at some point Dylan stopped screaming, and I was so very tired, my head drooping towards my chest as I waited for him to fall back asleep, but every time I thought he had, I'd get up as quietly as I could and tiptoe towards the door, only to have him whimper and fling a hand out towards me. It was like having a newborn baby again.

Eventually, too exhausted to continue the same futile pattern, I stretched out next to him and fell asleep. When I woke, it was past dawn, greyish early-morning light filtering through the curtains. From outside, I heard the clatter of bottles as the recycling bins were being emptied; we'd forgotten to take ours out. My body ached and my head pounded, but at least I'd slept.

I turned on my side and saw that Dylan was still asleep, long, dark lashes fanned out on his cheeks, which were as round and smooth as peaches. His lips were slightly pursed and he had his bunny tucked in close to his chest. He looked so young, so innocent, that my heart broke all over again for whatever he'd seen and endured in his short life. I wanted to make our house a loving home for him, for however long I could.

I slipped out of bed, grateful that he didn't wake, and headed downstairs for a much-needed cup of coffee. Nick was already brewing it as I came into the kitchen, still in his pajamas, his hair rumpled and his face bleary.

"How long was he screaming for?"

I prickled at that, although I wasn't sure why. "Not too long. He settled eventually."

"Did you sleep at all?"

"Yes, a bit." I opened the cupboard for a mug. "He must have woken up in the night and forgotten where he was. I'm not surprised he got scared."

Nick rubbed his jaw as he reached for a mug. "Yeah, I guess."

"There's bound to be an adjustment period."

Nick made a noncommittal noise and I felt myself getting irritated. "What is it?"

He looked at me defensively, a bit injured. "I didn't say anything."

"I know, but you're thinking something. What?"

He stared at me and I stared back; we knew each other too well to prevaricate. Finally Nick sighed. "All right, fine. I didn't expect him to be so… *weird*. I mean, I thought he'd talk."

"He does talk." Nick gave me an eloquent look of disbelief. "Apparently, he does. We just haven't heard him yet."

"You know what I mean."

Yes, I did, but that didn't keep it from annoying me. I wanted Nick to be more compassionate, more patient, more involved. And I wanted him to be all those things without me having to say so. "These kids aren't made to order," I told him. "They're bound to have issues. Insecurities. That's why they're with us. Why we're helping them."

Nick let out a sigh, as if I'd just said what he'd expected me to. "I know, Ally," he replied, and he poured us both coffee. The conversation felt over.

We developed a rhythm over the next few days, but it wasn't one I was completely happy with. I'd been planning to register Dylan for school, as Monica had suggested, but then she had called to tell me Beth hadn't agreed to the voluntary placement after all, and so I was to hold off putting him into school until the court hearing next week.

"And if the court decides he belongs with her…?" I ventured tentatively.

"Then he'll go back immediately. But if they don't, then we'll probably be looking at a slightly longer placement. A minimum of three months, rather than a maximum."

I didn't let myself dwell on either possibility for too long. Instead, I just tried to get through each day, and really, it wasn't that hard. Dylan was so very quiet, and when I got some old jigsaws out of the cupboard, he amused himself for hours putting them together and then taking them apart again.

But even when he was being quiet, I was conscious of his presence, and it made me anxious because I never knew what might set him off. One afternoon, I gave him a snack of grapes and he started screaming again and hurled them to the floor, breaking a bowl that had been part of my wedding china. Stupid of me to have used it, I know. It was only after I'd cleaned it all up that I remembered he'd indicated he didn't like grapes, but still. He didn't have to act as if I'd tried to poison him.

I knew those types of thoughts were unfair, and they made me feel guilty. I didn't want to think like that. I wanted to be magnanimous and generous and loving and patient, and for the most part, I think I was, but inside my head there was a snarl of unpleasant thoughts that I was ashamed to voice even just to myself. I certainly wasn't going to admit any of them to Julie now, even though I could tell by her alert expression and wide eyes that she wanted all the juicy details.

"Just okay?" she asks, and I shrug.

"It hasn't been easy, but it hasn't been terrible. About what I expected." And yet so not.

Julie nods and sips her wine. "So why was he taken into care?"

"I don't know." I called Monica once, hoping for a little more information about Dylan, but she didn't answer. I left a voicemail but she hasn't called back, so I'm as in the dark as ever.

"Do you think he was abused?"

"I really don't know, Julie." I love my friend, but I find her questions, this unabashed digging for details, unpleasant and distasteful. She's treating Dylan as if he is a guest on *The Jerry*

Springer Show, his life offered up as fair game to be analyzed and dissected, and then discarded.

"And you haven't met the mom?" She has either not registered my discouraging tone or chosen to ignore it.

"Not yet." Monica did text me that the planned visit had been postponed, which I was fine with.

"But you will?"

"At some point, yes, I think so."

Julie finally seems to register my unwillingness to talk about it, for she sighs and sits back. "Well, I admire you, Ally, I really do. There aren't many people who would do what you're doing."

"Which is part of the problem." I take a sip of my wine, closing my eyes briefly as I enjoy its velvety warmth. In the last few days, the Indian summer has given way to a more seasonable chill. This morning, there was a thick white frost on the ground, the maple leaves that had fallen from the big tree in our backyard scarlet rimmed in white.

"Yes, of course. I know more people should volunteer, but it is a big commitment, isn't it? You look tired."

I am exhausted. I've spent the last three nights sleeping next to Dylan. He starts off alone, but inevitably he wakes up in the middle of the night and I go in and sleep next to him. Whether it is allowed or not, I can't care about. It's what works.

Nick has told me I should just let him scream, that I have to set boundaries, but his well-meaning advice only annoys me. Somehow in the last three days, Dylan has become primarily my responsibility, which I realized is something I probably should have expected, yet still resent.

Nick and I have always had a fairly stereotypical division of labor—he takes care of the trash and the yard, the cars and our taxes, and I manage household stuff, laundry, cooking, and the minute details of kids' schedules, along with birthdays and Christmases and family vacations. And now I add Dylan to that list, while Nick satisfies himself with supervising bath time and the occasional "Okay, buddy?" It doesn't exactly feel fair.

Even tonight has been, on some level, Nick *letting* me go out, acting all magnanimous because he's going to stay in and babysit. Dylan was already asleep when I left, so it was hardly an onerous task, and it didn't have to be mine alone.

I don't feel like explaining any of that to Julie, though, even though we've compared and complained about our husbands on plenty of occasions, complicit in our understanding that we actually loved our spouses, that we knew how good our lives were. This feels different—too new, too raw, and I already feel as if I am being judged. I am judging myself.

The truth is, taking care of Dylan has forced me to start to reassess my own life, my own home. Having his silent gaze constantly on every aspect of both is nerve-wracking and deeply uncomfortable, and it makes me start picking holes in what I thought was a smooth, blameless blanket of privilege and blessing.

Dylan's presence makes me realize how little Josh talks to us, how his bedtime and phone use has somehow slipped out of my control without me even realizing it. It makes me see that Nick and I often exist day to day on a superficial plane of banal exchanges, and how we generally spend our evenings apart, on our laptops in separate rooms, not because we don't like spending time with one another, but because it just feels easier to surf the internet alone than make an effort with another person. It makes me count the days and realize that Emma hasn't called me in over a week. My happy, "#blessed" family seems to have lost a little of its glossy shine, and all without Dylan having to say a word.

I say none of that to Julie. As much as I love her, admitting so much weakness and doubt feels like handing her a knife to slip between my ribs. Although we've supported each other over the years, it has been with the sure and certain knowledge that we've never had anything serious to complain about.

Instead I ask about her kids—Brad in grad school down south, Tyler about to be married this spring. She is more than happy to tell me how well they are both doing, and I am more than happy to listen and think about someone else's happy life for a little while.

I've just said goodbye, with kisses on both cheeks, and am heading back down the street towards home when my cell rings—Emma. My heart lightens.

"Hey, Emma! We must be on the same wavelength. I was just thinking about calling you." I hear the smile in my voice and feel it on my face. Emma has been gone for less than two months, but I miss her terribly. We've always got along well together; even in the most difficult of the teen years, she was happy to hang out with me, always up for a movie night in or a girls' shopping trip out.

"Hey, Mom." She sounds a little subdued, but it is late after all, although maybe not by college-student standards. It is only a little after ten o'clock.

"You okay?"

"Me? Yeah. Josh texted to say you have a foster child staying with you?"

"Yes, his name is Dylan." Guilt needles me for not telling her sooner; I kept meaning to, but it all happened so quickly and somehow there never seemed to be the right time. "He's only been here for a few days. I was going to call you and tell you…"

When we started the fostering course back in June, Emma barely registered it. She'd just graduated from high school, and she'd scored a summer internship at a local law firm. She was in and out of the house, working, going out with friends, living life to the full before she headed off to Harvard.

She was also, I think, feeling very grown-up and like she didn't need to care about what happened at home. In her head, she'd already left. Now I hear a wobbly note of concerned wounded-ness, and I wish I'd made the time to call to tell her.

"So how long is he staying with you?"

"Hard to say. He might be gone next week, it might be for a few months."

"Months. Wow." I stay silent, sensing something more. "So will you be able to come to the Family Weekend?" she asks, and the raw note of vulnerability in her voice makes me ache.

I can't believe I've completely forgotten about that all-important weekend—it's been the highlight of my entire autumn, a weekend at Harvard to see university through Emma's eyes, to go to parties and concerts and receptions, as well as the big football game on Saturday afternoon. Nick and I had booked our hotel as soon as Emma had been accepted to Harvard. And yet somehow, since Dylan had catapulted into our lives, it has completely slipped my mind.

"Yes, of course we'll come," I say, because I can't say anything else. And yet right now I can't see how to make it happen, not with Dylan.

"Will you... bring him?"

"Dylan? I don't know. We need permission to take him across state lines." And, truthfully, I can't see how bringing Dylan could work. Everything will be so unfamiliar to him, and he has enough to deal with already. Besides, I don't want Emma's weekend to be all about Dylan, and not about her.

"So if you don't...?"

"There's respite care." But that doesn't feel right either, so soon after he's come to us. "And actually, he might be leaving next week, if the court hearing goes in his mom's favor." And right now I am hoping it will. That would make my life *so* much easier. All these thoughts jostle for space in my mind, making me feel guilty because they never feel like the right things to think, but Emma seems to brighten.

"Oh, well, if he's gone by next week..."

"He might not be. He's a lovely little boy, Emma. I think you'd like him."

She makes a "mmm" noise and I stop outside our front gate, frowning, counting the windows. There is a light on upstairs and I'm afraid it's coming from Dylan's room.

"Well, let me know either way," Emma says, "because if he comes, he'll need a ticket."

"Okay, will do." The light is definitely coming from Dylan's bedroom's window, and my heart leaps unpleasantly in my chest. "I'm sorry, honey, but I need to go. Can I call you back tomorrow?"

"I have class." Emma sounds the tiniest bit sulky, and I know she's hurt. I never cut short our calls.

"Text me a good time. I really want to hear what you've been up to, how everything is going. Please." She makes another "mmm" noise and I strain my ears, but I can't hear any screaming. "I love you," I say, too quickly. "Talk to you soon. Bye." And then I am throwing open the gate and jogging inside, to find out what has happened while I've been gone.

CHAPTER NINE

BETH

On Friday, three days after they take Dylan away from me, I get a letter in the mail, from the state. The court hearing is set for Tuesday, and I am relieved it is so soon, even as the days feel as if they pass endlessly. Still, one week from the time they took him, I could have my son back. I *will* have him back.

When I told Susan I was going to fight, she informed me that I could now have that lawyer I'd wanted. Dylan would have one, too. But when I met with mine, a nasal-sounding woman who droned on about the legalities of my case without seeming sympathetic to my cause at all, I felt worse off than before, as well as suspicious.

I ended up emailing Bruce, the webmaster of the CONN-spiracy site, and he sent me a long, informative email telling me I shouldn't trust any court-appointed lawyer, that they were all part of the failed system. He directed me to websites with information about representing myself in court—in fact, the Connecticut judicial site even has a page about it, and it's perfectly legal.

So I've spent my days preparing to represent myself in the court hearing for custody of my son. I've amassed all the information I can about how trustworthy and stable I am—printouts of my bank statements, my filed taxes, even my high-school report cards. Anything to show I am able to have the care of my son.

I know DCF will be amassing information too, and I can imagine what some of it is—missed appointments, Susan's previous visits, the testimony of neighbors, maybe even a statement from the preschool teacher Dylan barely met. All of it makes me burn with anger, because it is so unfair. There are so, so many worse parents out there than me, even just in West Hartford. Why has DCF—why has *Susan*—decided to go after me so hard?

It's not a question worth pursuing, and so I do my best to focus on my case. I've spent hours on the CONNspiracy website, scrolling through pages of legalese that make my brain hurt but are necessary for me to know. I've written down everything I can remember about Susan's visits, and what she did or didn't do that she should or shouldn't have. I've copied out laws that I struggle to understand but am determined to mention in court—even if the thought of standing up and speaking in front of a stern-faced judge is terrifying to me.

I've gone to the UPS store a couple of times to talk to Mike, because I need a friend and he's the only one I have. He's been encouraging, telling me he's sure I'll win, that the next time I come in I'll have Dylan back with me. I so want to believe him, but I'm not so desperate that I can pretend he has any idea what he's talking about. He has no experience of DCF, and I do.

I've also called Marco, to tell him what has happened. I didn't want to, but I felt he deserved to know, even if he hasn't seen Dylan since his sixth birthday, when he stopped by for fifteen minutes with a box of drugstore chocolates and a Matchbox car for Dylan.

"So how long are they going to take him for?" he asked when I phoned to tell him about the episode in CVS, and Susan. He sounded irritatingly unfazed that his son is being looked after by strangers.

"I don't know. I'm contesting it, though."

"Oh, Beth. Why?"

"*Why*? Because I want my son back."

"Don't you want a break?"

"This isn't a *break*, Marco." I couldn't believe he would phrase it like that, even as I remained completely unsurprised. All Marco has ever wanted is a break—an easy out, an easy life. He's been like that since I met him nine years ago.

In the spring of my senior year, when I was eighteen, a few months after my mom had just upped and left, I did something very stupid. I finished my shift at The Gap on a balmy Friday night in May, feeling lonely and adrift and also a little bit reckless. I was angry with my mom for leaving the way she did, for deciding that her life was so much more important than mine. And I was angry with my father for acting as if I no longer existed, working his shifts and spending every night in front of the TV with a six-pack of beer, utterly indifferent to me and my comings and goings.

So when a couple of guys in a beat-up Toyota Camry, parked in the corner of one of the empty West Farms Mall lots, the windows down and all the doors open, invited me over to have a beer with them, I said sure. Why not?

Normally, I wouldn't have *ever* done something like that, but life hadn't felt normal since my mom had gone. My dad was monosyllabic at the best of times, and now he was acting as if I was invisible, or if not that, then an irritation. My friends didn't know what to do with me; they'd sympathized for a while, but it had been months since Mom had left and they were over it, even if I wasn't. I felt angry and misunderstood and alone, and so I shrugged as if I did this all the time, and took the can of Bud Light they offered me as though it were no big deal.

If it sounds sketchy, it wasn't as much as even I'd originally thought, with guys calling me over as I walked across the hot tarmac. They were actually in my year at high school, and after exchanging hellos we realized we very vaguely knew each other.

They were underage, yes, but the driver wasn't drinking and all they wanted to do was sit and shoot the breeze. We were all destined for college in September—me to Connecticut State, two of them to UConn, another guy to one of the SUNYs.

It was warm and balmy, the evening sunlight shimmering off the tarmac, a spring breeze blowing over us, the sounds of muted traffic in the distance. Sitting with them on the hood of the car, watching the sun set over Farmington Avenue, Avon Mountain silhouetted in the distance, I felt as if I almost had a future again. I just had to wait out the summer with my dad, get through a couple more months, and then I was free. I would go to college and I wouldn't come back. It wasn't what I had wanted originally, but now it seemed like a way out. I felt, for the first time since my mom had left, almost hopeful.

How wrong that feeling was. I drank three beers—I *know*—and then, assuring my newfound friends that I was fine, I drove home. I felt a little loopy but not actually drunk, although I didn't really know what drunk felt like. I hadn't been to many parties during my quiet high-school years, had never done anything wild or reckless… until then.

Because I *was* drunk. I was over the limit, in fact, and I was, according to reports, weaving all over Route 44 as I headed back to our split-level in Bloomfield. A police car pulled me over, made me take a breathalyzer test right there, and I was booked for a DUI.

The knock-on effect of that one careless—and yes, stupid, dangerous, idiotic, irresponsible, et cetera—choice was that I basically lost everything. I lost my license for a year and was sentenced to one hundred hours of community service in a local nursing home; Connecticut State withdrew their offer of admission, and my dad more or less threw me out of the house—although, to be fair to him, I wanted to go.

In the blink of an eye, the flip of a beer top, my whole life twisted shape and became something I no longer recognized or even liked. And yes, it was my fault. I have never sought to shift blame, as tempting as that could be. It was all my fault. And yet I can't begrudge any of it, because of Dylan.

I met Marco at the nursing home where I volunteered; he was the cook, and still is. He was charming and full of life, with curly dark hair and ridiculously long lashes, and even though he'd been born in Bloomfield like me, he liked to put on an Italian accent and play the dashing Romeo.

He swept me off my feet, both literally and figuratively. We first met when he accidentally tripped me up as I was bringing a lunch tray into the kitchen. He was effusive in his apology, helping me up, insisting he clean up all the mess. I was dazed and tearful, if unhurt; it was only my third day of community service and I was still reeling from the sea change. All the staff at the nursing home knew why I was there, and they treated me with varying degrees of sympathy or scorn. I kept wanting to say *this isn't me*, but I knew they wouldn't believe me and so I didn't.

The next day, he brought me flowers, and somehow the story of how I'd got the DUI came spilling out of me, and Marco was indignant on my behalf, insisting the police were *pazzo*—crazy— he liked to pepper his speech with Italian words, but he didn't actually speak the language—and that I didn't deserve anything that had happened to me.

I was so grateful for his understanding, and the fact that he actually seemed to *like* me, although in retrospect I think he probably just liked the adulation I so willingly heaped upon him. I'd never had a proper boyfriend before, and Marco seemed like a *man*. He had his own car, his own apartment; he was twenty-three, but he seemed older, worldlier, and far more experienced than I was. I was awed that he'd even look at me.

By the end of the week, we were dating; by the end of the month, I'd moved in with him. I'd been sleeping on my high-school friend's sofa, but it was hardly an arrangement that could last forever, and Marco was insistent that he had space, that he wanted me there. A year later I was pregnant, and although he was surprised at first, when I said I wanted to keep the baby—because I'd always, always been sure of that—he promised to support me, said we should get married, although of course we never did.

I think he had a vision of himself as some sort of savior, although it was surely misplaced, because the truth is, by the time Dylan was born, things had already started to go pretty sour.

Marco was restless and bored with our couple life, and I was too timid to ask for anything. So I cleaned his apartment and I slept in his bed and I made his meals, while he worked and partied and basically lived his life without me, except when he chose to suddenly lavish me with attention, like a spoiled toddler who has found an old toy, or perhaps like a smug cat with a desperate, pathetic little mouse. Either way, it wasn't working, even if I insisted to myself that it was, because I had nothing else.

And then came Dylan, like a ray of hope into my barren life, and I lavished all the love and attention on my little baby that no one else seemed to want—not Marco, not my mother, not my father. Meanwhile, Marco got more and more fed up, until, after a spectacular tantrum—Dylan's, not Marco's—he finally left.

In the four years since Marco abandoned us, he's visited Dylan only a handful of times—birthdays, and one or two Christmases. He does put two hundred bucks in my bank account more months than not, but it's not an official arrangement and I never ask for it. I know I could, and probably should, but it feels like too much trouble.

In any case, I wasn't surprised by Marco's response to DCF taking Dylan, merely disheartened, but it does surprise me when I open the door on Monday evening to find him standing there with a dozen roses, a bottle of wine, and a wide smile.

I stare at him dumbly, trying to take in all the disparate parts of his appearance—the slicked-back curls, the smell of soap, the gas-station flowers wrapped in plastic and already starting to wilt. "What are you doing here?"

"I thought you needed cheering up."

"I'm fine, Marco. I have the court hearing tomorrow." I doubt he remembered, but he takes it in his stride.

"Exactly. I thought you'd be nervous, and you might appreciate a little bit of distraction. How are you doing, Beth? You look tired." He saunters into my apartment without asking to come in, and even though I want to boot him out, I don't.

I should, I know that. Confidence seeps from his pores along with cheap aftershave, and I know his being here can't be anything good. But I don't say anything because I'm lonely, and I've spent a week on my own, a week of obsession and fear and solitude and study, and a little company, even Marco's, is far too welcome.

So I close the door behind him and watch as he walks to the kitchen to rummage in the cabinets for wineglasses. I don't have any, because I hardly ever drink, but he makes do with a couple of plastic tumblers.

"So, how have you been?" he asks as he opens the screw-top bottle and pours us both generous amounts. He's dumped the flowers in the sink, still in their plastic.

"How do you think?" I stare at him hard even as I accept the glass and take a sip of the cheap, vinegary wine. "What are you doing here, Marco?"

"Can't I visit?"

"You generally don't, unless it's Dylan's birthday. Even then I don't know if you'll feel like turning up."

"Ouch, Beth." He gives me a friendly grimace. "I do try, you know."

I just shake my head. Marco tries, but not all that much.

From where I'm standing, I can see the price tag left on the bouquet of roses—five ninety-nine for the whole dozen.

"How is Dylan doing?" Marco asks, dropping the breezy charm, so for a second I let myself be fooled into thinking he actually cares. I've always wanted to think, deep down Marco *must* care, at least a little, about his own son. How can he not? He's not a monster. The old ladies at the nursing home love him, although perhaps that's just because he flirts with them all.

And, the truth is, even if it doesn't feel like it, he *does* try, if only in his own small, pathetic way. He wouldn't if he didn't care at all. It's small comfort, but it's something, even as I get frustrated with how little he does.

"I don't know how he's doing. I haven't seen him." My voice is tight because I don't want to cry, especially not in front of Marco. "Susan, his caseworker, has given me a couple of updates, but they're brief." She's just continued with her line about him adjusting well, which makes me feel suspicious. It can't be that easy for him, surely. But if all goes well tomorrow, I will know *exactly* how he's doing, because he'll be with me.

"I'm sorry, Beth." Marco looks genuinely contrite, a hangdog expression on his face that I ache to trust. "I can't imagine how hard this is for you. I know how much you love Dylan…"

"And you don't?" The words slip out before I can stop them.

Marco doesn't even look abashed. "You know it's not the same. You'd be pissed off if I acted like it was." That much is true. "You were always closer to him than I was, you know. Right from the beginning. Sometimes it felt like you were obsessed."

"I was a first-time mother of a newborn baby, Marco. Of course I was a little bit obsessed." I remember those first weeks of Dylan's life—the joyous incredulity I felt at this little person who was now my whole world. I used to watch him sleep; it was better than a movie, tracking the up and down of his tiny chest, the little angelic pursing of his lips. He was beautiful. He still is.

"I'm not complaining," Marco says. "I'm just saying it's always been different for you, even before I left. It was like… the two of you had your own little world. Your own language."

I shake my head. "You're exaggerating."

"I'm not. Don't you remember? Even before he could speak. He'd make some little grunt and you knew what it meant. You filled in his words before he even said anything."

"That's just how mothers are." But it's true that I've always felt attuned to Dylan; the fact that he is mostly mute hasn't really bothered me. It's almost as if the words I know he'd want to say are already in my head.

Thinking about that makes a lonely sweep of sorrow rush through me. I miss him so much, it's a physical pain inside me, a gnawing away of my insides, until I feel hollowed out and empty. I take another sip of wine, but it tastes sour in my mouth. I still don't know why Marco is here.

"What is it you want, Marco?" I ask tiredly. "Because I've got a big day tomorrow and I need to be prepared. I need to get some sleep. I have to be at court at nine in the morning."

He smiles easily. "It's only seven. You've got the whole evening ahead of you."

"You haven't answered my question."

"I just wanted to see you." His voice softens as he puts his tumbler down so he can take me gently by the shoulders. The feel of his hands jolts me; it has been a long time since I've been touched like this. Marco smiles down at me, and I know that smile—sleepy, expectant, sure. This is a booty call.

"Don't," I say, and I am both shocked and ashamed at how half-hearted I sound. It feels so good to be touched, a warmth seeping into me, firing my very bones, reminding me that I am not alone. "Don't," I say again, and it almost sounds as if I am giving him permission, asking for more. I can't believe how weak I am being.

"Are you sure about that?" Marco asks, and his voice is like a lion's purr, velvety and seductive. "Dylan isn't here…" He bends his head and brushes his lips with mine, and for a second I am so very tempted. This is the father of my child, after all, and this aspect of our relationship actually worked, not that I had anything to compare it to.

Then his words reverberate through my brain. *Dylan isn't here.* That's why Marco is here—because Dylan isn't. Because he doesn't have to deal with him, and we won't be interrupted. He doesn't care about Dylan. He doesn't even care about me. He just figured on some free sex.

"You are a jerk, Marco," I say, my voice trembling as I yank myself away from his languorous yet assured grip. "A real jerk."

He raises his eyebrows, looking amused, unaffected. "What's the harm in trying?"

I shake my head. "Go away."

"I do care, Beth—"

"As if." My voice is shaking, as is my body. "Go away, Marco. You aren't going to get anything from me. *Leave!*" My voice rises in a broken cry, and Marco holds his hands up. He hates any kind of real emotion, any kind of awkwardness. He just wants to skim through life, taking everything easy, including me.

"All right, all right, I'm going." He heads towards the door, pausing with his hand on the knob. "For the record, I did come over here to see how you were doing. I do care, even if you don't think I do."

"Sure." The single word is full of loathing. I can't believe how close I came to being reeled in by him again.

Marco sighs as if he wants to say something more, but in the end he just leaves. As the door closes, I release a shuddering breath. I came so close to giving in, just because I'm lonely. How pathetic can I be?

More than that, apparently, because the next thing I do is walk into the kitchen. I mean to pour my glass of wine down the sink that is still full of flowers, but instead I glance at the cheap bottle Marco left on the table. The moment hangs in the balance, suspended, teetering. And then I drain my glass, reach for the bottle and pour myself another.

CHAPTER TEN

ALLY

The Saturday after Dylan comes to us, the one before the court hearing, I decide we need a family day out, and so we drive to Granby to pick apples at Bushy Hill Orchard.

It's a beautiful day, cold and clear, and the leaves are at their peak. In another week they will be gone, the ground littered with a carpet of ochre and crimson, scarlet and russet. Nick is up for the trip, but Josh is reluctant; he had a cross-country practice at eight in the morning and he wants to spend the rest of the day in his room, on his phone or his laptop, only to emerge for meals, squinting and surly.

But I'm not having it, not today. "You haven't spent any time with Dylan," I tell him, trying to keep my tone cheerful rather than scolding. "And it's too beautiful to stay indoors. It won't be all day, Josh. Just a couple of hours."

He sighs heavily, but he agrees to come, and I am buoyant, determined to make this work. The drive across the mountains to Granby, a quintessential New England town, all red barns and Colonial farmhouses, is gorgeous, and although Dylan is quiet, he seems alert and curious, looking out the window at the colorful flash of trees going by.

We haven't been to Bushy Hill Orchard since Emma was about twelve, but we used to go every year, a family tradition. You are taken out to the orchard in a wagon pulled by a tractor, and you pick as many apples as you please, loading them in gunny sacks. Then it's back on the wagon to have the apples weighed in the old-fashioned country store, before we sit outside at the picnic tables with paper cups of apple cider and a bag of hot, sugary donuts. I love it all, and I want Dylan to, as well.

It all starts out fine. Dylan is apprehensive about the wagon, but when I help him to clamber up and sit next to me, he seems okay with it. I've taken to giving a running commentary of what we're doing whenever we're together, and I do this now, raising my voice over the rumble of the tractor.

In the middle of my patter, Nick gives me a gently quelling look, and I realize that everyone on the wagon—all the other happy families—are looking at me a little strangely. Actually, they're looking at Dylan a little strangely. They can see he's different.

I shrug it off, telling myself I don't care. This is what works for Dylan, and I'm going to do it, even when a woman near me gives a heavy, pointed sigh and remarks how nice it would be to be able to hear the birds. She's being ridiculous, because there's no way you could hear the damned birds over the sound of the tractor. I ignore her and keep talking.

After about ten minutes of jolting down a rutted dirt road, the tractor drops us off at the orchard—a grove of apple trees, none any more than six feet high, every single one dripping with ripe fruit.

"Let's pick, guys," I say cheerfully, and with a sigh to rival the woman on the tractor's, Josh takes a gunny sack and starts chucking apples into it. Dylan's hand remains in mine as we walk slowly between the trees, the sky achingly blue above us, the air so clear it practically shimmers. I pick an apple, rosy red and perfect, and put it in the sack. "Do you want to try, Dylan?"

He doesn't respond, of course, but I've become used to that, and I can usually discern a frightened silence from a considering one, the touch of his fingers to mine as visible as a question mark. Now his fingers tighten in mine as he studies a tree and then slowly, so cautiously, plucks an apple from it.

"That's the way," I say with more enthusiasm than is probably warranted, but I'm just so happy he's actually doing this. He's participating, and maybe he's even enjoying it. I like to think he is. "You want to pick another?"

It's painstakingly slow work, as Dylan takes an age to pick just one apple, seeming to study each one in turn with an endearing intensity, but we get there in the end. Our gunny sack is so full, we have to drag it on the ground, which can't be much good for the apples, as we head back to the tractor.

"This is fun, isn't it?" I say to Nick as we all clamber back onto the wagon. He stayed with Josh while I went with Dylan, so he hasn't had the bonding time with Dylan that I've been hoping for, but I still feel happy.

"Yeah, it has," Nick says as he slings his arm around me and gives me a smile. "This was a good idea, Ally."

I smile back, feeling pleasantly proud, satisfied with how everything has gone and how I've orchestrated it. It's the same feeling I've had when I survey our Thanksgiving dinner table, complete with glossy turkey and glinting cranberry sauce, or a Christmas tree laden with ornaments with presents piled underneath—a glowing satisfaction that life is good, that I've worked hard to make it so.

So far, this day has exceeded my expectations, and at this point in time that is a *great* feeling, because I've kept my expectations relatively low. With Nick's arm around me and Dylan seated on my other side, Josh across from us *not* on his phone, I really don't think I could dare to ask for anything more from this moment.

After we've weighed and paid for the apples, we buy a bag of donuts and some cups of hot apple cider and take them outside to a picnic table, to enjoy the afternoon sun. The look of surprised pleasure on Dylan's face as he bites into a cinnamon-dusted donut makes me want to laugh out loud, but I settle for a smile.

Nick and I exchange a look over Dylan's head—not exactly a loved-up look, but something a little bit like it. Since Dylan came into our lives, our conversations have become somewhat fraught, a tense innuendo of accusation to almost everything we say—Nick needing to work, my insistence that he spend time with Dylan, who is going to do what when.

Even the pronouns we've used—*I* instead of *we*, *you* instead of *us*—have revealed our emotional distance. But right now, as I sip cider and feel the sun on my face, I feel like we're getting back to where we were. Where we need to be.

And then, in the sunny silence of the afternoon, Dylan suddenly lurches upright, knocking his paper cup of cider to the ground, his sugar-dusted mouth opened wide.

"Dylan—" I begin, but he's already scrambling off the bench and sprinting away from us. Nick and I exchange a panicked look before he rises from his seat, calling his name. I am frozen, my heart thudding hard, my hands full of cider and donuts. "Dylan…" I say again, weakly this time. Josh simply stares.

Nick catches up with Dylan, reaching for his shoulder, but Dylan flinches away and keeps running. I watch, open-mouthed, as he runs up to a dark-haired woman standing by a car in the parking lot and tugs urgently on her sleeve. She turns, frowning as she looks down at him, and even from where I am sitting, I see Dylan's shoulders slump, his face crumple. He drops the woman's sleeve and turns around, trudging back towards us while Nick watches helplessly.

"Dylan…" I dump the donuts and cider on the table and reach for his hand, but he shies away from me. "Dylan, did you think that was someone you knew?" Even as I ask the question, I know the answer. Who else could he have thought it was but his mother? *Beth.* And for some reason, the way he ran to her, the urgent longing I sensed in every reckless step and the ensuing deep disappointment and even despair writ large on his face, hurts me in a way I don't expect.

I feel achingly sad for Dylan, but it's something more than that, a sense of loss in me that I don't understand. I haven't bonded *that* much with Dylan, and I'm certainly not jealous of his own mother. But I feel some sort of empty ache that I can't identify.

The easy, optimistic mood of the day has fizzled, and we leave the farm without finishing our cider. We're all silent as we troop back to the car, and Josh mutters something about needing to do homework and how he really didn't want to spend *three* hours picking apples. I ignore him, and lean my head against the window, closing my eyes, as Nick starts the car and we head back to West Hartford.

Back at the house, Josh disappears into his room and I lug the apples to the laundry room, realizing I have no real use for twenty pounds of Courtlands. How many apple pies or vats of apple sauce can I really make? Dispirited, I dump them all by the washing machine, to think about later.

Returning to the kitchen, I see that Dylan has taken one of the new jigsaw puzzles out of the cupboard and is lying on the family-room floor on his stomach as he puts it together. The sight almost gives me that warm, satisfied feeling I had back at the farm—almost but not quite. I walk over to him and crouch by his side, watching as he carefully studies a piece before fitting it to another.

"That's really good, Dylan." No response, naturally. "You really like puzzles." I pause. "Back at the farm, when we were having our donuts… you seemed as if you thought you'd seen someone you knew." Again, no response, not even a flicker of acknowledgement. He simply keeps on with the puzzle, his head bent over it. "Who was it you thought you saw, Dylan? Was it your mom?" I speak gently, but the question still feels invasive.

Dylan doesn't respond—of course—but then, just when I think he's going to completely ignore me, he shakes his head, a methodical back and forth that keeps going, over and over again, until I think he might hurt himself.

"It's okay, Dylan." I touch his shoulder, fleetingly, because I still can't tell if he likes that or not. "I'm sorry. I didn't mean to upset you. I won't… I won't ask again."

Dylan shakes his head a few more times, and then he selects another puzzle piece. I think he's back to ignoring me, but, to my surprise, he offers me the piece, and it feels like an apology of sorts, or maybe some kind of truce. I smile as I take it.

"Thanks." I study the piece as carefully as Dylan has been. It's a puzzle of outer space, and most of the pieces are pure, unrelenting black. This one, however, is yellow, bright yellow, the color of the sun at the center of the puzzle. I frown exaggeratedly as I glance at Dylan. "Where do you think this one goes?"

There is a hint of a smile on his face as he takes the piece and slots it into the missing middle of the sun.

I slap my forehead. "Of course, that's where it goes," I say, and then I am rewarded by a sight I've never seen before—Dylan's face splitting in a grin. It makes me want to cry, but I choose to laugh instead.

Later, when Dylan is asleep, Nick and I curl up on the sofa with glasses of red wine and a series on Netflix we've been meaning to watch for ages—some gritty crime thriller, more Nick's taste than mine, but I don't mind. I'm just grateful to check out for a little bit.

But first I have to tell Nick about my conversation with Emma, which reminds me that she didn't text me a good time to call today, and also that I didn't call her. Both make something clench inside me, but I tell myself she would be busy on the weekend anyway. I'll call her tomorrow.

"Harvard's Family Weekend is two weeks from now," I say to Nick, and he frowns, his wineglass almost at his lips.

"Yeah? So?"

"What are we going to do?"

"What do you mean, what are we going to do? We're going to go. We've booked two rooms at The Kendall Hotel." A boutique hotel in a converted firehouse, it is a stone's throw from Harvard, pricey and in high demand.

"I know, but with Dylan…"

Nick's frown deepens. "Can't he go into respite care for the weekend?" He says it like we're putting a dog in a kennel, and already I struggle not to feel irritated, even though I know his question is reasonable.

"I don't think that would be good for him, so early into his placement."

Nick stares at me, his eyebrows drawn together, a look of surprise on his face, as well as a hint of annoyance. "So what are you saying? We just… *abandon* Emma?"

"No, I'm not saying we abandon her. For heaven's sake, Nick."

He shakes his head. "I don't get you, Ally. We've been looking forward to this weekend for months. And you must know how much it means to Emma."

"Yes, of course I do." I take a sip of my wine, not meeting his eyes. I'm not sure what I expected from this conversation, or even what I wanted, but I know it's not this.

"So what are you saying?" Nick asks.

"I don't know. I just wanted to discuss it, to try to think of a solution that works for everyone."

"And I have one. Respite care." He shrugs. "Anyway, this might not even be an issue, if his mother gets him back, right? When is the court hearing?"

It annoys me further that Nick doesn't even remember the date. "Tuesday."

"Right. So why don't we wait till then and see how it plays out? Dylan might be out of our lives in a couple of days, so…"

"Is that what you want?" I blurt before I can think better of it.

Nick sighs. "Do I *have* to be the bad guy here?"

"I don't want you to be. I'm just asking."

"Why?" He gives me a penetrating look. "Why are you asking, Ally?"

The question feels loaded, but I know mine was, as well. I wish I hadn't brought this all up; we could be halfway through the series Nick had lined up on the TV. Halfway through the wine, too.

Yet now that we've come this far in the conversation, I'm not willing to back down. There are too many things we've been skirting around for the last four days, and they need to be said, before our positions are set in stone, before we discover we've become too inflexible to bend to one another as we usually do.

"I asked because you don't seem as fully invested in fostering as I am. In fostering Dylan, in particular." Nick is silent and I continue steadily, "I know it was my idea in the beginning, but you were on board, Nick. You were fully on board. You wanted to do this, sometimes more than I did."

"I know," he says quietly. He doesn't look at me, studying the depths of his nearly-empty wineglass instead.

"So what happened? Because Dylan has only been with us for a few days, but I feel like he's become my sole responsibility. And part of me doesn't mind that, but it's hard. And I don't want there to be this… divide… between us. Because of Dylan." That isn't all I want to say, but at least it's a start.

I realize my heart is pounding, my fingers slick on the stem of my wineglass. I don't particularly like confrontation, and I know Nick doesn't either. His face is shuttered, his lips pursed. I'm not even sure he's going to answer me.

"I'm sorry," he says finally. He still isn't looking at me. "I know I'm not… giving this my all. It's just… I didn't expect Dylan to… to be so…"

"To be so what?" I ask when he trails off.

Nick sighs. "To be so weird."

He said it before, but it feels worse now, when we've had a chance to get to know him. I know that to most people, Dylan *is* weird. Really weird. But I still don't like Nick saying it.

"If you'd had a childhood like his, you might be weird too," I reply, whispering even though Dylan is asleep upstairs. It doesn't feel right, to talk about him like this.

"But we don't even know what childhood he's had. Monica hasn't told us a single thing, and that feels wrong."

"She will, if his mother loses the court hearing." At least, I'm assuming she will, that she's waiting to find out if this will be a longer-term placement or not. That's the only reason I can think of why she hasn't given me more information. I still don't even know his last name, and that *has* to be wrong.

"Whatever." Nick shrugs. "Look, I know I haven't been as involved as I should be. As I want to be. But I thought… I thought we'd be getting a kid I could *do* things with. Throw a ball in the backyard, or even build something out of Lego—"

"Dylan loves puzzles."

"Dylan doesn't *speak*. I'm sorry, Ally, but it's just all a bit too weird for me." He shakes his head, as if that's the end of the matter.

"So what, we send him back?" My voice isn't quite shaking, but almost. "'Too weird for us, sorry'?"

"I don't want to send him back," Nick protests, but he doesn't sound convinced. I think if we could get away with it, he would.

And wouldn't you too?

I can't ignore that damning voice, because part of me would. Dylan is hard work, no question, but he needs help. He needs love.

"You know," I say after a moment, when I trust my voice to sound level, "I was pretty weird as a kid, too."

"Oh come on, Ally." Nick rolls his eyes in exasperation. "I know you say you were a bit of a geek, but you were nothing like Dylan."

I don't reply, because what Nick says is true, but not entirely true. I really was a misfit as a kid—a brainy geek in a school of quarterbacks and cheerleaders. I had one good friend, Chenguang, a Chinese girl with limited English and a good heart. I still send her a Christmas card every year.

But from sixth grade onwards school was, for the most part, pretty miserable—the kind of *Breakfast Club* stereotypical misery that you might not think actually happens in real life. Being tripped in the hall, gross things shoved through the vents of my locker, peals of hard-edged laughter from the back of the classroom when I came up with the right answer—again.

I haven't told Nick all those unpleasant details, because who wants to admit what a nerd they were, especially after a much-needed college reinvention? We've been back to my hometown of Moorestown more times than either of us can count or remember, and we've even run into some of my former classmates, but time is the great leveler, especially when you've got a handsome, charming, well-connected guy on your arm. I'm no longer the nerd, at least not on the outside.

Yet part of me still marvels at the children I've produced—Josh, the double varsity star, Emma the valedictorian, popular and pretty. I'm amazed that they came from me, that they have half of my genes. And they do—Josh has my toes, Emma my dimples.

I've outgrown the shy, stammering geeky girl I was, and when I've laughingly told people I was a nerd in high school, brushing it off in an instant, they always looked surprised. *You, Ally? No…*

"Anyone who peaks in high school is going to be disappointed later in life," I'd quip blithely, but part of me would always feel hot with both shame and triumph at my admission, and I never want to go into it too much, to tell people how I was bullied, marginalized, made to feel like a freak.

Perhaps that's why I am able to empathize with Dylan now, in a way that Nick doesn't seem to be able to. I was the weird kid, too.

And yet so was he, surely, at least in a way? "Can't you sympathize," I ask him now, "considering your own childhood?"

Nick gives me the same sort of double take he did when I asked that question hypothetically, back during our training. It feels far more loaded now. "I don't know what kind of childhood you think I had," he says in a final-sounding voice, "but that wasn't it."

What was it, then? I almost say the words, but I'm too tired, and we haven't even resolved the issue of Emma's family weekend, not really.

I sigh and sip my wine, making no reply, and after a couple of tense seconds, Nick clicks play on the remote, and the opening credits of the TV show begin to roll.

CHAPTER ELEVEN

BETH

The morning of the court hearing, I wake up with a gasp and a jerk, staring at the ceiling as I try to reorient myself in reality. I'd been having one of those strange dreams where you're awake enough to control what's happening, and everything makes total sense, although as soon as you regain consciousness it absolutely doesn't.

In the dream, Dylan was small, maybe three or four, and although he didn't look like himself—he was blond and blue-eyed—I knew it was him. We were on a train, one of those old-fashioned trains you find in Europe, with separate compartments and sliding doors. I was holding his hand and stumbling along the corridor, looking for seats, but all the compartments were full of blank-faced people, utterly indifferent to us.

I could hear a conductor lumbering behind me, and I was afraid, even though I knew I had a ticket. I reached my hand into my pocket and held it, anchoring me to the reality that I was allowed on the train, that we were safe.

I had finally found an empty compartment, and slid open the door, filled with relief, when I turned behind me and saw that Dylan had disappeared.

I wake up with my heart thudding, the fear of Dylan just *disappearing* trickling through me as I blink at the ceiling and try to remember my real life. Then I look at the clock, and my heart seems to stop right in my chest. It is eight o'clock, and the court hearing is in an hour.

I scramble up from bed, my mind darting in a dozen different directions. I tell myself not to panic, but I already am. An *hour*… I was meant to be so organized. I was going to get up early and go through all my notes, practice what I'd say… as it is, I will be rushing just to get there in time.

Last night after Marco left, I drank two glasses of wine, and on an empty stomach, and with my low tolerance, it was enough to send me stumbling to bed at eleven o'clock, my mind dazed and spinning.

I can't believe I was that reckless, but I'd felt so unbearably low, so utterly alone, me against the whole world, with no one—except maybe Mike the UPS guy—that I could call on. No one to back my corner, no one to hold my hand. No Dylan to put my arms around, to feel his solid warmth. I couldn't stand it, the gaping emptiness at the center of my life, and in any case, I didn't think two glasses would affect me so much, although obviously they did.

I didn't even mean to drink two—I drained the one, and then I poured another, but I wasn't really intending to drink it. I turned on the TV, and at some point I must have drunk it all, barely realizing what I was doing. Then I'd forgotten to set my alarm, although that wasn't unusual since I'd never needed one with Dylan, but still, for the morning of the court hearing, you'd think I'd remember. You'd think I'd be on top of it, this morning that matters more than any other.

And now I'm here, racing just to be able to show up on time, never mind being organized and efficient and in control, showing the judge and everyone else that I am totally equipped to represent myself, and I should obviously have my son back.

I've already searched and copied down the bus route from here to the Juvenile Court in Hartford, and it takes thirty minutes minimum to get there, plus walking time from the station. If I don't leave in the next five minutes, I am almost certainly going to be late.

"Damn it!" I practically shriek the words, because I'm so furious with myself. This wasn't how today was meant to go at all. I force myself to calm down because I still have an hour, and panicking won't help me—or Dylan. I need to stay in control.

I throw on the clothes I'd already picked out—a plain white blouse and a black skirt. It makes me look like a waitress, but it's the most professional outfit I have. I drag a brush through my hair and shove some makeup into my bag to do on the bus. Then I grab all my notes and papers—fortunately I'd organized them all yesterday, with different color sticky notes and paper clips—and then I practically sprint out of my apartment.

I am breathless and sweating by the time I reach the bus stop on the corner of Farmington and South Main. There is not a bus in sight. I pace up and down, too jittery to stay still, and attract the suspicious looks of the handful of business-suited commuters waiting there.

Where is that bus? It's already eight fifteen—only fifteen minutes since I woke up, and it shows. My hair is still in a tangle and I haven't brushed my teeth. I'm a *mess*. What the hell was I thinking last night, drinking that wine? Stumbling to bed without setting the alarm? Feeling so damned sorry for myself?

I make a sound, sort of a moan, and a woman standing near me edges away. I take a deep breath and do my best to control myself, even though I feel like falling apart. I don't have that luxury now.

A bus finally lumbers up to the stop five minutes later. As I join the line, I see how crowded it is, and I am terrified the driver will make me wait for the next one.

"*Please…*" I mutter under my breath, and I get another strange look from someone in line.

Thankfully, the driver waves me on wearily, seeming to sense my desperation. I must look panicked, maybe even crazed—carrying a sheaf of crumpled papers, my shirt untucked.

The bus ride to Hartford, although only a few miles, takes half an hour as the bus judders to a stop what feels like every few seconds. I manage to tuck my shirt in and smooth out my papers; I brush my hair and dab a little concealer and lip gloss on. It's eight minutes to nine when the bus finally rolls into the Hartford station. According to my phone, it's a fourteen-minute walk to the Court for Juvenile Matters on Broad Street.

Still, I tell myself, I'll only be six minutes late. Five, if I hurry.

I half-walk, half-run down the street, stumbling in my heels. It's four minutes after nine when I get to the Juvenile building, and I groan out loud, nearly a scream, when I see there is a security check at the front door, and a line of at least ten people waiting to go through.

"Please, I'm late," I say a bit desperately to a man waiting in line. He has a baseball cap pulled low over his face and he wears baggy, low-slung jeans and an oversized T-shirt that hangs almost to his knees. "Please, can you let me go through?"

He gives me a dismissive look from under the battered brim of his cap. "We're all waiting, lady."

I take my place in line, biting my lips in frustration, tasting blood. They'll wait, I tell myself. They must be used to people showing up late. They'll have to wait. There might even be a law about it, a rule about *having* to wait.

It's an agonizing twenty minutes after nine before I get through security, and it's another four minutes before I finally locate the court where the hearing is taking place, a set of double doors amidst half a dozen others. As I run towards them, Susan steps from the shadows towards me. She'd been waiting outside, and the look on her face is sorrowful.

"Beth."

"I'm sorry I'm late," I gasp. There are damp patches under my arms and my shirt is untucked again, my face undoubtedly red and shiny. "The bus—"

"Beth, the case has already been adjudicated."

I stare at her blankly, refusing to let the words penetrate. "We can start now—"

"The judge has a policy of waiting fifteen minutes. After that, she makes a decision."

Fifteen minutes? I missed my chance, my whole life, by a mere five minutes? I simply stare at Susan, refusing to take it in. "But… but that's not fair. The bus—"

"Beth, according to the guidelines on the website, you are advised to arrive at the court at least forty-five minutes before proceedings."

I swallow. Had I read that online? I can't remember. Of course, if I'd had a lawyer, I'd have known that. If I'd had a lawyer, someone would have been here to represent me. But I chose not to have one, because I was so sure I could do this by myself.

"But…" I try again, and then I shake my head. "No."

"Beth—"

"*No.*" I shake my head, harder this time, the way Dylan does. All my work… all the research… Then, stupidly, a flash of wild, pointless hope. "What did the judge decide?" *Maybe…*

"Dylan will remain in custody," Susan states gently. "There will be another hearing scheduled in three months."

Three months! *Three months.* I let out a long, low moan, an animalistic sound that comes from the depths of my being. My knees buckle, and Susan grabs my arm to keep me from crumpling to the floor.

"Let me buy you a cup of coffee."

I turn to her, scrabbling at her arm, desperate now. "Can't I talk to the judge? I wasn't that late—"

Susan shakes her head. "Another case is being heard now. They schedule them very closely together. I'm sorry, Beth, but it's been decided. There's nothing you can do."

I close my eyes, bracing myself against the tidal wave of recrimination that slams into me. This is my fault. *Again.* All my fault. Once more a single, reckless decision has the power to make a shipwreck of my whole life, and this time it matters so much more. I can't stand it; I feel as if I could be sick, as if I could tear my hair out, as if I could scream like Dylan and never stop.

"Let me get you a cup of coffee," Susan says again, gently, and I am so devastated that I let her lead me away from the court doors like a child.

I'm not even aware of where we are going, lost in my own despairing haze, but somehow we end up in a coffee shop outside the Juvenile building, and Susan places a cup of coffee in front of me, a Styrofoam cup of a dark, oily, and unappetizing brew.

"Sorry," she says. "This isn't Starbucks."

I take a sip of the drink and wince. I can't speak; I can't even think. I feel frozen, something locked inside me. If I unleash it, I will fall apart; I will simply disintegrate.

"What happened?" Susan asks gently, and I shake my head. I don't want to explain about Marco, the wine. She'll just use it against me at some point, and anyway it sounds too pathetic.

"The bus was late," I say after a moment, my voice monotone.

"Yes, I understand that, but..." Susan pauses. "You look as if you'd been rushing anyway."

"I forgot to set the alarm." I look up from the disgusting coffee. "I never needed one with Dylan."

Susan nods, and I look back down. I wonder if she can smell the alcohol on me. A measly two glasses of wine and she probably thinks I'm a lush, a drunk. Tears prick my eyes and that locked part inside me starts to crumble.

"Isn't there any way..." I begin, and Susan shakes her head.

"Court decisions are final. But I'm very optimistic that there will be a different result in three months. *Very* optimistic."

She's *optimistic*? I realize then that even in three months I might not get Dylan back, especially now that I have this on my record. *Mother could not be bothered to show up to court.* And that's when I start to cry—not a few trickling tears, but a wail of anguish that rises in volume like a siren. I realize, as I hear it coming out of me, that I sound like Dylan.

"Beth." Susan touches my hand, more of a warning than a comfort. "Beth."

I shake my head, tears spilling from my eyes like a tap has been turned on. I manage to lower the sound of my sobs, to something soft and snuffling, but I am still a wreck. I am completely undone.

"I know this isn't what you wanted," Susan says in that steady voice I both crave and despise, "but I honestly think it will be better for you and Dylan. This gives you a chance to seek support, Beth. And for Dylan to, as well."

She's giving me her same old spiel, but I can't fight against it anymore. I can't tell her any longer that I don't agree, that I know what's best for Dylan, because that right has been taken away from me, and it's my fault that it was.

So I just shake my head and cry, because I don't have anything left but grief.

Susan murmurs something and then goes to get some crumpled napkins, which she hands to me wordlessly. I mop my face, trying to get myself under control. After a few minutes, I do. Sort of.

"So what now?" I ask in a raggedy voice.

"I assemble an action plan to determine the steps you need to take in the next few months. When I've done that, I'll meet with you and we'll go through each one." Susan smiles at me. "Remember, Beth, we're here to help."

You're here to take away my kid, I think, but I don't have the energy to say it.

I bunch up the damp napkins as I take a steadying breath. "When can I see Dylan?"

"I can call Monica and try to arrange a visit for this afternoon, if you like," Susan says, still smiling. "You wanted to see where Dylan is living…?"

"Yes." I almost can't believe it's that easy. I can see Dylan *today*. "Yes, I'd like that. Thank you."

"Of course. According to the terms of the judge's decision, you are entitled to see Dylan for an hour once a week for the next four weeks. After that, we can review the visitation schedule."

I know she means well, but she makes me feel like a complete criminal.

I nod, not trusting myself to say anything—or break down again.

Susan's expression softens. "Would you like me to drive you home? And I can call Monica and let you know the details of the visit, before I drop you off." Susan glances at her watch. "I have another appointment in half an hour, but I should have time if we leave now."

"Okay. Thanks."

As Susan smiles at me again, I realize all that she's doing for me—the coffee, the conversation, the ride home. I wonder if I am right to trust her, and then, with a sickening lurch of fear, I wonder if I made a huge mistake in not trusting her from the beginning.

But she took away Dylan.

I rise from my seat and dump my barely drunk coffee in the trash. As I look around the café, I see it is full of down-and-outers, people passing time with defeated looks on their faces, probably all of them waiting for their turn at the court next door. I'm one of them, and they all know it, and the thought depresses me unbearably.

This isn't me—and yet it is. Now, it is.

CHAPTER TWELVE

ALLY

When Monica calls me on Tuesday morning, it's to tell me that the judge decided in favor of DCF, and can Beth come visit Dylan this afternoon?

For a second I simply stand there and blink, my cell pressed to my ear, as I try to process all that information. "Um, yes. Of—of course," I finally stammer. And then: "So… if she's lost custody…"

"The next court hearing will be in three months, and we anticipate reunification happening at that time." A pause, weighted. "Is any of that a problem for you?"

"A problem? What? No." None of this is exactly a surprise, but it still feels like something new. This morning, Nick tousled Dylan's hair and said goodbye to him before going to work, in a way that I knew was meant to be taken as final.

Last night, as we were getting ready for bed, he told me his views on the matter: "She'll get him back. He's got some behavioral issues, sure, but he seems like a fairly normal kid." I pressed my lips together, not wanting to remind Nick that three days ago Dylan had been too weird for him. Now that he was possibly going, he was normal again? "It's not as if he's been abused," he continued as he unbuttoned his shirt. "He doesn't have a mark on him."

"There are different forms of abuse."

Nick shrugged. "He looks pretty healthy to me—well-fed, clean. You know. Anyway, the government can't take kids away for no good reason. It's got to be something serious."

I didn't answer, because his vague, sweeping statements were completely absurd. DCF *did* take kids away, for all sorts of reasons. You heard the horror stories—innocent parents whose child had a bruise from a stray ball during gym class and all of a sudden DCF swept in and removed him. And then the flipside—the poor children who were horrifically abused and somehow the social workers missed it. I didn't understand how both could exist simultaneously, but I knew they did.

"What time would Beth like to come over?" I ask Monica.

"Two o'clock?"

That's in less than two hours. "Okay. Should I... should I tell Dylan?" I lower my voice because he's in the family room, absorbed in building a tower of Lego, just as Nick wished he would.

"Yes, I think that would be a good idea. The visit will last an hour, and Beth would like to see Dylan's room, hear a little bit about how he's been doing."

"Okay."

As I end the call, I wonder why I feel so nervous, the way I did the first day Dylan came to us—only a week ago, but it feels like a lifetime. I feel almost like a different person.

I'm certainly a lot more confident with Dylan. He's still waking up at night, and I'm still spending most nights sleeping next to him, but the days have been going pretty well.

Well, they're *okay*. He still screams sometimes and at least once or twice a day he has a complete and total meltdown—on the floor, kicking and screaming, spending himself utterly, but I wait it out and we are able to move on.

Of course, the rest of my life has been put almost completely on hold. I still haven't managed to call Emma, and I can't remember the last time I had a proper conversation with Josh, or even Nick, about something other than foster care.

My work, which usually takes twenty hours a week, has been whittled down to two and I am way behind the accounts for several of the firms I work for. I haven't had a catchup with any of my friends, except for that semi-awkward drink with Julie, since Dylan came to us, and I can't see it happening anytime soon.

I've already RSVPed to my book club, saying I couldn't come to our meeting this month. I hadn't even read the book, and the thought of discussing plot elements and literary themes makes my brain hurt. I'm way too tired for that.

I glance around the kitchen, which is pretty clean, and then I head over to where Dylan is lying on the carpet.

"Hey, Dylan." He doesn't look at me, but he tenses a little, so I know he's listening. "Guess what? Your mom is going to come visit you today." I've injected a note of enthusiasm into my voice, expecting Dylan to perk up a little, but he scrambles off the floor, knocking the tower apart in the process, and runs to the front door and starts yanking at the handle; thankfully I've already taken the precaution of locking it, after Josh left for school.

"Hey, not so fast." I try for a laugh, although I am discomfited by the intensity of his response. "I can see you're excited to see her, but she's not coming yet, Dylan. Not for a couple of hours." I touch his shoulder gently. "Why don't you come finish the tower with me?"

Dylan flinches away from me, shaking his head firmly. He is standing by the door, his hands resting on the window ledge as he stares out at the driveway with focused determination, a sentinel at his post.

I try again. "Dylan, your mom isn't going to be here for a long time. Why don't you come back into the kitchen?"

Another shake of his head, firmer and longer this time, a back and forth that must make him dizzy. I sense we are skirting close to a meltdown, and I decide not to push it. If he wants to wait by the door for two hours, then fine, I'll let him.

And that's exactly what he does, standing there rigid and unmoving, almost unblinking, for nearly two hours. It's unnerving to see him so still, so purposeful. He must be exhausted, but he never moves from his post. If I thought he was settling in here, that he was happy, then right now I realize I've been mistaken. All Dylan has been doing with me is biding his time.

A little before two, I join him at the window, waiting and watching for Beth's arrival. I have no idea what to expect, or even how to be. I've put some cookies out, and made lemonade, but it all feels a bit strange and surreal.

A few minutes after two, the same beat-up Ford Focus from before pulls into the driveway and Susan, Dylan's caseworker, climbs out of the driver's side. Dylan tenses, his body making me think of an arrow poised for flight, and then he scrabbles at the door handle. For the first time, I hear him speak.

"Mama—*Mama!*" He is belting it out, his voice an unsettling mix of joy and savage determination, as he tries to wrench the door handle right off.

"Let me unlock the door, Dylan," I say as I fumble with the key. "Just a sec—"

The millisecond the lock turns, he is opening the door and flinging himself outside so hard he trips and nearly falls, but he rights himself before he takes a tumble and sprints towards the car, and the door that is just opening.

I stand on the stoop and watch as a woman emerges from the car; I can barely see her because before she's straightened, Dylan has thrown himself at her, and they are a tangle of limbs, their heads, hair the same color, so close together I can't tell them apart.

I glance at Susan, who gives me a wry smile. She does not seem surprised by the joyous ferocity of Dylan's greeting, and for the first time, I wonder why the hell she decided to take him away from the mother he so obviously adores.

"Nice to meet you," I call, futilely, because Dylan and his mother are in their own world. They are both laughing and crying at the same time, and Dylan is clinging to her like a monkey, his arms wrapped around her neck, his legs around her waist. She hoists him on her hip as if she's carried him like this a million times before, even though he's a bit too big to be carried like that—especially for someone so small.

I realize, as Beth comes towards me, her face tilted towards Dylan, barely aware of anything else, she is not what I expected at all. In my vague imaginings of what Beth looked like, I unthinkingly bought into some unfortunate stereotypes. I pictured tattoos, piercings, dyed hair, a slouching, vacant manner, a low-educated woman who was somewhat indifferent to the plight of her child, maybe a hint of drug or alcohol abuse, although neither had ever been mentioned. I didn't realize I'd been holding onto these offensive clichés, constructing a framework around them, until I see Beth and acknowledge she doesn't fit any of my ill-conceived notions.

She is slight, like Dylan, with long, wavy hair the same shade as his—a chocolate brown—and a petite, heart-shaped face, with wide, deep-set hazel eyes. She is wearing a dark green sweater and a pair of jeans, both a little worn-looking but nice enough, and so very normal. She looks like a well-brought-up, middle-class kid—like one of the young women I used to hire to babysit Emma and Josh when they were young.

As she comes towards me, she finally looks up at me, and something flickers in her eyes. She is taking me in just as I was taking her in, and I wonder what she sees. *Middle-aged housewife whose hair needs coloring, trim enough, wearing clothes that aren't quite preppy or funky, as if she can't decide who she wants to be.*

"Hi!" The word shoots out of me like a bullet, and my smile feels too wide, too fake.

Beth nods her greeting, not quite meeting my eyes or giving a smile back. "Thank you for taking care of Dylan." Her voice is low, pleasant, another surprise.

"Of course. It's been my—our—pleasure. He's a wonderful boy." I aim a smile at Dylan, but his head is buried in Beth's shoulder.

"Shall we go inside?" Susan asks in the comfortable tones of someone who is used to these meetings, and how to smooth over the inevitably awkward moments.

"Yes, yes," I say quickly, almost babbling. "Come through."

I lead them back towards the kitchen, my mind racing as I try to think of something innocuous to say. "Maybe Dylan can show you some of the puzzles he's been doing…" I begin, only to realize Dylan is not going to budge from Beth's lap, and neither is she going to encourage him to do so.

Beth sits at the table, still holding Dylan, and I offer lemonade and cookies, both of which are refused by Beth, although Susan takes a glass with a kindly smile.

"So, Beth, you can see Dylan has been very well cared for here," she says in a slightly teacherish tone.

Beth doesn't reply. She rests one hand on top of Dylan's head, as if she is anchoring him to her. He is nestled against her, as if he is trying to fuse himself to her body. It's touching, but it's also a little strange. A little much.

"We're enjoying having him here," I say in the same jolly tone I struggled not to use when Dylan first came to us. "Are there any questions you'd like to ask me?" I give Beth what I hope is an encouraging smile.

She stares at me for a long moment, her eyes so very dark—they are the same hazel as Dylan's, glinting with gold—and doesn't say a word. Okay, that's a little weird, too.

I shift in my seat and hold onto my smile.

"Beth?" Susan prompts gently. "Is there anything you want to know?"

"Has he been—happy?" she asks after a moment, her voice catching.

"Yes, I think so. We went apple picking this weekend and he seemed to really enjoy that." I think about mentioning the woman he mistook for her—I can see the resemblance now—but I don't.

"Apple picking, how fun," Susan says. "I haven't had a chance to go this year."

Beth says nothing. This is starting to feel torturous, but I try to stay upbeat.

"He's been enjoying puzzles while he's here," I try again. "Does he do puzzles when he's with you?"

Beth gives me what can only be called a scathing look, so I can't keep from cringing a little. "Yes, he does puzzles," she says shortly, and I feel I've offended her with my question. Was I being patronizing? I can't even tell. What am I *supposed* to ask her?

"Maybe you'd like to see Dylan's bedroom?" Susan suggests and Beth gives a brief nod.

Gamely, I take them upstairs, Beth still holding Dylan. I try to think of something to say to ease the moment, but my mind is blank.

"Here's his room," I practically sing out, and step aside so Beth can see the guest room. It hasn't changed much in the week since Dylan arrived. The two backpacks are in the closet, and his clothes fill up only one drawer of the dresser. His bunny is on the bed, propped against the pillows.

Beth catches sight of it, and she draws a quick, hitched breath, leaning closer as she clutches Dylan. I realize she is taking in the sewn-on ear, and I can't tell how she feels about it. Should I have done a better job, or not done it at all? I have no idea.

"This is a very nice room," Susan says, like it's a hint for Beth to chime in, but she doesn't say anything. She just turns away and heads back downstairs with Dylan, leaving us to follow. "This is challenging for her," Susan says to me in a low voice as we walk back down the stairs. "She's very… possessive… of her son."

I don't reply, because aren't we all possessive of our children? They're *ours*. It occurs to me then, in a way it never has before, how offensive it must be to Beth, that I am taking care of her child. That I am sewing on the ear of the bunny that she must have lovingly picked out and held and washed, that I am asking her if he likes puzzles when she probably helped him complete his first one, bought them for birthdays. She knows everything about her own child, and here I am, acting as if I can tell her something about him that she doesn't already know by heart.

I feel a rush of shame, and even anger, although I'm not sure who it is directed at. Myself? Susan? The whole broken system? I can't make sense of my feelings, and so I push them away, trying to focus on the present, which is surely hard enough.

When I come back into the kitchen, I see that Beth has moved to the sofa in the family room, and Dylan is on her lap. She is murmuring to him, but I can't make out the words, and I glance at Susan, who is standing in the kitchen, looking a bit bemused.

"I think Beth would like some time alone with her son," she says. "Would you like to show me the rest of the house, Ally?"

I can't tell if this is just to give Beth and Dylan some privacy, or if she needs to inspect it for some reason.

"Sure," I say after a moment. I look around the kitchen, and then gesture to my office. "Here is my office…"

We go through the downstairs—office, laundry room, living room, dining room—and then I head upstairs. Does she need to see Josh's room? It's probably a mess.

But as we get to the top of the stairs, Susan touches my hand. "I'm sorry. I just wanted to give Beth some space."

"Oh." I let out an undisguised sigh of relief. "Right."

"How are you finding all this, Ally?" Susan cocks her head, her smile so sympathetic that I feel weirdly on my guard. "Monica mentioned this is your first placement. I know there can be quite an adjustment period, not just for the child in care, but for the family."

"Um, yeah, we're okay." At least I think we are, mostly. I certainly don't want to burden Susan, who must see families hard hit by tragedy, with my small concerns and petty troubles.

"You have a son?" Susan asks.

"Yes, Josh. He's a junior in high school. And Emma… she's at college."

"How lovely. And how have things been with Dylan?"

"Um, yeah, good." I sound so nervous, as if I am lying. "He's a really sweet boy, but, um, you know, he has his moments."

"Yes." Susan is unfazed by my veiled criticism. "He's been having tantrums? Screaming?"

I think of that high, piercing note. "Yes, but only a few times a day."

Susan nods slowly. "And he's eating and sleeping okay?"

"I think so. He doesn't eat very much and he wakes up in the night sometimes, but it's… manageable." I'm not going to tell her that I sleep next to him most nights, but the omission makes me feel guilty, and I can feel myself blushing. I know I'm probably breaking some rule.

Susan nods again. "Monica and I would like to meet with you together, to discuss Dylan's action plan. Now that we know he'll be staying with you for at least three months, he should be registered for school, as well as scheduled for certain therapies and assessments we believe he needs."

"Yes, of course."

"Would four o'clock tomorrow afternoon be all right?"

"Yes, fine." I hesitate, and Susan raises her eyebrows, sensing my question. "It's just… why did you take him away?" I ask, lowering my voice to a whisper. "I don't understand it. They seem so close… she obviously loves him, and he loves her." I swallow hard. "He stood by the door for two hours, just waiting for her, when I told him she was coming to visit."

"Yes, I can believe that." Susan sounds so unsurprised, I have a sudden urge to shake her, or at least wipe that bland look off her face.

"So why did you separate them?" I ask, and I almost sound aggressive.

Susan just takes my tone in her stride; she must be used to it all by now.

"Did Dylan's response to his mother seem at all… odd… to you?" she asks after a moment, her tone diffident.

"Odd?" I'm not sure what she wants me to say. "I mean, yes, I suppose it was a bit… intense. On both sides."

"Yes." Susan nods as if I've given the correct answer. "It's my belief that their relationship has an unhealthy level of intensity. Beth has isolated Dylan from everyone but herself. She's refused to allow him to go to school, to make friends, or even to receive the appropriate medical care he needs."

I absorb this, trying to fit it in to what I know of Dylan, what I've seen of Beth. "Does he want to go to school?"

"I don't think Dylan has ever been able to figure out what he wants," Susan says quietly. "He's so wrapped up in what Beth wants… in pleasing her, in following her unspoken rules."

"But…" Something about it all doesn't make sense. "Why did you take him away? I mean… how did you figure this all out?"

"It's just guesswork at this point," Susan concedes with a sigh. "Based on observation. I will be very interested to see how Dylan does away from Beth for a significant length of time. If he is able to thrive in school, as well as in a more regulated household. If the tantrums and shrieking stop, because he isn't so anxious about Beth and her reactions."

"That's why he screams? Because of Beth?" That can't be right, since he's done it here, too.

"I think Dylan experiences a lot of anxiety," Susan says. She sounds sad. "Anxiety that Beth, most likely unknowingly, feeds. I'm hopeful that, with the right support and therapy, he can begin to address those anxieties, and Beth can learn to recognize her own unhelpful behaviors." Susan touches my hand briefly. "But we can talk more tomorrow, when we go through Dylan's action plan. Thank you for everything, Ally. The lemonade was delicious."

My mind is still spinning as I follow Susan downstairs. Beth is still in the family room with Dylan, and Susan suggests we sit in the living room, a room we hardly ever use, to give them some privacy. We sit stiffly on armchairs and make awkward chitchat while I instinctively strain to hear Beth's murmurs from the other room.

Finally, after what feels like an age, Susan rises and heads back to the family room. After an uncertain moment, I follow. Susan tells Beth they need to go, and Beth looks stricken for a single moment before her expression hardens into resolve and she stands up, Dylan still clinging to her.

I realize the farewell is not going to go smoothly, and I have about six seconds to brace myself before Beth tells Dylan she has to go, and Dylan starts screaming. Beth is trying not to cry as she attempts to pry her son off her, and I stand there, feeling useless.

It's Susan who steps in, removing Dylan with a calm forceful-ness as she explains the whole process. "Your mom has to go now, Dylan, but she'll see you next week. You're going to stay here with Ally. Maybe you can have some lemonade and a cookie?" She gives me a pointed look and I rush in.

"Yes, yes, a cookie, Dylan. Let's have a cookie."

Susan hands him to me and I find my arms full of flailing boy; I haven't actually held Dylan since he's been with us, and

I feel as if I'm trying to catch hold of a giant grasshopper, or a writhing snake. Susan takes Beth by the elbow and steers her towards the front door; she is crying now, one fist to her mouth. Dylan elbows me in the eye and I bite my tongue to keep from swearing out loud.

Then I hear the front door close, and I put him down, only to have him sprint for the door, which, of course, is unlocked this time, since they've both just left.

I rush after him, nearly falling in my haste, and manage to close the door with the flat of my hand before he's gotten out. Thank God I didn't trap his fingers or worse.

"*Mama!*" Dylan starts pounding on the window, hard enough to make the pane rattle, as Susan reverses the car out of the driveway.

I lock the door.

"*Mama!*"

We both watch the car disappear down the street, and then Dylan starts to scream. I want to cover my ears; I want to scream myself. *Three more months*, I think. *Three more endless months.*

CHAPTER THIRTEEN

BETH

"I know that was hard, but it will get better."

Susan sounds offensively calm as we drive away from Ally's house. From my son. I can't reply, because my throat is clogged with emotion and tears are trickling down my cheeks. How many times will I fall apart in front of this woman? I really do want to be stronger than that.

And so I take a breath, and wipe my face, and will my voice to sound even. "I don't know how you can see how much he misses me and still think you're doing the right thing."

"Doing the right thing isn't always easy, Beth," Susan says. "And it isn't always clear. But I still believe Dylan needs this time away from you."

I don't bother asking why, because I know she'll blather on about support, and I really don't want to hear that now. I want to remember how Dylan felt when I was holding him, his arms wrapped around me, his heart beating against mine, his body as fragile as a bird's.

He was so glad to see me, so wonderfully happy, and it filled me with equal parts joy and grief. I remember his stricken expression as I left and I nearly double over. How could I leave him like that? Again?

I almost didn't. There was a moment, when I was holding him and Susan and Ally had gone upstairs, that I thought about leaving the house. Running away with him. I could go back to my apartment—it really isn't that far—pack a bag of clothes and then just *go*. We'd take the bus, like I did this morning. We'd find somewhere safe, out of state, where DCF wouldn't bother looking for us. It would be just the two of us again, the way it always was.

I was so close to actually doing it—not just the wistful what-if you know you're never really going to act on, but actually *doing* it. I felt my heart start to pound and I half-rose from the sofa, Dylan clinging to me. It was five seconds to the door. *Five seconds.*

But even as I thought that, I heard the creak of the stairs and I knew they were coming back down. I sat back on the sofa and my heart rate slowed and, as I hugged Dylan, I wondered how I could have seriously thought about it at all.

What if I'd been caught? They would have taken Dylan away from me forever. Now, as we drive back towards my apartment, I feel something in me harden.

I'm not going to fight Susan anymore. I'm not going to rage against the heartless machine that is the Department of Children and Families, because it's futile. The judge has decided, the deed is done. Dylan will be living in that house, with that woman, for the next three months. I need to focus on getting myself into a position where they have no choice but to give him back to me. Where it's *obvious*. I have to do everything right.

"Ally seems nice, doesn't she?" Susan says, and I force myself to respond levelly.

"Yes, she does."

Actually, I hate Ally. I hate her instinctively and utterly, because she has my son, and because I could tell from the moment I set eyes on her that she was surprised by me. She'd been expecting some druggie, no doubt, some pathetic loser of a mother who doesn't deserve to have her child. She'd made assumptions about me and I could tell she wasn't ready to let go of them. She kept looking at me as if I were a puzzle she had to solve, as if the pieces of me didn't fit.

And as for *puzzles…*! The way she talked about them—as if I wouldn't know what they were, as if she'd discovered this great interest of Dylan's that I had no clue about, because I clearly didn't care about my son. It made me furious, along with the lemonade and the stupid cookies, Dylan's big bedroom, the smell of air freshener, even the ear stitched on his beloved bunny—I resented all of it. Who does she think she is, June Cleaver? Betty Crocker? She stood there like she thought she was the perfect mom, as if I should be taking notes, *and she had my son.*

I will always hate Ally, but I know I need to be nice to her, because right now she is taking care of Dylan, and his well-being is the most important thing. I can never forget that. So I swallow my vitriol and give Susan what I hope looks like a smile.

"She seems really nice," I say. I have to force each word out, but I think I sound as if I mean it.

Susan smiles back, but I can't tell what she is really thinking. I never can.

She drops me off a few minutes later, after arranging a meeting tomorrow morning to go over my "action plan," which makes me sound like a CEO or a superhero, I'm not sure which. Obviously I'm not remotely close to either.

I trudge towards my apartment, my heart feeling as heavy as my feet, everything hard to move. I don't want this to be my pathetic reality. I just *don't.*

"Beth… Beth!"

As I'm unlocking my door, I see my upstairs neighbor Angela, waving from her doorway with a slightly vacant smile.

"Hi, Angela," I say dutifully, but my heart's not in it. She's going to ask me where Dylan is, except she'll forget his name, and I really don't want to explain everything to another person right now.

"How are you, dear? How is…" Her forehead wrinkles and I fill in,

"Dylan."

"Yes, Dylan! How is he? Such a sweet boy. So quiet."

"He's out with his dad at the moment," I lie, and I don't feel guilty about it at all. I can't face the painful awkwardness of the truth, not right now.

"Oh, is he?" For some reason, this makes Angela brighten. I realize why when she asks, "Why don't you come upstairs for a cup of tea, then?"

I know she's only asking because Dylan isn't here; he doesn't like her apartment, with all its fragile knickknacks and the stuffy, medicine-laced smell it has. I want to refuse, because I'm exhausted and sad and fragile, but the naked hopefulness on Angela's face makes me pause. I think she is about as alone as I am. She doesn't have any family to visit, as far as I can tell, and the only person who ever comes to her apartment is a gum-chewing care worker who helps her with some errands and housework, and is paid by the hour.

"Sure," I say, pitching my voice loud enough for her to hear, as she's a little deaf. "That would be nice. Thanks."

Upstairs, I follow Angela into her apartment—a shrine to decor circa 1981. Clashing floral patterns and lace doilies feature heavily, along with porcelain figures of shepherdesses and milk-maids. It's the same configuration as my apartment downstairs—a long, narrow living room, the kitchen in the back, a bedroom and bathroom to the side—but it feels completely different.

"Hasn't it gotten cold?" Angela remarks as she bustles back to the kitchen on slippered feet. "There was a frost this morning."

"Yes, funny to think it's almost November." And it will be almost February before I can get Dylan back. That feels ages away—and what about Thanksgiving and Christmas? Where will he be for the important days, the family ones? All of it—the uncertainty along with the knowledge--gives me a physical ache in my middle, a sharp pain that feels like a drill burrowing into me.

Angela gives me a sympathetic look, although she can hardly guess what I'm thinking. "It's hard, isn't it?" she says as she puts the kettle on the stovetop. I stare at her blankly; she can't know what I'm going through… unless she was the neighbor who said something to Susan? Looking at her now, smiling so benignly, I can't believe it of her. It has to be Mr. GT5 from the top floor.

"Yes," I finally say, because it's the only response I can give. "It is hard."

"I was a single mother, you know," Angela continues. "My husband left me when I was only twenty-four. It was the early sixties then. Single mothers weren't looked at all that kindly, I can tell you."

I try not to gape. "I didn't know…"

"No, I never like to say." She lets out a little sigh. "People make assumptions, don't they?"

"Yes." I know that much is true. I just didn't think they made those kinds of assumptions about people like Angela—gentle old ladies with china shepherdesses and lace doilies everywhere.

"Anyway, it can be difficult, when it's just you, making all the decisions, shouldering all the responsibility. Second-guessing yourself, and there's never anyone to ask if you're doing it right." She smiles and shakes her head.

She's captured my feelings so accurately, I struggle to find something to say. I want to thank her for understanding, for stating it so simply, yet I can't quite find the words. "Where is your daughter now?" I ask. Angela is around eighty, so her daughter must at least be in her fifties, yet I haven't seen anyone come by in the four years I've lived below her.

Angela's face crumples into sadness. "She lives out in California now. She won't visit." The kettle boils and she pours hot water into a floral-patterned teapot.

"Why won't she visit?" I ask as Angela shuffles to the fridge to get milk.

"We had an argument a long time ago. Twenty or twenty-five years ago now, I'd say." She squints, smiling sorrowfully, as she shrugs her bony shoulders. "Do you know, I can't even remember what it was about? But I must have done something, mustn't I?"

I stare at her for a few seconds, overwhelmed with sadness for her as well as for myself. How can her daughter be so estranged, for something Angela can't even *remember*? How can she leave Angela to get by on her own, when she's so ill and frail and obviously lonely?

"Here you are, dear." Angela smiles at me as she hands me a porcelain cup of very milky, very weak tea.

"Thank you, Angela."

As she sits down across from me at the little round table, a sudden horrible thought occurs to me. I've been so focused on getting Dylan back, and dealing with DCF, that I haven't really considered how he'll react when he's back home with me. What if he's angry with me? What if he resents me now or later in life, for abandoning him? I think of how tightly he held me earlier and I want to be reassured, but three months is a long time, and I only get to see him for one hour a week, at least for the next month. What if, like Angela's daughter, Dylan ends up estranged from me, bitter and angry, refusing to visit?

"I used to write her," Angela says, breaking into my thoughts.

"Your daughter?"

"Yes. Every week, until I couldn't anymore." She gives me an apologetic smile as she taps her head. "The brain isn't what it used to be, I'm afraid. I can't write anything but my name these days. The letters just don't come out right. It's so frustrating."

"I could write her for you, if you want." The suggestion slips out before I've thought it through, but it feels right.

Angela looks surprised. "Oh…"

"You could tell me what to say. I don't mind. But only if you want to."

"Oh, Beth." She sniffs and then laughs and takes a little lace-edged hanky from her sleeve and dabs her eyes. "That's so very kind of you. Thank you."

"It's no trouble."

"Really very kind." She smiles and sighs and tucks the hand-kerchief back in her sleeve as she looks around the little kitchen, her forehead crinkling. "Now, where is…"

"Dylan. He's not here." I try to smile. "He's with his dad."

About twenty minutes later, I'm back in the emptiness of my own apartment, having promised to visit Angela tomorrow to help her write a letter to her daughter. I wonder if she'll even remember the conversation, but I am determined to follow through. It feels good, to help someone with their problems, rather than just focus on my own.

However, any sense of purpose or goodwill I felt helping Angela drains away as I gaze around the barren space and miss Dylan. Missing him is an activity that takes up all my emotion, all my energy, and yet still leaves me so empty. It's only four o'clock in the afternoon and I can't stand the thought of another evening alone. For the last few days, I'd been so busy preparing for the court hearing that I didn't let myself feel lonely. Now there's nothing but the prospects of three months of nights like this one.

Then my phone rings, and when I look at the screen, I see, with a surprise verging on pleasure, that it's Mike. I gave him my number a few days ago, when he was asking about the court hearing… and now I'll have to tell him the judge's verdict. That little flicker of pleasure evaporates.

"Beth? How did it go?"

He sounds so eager, I don't want to disappoint him, but of course I have to. "The judge decided that Dylan should stay where he is, for now."

"What...!" Mike's shock is almost gratifying, even though I don't feel I deserve it after my shameful no-show this morning. "But how? Why?"

I can't bear to tell him that I actually missed the whole hearing. "She just did."

"Aw, Beth." Mike sounds genuinely upset. "That's so unfair. I'm so sorry. Is there anything I can do?"

"Thanks, but I don't think so. There's nothing anyone can do but wait." And jump through all the hoops Susan is going to set me.

"When do you get him back?"

"There's another hearing in three months. Hopefully then."

"Aw, man. I really am sorry."

"Thanks."

We're both silent, the only sound our breathing. I don't feel so alone, and yet at the same time I feel more alone than ever. Mike is the only person in the world who cares about me right now, and I don't even know his last name.

"Look..." he says after a moment. "I know this might not be the right time... but I get off work in another hour... do you want to get a pizza or something?" There's a slightly wobbly note of vulnerability in his voice, and he sounds so sincere and so nice that I almost say yes.

But part of me feels as if doing anything like that would be a betrayal of Dylan, and another part can't even remember how to socialize. Would it be a date? And even if it wasn't, how am I supposed to act? What would we talk about? It's been way too long since I've done anything social. Since I've had a friend.

"Beth?" Mike prompts, and I realize the silence has gone on too long.

"That's really nice, Mike, but I think I'm just going to stay home tonight. But thank you for thinking of me."

"No problem. I understand totally. That's cool." He trips over his words in his effort to assure me it's all okay.

But it doesn't feel okay as we say goodbye, promising to talk soon, and when I end the call, the silence in the apartment seems weirdly loud, like a ringing in my ears. I have a sudden urge to make a noise, to scream, but I don't.

I half-wish I'd said yes to Mike, even as it feels impossible. Yet the whole evening empty in front of me feels impossible too. And another and another and another—nearly ninety evenings like this at least.

What will I do? How will I survive?

And then I think about how if I can't go back to the beginning and reset, then I want to skip to the end. It would be so easy. I'd go to the doctor, I'd tell him how I'm not sleeping, how I'm depressed. He'd prescribe something—I've never taken anything before, so I don't think I would be seen as a risk.

And then I'd sit on my bed and swallow all the pills with a mouthful of water. I'd curl up on my side and just drift away. It really would be that easy.

But of course I can't do that, even though right now I want to, with that same gut-kick sense of urgency I had at Ally's, when I almost ran out of the house. But I didn't, and I'm not going to do this, either.

Because of Dylan.

Dylan. I need to remember why I'm here, who is important. Dylan. Everything I do is for him.

CHAPTER FOURTEEN

ALLY

"You ready, bud?"

I give Dylan what I hope is a cheerful smile as I unbuckle my seatbelt. It's eight-twenty in the morning and we're parked in the lot in front of the local elementary school that Emma and Josh used to attend. A line of long yellow school buses has pulled up in front, and children are trotting in with backpacks and lunchboxes, all under an azure sky, the scene framed by the scarlet leaves of the trees in the school yard. It's a quintessential American moment, and yet I don't yet know where we fit into it.

Two days ago, Susan and Monica both came over and went over Dylan's action plan with Nick and me—I asked him to stay so he'd know what was going on, and thankfully, with some badly masked reluctance, he agreed.

He'd been surprised that we still had Dylan on Tuesday evening when he'd come home from work, but he'd tried to cover it, giving Dylan a cheerful smile and then sitting down and doing a puzzle with him before dinner. I appreciated the effort, even if things were a little strained between us still.

There was a lot to take in from Susan—a plan for Dylan to go to school, and a raft of appointments over the next few weeks—pediatrician, dentist, psychiatric assessment, and weekly sessions with a cognitive behavioral therapist.

Susan had been liaising with the school, so Dylan would have his own special education assistant to help him, at least at the beginning, but the truth is, I cannot imagine him going into school willingly, and staying there all day.

"What if school doesn't work out?" I asked Susan and Monica, as we sat at the kitchen table with the papers spread out before us.

"Helping Dylan assimilate to a school environment is a crucial part of his action plan," Susan said, which wasn't actually an answer. "It's important that we are all committed to it."

"Is Beth committed to it?" Nick asked unexpectedly, and Susan nodded.

"She has agreed, yes."

"Well, we'll certainly do our best." I lifted my gaze to the view of the backyard, where Josh was attempting to kick a ball with Dylan. Dylan wasn't really playing, but it heartened me to see them together, and that Josh was at least trying.

Yesterday we'd spent nearly two hours at the pediatrician, getting all Dylan's health forms filled out, including giving him a boatload of vaccinations he'd never had.

"He has no record of *any* vaccinations?" The nurse had asked me with more than a hint of censure in her voice and I'd shrugged apologetically.

"He's… he's not mine." I regretted phrasing it that way as soon as I said the words. Dylan's expression didn't change, but I felt something from him, a sort of mental flinch. "I'm his foster mother," I amended. "He's been living with us for the last nine days."

Dylan did spookily well with the needles. I remembered having to hold a screaming Emma down with the help of two nurses, but Dylan simply sat there, and he didn't even make a sound when the needle went in—again and again, because he had to have so many. By the time we were done, both arms were speckled with colorful Band-Aids, and he'd stayed completely silent.

"Aren't you a brave boy?" the nurse said, thawing from earlier, but then she gave me a look of sympathy, as if she knew Dylan's reaction, or lack of it, to having the vaccinations was a bit off. It had made things easier, especially since he had to have another round in two months, but it seemed weird; I'd been fully expecting to have to have him in a wrestling hold while the nurse administered the shots. I realized then how little I understood him; I didn't know what upset him, or what didn't.

We went to Dunkin Donuts afterwards for what was meant to be a post-doctor treat, but as soon as the door closed behind us, Dylan started screaming. I hustled him out as quickly as I could, wondering why Dunkin Donuts set him off and four needles into his arms didn't, and we had a chocolate milk at home instead.

And now we're here, and I really am wondering how this is going to work.

"So this is your new school, Dylan," I say as I help him out of the car. He has a new lunchbox—a *Cars* one, like his backpack—and he carries it carefully, like a briefcase. He hasn't responded to any of the changes in the last few days how I expected him to—with resistance, screaming, tantrums. He'd just been eerily silent and wide-eyed, blank-faced. It's definitely a little spooky, but at least it makes it easier. Still, I'm worried about leaving him. He looks so small.

We walk hand in hand to the doors; the principal, a friendly, round-faced woman, and Dylan's special ed assistant, a hip-looking African-American woman with braided, waist-length hair, are waiting for him in the office as we come in. They both give him wide smiles as we enter the room, and while Dylan doesn't smile back, he doesn't scream, either.

I feel myself start to relax just a little. Maybe this is actually going to be okay. I fill out a bunch of paperwork, and listen to the principal explain the plan for Dylan's adjustment to school, but at this point it's so much white noise. I've heard it all before from

Susan, how he needs a 504 plan until he can get an IEP—phrases I'd never heard before now, but meant he would get the help he needed in school. The IEP, or Individual Education Plan, comes with an official diagnosis, and how the steps of the plan will be reviewed weekly, in a meeting with the principal, the classroom teacher, the special education assistant, and Susan, who will inform me of any changes.

It reminds me that even though I have the most responsibility for Dylan right now, even though I'm the one tucking him in at night and making sure his teeth are brushed, I don't get any say in things like this. I just get to be kept informed.

Ten minutes later, it's time for me to say goodbye, and suddenly my throat goes tight. I've only known this little boy for a week and a half, but right now he's looking at me with his big hazel eyes full of so much trust and yet also fear, and I feel as if I'm betraying him... which makes me wonder, uncomfortably, how Beth must feel.

"So you're going to stay at school, Dylan," I say, crouching down so I'm eye-level with him. I've told him this before, but it bears repeating now. "And I'll pick you up at the end of the day, at three-twenty. And then you can tell me everything that happened, okay? All the exciting things you did." Why I'm suddenly acting as if he talks, I don't know, and yet I know he'll find a way to communicate with me, just as I'll find a way to understand. "All right, bud? Okay?"

"Say goodbye to Ally now, Dylan," the principal says firmly. She's put one hand on his shoulder and I can tell he doesn't like it, although he doesn't move. He simply looks at me with that fathomless, unblinking stare, and I want to hug him, but I don't know he'll react and it's clear the principal and special ed assistant both want me to leave as quickly as possible.

So I do, straightening with a smile, giving him a little wave, and then walking quickly out of the building. I don't know why

I'm so close to tears as I head back to the car, forcing myself not to look back even once.

Two weeks ago, I'd never even heard of Dylan McBride—now I know his last name, along with his birthdate, his height, his weight, the bedtime stories he likes, the fact that his favorite color of Lego brick is green. A couple of days ago, I was half-hoping his mother would get him back. What has changed now, that is making me feel as if I've left part of my heart back in that school? Everything and nothing, and I don't even know why.

I think of his grin as he handed me the puzzle piece a few days ago; the feel of his little hand limp in mine. The way his eyelids flutter when he sleeps. That trusting, unwavering stare. I draw a shuddering breath and then I get in the car.

The house is quiet as I unlock the front door and step inside; it's the first time I've been alone in it in nearly two weeks, and it feels both unsettling and like a relief. I drop my keys on the kitchen counter with a clatter and I look around the gleaming, yawning space of the empty kitchen and wonder what to do.

Of course, there are a million and one things I could be doing. Work, for one. I'm more behind than I ever have been, and while the firms I work with have been understanding, they won't be forever. And then there's laundry, which has piled up for several days, along with the sacks of apples, and all the other housework—I don't think I've changed Josh's sheets since at least a week before Dylan came.

With a sigh, I decide the first thing I'm going to do is make myself some coffee and simply sit in the sunshine streaming in from the French windows and just *be*. Breathe and sit and think. It sounds wonderful.

I've just switched the coffee maker on when the front door opens and I hear Nick sing out a jaunty, "Hel-*lo*!"

"What are you doing home?" The question sounds a bit ungracious, but I'm surprised. He left for the office less than two hours ago.

"I thought I'd come back and see how the morning went." He seems strangely buoyant as he comes into the kitchen, shedding his briefcase and then his suit jacket like a man who has been let off the hook.

"You could have just texted—" I feel slightly grudging of losing my solitude for the first time in weeks, although I try to hide it, because Nick seems so cheerful.

"And I wanted to see how you were doing." He shimmies over to me and snakes his arms around my waist, pulling me into him. I put my arms around his neck, trying to smile, but the truth is I'm not really in the mood.

And I can tell Nick is, as he nuzzles my neck and says in a voice full of deliberate, Casanova-like swagger, "We're alone for what feels like the first time in months."

"Weeks, Nick, not months…"

He reaches down to pop the button on my jeans, and I manage a half-hearted laugh.

"Nick, it's not even ten in the morning."

"So?" He gives me a teasingly lascivious look, and I wonder how I can feel so utterly unsexy. This is really just about the last thing on my mind. Nick hasn't even asked how it went, if Dylan settled, if he screamed.

He unzips my jeans. "Nick…"

"Come on, Ally. Don't you want to?" He gives me a little boy look and I try to smile. "I came home specially."

"I know you did." I can feel myself crumbling, because he did come home specially, and we haven't had any time together. If we can't work in this way, how can we work in any other?

And so I nuzzle him back and, flushed with victory, he scoops me up in his arms and grandly carries me upstairs. It all feels a bit forced, a bit too much, but I make myself go along with it, laughing and putting my arms around his neck as he lumbers up the stairs.

In the bedroom, we shed clothes quickly—the mundane details of this sexy morning—and then slip under the covers. Nick draws me towards him, and after ten days of sleeping in the guest room with Dylan, the bump and slide of flesh on flesh shocks me. But it does feel good to have Nick's naked body next to mine, to remember how we fit, how we work. We need this, even if my heart hasn't been in it. I pull him closer, determined to make up for my lack of feeling. In any case, I don't think Nick notices.

Afterwards, he rolls onto his back and lets out a deep, satisfied sigh, before he checks his watch and makes a clucking noise, like he needs to get going.

"You haven't asked how Dylan got on at school," I say before I can stop myself.

Nick rolls out of bed and reaches for his boxers. "How did he?"

"I'm not sure I even know. I left quickly. It seemed as if they wanted me to."

"Okay, then," Nick says, as if that proves he didn't actually need to ask, and maybe he didn't. I feel as if I've been trying to pick a fight, but I don't want to. I just want him to care.

"So back to work?" I say, trying for a light tone.

"I've got a meeting at eleven."

"Wow, this was a quick one."

He flashes me a quick smile. "But definitely worth it." He leans over and kisses me, and I close my eyes, wanting to savor it. "Love you."

"I love you, too." No matter what tensions have been between us lately, I mean it.

"See you tonight. Text me when you pick up Dylan and let me know how his day went."

"I will." I stay in bed as I hear Nick jog down the stairs and then the front door close. This wasn't how I planned my morning at all, but now that I'm in bed I feel like I could just curl up and go to sleep. I'm tempted to do just that, but necessity compels me to get up.

I take a quick shower and dress again, and then, not ready to face work, I decide to do some housework. I have, strangely enough, always enjoyed cleaning—the satisfaction of seeing the results, of putting some elbow grease into something and making it shine. I blitz the downstairs with cleaning spray and then vacuum, and then I decide to brave the pit of despair that is Josh's room.

Once upon a time it was a cute, boyish bedroom with a solar system theme, a wicker basket full of Legos, and framed pictures that Josh had drawn in elementary school. When Josh started junior high, sports trophies—the kind all the kids got—decorated the top of the dresser.

At some point—four or five years ago—all that went into a storage bin and was replaced by a plain black duvet, a black varnished desk from IKEA, and a laptop. Josh's baseball and cross-country trophies are in Nick's study. I think he's prouder of them than Josh is.

Now I open the door, take a deep breath, and step inside. The curtains are drawn, the duvet a rumpled lump on the bed, clothes in dirty heaps on the floor. The room holds a stale, sweaty smell of unwashed clothes and cheap deodorant. I push the curtains open and crack the window, grateful for the cold, fresh breeze that blows over me.

First, I strip the bed, bundling the sheets into the laundry basket I've brought with me. Then I quickly spray the dresser and desktop with furniture polish and wipe them down. Lastly, I start sorting through the piles of clothes on the floor to try to determine which are actually dirty and which are clean but never made it into the drawers. It requires the unenviable sniff test, and I wince every time I get it wrong, before hurling the offending item into the laundry basket.

I am refolding the clean clothes and putting them in the drawers, thinking about how I need to get started on my own work, when I feel something lumpy and solid underneath Josh's boxers.

At first, I'm just naïvely curious, wondering what made it into his underwear drawer, until my hand closes around the object and I take it out. It's money—a wad of bills tightly rolled and held together with a dirty rubber band. I blink at it, not understanding, because Josh has a bank account and a debit card. He gets an allowance of fifty bucks a month, and he made some money from his summer job of mowing lawns, but it all goes into his bank account.

I remember when he was about eight, and Nick and I took him into Webster Bank and helped him fill out the form for a junior savings account. We were so proud, watching our young son achieve this little milestone of maturity.

I take off the rubber band and start smoothing the bills, feeling as if I am outside of myself, watching this unfold. It's mostly tens and twenties, but there are a lot. When I finish counting, it's over six hundred dollars. Six hundred and fifty-four, to be exact. There's no way my son has this sort of money... except he does.

Not knowing what else to do, I roll the bills back up and fit the rubber band around them, my fingers shaking. It's not an easy task at the best of times; there are a lot of bills and they're crumpled now.

I stand there for a moment, the money in my hand, my mind spinning. What should I do—take the money? Call Nick? I feel frozen, my mind skating off to various possibilities and then scurrying back. There has to be a reasonable explanation. Plenty of reasonable explanations.

It's not his money; he's keeping it for a friend. He withdrew all his money from his account—but why? My mind continues to skate and scurry, and then, because I really have no idea what to do, I shove the money back under my son's boxers. I'll leave it there until I've talked to Nick, until we figure out how to approach this. But as I go downstairs, I push thoughts of that money out of mind. I can't think about it now. Not on top of everything else. Not on top of Dylan.

And so I pour myself the cup of coffee I forgot about earlier, and heat it up in the microwave, and take it to my office. I open my laptop and try to focus on bookkeeping, and other people's money, and not the six hundred and fifty-four dollars fairly pulsing with malicious purpose upstairs in my son's underwear drawer.

CHAPTER FIFTEEN

BETH

The Positive Parenting Program that Susan signs me up for is in Wethersfield, which is an hour by bus from West Hartford. It was the only one with space available, and she asks if I mind taking the class with two other people. Apparently, because this is a Level Four class, I'm meant to take it one-on-one with the instructor, but there aren't enough instructors, or maybe just too many crap parents. I don't even know how many levels there are, or whether four is good, bad, or in the middle.

In any case, I say I don't mind, both because I hate the thought of some sanctimonious teacher spending a hundred percent of her time scrutinizing me, and because I am determined to be agreeable to everything Susan says. I've also consented to see a counselor, over in Simsbury, because it's the only one with space who works with DCF. By the end of these three months, I'll have travelled all over the state by bus just to satisfy Susan.

But I don't complain; I didn't protest a single point when Susan went through her action plan—all the things both Dylan and I need to do to be reunited.

"So counselling and a parenting class," I said, trying to keep my tone positive even though I could feel my hands curling into claws in my lap. "Anything else?"

Susan folded her hands on my kitchen table as she gave me one of her smiling looks. "I'd like to see you developing some community support, Beth. Maybe a local parenting group or even a religious community?"

I stared at her in disbelief. "So you're saying I have to go to church to get my son back?"

"No, of course not. But it's important that you don't continue to be isolated."

"So I need to make friends."

She raised her eyebrows. "Do you have friends?"

What a question. "A few." I thought of Mike, and maybe Angela. Wow. "Actually," I told her, "I'm friendly with my upstairs neighbor. I'm helping her write a letter to her daughter this afternoon." I said this a bit belligerently, even though I didn't mean to. It was just so hard not to sound defensive when someone was analyzing your every move.

"That's great," Susan enthused. "I'm so pleased."

Now, as the bus trundles down the highway to Wethersfield, past a monochrome near-winter landscape, I let my mind drift. I have no idea what to expect from this parenting class, and it makes me think about when I first became a parent.

I didn't even realize I was pregnant for a little while, because I was that naïve. Marco had been using protection but not reliably and I hadn't let myself think that way—that I could have a baby. It just didn't seem possible. I had only just turned nineteen; a few months before, I'd been in high school.

And then my period was late, and I started feeling tired and achy and nauseous, and I'd been watching some stupid romcom, I can't remember the name, but the main character had all the classic symptoms and had a well-duh moment and then I did too.

I didn't say anything to Marco; by that time I'd finished my community service at the nursing home and I'd got a job working at Michaels Crafts in Farmington. I just restocked shelves and mopped the floors, but I loved the atmosphere—the reels of bright ribbon, the swatches of fabric, the Styrofoam shapes and fake flowers and jars full of beads and crystals.

After my shift one evening, I walked to the nearest CVS and bought a pregnancy test. The cashier was a guy my age, the kind of guy who probably played football and dated a cheerleader, and I went crimson with mortification as he searched the slim white box for a barcode. It seemed to take ages, and when I accidentally met his eye, he gave me a little smirk.

Funnily enough, it was that smirk that made me realize I wasn't actually worried or scared about being pregnant. I was excited. I met his smirking expression with a proud one of my own, and then I put the test in my bag and took the bus home, feeling as if everyone must be able to see it even though it was safely tucked away.

Marco wasn't home yet, which was just as well. I took the test and stared at that magic little window and even though the instructions had said to wait for three minutes, it only took about ten seconds before two blazing pink lines showed up—and I laughed out loud.

I'll never forget the feeling I had just then—of joy, and excitement, and hope, all untainted by any fear or uncertainty. It felt so clear to me then. I wasn't alone. I had someone to love, someone who would love me. I wasn't just Beth McBride, drifting through life. I was Mommy. Or I would be soon. I didn't even think about Marco—not as a father or a husband or anything at all. I just thought about me and my baby. Which, I suppose, was pretty indicative of the problems between Marco and me.

In any case, he was shocked, and then he was worried, and then he decided to embrace it all and talked about getting married, although he never actually asked me or bought me a ring.

I read everything I could online about pregnancy, and sometimes I would tell Marco things—when the baby was the size of an egg, or a lemon, or a pear, but after that first dazzling display of solidarity, he wasn't really interested. In fact, as my lovely bump grew so did his discontent. I was tired; I was fat; I was boring. He never said as much, but I could feel it emanating from him like something toxic and I didn't care. I think, in some dark corner of my heart, I was actually glad. Some part of me just wanted it to be my baby and me.

When the birth came, it was actually easy. My OB had warned me I could have a hard time because I was small and slender, but Dylan was born in less than two hours, which the nurse said had to be a record for a first baby. I didn't even have to have any pain relief. I didn't want any; I didn't want anything to dull my senses or take away from the perfect clarity of the experience.

And then the nurse put Dylan on my chest, all red and squalling, his face scrunched up and his fists bunched by his chin waving furiously, and I fell in love.

I'd thought I loved my baby before, with the swelling of my bump and every precious kick, but I didn't even know the half of it then. When I looked into Dylan's deep blue eyes, his little reddened, wizened face, it was like my heart tipped right over and fell into his. I knew I'd never know what it was to be separate again.

I try to remember now how those first few weeks and months of Dylan's life were—a blur of sleepless nights and endless feeds, and Marco stomping around, annoyed that life wasn't as easy as it had once been. Looking back, I know I was a bit too indifferent to him; I was entirely wrapped up in Dylan; I couldn't have cared less about his father. But now, as the bus takes the exit for Wethersfield, I do my best to recall when Dylan started having challenges. When was his first tantrum? When did I realize he wasn't speaking, that he was scared of so much?

I'm not sure I can pinpoint a time or even a year. I suppose I thought all babies needed to be held all the time, and fed almost as much. I thought all mothers watched their babies sleep and made sure they were breathing. I didn't think I was different, because I didn't know what *same* looked like. If normal has a definition, I never knew what it was.

And in any case, I didn't mind any of it. I wasn't looking for a break from Dylan; I was never annoyed that he took so much of my time. I remember standing in a checkout line at the supermarket behind a woman who had a baby the same age as Dylan—about a year old, then. Her little boy was plopped in the front seat of the shopping cart, sticky hands reaching for everything, bright button eyes alight with interest.

"What a cutie," the checkout lady said, and the woman rolled her eyes.

"He never sleeps. Never stops moving. I can't get a second's peace, honestly." She let out a heavy sigh and shook her head, as if in regret.

I remember watching her with a sort of repulsed curiosity. What kind of mother talked that way about her baby? Of course, I knew what kind of mother did something like that. What kind of mother chose her own comfort over her child's. Mine.

But I was never, ever going to be like my mother. And in any case, I was happy. Sometimes I think that was the happiest I've ever been, when Dylan was small and utterly dependent on me, when every young mother was stuck at home, attached to her child, and neither my son nor I felt like a freak.

The bus rumbles down Wethersfield's main street, which is as quaint as a postcard, all painted wooden buildings and the typical New England white spire. The Positive Parenting Program (Triple P, as Susan called it) meets in the town's community center, which is only a few minutes' walk from the bus stop.

It's a huge building, as big as a school, with a fitness center, a banqueting room, and several other spacious meeting rooms. A woman at the front desk raises her eyebrows inquiringly and I tell her I'm here for the Triple P course, because I don't want to say out loud that I need to take a parenting course, but it doesn't matter because she knows exactly what I'm talking about.

When I approach the function room at the end of a long, carpeted hallway, I see there are two women already there, sitting at a conference table, looking uncertain and out of place.

The first one looks about fourteen—she's chewing gum and is heavily pregnant, her dyed blond hair pulled back into a high ponytail. The second is a type similar to Ally—mid-forties, trim, highlighted hair, a lot of nervous energy. As I step into the room, I can't help but think what a trio of misfits we are, but I suppose that is to be expected, considering the circumstances.

They both nod a greeting as I take a seat, but none of us speaks or makes eye contact. The young one takes out her phone and starts swiping with the sort of vigorous boredom that suggests Instagram or TikTok—not that I have either, but I know about them.

I take a seat two down from the teen, glancing around the nondescript room—conference table, chairs, a blank-faced whiteboard. There is a stale smell of old coffee in the air, which makes me wonder if we'll get refreshments. This course is two hours long, after all.

After a minute or two, a woman sweeps into the room. She's in her fifties, with gray hair piled haphazardly on top of her head and a smiley sort of face. She's wearing a loose blouse and a long skirt, and she has hippie jewelry—a beaded necklace and dangling earrings. I'd think she was trying too hard, but somehow it works, and I like her, although part of me doesn't want to.

"I see I'm the last one here." She gives us all a wide smile as she puts a battered messenger bag on one end of the table. "Have you been able to get acquainted?" Silence as we all shrug. "Why don't we go around and say our names? I'm Margaret, and I have two daughters, Stella and Verity, aged twenty-one and twenty-four."

She turns to me expectantly, and I half-mumble, "I'm Beth and I have a son, Dylan, who is seven." Just saying that much makes my voice catch and I look down at the chipped Formica table, blinking hard, as the teenager introduces herself.

"I'm Angelica, and I have a son who is two and this one here." She rests one hand on her large bump. "Due in two months." I can't keep from looking up in surprise. She has a son who is *two*? She looks so young.

The last woman takes her turn. "I'm Diane, and I have a son, Peter, who is eleven." She swallows hard, as if she is going to say more, but then decides not to. She presses her lips together and looks at us all defiantly. I wonder what her story is, and if I want to know it.

"Great," Margaret enthuses. "This is a great start." We all stare at her blankly, because all we've done is say our names. "Now I'll just say a few words about the Triple P course, in case you haven't had a description of it yet."

We all settle back into our seats in a way that makes me think we've all had the description, but Margaret's got to tick this box anyway.

I tune out a bit as she explains about how we're going to learn about positive parenting techniques before we tackle any challenges, even though she expects we'll want to rush ahead to deal with any issues we're facing currently. We're in the Level Four course because we're dealing with, as she says, "significant challenges". I can't argue with that, but I want to.

Then she gives us each a checklist to make sure we're really Level Four worthy. I scan the list and inwardly squirm at each description: *Do you struggle to take your child out in public? Does your child wake repeatedly at night, or need an extended routine to fall asleep? Do you find yourself arranging your life to meet your child's emotional needs?*

Yes, yes, and yes, I think, but does that have to be a problem? Clearly it does, since I'm here, and I wonder then why I am so resistant to this course. Surely I want to be a better mom… even if it means admitting I wasn't a great one already. My thoughts go round and round in an unpleasant circle, and I force myself to listen to Margaret as she launches into the positive parenting techniques, talking as if it is both elementary and rocket science at the same time—obvious, yet clearly completely beyond us.

I try not to get annoyed as she talks about spending quality time with our children—"it only has to be ten or fifteen minutes at a time, but really invested, without your phone or the television on"—and how important physical affection is—"hugging, cuddling, tickling."

Angelica is already looking bored and Diane is chewing her nails. I am silent, because I know I don't need this. I already spend plenty of quality time with my child, never mind ten or fifteen minutes. And physical affection, or lack of it, has never been an issue. Did Susan really think I needed to be told this?

By the end of the two hours, I am feeling restless and definitely annoyed, because Margaret hasn't said anything I don't already know, that I don't already *do*. She must have picked up on my irritation because as I'm standing up, getting ready to leave, she smiles at me, cocking her head, and says, "I got a feeling I was preaching to the choir today, Beth."

I shrug, glancing at Angelica and Diane, who are doing their best to hightail it out of there.

"I know some of the things I say will seem obvious," Margaret continues in a gentle tone. "But they're still important to reiterate."

I shrug again, because I don't know how to respond. I feel like the naughty kid being kept after school. Angelica has already slouched out of the room, and Diane is sidling past us with a nervous smile. Why did I merit singling out? It wasn't as if those two were stellar students.

"Anyway," Margaret says with another smile, "I just wanted to reassure you that we will move on next week to some topics that might feel a bit more practical and relevant."

"Okay, thanks," I mutter, and then I follow Diane out the door, breathing a sigh of relief. One down, nine more to go.

Twilight is already settling over the town as I wait at the bus stop, hugging myself because the day has developed that sharp, wintry coldness that comes in a New England November, always seeming to take me by surprise. One minute it's all golden sunshine and autumn leaves; the next you're freezing your butt off and everything looks gray, like the color has been leached out of the world. The next bus isn't due for fifteen minutes; I'm not going to get home till five-thirty at the earliest, not that I have anywhere to be.

"Hey, where are you headed?"

I blink in surprise at the car that has slowed down in front of the bus stop—a big, shiny white SUV. Diane is in the driver's seat, smiling uncertainly at me.

"West Hartford," I say, unsure why she wants to know. "Near the town center."

"I'll give you a ride if you want. I live in Simsbury."

"Oh…" I'm so surprised that I just stare at her for a moment. Judging by her nervy manner in the class, I didn't expect her to be friendly. "Okay," I say. "Thanks."

I open the passenger door and slide into the leather interior, realizing at the last second that Diane might be a serial killer and I'm her next victim.

"I love West Hartford," she says as she pulls back onto the street and heads towards the highway. "The town center is so cute."

"Yeah, it's really nice." I feel a bit more relaxed. She looks so normal, with her button-down blouse and artfully tied scarf. She can't be a serial killer. But why is she having to take the Triple P course, Level *Four*? She hardly seems like the type, but then I didn't think I was, either.

"So." Diane flexes her hands on the steering wheel. "You're probably wondering why I'm taking that course."

I can't keep from letting out a little laugh because, of course, that is exactly what I've been wondering. "Well, yeah," I admit. Then I ask bluntly, "Have you wondered why I am?" I'm afraid she might say no, that I look exactly like the kind of bad mother who would end up in a class like that, but she nods and shrugs at the same time.

"Yes, I mean... I suppose on some level everyone should take a parenting course, right? It doesn't always come naturally. At least it didn't to me."

It did to me, I think, but don't say. But I can't remember a moment's doubt after I held Dylan in my arms. Being with him felt as natural as breathing, even when it was hard. I never doubted myself, never thought I was doing it wrong, although I certainly worried about all the things out there that could hurt him—all the dangers he would face. But isn't that what a loving mother does?

"My son Peter is adopted," Diane says. She is staring straight ahead as she navigates onto I-91. "I got him when he was five, from Georgia. The country, not the state."

"Okay," I say after a moment. I'm not sure what response she's looking for.

"He'd been in an orphanage since he was a baby. I'm sure you've read about what they're like." She shakes her head. "Horrible places. They just... *leave* the kids in cribs, crying all day. They don't even change their diapers. I'm sure not every place is like that, and I know they're understaffed and all that, but... it was terrible."

"I'm sorry." That doesn't seem like the right response, but again I'm not sure what is.

"The thing is, you can realize all that and it still doesn't make it easier, you know? Peter has issues, of *course* he has issues, from all the neglect and abuse. But heaven help me..." She shakes her head slowly. "I had no idea how hard it would be."

"I don't suppose you would have been able to," I say after a moment.

"I thought I was going to be so patient. So understanding. I read books, I went to support groups, I did it *all*."

"So what happened?" I ask, because obviously something did.

"It got to be too much," she says simply. "First he was suspended, then expelled from school, kicking, screaming, biting… often non-verbal, breaking everything. I don't have a single piece left of my mother's Meissen set. Not one piece."

I have nothing to say to that, so I stay silent, and after a few seconds she continues.

"I couldn't take it. I just *couldn't*." She turns to me almost wildly, taking her eyes off the road, so the car starts to career into the next lane before I draw a quick, sharp breath and she quickly rights it. "Sorry. Sorry. You must think I've completely lost it."

I sort of do, but I understand, as well. How can I not? I'm the mom who grabbed her son's wrist in a CVS, hard enough for someone to call the DCF hotline. I'm the mother who drank too much the night before and couldn't show up for a custody-hearing case on time. If anyone's *lost* it, it's me.

"I understand," I say quietly.

Diane seems to sag, the fight drained out of her. "In the end, I put him in a voluntary placement. I just couldn't hold out any longer. And I'm going to this class because I have to, in order to get him back, but the truth is… the terrible truth is…" She pauses, her face haggard, and I already know what she's going to say, but I don't want her to put it into words. Make it a fact. "The truth is," she finishes heavily, "I'm not sure I want him back."

CHAPTER SIXTEEN

ALLY

"Isn't this fun?"

Nick's voice is full of cheer as we stand on the sidelines of the Harvard–Dartmouth football game, clutching travel mugs of coffee and trying to stay warm. It's a beautiful day—crisp, clear, and very, very cold. Every time one of us speaks—not that I've said much—our breath comes out in frosty puffs of air.

We arrived in Boston last night, and took Emma out for a pizza in Harvard Square before heading back to our hotel. A week ago, I called Monica and asked her if Dylan could be put in respite care for this weekend. I could tell Monica was a bit taken aback by the request; after all, at that point we'd had him for less than two weeks. I explained about the parents' weekend at Harvard, and she said she understood, and then, after a delicate pause, asked if I'd consider taking Dylan with us, if Beth gave permission.

I struggled with an answer, because I *had* thought of taking Dylan, and I'd asked Nick about it, and he'd said, quite firmly, that this weekend was about Emma and if Dylan came with us, it would have to be about Dylan.

I understood his reasoning, and I knew it was true, but it still tore at me, to think of sending Dylan away when he was just getting used to us. When he was just starting to trust me.

That first day I picked him up from school, he ran over to me and threw his arms around my waist, burrowing his head into my stomach. It was the first time he'd hugged me, or touched me in any way, and I let out a little laugh of pleased surprise.

"Dylan… how was your day?"

He didn't answer, of course, but his special ed assistant, Larissa, did. "He had a good day," she said firmly. "A really good day. There were a few ups and downs, but everyone has those, right, Dylan?"

Dylan, his head still buried in my stomach, didn't reply, but I felt both hopeful and worried by her response—what were these ups and downs, exactly? I didn't ask and she didn't tell me, but that evening, Dylan seemed especially cuddly and close to me, and we read an extra three stories at bedtime. I didn't mind—Dylan's head on my shoulder as I read *Sylvester and the Magic Pebble*—one of my favorites—for the third time felt like an unexpected and poignant bliss.

I was thinking of all that when Monica had prompted me on the phone. "Ally? Would it be possible for you to take Dylan with you, if Beth agrees?"

"I don't think so, no," I'd said, my tone firm but also full of regret. "It's a very hectic weekend… a lot of moving around… and my daughter…"

"I'll see if I can find some respite carers." Monica's voice was brisk; she knew when not to push. A few hours later, she called me to say she'd found an older couple in Middletown who would take Dylan for the weekend. She didn't tell me anything else, but already I had an image of some broken-down hovel with a grouchy old couple, and I nearly blurted that we'd take him to Boston, or that I wouldn't go.

But of course I couldn't do that. I'd finally called Emma back and she'd sounded so dreary on the phone, expecting me to back out of the weekend. "You're not coming, right?" were the first doleful words out of her mouth. I couldn't let her—or Nick—down. Or Josh, for that matter, although when it came to my son and the six hundred dollars I'd found in his drawer, I felt paralyzed, my mind frozen into a terrified stasis. I couldn't think about it, and so I hadn't, which felt like a terrible oversight. I had to tell Nick about it. I had to find the time.

Now, as we watch Dartmouth score a touchdown, I still haven't let myself think about that money at all, and yet at the same time it feels like I'm always thinking of it. It's there in my mind, like a lingering shadow. Why on earth does he have it? Does it belong to someone else? Has he been tutoring kids or mowing more lawns than I realized...? There *has* to be an innocent explanation for that money. I feel guilty for wondering for even a second that there might not be, for making it a thing.

"Emma's going to meet us here, right?" I ask Nick, not for the first time, as I scan the bundled-up crowds along the side of the field. There is a jolly mood of slightly snobby camaraderie between everyone that I'd encountered when we'd come for a prospective parents' weekend last May, a sort of smug, well-heeled attitude of having made it at last.

Last spring, I'd been thrilled to be part of that exclusive club, to join in the cabal of satisfied smugness, but now it all just makes me feel annoyed and restless.

"Yes, she's coming, Ally," Nick says as he stamps his feet to keep them warm. "She said she was. She'll come when she comes."

We'd seen Emma for a freshman families' brunch that morning—an impressive buffet in one of the college's oldest buildings. Emma had nibbled a bagel and spoken very little, and I hadn't been able to help notice how thin she looked. She'd always been willowy, but the wrists poking out of the frayed cuffs of her sweater looked positively scrawny, and her face, usually heart-shaped and lovely, looked gaunt. Weren't freshmen supposed to *gain* weight?

I hadn't said anything about her weight, not wanting to fuss. Emma has always been highly motivated, highly strung, and while we've never really argued seriously, managing her moods sometimes feels like a bit of a tenuous high-wire act. Too sympathetic, and she gets annoyed and huffy. Too unbothered, and she becomes wounded and teary.

Over the years, I think I've figured out how to pitch it mostly right; of course I've had my missteps, as every mother has, but I've learned how to manage my daughter without seeming to do so. It is only now, as I reflect on how powerless I feel in this moment, that I wonder if managing someone is really ever a worthy goal.

This morning, while she picked at her bagel, I tried to act as if her silence was normal, and Nick filled it in with paternal bonhomie, while Josh kept sneaking glances at his phone. It all felt so much less than I wanted it to—where were the jokes, the laughter, the bonding and fun? It was challenging to get Emma to say anything more than "fine" or "okay." While other students were still milling around with their parents, Emma said she had to meet some friends and she'd see us at the football game.

"She's with friends, she's having a good time," Nick says now, in answer to my silent worry, and he gives me a reassuring smile. "This is what we've always wanted for her."

I know that, and yet it doesn't feel the way I expected it to. I glance at Josh, who is here on sufferance and standing next to me looking as bored as ever. Football is not his sport, and I know he feels self-conscious because he's clearly not a college student, and all these suddenly, seemingly mature freshmen are looking down on him laughingly, or so he thinks. I doubt they're taking much notice of him at all, ensconced in their own happy bubbles.

I know I need to ask him about the money, but I don't know how. Start serious or keep it light? Assume there's a reasonable explanation, or prepare for the possibility that there isn't? And, of course, I should tell Nick, but somehow I haven't done that either.

I let out a heavy sigh without realizing it, and Nick gives me a sideways glance, a combination of concern and faint annoyance.

"Ally? Everything okay?"

"Yes." I sound unconvincing even to myself.

"Are you worried about Emma?"

"A bit. She seemed so quiet. And didn't you think she looked thin?"

Nick considers this for a moment. "Harvard is intense. We knew that."

His matter-of-fact statement causes me to instinctively recoil with worry. "Do you think she's stressed about it? The academics?"

"Probably, a little?" Nick shrugs. "I mean, *Harvard.*"

"I know, but…" I lapse into silence as I consider the possible causes of Emma's stress. She worked hard all through high school, and yes, there was definitely some anxiety involved, but, stupidly, perhaps, I thought we'd be past all that now. Once you've been accepted to Harvard, you've made it, right? "I wish she could talk to us about it." Emma used to talk to me about everything. Well, most things. And sometimes it took some patience and prying, but still. We've always had a good relationship. I really do believe that, which is why things feel so strange and uneasy now.

I shift where I stand, trying to get some feeling into my freezing feet. I can't concentrate on the game, because even though it's between Harvard and Dartmouth, it's still football and I've never liked it. Vague fears keep swirling through me—Josh's money, Emma's quiet, Dylan. I purposely haven't mentioned Dylan to Nick and yet somehow that is a worry, too. Why can't we talk about him normally? Why do I always feel like mentioning him annoys Nick in some way? And how is he coping, in respite care?

When I dropped him off at the respite house yesterday afternoon, he clung to me and cried, the way he had with Beth the week before, and it took all my effort not to cry, too. The couple having him for the weekend seemed very nice—grandparent types with a calm and soothing manner. But it was still a change, and it made my heart ache to walk away from him as tears streaked down his cheeks. At least he wasn't screaming. Nick didn't even ask how it went.

I glance at him now, my handsome husband—light brown hair with distinguished salt-and-pepper sides, a still-strong jaw and friendly blue eyes. He's forty-seven, but he looks good, keeps himself fit. He's clapping now, his gloved hands making a muffled thump, as he shouts encouragement to Harvard's side. He fits in here effortlessly, and I feel like I don't. I think, on some level, I've always felt like an imposter as an adult. I have the right clothes, and mostly the right hair when it isn't frizzy. I have the right house and the right husband and definitely the right kids, and yet somehow, at the heart of it all, I feel wrong.

The thought, coming to an almost empty-nester at aged forty-six, feels incredibly depressing. Am I having a midlife crisis? Is that what this is about? Or is it something more?

"There's Emma!" Nick starts back, towards the crowd, and I follow, with Josh shuffling along behind me.

Emma looks beautiful, her dark hair pulled into a messy bun, a rainbow-colored scarf thrown carelessly about her neck. She's wearing a vintage corduroy coat and a long, patchwork skirt, the epitome of funky college artiness.

Last year, she was, like just about every other girl in her school, preppiness personified, but now she's trying on clothes along with personalities, and it makes me both proud and anxious. I know this is part of growing up, but I just hope she finds herself in the end.

"Hey, sweetie." Nick pulls her into a hug; somehow it's easy for him, in a way that it isn't for me right now, although it always was before. Wasn't it?

"Emma." I pat her shoulder clumsily, wondering why on earth I'm being so awkward. This is *Emma*. "You look wonderful."

She gives me a look, wrinkling her nose, like I said something I shouldn't have. I realize it was probably unwise to comment on her fashion choices, to make a point of the change.

"What have you been up to?"

She shrugs, and then nods towards the game. "Who's winning?" she asks Nick.

"Dartmouth, but we've got them on the ropes."

He's mixing his sports, even I know that, but Emma doesn't mind. She tucks her arm in Nick's and they watch the game together while I stand there, freezing and awkward. I wonder if I've done something, if my hesitation about coming this weekend was hurtful, and this is some sort of punishment. Or am I just being way oversensitive, because everything feels so fragile right now?

I glance at my son, who is watching the game with an indifferent look on his face, his hands jammed into his pockets.

I decide to make an effort. "How are you, Josh?"

He glances at me, surprised, a bit disbelieving. "I'm okay," he says in a tone that suggests *why are you asking?*

"Did you miss a practice, coming here this weekend?" I should know if he did, but Nick handles the weekend practices and I've forgotten the schedule.

Josh shrugs an affirmative; at least I think that's what he does.

"I'm sorry about that." Another shrug. "How is cross-country going?"

"It's okay." He stares straight ahead, seeming to be willing this conversation over.

I sigh.

"Well, we're really proud of you, you know," I tell him. "For all you do. Cross-country and baseball and, of course, your grades…" I trail off, because this is clearly agony to Josh, and frankly it's agony to me. Why do teenagers have to be such hard work? I get more back from Dylan, even when he doesn't speak.

I do my best to shake off my dark mood as we walk back to campus after the football game, for a families' tea. Emma seems to sparkle as she chats with some friends, and Nick is all manly handshakes and relaxed laughter as he talks to another dad about the insurance business and then football. Josh has taken his phone out unabashedly, and I don't tell him to put it away.

I make some desultory chitchat with another mother, a sleek, bobbed woman who is painfully thin and glossy-nailed, a criminal lawyer in Manhattan. My twenty hours' bookkeeping for a couple of independent clothing and jewelry shops in West Hartford feels pathetic in comparison, and I am conscious that my nails are raggedy and I need to get my roots done. I'd been planning on splurging on some beauty treatments, but, of course, since Dylan came, I never got around to it.

I tell myself not to mind; both our daughters are at Harvard, after all. It's a level playing field in that way, at least.

Later, as we head back to the hotel to change for dinner, Nick slings an arm around me. "Did you have a nice time?" he asks. We barely spoke to each other for the whole event; he stayed with the jovial dads and I listened to the preening mothers.

"Yes, a very nice time," I say dutifully, because what else can I say? I don't want to feel so out of sorts, I really don't, but I do. It's like a weight dragging me down, and Nick notices.

"Are you still worried about Emma?" he asks as we change in our hotel room for dinner at one of Cambridge's best restaurants. "Or Dylan?" There's no censure in his voice, but I tense anyway.

"Both, I suppose." I slip on the little black dress that has done trusty service for nearly twenty years, wishing I'd bought something new for the occasion. "And Josh."

"Josh?" Nick stills in buttoning up his crisp blue Ralph Lauren dress shirt. "Why are you worried about Josh?"

I hesitate, knowing now is not the time to mention the money I found. "Don't you find him a bit… monosyllabic?"

Nick shrugs. "He's a teenaged boy."

"And maybe even a bit—hidden?"

"Hidden?"

"Secretive."

Nick shakes his head slowly as he reaches for his tie. "Ally, sometimes it feels like you're looking for problems. Josh is fine. He works hard, he does well. I was thinking of encouraging him to apply to Dartmouth, actually. Just think. In two years, we might have one on each side for the football game. Wouldn't that be something?"

"Yes, it would." I smile, trying to share his mood. I know I'm being a killjoy, and I really don't want to ruin this weekend. Dylan is probably fine, and I'm sure Josh has an explanation for the money, and as for Emma... I'll make an effort tonight at dinner. Get to the bottom of whatever is going on with her, if anything. Maybe it's just PMS, or typical teenaged moodiness. I don't need to take it to heart.

An hour later, we are at a table for four in the back of the restaurant, all candlelight and clinking glasses. Nick orders a particularly expensive bottle of champagne and toasts Emma, giving both Emma and Josh half a glass each with a wink for the waiter, and as we all raise our glasses, I catch her eye and smile. She smiles back, faintly, and I choose to be encouraged.

I look around at my family, our glasses raised, our smiles out, the whole world before us, and I remind myself to stop worrying and be thankful. I really am blessed. Nothing, I tell myself, has changed about that.

CHAPTER SEVENTEEN

BETH

In the car on the way to my third visit with Dylan, Susan asks me how the Triple P class is going. We've had two sessions now; more forced sharing and positive parenting tips that I don't need, but I like Margaret and Diane feels like a sympathetic soul. She drove me home again, but she didn't talk about her son or the fact that she might want to give him back, and I didn't ask.

Still, I think of Diane's wild confession in the car, of Angelica chewing her gum, and Margaret telling us all yet again to be nice to our kids, and I struggle to say something positive about the experience.

I'm determined to be upbeat, though, to show Susan that whatever she's suggested I do is working. I know now that she's actually doing a lot for me—after talking to Angelica and Diane about their caseworkers before the last class, I realize Susan is going above and beyond for me—taking me to visit Dylan, checking in with how I'm doing. I don't know whether to be appreciative or not, though; *why* is she being so nice? Is it because I need so much help, or because I don't?

I can't second-guess myself or Susan too much, though, or I'll drive myself crazy. It's been hard enough keeping an even keel—going to the parenting classes, keeping my jewelry business afloat, getting through my endless evenings without falling into despair. I've gone up to Angela's a couple of times to write letters for her, which is a poignant and painstaking process. She struggles to think of something to say, and I end up making so many suggestions that the letter might as well have been from me. There's been no reply yet, as far as I know.

"The class is okay," I tell Susan, because I don't want her to think I'm being completely fake. "I'm not sure why I have to take it, though, to be honest."

"Oh?" Susan gives me a friendly smile, encouraging me to say more. "Why is that?"

"Well, it's not as if I neglect Dylan," I say a bit recklessly. "I mean, Margaret, the teacher, is always going on about how we have to spend time with our kids, even if it's just ten quality minutes. That's not exactly my problem, is it?" I was trying to speak levelly, but my voice has risen.

I take a calming breath and look out the window. I wasn't trying to pick a fight, but I *love* spending time with Dylan. I give him affection, and positive reinforcement, and hugs and cuddles all the time. Or at least I did, when he was with me. The two times I've seen him with Ally have been so short, they hardly count.

In fact, the visit last week was a bit of a disappointment. Dylan had just had his third day at school—which seems so *strange*—and he was really tired. He hugged me hello, but he didn't want to do anything, and so we ended up cuddling on the sofa in the family room while Susan and Ally drank coffee and made chitchat at the kitchen table. When I said goodbye, he hugged me but he didn't cry or scream—which is a good thing, obviously, but it still hurt.

Susan is silent for a long moment, and I sneak a look at her. She is staring straight ahead, her lips silently pursed, her forehead crinkled. She looks both thoughtful and troubled, and I feel a sudden tremor of fear. What is she thinking right now, about me?

"I wouldn't say that's your problem, no," she says at last. "But, Beth…" Again I feel that flutter, wild and uncontained, and I have a sudden certainty that I don't want to hear what she's going to say next.

"What?" I ask, even though I don't want to know.

"Have you started your counselling sessions yet?"

"No, there wasn't an available spot until next week." Why is she asking me about that *now*? What does she think is wrong with me? "What were you going to say?" I demand, because now I realize I do want to know.

"Have you ever considered that your relationship with Dylan might be… a bit too intense?" Susan asks, choosing each word as if it's fragile and likely to break.

"Too intense?" I stare at her blankly. What does that even *mean*? "What are you trying to say?" I ask, and now I sound aggressive.

"I'm not saying anything definitively, Beth. I just want to encourage you to think about that."

"Think about what? That I'm too intense? That I'm somehow bad for my son?"

"You and Dylan have lived very isolated lives. I think it's lent a certain intensity to your relationship that might not be very helpful to Dylan." She gives me a quick smile that I think is meant to be reassuring. "But perhaps this is something you can discuss during your counselling sessions."

She turns into Ally's driveway, leaving me both reeling and defensive, and when I unbuckle my seatbelt, she doesn't unbuckle hers.

"I thought you could have an unsupervised visit with Dylan today," she says. "Since the last two visits have gone so well. If you'd like to take him for a walk or to the park… In another week, we can discuss a longer visiting arrangement—I'm planning to recommend two hours, twice a week."

"You're not coming?" I say dumbly.

"Not this time. I've got an appointment in Bloomfield. Are you okay to walk home?"

"Oh… yes." I feel as if I've been let out of prison, but it also feels as if I'm in free fall. Susan is abandoning me. I'm used to her walking me into the house, chatting with Ally while I sit with Dylan. It's only happened twice, but already it has become a routine. "So… is that how it will go from now on?"

"That's the hope." Her smile widens, as if to include me. "The goal for *all* of us, Beth, is reunification."

"Right." I feel weirdly nervous about seeing Dylan alone, and that makes me anxious. How can I be nervous? And yet how can Susan drop that bombshell about me being too intense, and then in the next breath tell me she's not coming in with me?

"Beth?"

I realize I'm just sitting there, staring. "Sorry." I try for a smile. "Thanks."

And then I am out of the car and walking up to Ally's house as Susan drives off, feeling strangely light, a bit empty, as if I am missing something, my purse or even an arm.

"Beth!" Ally looks surprised to see me even though this visit has been arranged. I realize, as she cranes her neck to look behind me, that she's been expecting Susan too.

"I came alone. Susan had another appointment, and she's said that my visits with Dylan can be unsupervised."

"Oh…" She hesitates, and I wonder if she thinks I'm lying, and just like that, I'm annoyed. I'm reminded of how much I don't like this woman.

Last week, I recall, she fussed around, hovering over Dylan and me until Susan called her back and asked for a cup of coffee. I saw that Dylan had a new lunchbox, to match his backpack. I knew he'd started school, but the sight of that shiny lunchbox unnerved me. And when I asked Ally about school, she was way too enthusiastic, telling me how absolutely wonderfully he was doing, which made me feel worse. Maybe it shouldn't have, but it did.

Now, without Susan here, I drop any pretense of friendliness. "May I see my son, please?" I ask with pointed iciness, and she blinks.

"Yes, of course." She steps aside and I stride in, looking for Dylan. "He's in the family room," Ally says, trotting behind me as I head to the back of the house.

The house is even nicer than I remembered from the last two weeks. Everything smells lemony and clean, with underlying homely aromas of coffee and dinner cooking—something beefy and comforting that makes my mouth water—and also makes me unreasonably angrier.

I take a deep breath, willing myself to be calm. It's a *good* thing that Dylan is in a place like this. I'd much rather he was in a place like this, warm and clean and comforting, than somewhere that was dirty or dangerous or just plain unwelcoming. Of course it is, and yet still, my hackles rise.

And then I see Dylan. He's curled up on the sofa, watching *Wild Kratts* on PBS Kids. He's holding his rabbit by its good ear, and he is absorbed in the show. He doesn't even see me come in, unlike the last two weeks when he ran to give me a hug.

For a second, I stand there, feeling lost, rootless. I watch my son, looking like any other kid. He's wearing clothes I don't recognize—a striped polo shirt and khaki pants. His hair is brushed to the side in a way I never comb it. His gaze is on the screen. I can't speak.

"Dylan," Ally says, seeming to sense something of what I feel—although I'm not even sure what I feel. Am I happy or sad, resentful or thankful? It is as if my world is a snow globe that someone just turned upside down and shook hard, or a kaleidoscope whose image has just changed, so for a second it's all brilliant colors and swirls that don't make sense. I also feel rage—red-hot and real, coursing through me in a river, but I'm not even sure what I'm angry about.

"Dylan," Ally says again, raising her voice, and finally my son looks at me. Our gazes lock and clash and for a second nothing happens. He just stares while Ally watches and again I feel as if the floor, the whole earth, is falling away from me. I reach out to the kitchen island to steady myself, my hand sliding across the slippery granite.

"Dylan," I say, and it almost sounds like a whimper.

"Dylan, aren't you so excited to see your mom?" Ally interjects in an overly cheerful voice, and I want to slap her. I don't need her interference, well-intentioned though it might be.

Slowly, Dylan uncurls himself on the sofa, still clutching his rabbit.

I walk towards him, and all the while Ally watches, a spectator to our sad little drama.

"Hey, Dylan." I sit next to him and touch his head briefly, messing up his child's combover, so his hair springs back across his forehead and slides into his eyes. He looks more like my son now, but then he shakes his head and pushes the hair back, and somehow that stings. It's only been a week since my last visit, and already he's changed so much. How? *Why*?

"How have you been, Dyl?" I ask, unable to keep from touching him. My fingers skim his cheek and then I put my arm around his shoulders and draw him closer. He comes, but after a second's hesitation that cuts deep, even though I am trying not to let it. I'm already losing him, after just a few weeks. What is it—he—going to be like after three *months*?

I swallow hard. I can feel Ally staring.

"Why don't we go for a walk, Dylan?"

"Oh…" Ally trails off uncertainly. She is probably wondering if I'm *allowed*. But Susan suggested it, and in any case, I'm tired of feeling like I need permission from some stranger to simply be with my child.

"Would you like that, Dylan?" I ask as I reach for his hand. He lets me take it, lets me draw him up to standing. "Where's your coat?"

"I'll get it," Ally says, and she comes back with a navy blue puffa parka that I've never seen before. I stare at it blankly before I look at her in silent accusation. "I bought him a coat," she explains awkwardly. "The jacket he had was so thin…"

Thin? It was fine. Maybe it wasn't one hundred percent down from Nike like this one, but it did the job. I take the parka without a word and help Dylan into it. He's silent, but not in a way I understand. I usually know exactly how he's feeling, I can translate every sigh or twitch, but right now I'm adrift. We both are. I feel an urgent need to get out of this house with its underlying and cloying, lemony scent, its smug neatness. Even the smell of the dinner cooking offends me somehow.

"You could walk down to the park by the elementary school," Ally suggests. "Fernridge…"

As if I don't know it. We're only a ten-minute walk from my house, if that. I don't bother replying, even though part of me knows I should. I can't afford to antagonize Ally, even though she's antagonized me with the coat and the clothes and the way she brushes his hair.

I take a deep breath and nod. "Thank you," I say, and then I lead my son out of the house.

Dylan and I walk in silence down the street, in the last of the afternoon's mellow light, although there's a nip to the air and shadows are gathering. It will be dark by the time we get to the playground, or almost. It's mid-November, Thanksgiving next week, and in New England it is starting to feel like winter.

"Do you like school, Dylan?" I ask. Ally and Susan have both told me the basics, that he has a special-education assistant and that it's been going well, but I don't know anything else.

Dylan, of course, doesn't answer, but I can usually tell what he's thinking. I see it in his eyes, in the duck of his head or the way his hand tightens in mine, but he doesn't give me any of these signals, and for the first time I feel as if we're speaking different languages.

"Dylan?" I crouch down on the sidewalk and put my hands on his shoulders to turn him towards me. I want him to look me in the eye; I want to feel that connection. He stands still, staring at me steadily, but something feels off, *less than*. I think about what Susan said, about our relationship being too intense, and then I don't know what to think, because it certainly doesn't feel that way now. "Do you like school, Dylan? It's okay if you don't." No reply, nothing, just a steady, blank blinking. "And it's okay if you do," I say, surprising myself with the words, and, I realize, surprising Dylan. His eyes widen and then he leans forward a little, so his head almost touches mine. I put my arms around him in a hug that he submits to rather than participates in, but I tell myself not to mind.

After a moment, the cold seeping through the knees of my jeans, I stand up and we walk hand in hand to the park, through the lengthening shadows.

We stay for half an hour, sitting on the swings. Dylan has always loved the swings, just as I used to. When he was a baby, I used to swing with him on my lap, one arm wrapped around his chubby middle, and fly high—higher probably than I should have, considering how little he was—but it felt so freeing. As soon as he could, he started going on the swing on his own, painstakingly learning how to pump his legs, his one real act of independence, and one I always encouraged.

As we sit and swing in silence, my thoughts veer from fear to anger to simply wanting to be with Dylan. *Am* I too intense? Is there something *wrong* about my relationship with my son? I reject the idea instinctively; everything I've done with Dylan, the way I've been, has always felt right.

I never second-guessed myself, until he was taken away. Not even when Marco lost his temper and called DCF, not even when Susan came poking around that first time. I knew I had to appease the powers that be, and I knew life with Dylan could be hard, but I didn't *doubt*.

Now I am full of doubts. I look at Dylan in his parka and khakis, his hair brushed back like a little businessman, and I wonder if he's been tolerating me all along. What if he prefers Ally and her neat house, his big bedroom, his brand-new lunchbox? What kid wouldn't?

But those are just things. They're not love. They're not his mother.

By the time we walk back to Ally's house, it is dark. Cars are turning into driveways, lights flicking on in houses, giving me even more of a sense of being on the outside looking in. As we walk down Ally's street, my steps slow. I don't want to give Dylan back. I'm afraid of what will happen if I do. What will he be like next week? Will he hold my hand? What about a month from now? Two months? What if, by the time I get him back, he doesn't want me anymore?

The powerlessness I feel is choking. I struggle to breathe. My hand tightens over Dylan's, and he squirms a little.

"Sorry, buddy." I give him a smile as I determinedly loosen my grip. I can't cling; I can't lose him, and the result is I don't know how to be.

Ally opens the door as soon as we turn up her driveway; she must have been waiting and watching, even though I'm only a few minutes late.

"It's so dark," she says, as an explanation, and I don't reply.

Inside, the house feels warm and welcoming, like a huge hug enveloping me that I instinctively resist. The kitchen is full of inviting smells and sounds; the rest of Ally's family is there, and I do a double take at the sight of her husband standing at the counter, opening a bottle of wine, and her son, a dark-haired teenager, setting the table.

"Beth." Her husband sounds delighted to see me. "I'm Nick. I'm so glad to meet you." He holds out his hand and when I take it, he gives me a firm handshake. He's that kind of man—purposeful, assured, with an effortless friendliness. "Do you want to join us for dinner?"

That's the last thing I expect, and I glance at Ally, who looks surprised, but quickly masks it with a friendly smile.

"Yes, Beth. Why don't you join us?"

The unexpected invitation puts me in a ferment of surprise and discomfort; I really didn't expect this, and obviously Ally didn't either. Is it even allowed?

The table is set for four, but Nick is already beckoning to the son to lay another plate, although I haven't said anything. Part of me desperately wants to say yes, and another part of me wants to run away as fast as I can. I don't belong here—*and yet my son does*?

I look down at Dylan, and he smiles at me, shyly, hopefully, and I am decided.

"Thanks," I say. "That would be really nice."

CHAPTER EIGHTEEN

ALLY

I am silent as I serve out the beef stew. Nick has gone into genial host mode, which he does so well, far better than I ever can, especially in these unusual circumstances. He is chatting easily, offering Beth wine, which she accepts, taking a sip from her very full glass almost immediately. I shouldn't judge, I *know* that, and yet part of me still does.

Even Josh is rising to the occasion, helping Dylan cut the chunks of beef in his stew, something I've never seen him do before, although he has been making a bit more of an effort with Dylan—saying hello, or putting on PBS Kids in the morning. We've developed a rhythm over these last few weeks; it's not perfect, but it works. Dylan has settled into school, even if he is still silent.

Last week, he had a psychiatric evaluation, and on Thursday afternoon, I took him to his first cognitive behavior therapy session. I don't know what his diagnosis is, if any, but Monica said she'd keep me informed.

His therapist, Mark, is a very chilled guy, who seemed to feel the session was successful. Apparently Dylan drew a lot of pictures. He was happy to go in, and just as happy to come out. In fact, in the week and a half since Dylan started school, he's had far fewer meltdowns, and he's mostly stopped waking up at night. He still doesn't talk, and he occasionally falls apart, but it's all been easier than I expected.

In fact, it feels as if it's my own family that's falling apart, although no one is noticing but me. I still haven't talked to Nick about Josh, and when I went into his bedroom a few days ago, the roll of money was gone. I didn't know whether to be relieved or more worried than ever. I knew I should have dealt with it sooner; what actually happened to that money? Do I ever want to know?

And as for Emma... I tried to talk to her during our dinner in Boston, but she remained monosyllabic, not meeting my eyes. I even asked if she was angry with me, braving that honesty, and she shrugged and asked me why I would think that. But when I said because she hadn't really been talking to me, Emma just rolled her eyes and told me I was overreacting, as usual. The *as usual* stung, and I tried to pursue it; we went around in circles for a few minutes before, defeated, I finally dropped it.

Beth takes a seat next to Dylan, sipping her wine as her gaze darts around, taking us all in. From the outside, it looks like a perfectly pastoral scene—the stew in the center, the warm lighting, the full table. I want to believe in this scene, I want to take it at face value, but at the same time, I am afraid to. I am afraid it will collapse like a cardboard cutout, leaving nothing behind.

"So, Beth, do you live in West Hartford?"

"Yes, just off Boulevard."

So close? I am discomfited by this realization, while Nick takes it in his stride. As he chats to Beth, I learn that she grew up in Bloomfield, where her father still lives. She works freelance making jewelry to sell on Shopify, and Nick duly writes down the address of her website, and even intimates he'll buy some pieces for Emma or me.

"What about you?" Beth asks after we've finished our beef stew and the conversation has started to dry up. "You have a daughter... Emma?"

"Yes, she's at college in Boston. Freshman." Nick's voice rings out with pride.

"And you're a junior?" she asks Josh, who mumbles something in the affirmative. "You're going to go to college?"

"Um, yeah." Josh looks nonplussed by the question; of course he's going to go to college.

"That's nice." There is something wistful about Beth's tone and she doesn't ask anything more as she rises to help clear the dishes.

"You don't have to…" I begin, but Beth just ignores me. She's been ignoring me all evening, at least I think she has. Maybe I'm just overreacting. *As usual.* But she hasn't addressed me directly, and she doesn't reply now, as she clears plates and I get some ice cream out of the freezer for an impromptu dessert.

Dylan has stayed silent through the whole meal, as usual, and his gaze tracks Beth as she moves between table and counter before coming to sit beside him. She gives him a reassuring smile and he looks away.

I can't help but feel guilty about his new clothes and coat, the way I brushed his hair. I saw Beth take it all in, and I knew she didn't like it, but the truth was, Dylan's clothes were practically threadbare, and his coat wasn't appropriate for winter. As his foster parent, I have a duty of care to make sure he has suitable clothing. As for his hair… well, I didn't cut it, I know I'm not allowed without her permission, but I do like it better that way. I can see his eyes. But I knew Beth resented each and every thing, and I couldn't blame her for it, even as I felt defensive.

I dole out the ice cream, and Josh gobbles his in a few seconds before saying he has homework. Nick pours out the last of the wine, but nobody but he drinks it.

"I should go," Beth says reluctantly. She gives Dylan what I can only describe as a hungry look. "Maybe next week, Dylan, we can go back home for a bit? I've got some new craft stuff you'd like. Some Play-Doh…"

Dylan hesitates before giving a quick nod.

Beth reaches for him, wrapping her arms around his slight body and drawing him close. "I'll see you soon, Dyl," she whispers and I busy myself stacking plates in the dishwasher, trying not to seem invasive. Nick is watching them openly, a slight frown on his face. I feel like telling him to stop, but I can't without being obvious.

A few minutes later, with a brief goodbye and mumbled thanks, she leaves, and I let out a little sigh of relief. I didn't realize just how tense I was, having Beth here, until she's gone.

"That was nice," Nick remarks as he comes back into the room. He raises his eyebrows at Dylan. "Bath time, buddy?"

Dylan trots off happily enough; it's become their thing. Pretty much their only thing, but that's okay.

I keep cleaning the kitchen, trying to sort out my thoughts even as I try to keep from thinking at all. I should log Beth's visit, along with the rest of Dylan's day, something I've had to do every day since he came here. I am tempted to go onto one of the online foster parents' message boards and surf for posts about socializing with birth parents, but I know I'll get a lot of complaining and then a lot of sanctimonious responses and I don't feel like reading either.

"That went pretty well, I think," Nick says as he comes back into the kitchen. I realize I must have been staring into space for a while, if bath time is already over.

"Where's Dylan?"

"Playing in his room."

I nod slowly. Ever since I bought some puzzles and Lego for Dylan's room, he'll play there quite happily, sometimes for hours.

"It does make you wonder," Nick continues as he heads for the sofa and the TV remote, "why she had Dylan taken away from her. She seems pretty grounded and normal to me. A little quiet, maybe, but then so is he."

I wipe the kitchen island with slow, circular motions. "I don't know. Don't you think there's something…" I hesitate to put it into words. Nick waits, eyebrows raised. "Something a little… off about her?"

"Off?" He sounds nonplussed.

"I don't know. Just… a bit… much." I can't explain it better than that.

Nick shrugs. "I suppose it's a complicated situation. I mean, we're taking care of her child."

"I know."

"Do you know why Dylan was taken?"

I shrug. "Sort of. Susan told me that he has anxiety issues, as we obviously know, and she thinks Beth feeds into it." I pause. "He has seemed better here, hasn't he?"

"It's not like we have anything to go by, from before."

"Well, just those first few days. The screaming…"

"He's settled in pretty well," Nick admits. "But that's not necessarily a reflection of Beth's parenting skills, or lack of them." He sounds reproving, and I drop it. What am I trying to say, anyway? That Beth is a bad mother? Will that make me feel better about myself? Hardly. I knuckle my forehead, my eyes closed. "Ally?" Nick sounds concerned. He hasn't turned on the TV yet, although I'm sure he wants to. "Is everything all right?"

"No," I say heavily. I have to tell him about the money. It's been too long as it is. "No, I'm afraid that it might not be." I open my eyes and stare at Nick. He looks back with a frown.

"Okay…" he says guardedly.

"Let me put Dylan to bed first." I go upstairs, dreading the upcoming conversation with Nick. I have no idea how he'll react. In our nearly nineteen years of parenting, we haven't really had any big issues—and maybe we don't now. Both Emma and Josh have pretty much sailed through their teenaged years, with just a few of the basic bumps. Yes, Josh is a bit monosyllabic, and

Emma has her moods, but compared to the friends we have with daughters in eating-disorder clinics and sons addicted to porn or pot or worse? We've had it easy. *Easy.*

As I come down the hallway, I hear humming, and I realize it's coming from Dylan's room. Besides the one time he said "Mama," and of course the screaming, it's the first sound I've heard him make. I stand in the hallway and peek around the doorway to see him kneeling on the carpet of his bedroom, constructing a village made of Legos and humming under his breath. That cheerful, industrious sound makes me smile like nothing else could in that moment. I simply stand there and listen, letting it fill me up and buoy my heart.

Then I step into the room and it stops. Dylan looks up, alert, almost guilty, and I smile at him.

"Hey, Dylan. That looks amazing." I nod to the eclectic assortment of Lego buildings—some square and squat, some tall and narrow. "You've been busy. Should we leave it all the way it is so you can work on it again in the morning?"

He nods and smiles shyly, and I reach for his hand to draw him up to his feet. We've developed a way of communicating over the last few weeks, a kind of silent conversation of looks and shrugs, nods and smiles. When Dylan comes up to me and silently holds my hand, I know he's asking me a question. When he smiles, he's saying yes.

Now he walks with me to the bathroom and I help him brush his teeth, thinking how wonderfully simple this all is, compared to the current minefield of my own children's lives, which seems a particularly odd thought, considering how complicated Dylan seemed just a few weeks ago.

"Was it nice to see your mom today?" I ask, and Dylan freezes, giving me a guarded look that makes me pause, toothbrush in hand. I study his face, the way worry clouds his clear, hazel eyes as he ducks his head. "It's okay, Dylan," I say softly, but he doesn't relax, still hiding his face from me. "Whatever you're feeling, it's okay," I tell him. I don't know what he's feeling, and I don't want to project anything onto him, but it's strange and a bit concerning that a mention of his mother makes him tense so much.

He certainly didn't hug her today the way he has before, and he didn't seem particularly sad to see her go. I think of that first visit, and the two hours he spent waiting by the door, the hour of screaming afterwards. We've come a long way since then, but I wonder if Beth would see it as progress. I certainly never expected him to assimilate so quickly.

"Time for bed," I say, and Dylan relaxes a little bit. Back in the bedroom, I turn back the duvet as he scrambles into bed, reaching for his rabbit, and then I sit on the end and sing several lullabies, the most relaxing part of my day. I don't remember when I started doing this, maybe in the middle of that first night when I had to sleep next to him. I sing all the old songs—"Hush Little Baby," and "Twinkle Twinkle Little Star," all three verses. I hadn't realized I still knew them until I sang them to Dylan. "*Then the traveler in the dark, thanks you for your little spark. Would he know which way to go, if you did not twinkle so?*"

He drifts off by the last verse; a full day of school, plus Beth's visit, has wiped him out. I watch him for a few moments, his face softened and relaxed in sleep, his breath coming in and out in soft little sighs. One hand is curled around his rabbit's good ear; the one I sewed on is still hanging on, but it's gone even floppier.

Outside, the stars are pricking the sky with their tiny sparks, just like in the lullaby, and I have a weary desire to stay in this darkened room with this sleeping child, where life seems so simple and sweet. But I know I can't, and after another few peaceful moments, I rise from the bed and head downstairs for my conversation with Nick.

He snaps off the TV the second I come into the kitchen, already frowning. "So what's going on?" he asks, sounding a bit belligerent.

I sigh heavily. I want a glass of wine, but we finished the bottle at dinner, even though I only had a few sips. Nick kept filling Beth's glass as well as his own.

"Last week I found something in Josh's room," I say quietly, and Nick's frown deepens into a severe crease in his forehead.

"Last week? And you didn't tell me?"

"I'm sorry. There never seemed to be the right time." Nick just gives me a look, and I recognize that as the feeble excuse it is. "I suppose I didn't want to have to think about it, and it might be nothing."

"Okay." He absorbs that for a moment before asking, "So what did you find?"

"Money."

"*Money*?" He sounds incredulous, very slightly sneering.

"Six hundred and fifty-four dollars, to be exact, rolled up with a rubber band and hidden under his boxer shorts." I collapse onto the sofa, exhausted by everything. I want Nick to take control of this, to have a man-to-man chat with Josh, to sort it out, make it better. But I can already tell from his frowning expression, the way his gaze is darting around as if searching for probable answers, he's not going to do that. I suppose it isn't really fair for me to expect him to.

"Obviously there's a reasonable explanation," he states.

"Yes." The word escapes from me like a sigh.

"What are you thinking? Drugs?" He sounds accusing, but of me.

"It crossed my mind," I admit. "I mean, it *would*, Nick. He doesn't have six hundred bucks. He has no way to make that kind of money."

"He mowed lawns last summer…"

"At ten bucks a pop, that's what? Sixty-five lawns? No way." I shake my head wearily. "I thought maybe he was keeping it for someone, but why would he?"

"Maybe he sold something. His phone…?"

"He hasn't sold his phone."

Nick shrugs. "There has to be a reason. Josh isn't into *drugs*, Ally. He's varsity cross-country and baseball. They get tested for doping. Anyway, he wouldn't be that stupid."

He isn't thinking anything I haven't already considered, several times. "You don't know that," I tell him. "Besides, the anti-doping tests are random, and only once in a blue moon. Josh hasn't actually had one yet."

"And you just want to assume he's into something bad? That he's some *druggie*?"

"No, of course I don't want to. I don't want to at all. But it's the first thing that leaps into your head…" I rub my forehead wearily. "Why are we fighting about this, Nick?"

Nick slumps back against the sofa, the TV remote control sliding out of his hand and onto the floor with a thud. "I don't know."

We are both silent, absorbing the fact of that money, of the disconcerting ripple on the still surface of our lives that hints at something darker and deeper. Am I wrong to be suspicious? Does it say something about me? Maybe drugs wouldn't even cross most mothers' minds.

"Do you honestly think he's doing drugs?" Nick asks at last, his voice low and drained. He is staring blankly ahead, looking somehow smaller.

"Doing or dealing?" I shrug. "Most people doing drugs don't have the money, do they? They're the ones spending it." Although I'm no expert; I'm garnering my information from half-remembered episodes of *The Wire*. This is so outside my realm of experience… and yet now perhaps it isn't.

"Dealing drugs? Josh?" Nick lets out a huff of hopeless laughter. "How can you even think that?"

"I don't know." I shiver suddenly, even though the room is warm. "I don't think I ever would have before."

"Before what?"

I shake my head. I'm not even sure how to explain it, how sometimes, since Dylan came into our lives, everything feels so *fragile*. It only takes a moment for something—everything—to shatter, like it did for Beth. Like it could for us. Or am I just being paranoid?

"Ally, what?" Nick leans forward. "Do you know something I don't?"

"No, I don't think so." I know I don't. "I just have this… feeling."

"A feeling."

"I'm just scared, Nick."

His expression softens then, and he leans forward and puts his hand on my knee. I cover his hand with my own, grateful for the touch bringing us together, anchoring me to our marriage, our real lives.

"I'm sorry," he says quietly, but I'm not sure what he's apologizing for.

"He's been kind of secretive lately, don't you think? I know he's sixteen and all that, but even a year ago he talked to us more. Didn't he?"

Nick's hand tenses on my knee. "I don't know…"

"Last winter, we went ice skating in Avon, remember? He and Emma were joking around the whole time. He was laughing." I can't actually remember the last time I heard Josh laugh.

"Maybe it's hard for him without Emma here. Harder than we realize."

"Maybe, but he didn't really talk to Emma last weekend. And he hardly ever talks to us now. Just grunts and goes up to his room."

"Ally, that's a whole other issue than some hidden money."

"Is it?"

He sighs and sits back, taking his hand off my knee to run it through his hair. "I don't know."

We lapse into another unhappy silence. Part of me wishes I never found the money. Ignorance is bliss and all that, and yet now that I've found it, I know I wasn't as ignorant as I wish I'd been. I know that I thought of drugs right away not because I'm so distrusting, but because I've sensed all along that something has been off. I just haven't wanted to acknowledge it.

"Well, we'll just have to talk to him," Nick says decisively. "And see what he says."

"And you think he'll tell us the truth?"

"I think we'll know if he's lying."

I quake inside at the thought of that conversation. "I never thought we'd be in this position."

"It might be nothing," Nick insists stoutly. "And anyway, most parents have some issue or other with their teenagers. We've been lucky so far."

Yes, I think with an inward shudder. *So far.*

CHAPTER NINETEEN

BETH

Three days after my dinner with Ally and her family—three long, lonely days—I am sitting on a plaid-patterned sofa in a comfortable room, winter sunlight streaming through the window, about to have my first counseling session.

Anna, my counselor, is a mild-looking woman in her late thirties, with her dark hair swept back in a loose ponytail. She is tall and slim and elegant without being intimidating; her movements seem almost balletic as she puts a box of tissues on the coffee table between us.

"Am I going to need those?" I ask, meaning to sound wry, but it comes out aggressive instead. Four days on, I am still feeling raw from that awful dinner—although the reality is, there was nothing awful about it, and that is what hurts.

Ally's home, Ally's family, seem pretty picture-perfect to me. Why wouldn't Dylan be happy there? And he obviously is. When I said goodbye, he barely put his arms around me in a hug. I struggled not to clutch at him, to cling, to hold him as tightly as I could. And all the while, Susan's words rang in my ears. *Do you think your relationship might be a bit too intense?* What is that even supposed to *mean*?

"So." Anna smiles at me. "These sessions are really for you, Beth. What would you like to talk about?"

"I…" I stop, my throat going alarmingly tight *already*. I'd come into this room, into this whole concept, determined to be strong. I wasn't going to give anything away. I was going to convince Anna how capable I was, how strong and with it and everything I need to be to get Dylan back.

Yet here I am, having barely said one syllable, and already tears are crowding my eyes and my throat feels too tight to speak. *What is happening to me?*

"Beth?" Anna prompts gently, and that alone tips me over the edge. I start to cry, and not just cry, but properly blub, with snot and hiccuppy noises and all the rest. Blindly, I reach for the tissues and try to mop up the mess.

"I'm sorry," I gasp out. "I wasn't… I don't know why…"

"You'd be surprised how often this happens," Anna says with a small, sympathetic smile. "People finally get into a safe space, where they can actually talk about what they're feeling, and it is overwhelming. Don't worry. Tears are good."

Are they? Because they keep coming. And I realize, as I uselessly wipe my face, how many things I am sad about—Dylan already growing apart from me, and the swamping loneliness I feel when he's not with me. The terrible, gnawing fear that I'm not a good mother, and worse than that, maybe I'm actually a bad one. The grief I feel over everything—losing Dylan, losing my chance at college, even my failed relationship with Marco. *My parents…*

There's so much, and it feels like a heavy weight on my chest, and I don't even know how to begin. And, meanwhile, Anna simply sits there, smiling sympathetically at me and waiting for me to say something.

"I want to talk about my dad," I blurt, and she nods, completely unfazed by this, waiting for more. It's the last thing I expected to say, to want to say, and yet, weirdly, it feels like such a relief to say it.

And so I begin.

*

Three hours later, I'm back in my apartment, boxing up jewelry orders and feeling utterly drained. I spent the entire hour with Anna talking about my father, which I really didn't expect at all. I mean, surely there are more pressing, current matters to worry about?

And yet revisiting all those old wounds, hurts I'd thought had scarred over and were *fine*, felt painful but necessary. There were a lot of tears, and I don't actually feel much better, but for once, I don't feel worse. Truthfully, as I load all my packages into a canvas bag and head out to the UPS store, I don't know how I feel, but I try not to worry about it too much. I've had enough self-analysis for one day, surely.

Mike is behind the counter when I go into the store, his expression brightening when he sees me. We've brushed over his invitation for a pizza that he made a few weeks ago, acted as if it never happened, although he's still as friendly as ever.

"Hey, Beth. How's it going?"

"Okay, I guess." To my surprise, I realize I mean it. Things aren't great, not even close, but they're not horrible, the way they've sometimes felt. "How are you?"

"Pretty good." Mike gives me a lopsided smile as I unload the packages onto the counter. "Though my mom is having her third round of chemo."

"What?" I look up in surprise. He's never told me about his mother before.

"Yeah." Mike scratches his cheek self-consciously. "She was diagnosed with breast cancer five months ago. Stage four."

"I'm so sorry."

He hunches his shoulders. "Thanks."

I feel guilty, like I should have asked about his mom even though I didn't know she was sick. Yet even though I obviously couldn't have done that, I realize our conversations have always been about me and my problems. I've never once asked Mike about his life. I've never even wondered about it. Life with Dylan has made me completely introspective.

Mike is ringing up each package, and I feel any moment of connection slipping away from us. As he does the last one, I take the plunge, blurting out awkwardly,

"If you're done with work soon… do you want to go for that pizza?" Mike stares at me in surprise. "I mean… if you're not busy." I feel my cheeks heat. I can't remember the last time I've asked someone to go out, if ever. This is completely new territory for me; Marco managed our entire relationship, not that Mike and I have one of those.

"Yeah, that would be good," Mike says at last, and I nearly sag with relief. Surely this doesn't need to be so hard. "I don't get off for another hour, though. Could I meet you somewhere?"

"Sure."

"What about Barb's? That's where I usually go."

"Yeah, that would be great."

We agree to meet and then I head home, a flurry of nerves taking residence in my stomach. Should I change? Put some makeup on? I barely have any. And if I look too dressed up, will Mike think it's weird? It's not as if this is an actual date.

I end up changing my top and adding a bit of lip gloss, which isn't much effort but still feels like too much.

When I walk into Barb's an hour later, Mike is already sitting in one of the booths with a Coke, and he rises as I walk towards him.

"I got off a little early. Let me get you a drink."

"Um, okay." I nod towards his Coke. "That looks good."

I slip into the other side of the booth, feeling incredibly self-conscious. Already this is feeling more like a date than I expected it to.

Mike signals to the waitress and then orders me a Coke, before turning to me with a smile that spreads across his whole face and crinkles his cheeks. He's so friendly-looking that I can't help but relax and smile back.

"So, what did you get up to today?" he asks and I surprise myself by answering honestly, by wanting to.

"I went to my first counseling session. It was… intense." Kind of like me, then, apparently.

"Intense?" Mike repeats with a frown.

"I've never done any kind of counseling or therapy before. The whole thought of it freaked me out, to be honest."

"Yeah, I can see how it could. I've never had any, either." He props his elbows on the table. "So were you glad you went, in the end?"

"Yeah." I pause to take a sip of my Coke that the waitress just delivered. "I ended up talking about my dad, which I didn't expect at all."

"Why not?"

"It's just such old history. I thought I was over it."

Mike tilts his head, his expression all sympathy. "Over what?"

"Just… the rejection, I suppose." My throat is getting tight again and I take another sip of Coke to ease it. "He asked me to leave home when I was eighteen."

"That's tough." Mike doesn't sound surprised, though, and I wonder if he has a similar story with his own dad. "How come?"

Haltingly, painfully, I tell him about my mother leaving, the DUI, the way my life fell to pieces all around me, and how my dad seemed indifferent to it all, to me. In the nine years since I've left home, I've seen him three times—once early on, to get my stuff when I was moving into Marco's, once when Dylan was born, and a last-ditch effort when Dylan was four. Each time, my dad acted as if he couldn't care less.

"I really did think I was over it," I tell Mike. "He's a jerk, I get that. It shouldn't hurt, but it does." I try to smile but sniff instead, and Mike reaches over and holds my hand. It feels both weird and right, and I don't want him to let go.

A few minutes later, the waitress comes to take our order, and we agree to split a medium buffalo chicken, which is both of our favorite pizza topping. After she leaves, the intensity has thankfully broken, and I've avoided crying, which is definitely a good thing.

"Anyway, that was all a long time ago," I say in the tone of someone who is finishing a conversation. "What about you? Are you close to your family?"

"My mom, yeah." Mike picks at the peeling corner of the laminated menu. "My dad walked out when I was nine."

"Oh, I'm sorry."

He shrugs. "I didn't mind so much. He wasn't a great guy, you know?" His mouth twists and he looks away.

"Still, it's hard. My dad isn't that great a guy, at least I don't think he is. But I've still wanted him to love me." It's basically what Anna said to me earlier, and I realized how true it was.

"Yeah." He sighs. "I guess so. I didn't really want him to stick around, because he had a hell of a temper, but I didn't want him to want to go, if that makes sense."

"It does." I almost reach for his hand again, but I'm not quite brave enough.

"Have you seen Dylan recently?" he asks and I tense right up. It was actually kind of nice, not to think about Dylan for a little while. To think about myself not in relation to my son, which is something I hardly ever do. The realization makes guilt trickle through me like acid. "I saw him on Tuesday." I pause and then blurt recklessly, not sure if I want to ask and really not sure if I want him to answer, "Do you think... do you think I'm too intense?"

Mike stares at me blankly. "Too intense?"

"With Dylan." He doesn't say anything and I explain, "Susan—the caseworker—suggested I was. I'm not even sure what she meant." Mike remains silent and I start to feel uneasy. "Do you think I am?"

Mike rubs his neck. A frisson of fear runs through me like a shiver. "Mike?"

"I haven't seen you together enough really to know if you are or not." Which is *not* an answer.

"I've come into the store several times a week for four years, always with Dylan. The truth is, you know me—us—better than just about anyone." Better even than Susan, maybe, which is a strange thought. "So?" I ask, a truculent note entering my voice. "What do you think? Am I?"

"Beth…"

"*Mike.*"

"Maybe, a little?" He gives me a sheepish and unhappy look. "I mean, not in a bad way. I don't mean in a bad way at all."

I take a sip of my Coke, trying to compose myself. "So what do you mean, then?" I ask when I trust my voice to sound steady. I feel unaccountably hurt, and I don't want to show it.

"Just that… whenever the two of you came into the store… it was clear you only had each other."

"We *do* only have each other." And now I do sound hurt.

"And sometimes… I don't know… the way you always know what he's saying, even though he doesn't speak?"

"What's wrong with that?"

"Nothing. Beth, I'm not criticizing. Honestly. It's just… it's what I'd call intense." He pauses while I struggle to find a reply. "It doesn't mean it's a bad thing."

"It sounds like it does." The hurt vibrates in my voice even though I don't want it to.

"I'm sorry. I shouldn't have said anything. I just wanted to give you an honest answer, because… well, because I think it's important to be honest."

I shake my head, taking a sip of my Coke, and Mike reaches for my hand. I let him take it; I crave the contact, the comfort, even though I still feel hurt.

"I didn't mean to upset you. I really am sorry."

"Don't be sorry." My voice sounds clogged and I draw a heavy breath. "It's okay."

"I shouldn't have said anything." Mike looks miserable, and I squeeze his hand, recovering myself.

"It really is okay, Mike. I wouldn't… I wouldn't be in this position if something wasn't wrong, would I? I mean, I know you think DCF have been unfair, but…" This feels like the hardest, most honest thing I've ever said, and yet some part of me needs to say it. "Maybe… maybe they haven't been." The words seem to fall into the stillness between us, like stones in a pool, the ripples going endlessly outward.

Mike doesn't say anything, but he keeps holding my hand.

After a minute or two, the waitress comes with our pizza, and we stop talking about heavy stuff as we dig into the huge slices. The food and the lighter conversation are both a relief. I've definitely had enough soul-searching for one day. More than enough.

By the time we finish at Barb's, it's dark and starless outside, the air holding the cold, metallic edge that promises snow. I tilt my head to the sky, looking for stars, but there's only a pale sliver of moon, looking impossibly small and distant.

"It's Thanksgiving next week," I remark. "Will you be with your mom?"

"Yeah, she always does a turkey and all the rest. It's nice. What about you?"

I don't want to tell him that I'm going to be on my own for the holiday. I probably could have asked Susan if I could have Dylan for Thanksgiving, but the truth is I was afraid of him not wanting to be with me, especially when Ally and her family could give him so much more. Still, I don't want Mike to think I'm fishing for an invitation.

"I'll probably see some friends," I murmur, but Mike isn't fooled.

"Look… you could come with me." He sounds uncertain, which makes me even more so.

"I don't know…"

"It would be casual. My mom is really relaxed. It wouldn't, you know, have to mean anything." He sounds embarrassed, and I duck my head and start walking without replying, because I don't know how to handle any of this. I'm twenty-seven years old, I have a child, for Pete's sake, and yet dating—if this even is that—is beyond me.

"Think about it," Mike says as he falls into step next to me.

We walk in silence back towards Boulevard, and it isn't until we turn onto my street that I realize he's walking me home, and I start to panic. Is he expecting something? Should I ask him in? I can't. I don't want to; I'm not ready for anything like that. My steps slow as we come to my building; I feel frozen with uncertainty.

"This is me…" I finally say with one of those awkward little laughs and Mike turns to me, his hands jammed into the pockets of his parka.

"This has been fun," he says. "I'm glad you asked me. So, I'll see you soon?"

I exhale in relief that he's leaving it at that and Mike's mouth twitches in a smile. I wonder how much he realizes of what I was thinking. I give an embarrassed laugh and his smile widens. I have a feeling he's been privy to my entire thought process.

"I really did have fun," he says quietly.

"So did I." And for once I don't feel guilty, for enjoying something without Dylan.

We smile at each other and then Mike leans forward and kisses my cheek. His lips are cold and the kiss is so quick, but somehow it feels exactly right. Anything more would have been too much. Anything less would have been a disappointment.

"Bye, Beth," he says, and then he's walking back down the street, his hands still in his pockets, his head lowered against the bitter wind that's blown up.

I stand there for a few seconds, letting myself feel the wonder of a first kiss, even if it was just on the cheek. It was still sweet, still precious.

I tilt my head upwards, but there are still no stars. Yet as I gaze at the heavens and that pale slice of moon, the first snowflakes begin to fall.

CHAPTER TWENTY

ALLY

Nick and I don't have a chance to talk to Josh for three days. I've been on high alert the whole time, full of nervous energy, unable to concentrate on work, even though now I have the luxury of six hours to myself every day. Still, our schedules demand we wait till Friday.

On Wednesday, Nick has a conference call in the evening, and on Thursday Josh has training and I have to take Dylan to the dentist after school. Apparently Dylan had never been to the dentist, so I suppose it should not have been a surprise that he needed four fillings, but I still felt shocked. That little voice of judgment I kept trying to silence spoke a bit louder. *What kind of mother doesn't even take her son to the dentist?*

What kind of mother has a son who deals drugs?

I schedule the fillings for the next week, dreading how Dylan might handle the whole process—the Novocain, the needle, the drilling. All with the potential to set him off.

Admittedly, he's gotten so much better. He only had one meltdown today, when the dentist closed the door behind him, and it ended as soon as I asked him to leave the door open a little bit. I do think Larissa, his special-ed assistant, along with the therapy sessions, are helping him. They seem to be.

So all that meant we couldn't talk to Josh until now, and I think both Nick and I have been feeling the strain of not knowing. We are certainly both edgy by the time I put Dylan to bed and we call Josh down to the family room for the Big Talk.

Josh slouches into the room, wearing a black hoodie and sweat pants, his brows drawn darkly over his eyes as he looks between us suspiciously. We are caricatures of concerned parents—Nick standing self-righteously in front of the fireplace, and me perched on the edge of the sofa, my hands tucked between my knees, deferring to my husband for the initial attack.

"What's up?" Josh asks. He stands on the step leading down into the family room, clearly not wanting to go any further and commit to this conversation.

"Come sit down, Josh."

Josh doesn't move. "What's up?"

"Come sit *down*," Nick practically barks, and I wonder why we are arguing about this instead of the money that is no longer in his drawer.

Josh looks between us both and then silently steps down into the room. He doesn't sit down. He and Nick lock gazes for a moment before Josh drops his, shifting impatiently where he stands.

"What is this all about?" he asks in a surly voice.

"Josh, your mother found a rather large amount of money in your underwear drawer." Nick has a tendency to sound pompous in moments like this, his instinctive default when he's uncertain or nervous, but right now it feels needed. It lends an import to this moment that would otherwise feel like just another battle about Josh's phone or the PlayStation, except we stopped bothering with those battles, and I'm not even sure when.

Josh lifts and drops shoulders, a negligent gesture. "So?"

"Where did you get that money?"

His gaze slides away before returning inexorably to the middle space between us. "I saved it."

"How?"

"Why does it matter?"

"Because I can't imagine how you've managed to save that amount of money."

Another rise and fall of his shoulders. "Well, I did. Allowance... birthdays... Christmas. Grandma gave me a hundred dollars when I turned sixteen."

For a second, Nick and I both tense and I know he is wondering if we've got this all wrong. It would be such a relief, but based on the way we've approached this whole conversation, it would also be a major mistake. I am already bracing myself for Josh's sneering fury—*what, you thought I was doing drugs?*—when I remember that I deposited my mother's birthday check to him into his savings account.

"No, Josh," I say quietly, the first time I've spoken. "That money from Grandma is in your savings account."

Josh shrugs yet again. "I don't know, then. I just saved it, all right?" His bullish defensiveness rings a horribly false note. We've already got him on the ropes, and that is *not* good.

"How?" Nick says quietly. He's dropped the imperious bluster, replaced it with something more serious.

Josh lowers his gaze, looks at the floor. "I don't know. I just did."

Why can't he come up with a decent excuse? I feel oddly disappointed; I wanted something from him that I could at least *try* to believe in.

"Over six hundred dollars, Josh," I interject. "Help us understand."

"Why does it matter?"

"Because," Nick answers levelly, "as your parents, we need to know how you got that money."

"I just saved it." Josh raises his voice, trying to sound impatient now. "Like I said. Birthday money and allowance and stuff. Who *cares?*"

We're going to go around in circles now, just like I did with Emma. I haven't even talked to her since the parents' weekend, although I've texted her a couple of times. She replied only once, a few words that told me nothing. Now, with Josh, we'll keep pressing and he will keep deflecting and we'll never get anywhere.

"Is it drugs?" I ask, and it's as if I've just done a poo on the floor. Both Nick and Josh look at me in blank-faced shock. I am not following the script for this particular family drama, and suddenly I don't care. I meet Josh's stunned gaze with a calmness I didn't expect to feel. "Are you dealing drugs?" I ask evenly, with an almost-serenity that is bewildering to my husband and my son. "Is that where you got the money?"

"Ally..." Nick begins, and then stops.

Josh shakes his head. "Why... why would you think that?" He sounds wounded, and Nick looks torn, as if he wants to come to his son's defense, but I see right through it. Right now, Josh looks like he did when he was four, and he'd broken a crystal vase in the hall, one of our wedding presents. He tried to convince me the neighbor's cat had somehow got into our house and knocked it over, all wide-eyed innocence with a guilty darkness lurking beneath. It was kind of cute back then. It isn't now.

"Josh. That's not an answer."

"Ally," Nick says again, and again he stops.

A silence stretches on, elastic, stretching thinner with every second, until I'm sure it's going to snap. No one says anything, and Josh keeps looking at anything but us. Nick's body is soldier-straight, his shoulders thrust back, every muscle practically vibrating with tension.

Josh lets out another sigh, one of defeat rather than impatience. "What does it matter?" he says, clearly not expecting an answer, and that is when I know for certain.

Of course, some part of me has known all along. Some part of me knew the second I looked down at the roll of bills, even though I didn't want to. But now I *really* know, a leaden certainty that lines my stomach and weighs me down, and I can't bear it.

My son, my dark-haired golden boy with the impish smile and the lovable lisp, sells drugs. He is a drug dealer. I know it, and yet I still need him to say it.

"Josh," I say quietly, a command.

Another silence ticks on, and each second feels fraught. Nick takes a deep breath, as if he is about to speak, to *burst*, and then Josh shrugs and says, "Fine. All right. Okay?" He gives us as a "happy now?" look, as if that's the end of the matter, but of course it is only the beginning. The awful, awful start of something I can't bear even to think of.

Yet another silence, this one like a thunderclap, or maybe the explosion of a bomb. I can almost see the wreckage strewn around us. Josh stares at the floor, and Nick opens and closes his mouth like an indignant fish.

"What," he asks after a few endless seconds, "is that supposed to mean?"

"What do you think it means, Dad?" Josh asks and there is a snarl in his voice that makes Nick recoil like a wounded animal. I can picture the sepia-tinted montage that is going through his head right now—the camping trips when Josh was little and Nick was a Boy Scout leader; the soft summer evenings in the backyard, tossing a baseball back and forth. The half-marathon they did together last year, for charity. Their love of Marvel movies, which neither Emma nor I can stand. I see it all playing in Nick's head, and then I see it going up in smoke, crumbling to ash, because we are now in this place—a place I never thought we'd be, one I never would have been able even to imagine.

"Josh…" Nick says helplessly, and now he sounds like the child.

I stare down at my lap. I am dry-eyed, heavy-hearted, the blood rushing in my ears. I am strangely unsurprised and yet I am also in shock. I know I can't even begin to consider all the ramifications of this.

"What kind of drugs?" I ask quietly, more of a statement than a question. Nick makes some small sound of helpless protest.

Josh sighs. "Nothing major. It's no big deal, you know. Everybody does it."

"Everyone sells drugs?" I lift my head to stare at him hard. "I don't think so. What drugs, Josh?"

Another restless shrug as he refuses to meet my eye. "Just some prescription stuff. Adderall, Xanax, Valium. Some Special K."

Special K? "I assume you don't mean the cereal," I say coolly, and Josh lets out a huff of laughter.

"Ketamine," he says, and there is something of a smirk about him, as if he is enjoying my confusion and outrage, at least a little, and that is almost as bad as the rest of it. Who is this unabashed man-child, talking about these drugs so offhandedly, scornful that I don't know the slang? And yet at the same time I feel a shaming rush of relief. Ketamine is a little different ballpark than crack cocaine, after all. Isn't it?

"Where do you get these drugs?" Nick demands. He's recovered his composure, mostly, although he still looks winded.

"Around."

"Come on, Josh."

"I get some from online pharmacies."

"You can't get—ketamine—from an online pharmacy," Nick says in a voice of authority, and Josh laughs again.

"Shows how much you know." There is such contempt in his voice, I marvel at it. Where did it come from? When did we lose Josh's little-boy love, the adoration a child has for his parents? A long time ago, of course I know that; it's normal, a natural process of growing up, letting go. Yet underneath the teenaged silences and sulks, I thought there was a solid bedrock of familial devotion. Now I wonder if there is a bedrock to anything. *How on earth did we get here?*

Nick does his best to recover from his misstep. "Where else?"

"Nowhere."

"You said *some* from online pharmacies. What about the rest?"

"What does it matter?"

"Whenever you ask that, Josh," Nick says, "it's because it *does* matter. Why don't you just tell us, because we'll find out one way or another?"

"Are you going to punish me?"

Now Nick is the one to let out a huff of hard laughter. "Are we going to *punish* you? You're dealing drugs, Josh. You're breaking the law. What do you think?"

I see a calculating look creep onto my son's face. "If school finds out, they'll kick me off the team."

Nick stares at him blankly, but I know what Josh is getting at. Having a son doing two varsity sports—maybe even playing one day for a college team—is a major point of pride for Nick. Whenever we meet someone new, he almost always works Emma's college admission and Josh's sports into the conversation.

But every parent in this town, in this whole *state*, does the same thing, or some version of it. I've never faulted him for it, never even minded, yet now I feel sick, because I realize Josh knows this as much as I do. He stands before us with his arms folded and an expectant smirk on his face, seeming utterly assured of the power of the trump card he's just played.

Nick still looks blank, impervious. "Then you're kicked off the team." He speaks as if it's obvious, but then I see the realization seeping through him like poison. Josh kicked off the teams, suspended or even expelled from school. No Dartmouth, maybe no college. All our hopes for our son extinguished.

Or am I being overdramatic? Maybe this is the new normal. Maybe, if I dared to talk to Julie or my other friends about this, they'd laugh at my floundering innocence. *Oh come on, Ally. All teenagers experiment a little. It's different drugs, maybe, but it's the same kind of thing. Didn't you ever try a joint?*

Actually, I never did. It wouldn't have been possible, even if I'd wanted to; I wouldn't have known how to procure any drugs, whom to talk to at school. Presumably everyone at Josh's high school knows to talk to *him*. The thought makes my stomach churn and I feel as if I could be sick.

Nick draws himself up. Again. "You need to throw out all the drugs," he states. "*All* of them."

Josh gives an indifferent shrug. "I don't have any now, anyway."

"And we'll need your laptop. I'll have to go through it."

Josh tenses for a second, but then he acquiesces—too easily, I think. Whatever damaging stuff he's got on there, he must think we won't be able to find it.

"And you must promise never, ever to sell any drugs again, Josh." Nick speaks severely, like he's telling Josh to stop telling lies, or stealing cookies from the jar. I have an absurd urge to laugh, except I know I will actually sob. I press my lips together tightly enough to hurt. "If people ask, you tell them you've stopped selling. Period. Got it?"

"Fine."

I stare at Josh, and then Nick, and I wonder if my husband actually thinks this is going to work. How on earth will we know if Josh is dealing drugs or not? And even if he isn't, we haven't so much as approached the terrible root of the problem—*why* he's doing this, how he could do it at all, how he came to it in the first place.

"So that's it?" Josh asks for another tense moment. "You won't tell school?"

"I haven't decided," Nick says sharply. "I haven't decided at *all*. It might be that I have a legal obligation to inform the school," he adds, a bit sanctimoniously, but I realize that he surely does. And then I realize I probably have a legal obligation to inform Monica. Maybe Dylan will be removed from our home. In fact, he probably will.

"Well, when will you decide?" Josh asks in a bored voice, and I feel as if we've lost him, as if we lost him a long time ago. He doesn't care what we think; he's not upset that he's disappointed and hurt us. He just wants to jump through whatever hoops we've deemed necessary so he can keep on living his life the way he wants. The realization is so painful, it actually takes my breath away.

Looking at this sulky-eyed boy-man with a fuzz of hair on his upper lip and the sullen cast to his features, I am reminded of a different Josh—four years old, apple-cheeked, innocent. Once he slipped out the front door and across the street while I was putting in a load of laundry. Someone saw him alone and stopped their car, and brought him to my front door with a friendly smile, along with a flicker of judgment. As a result, I scolded him sternly, more than I usually would have, and a tearful Josh presented me with the crumpled tulip he'd picked from our neighbor's flower bed.

"For you, Mommy. I crossed the street so I could get you a flower."

My heart and anger both melted, and I scooped him up in a hug and made him promise not to do it again. I treasured the flower, pressed one of its petals between the pages of a dictionary, and related the whole story to Nick later, my heart bursting with love for this little boy of mine, impish and so very sweet.

That moment now feels as if it happened to someone else. Someone's else son, another mother. There's no flower now.

"So when?" Josh asks, impatient.

"I don't know," Nick snaps. "It depends on you, Josh, and whether you can respond the way we need you to respond. Because right now you're not seeming very sorry about what you've done. You've been supplying illegal substances to minors—"

"Oh come on," Josh scoffs, "it's just stuff you could get online if you wanted to. It's not like it's cocaine." Which is what

I thought a few moments ago, and yet I don't like it coming from him.

"I read an article about teenagers who bought what they thought was Adderall online and it *killed* them," Nick states. I think I remember skimming it in *The New Yorker* a few months ago, when such sordid dealings seemed a world away from me and my charmed life. "These drugs from China—"

"I'm not buying drugs from China," Josh interjected, rolling his eyes.

"Where, then?"

He shrugs, shoving his hands in the pockets of his jeans. "Different places."

Nick stares at him for a moment, his whole body seeming to sag. "Don't you care?" he asks after a moment and Josh shifts from foot to foot impatiently.

"Can I go?"

"Are you even sorry?"

"Dad—"

"*Josh*. Answer me. Are you sorry?"

Josh sighs and stares at Nick. "Not really."

Nick deflates further, his expression bewildered, his face looking almost gray with pain and disappointment. "But…"

"It's not like I'm doing any harm. Everyone takes this stuff, Dad. It's like—it's like Skittles were in your day, all right? Or caffeine pills. It's no big deal. No one *cares*."

Josh speaks with the most emotion I've heard from him in months, a kind of evangelical zeal that repulses me even as I long to be convinced. *It's no big deal.* This doesn't have to become a big deal. If we can just handle this, move past it, then life can continue on as it has been.

Except already I know that's not true. Already I know that everything has changed, our perception of everything has changed—of Josh, of our family, of all that we've lived for and believed in.

How could *our* son do something like this? He had a good upbringing. He had all the quality family time a child needs—family dinners, camping trips, stories at bedtime, bike rides and board games. He had security and stability, affection and love. *I did everything right.* And now this? A white-hot flame of anger shoots through me like a fiery geyser, and then it flickers out. Surely I know by now there are no guarantees in this life, not for anything. Not for anyone.

"Go get your laptop," Nick says flatly. "And your phone. I'm taking both until further notice."

"What?" Josh's jaw drops as outrage flashes across his face. "Dad, I need my phone—"

"No, you don't," Nick says in that same final tone. "Not if you want to stay in school, and on the baseball and cross-country teams."

"I don't even care about the fucking teams," Josh explodes, making us both flinch from both the expletive and the emotion. "I don't even *like* baseball, okay?" Then he storms upstairs while Nick and I look at each other helplessly, swamped with confusion and grief.

CHAPTER TWENTY-ONE

BETH

In the end, I decide to go with Mike to his mother's for Thanksgiving. I wasn't planning to, but the thought of being alone for the whole holiday felt more and more dismal, and more significantly, I was realizing that I wanted to start being proactive—about a lot of things.

I think it started with the counseling I was skeptical about but have come to, not *enjoy*, never that, but need, and perhaps that's better and more important.

During the second session, I talked about my mother and then about Marco, and first there were tears and then, to my surprise, there was anger—a consuming rage I never expected to feel. I was nearly shaking with it, and as ever, Anna seemed unfazed by my reactions.

"Who are you angry with?" she asked, and to my surprise I said, "Me. For caring so much. For letting myself be hurt. And for being taken in by Marco. He was so shallow. He's always been so shallow." It was such a relief to say it, and yet it led to more tears and tissues, until I sagged against the seat, utterly spent, and Anna told me she'd see me next week.

In some ways, it's been easy to talk to her about my distant, sorrowful past—my dad, my mom, Marco. All those relationships are essentially over. Neither of my parents even know Dylan has been taken from me, and I haven't spoken to or heard from

Marco since the night before the court hearing, when I booted him out of my apartment.

Talking to Anna about the present feels much more frightening. Much more dangerous. I don't want to tell her about what Susan said and Mike admitted—that maybe I've been too much as a mother, that maybe I've got so much wrong, even things I don't know about yet. I don't want to tell her that I both hate and envy Ally and her perfect house, her perfect life, and how, in the dark and despairing middle of the night, I wonder if Dylan is happier there than he's ever been with me.

The day after I had dinner with Mike, I called Susan. She sounded tired and hassled, a reminder that Dylan and I am far from her only case.

"Beth? Is everything all right?"

"Yes. I was just wondering how Dylan has been doing."

A pause and I suspected she was trying to gauge my tone, the reason for my call. Was I gathering ammunition or just in a funk? The truth was neither. I simply wanted—*needed*—to know.

"He's doing well, Beth, but I haven't seen him in a while. In fact, I haven't seen him or anyone associated with your case since I last drove you to Ally's house. Is there a reason you're asking?"

So Susan hadn't seen him since before I had? That shouldn't really surprise me; Angelica and Diane both saw their caseworkers only once a month. "He's in therapy?" I pressed. "And you mentioned he had an… an evaluation?"

"Yes, but I don't have the results yet. As soon as I do, I will certainly discuss those with you."

"What about the therapy? Is it helping? Have any… issues come up?"

Another one of those pauses. "The therapy is for Dylan to process his own feelings and experiences, Beth, but I do believe it is a helpful resource for him."

I felt chastised, but I did my best to shake it off. "I'm not asking to be difficult," I told her. "I just want to know. I want to be sure that this is all working. I'm doing my part."

"I'm very glad to hear that."

"How many cases do you have right now?" I asked, and I felt Susan's wary surprise, even through the phone.

"I'm afraid I can't discuss my other cases with you, Beth."

"I was only asking because you sound tired," I explained quietly. "That's all."

The Tuesday before Thanksgiving, when I went to see Dylan, I braced myself for another lukewarm welcome. Ally seemed distracted, fluttering around the kitchen as if she didn't know where to go, and neither Nick nor Josh were at home.

"Is everything okay?" I asked her, and she gave me a sharp look.

"Yes. Why wouldn't it be?"

"I don't know." I backed off immediately. Who was I to comment on her life? Besides, what could be wrong in Ally's perfect world? A broken nail?

I took Dylan by the hand; he didn't resist but he didn't seem to enjoy it, either, his little hand limp in mine as we went outside into the darkening twilight of a wintry afternoon. The snow from a few days ago had been no more than a dusting, but it was certainly cold enough to snow, with a hard, steely edge to the air, the sky already turning impenetrably black.

It was only a month until Christmas, but I couldn't think about that yet. Christmas without Dylan would be grim indeed, although the holiday had always been quiet for us—a small tree, a present or two, a nice meal. Did anyone really need more?

"I thought we'd go to the library, Dylan," I said as I started down the street, towards Farmington Avenue. "It's open till six on Tuesdays. Have you been to the library since…?" I couldn't bring myself to finish that sentence.

Dylan shook his head. His eyes were wide, and he was watching me carefully, as if looking for cues. Had he always looked at me that way, or was it new, because I was becoming a stranger? I told myself not to overanalyze everything, and just try to be with my son.

The library was thankfully quiet, the afterschool crowd having gone home for dinner, the toy area wonderfully empty. Sue, the main librarian, was behind the main desk, and she half-rose from her chair as we came in, giving us a wide smile.

"Dylan! Beth! I haven't seen you in a while."

It was over a month since I'd lost Dylan. I managed a smile back. "We've been busy."

"How are you, Dylan?" she asked, knowing not to expect an answer, but Dylan gave her a smile and a nod, which was a lot for him.

I knew I should have been gratified and even excited by this progress, but it scared me. Why had it taken Dylan leaving me for him to start making these strides? What had I missed? What had I *done*?

"How have *you* been, Beth?" Sue asked as Dylan went to play with the ever-enticing train table. "Busy, you said?"

"Um, yeah." I glanced at Dylan; he was happily running a train along the wooden track. If there were any other kids here, I'd be nervous of a screeching meltdown, but I thought he should be fine on his own. Still, I felt a little nervous, as I always did in public places. At any moment, some snotty-nosed kid could swoop in and swipe his train.

"Things okay?" Sue asked, eyebrows raised, and I forced myself to look back at her.

"Yes, they're fine. Good." I was not about to explain.

"Dylan seems well." She nodded towards the train table. "A little less shy than he usually is."

"Yeah." My stomach churned at the thought. "Yeah, he does."

I kept a discreet eye on Dylan as I moved around the children's sections of the library, selecting books for him. He was involved in the trains, and not once did he glance up and look at me, as he usually would.

Normally I wouldn't venture far, making sure he could always see me, and I'd rush forward if I sensed anything that could be a threat. Wasn't that the right thing to do? How else is a mother supposed to manage, with a child who can scream for over an hour without stopping, provoked by the smallest or most unexpected thing?

Yet right then, watching Dylan from afar, I second-guessed everything. And when a boy came into the library with his dad and careened towards the train table, I hesitated for a fraction of a second, just to *see*.

The new kid started commandeering all the trains on the table except for the one clutched in Dylan's hand. I couldn't see the expression on my son's face as this new boy began to take over the table, but I could feel myself tense with both outrage and fear. Normally by now I'd be over there, hustling Dylan away, glaring at the other child. This time I stood frozen, waiting, although I wasn't sure what for. Then the kid made a grab for the train in Dylan's hand. There were a dozen or more trains on the table, but he wanted my son's. I didn't wait for Dylan's response, I just charged over.

"Come on, Dylan, sweetheart." I touched his shoulder, and he turned to me, his mouth opening in what I *knew* would be that unholy screech. "Dylan…"

Dylan started to scream, and the kid backed away, looking shocked, and I took Dylan's hand and led him out of the library without checking out any books.

It was only when we were walking back towards Ally's house that he finally stopped screaming. And it was only when we were going up the path to her front door that I wondered if he'd started not because of that boy, but because of me.

The day after the library incident, Susan called me to set an appointment to go over Dylan's psychiatric evaluation sometime after Thanksgiving. I asked for the bottom line over the phone, and with a sigh, she said, "It's clear Dylan has severe anxiety issues. The psychiatrist believes most of his behavioral challenges stem from an underlying anxiety."

Well, I basically knew that—I knew Dylan was afraid of a lot of things, that situations and people and even *grapes* made him anxious. Yet somehow it felt different, hearing it from Susan.

"Underlying anxiety about what?" I asked.

"We can go over this next week, Beth. I really don't know that it's an appropriate conversation to have over the phone."

I didn't press, even though I wanted to. Of course Dylan had anxiety. He'd been scared of so much ever since he was small, just a toddler. Susan wasn't telling me anything I didn't know, so why did it feel so different now?

It was a question I didn't want to examine too closely, never mind actually answer. I didn't want to be alone with my thoughts spiraling through me, and so I texted Mike and asked him if I could come to his mother's for Thanksgiving after all. I didn't entirely want to go, but I definitely didn't want to be alone, wondering if I was the worst mother in the world.

So now I'm here, in the passenger seat of Mike's Toyota, driving towards his mother's house in Windsor, about twenty minutes from West Hartford, having no idea what to expect.

It's a bright yet bleak day, the grass all withered and brown, the trees stark and leafless. It's always been a difficult time of year for me—this month sandwiched between family holidays where the world stops as everyone comes together. I haven't had a family holiday in years; my mother has invited me to New Hampshire a couple of times and I went when Dylan was a baby, but it felt too difficult after that and she didn't seem particularly heartbroken when I said no. My father, of course, never made the invitation.

"So it will just be you, me, and your mom?" I ask a bit anxiously as he heads down the I-84.

"Well…" Mike gives me a sheepish smile. "My sister and her kids will be there too. But they're very relaxed."

"You didn't tell me that before!"

"I thought it might make you nervous."

"Well, it does," I say a bit tetchily. "So it would have been good to know beforehand."

"Beth." Briefly, Mike rests his hand on mine before returning it to the steering wheel. "What's wrong?"

I look out the window at the brown, barren landscape of almost-winter. "I'm just tired. And nervous."

"Something else," Mike says astutely, and I wonder how we've leapfrogged to this stage of a relationship, where we sense each other's moods, where we care so much. I don't think Marco and I ever got there. I doubt he even tried. It makes me feel even more anxious, and I wonder if I should have agreed to this Thanksgiving. It feels like a step too far.

"Have you told your mom and sister about me?" I ask, my face still turned towards the window. "About Dylan?"

"No. I didn't think it was my information to share."

"Thank you."

"But they wouldn't judge you. I don't judge you." He pauses, an unhappy silence. "I feel like I shouldn't have said that thing about you being intense, back at Barb's."

"You were just stating your opinion."

"I didn't mean it badly—"

"I know." I draw a raggedy breath. "Anyway, it's probably true. You're not the only one to say it. Susan said the same thing. She… she sort of implied that his anxiety is… my fault."

"What?" Mike looks outraged. "Beth, that can't be true."

"Why would they have taken him away from me otherwise?"

"Because they're dumb," Mike says robustly, and suddenly I am laughing, a creaky, unpracticed sound.

"Yeah," I agree, shaking my head. "They're dumb."

He smiles at me, and I smile back, and even though I know that's not the real reason, I feel it in my gut, today I need to believe it. Today, just for a few hours, I need not to live under the shadow of my own failure.

Mike's mother, Deb, lives in a hundred-year-old house of white clapboard with a funny little round tower room in front, on a street near the center of Windsor with a lot of pickup trucks and barking dogs leashed on chains. It's a funny mix of quaint and hick, and as we get out of the car, she comes to the door, wreathed in smiles.

She's completely hairless from the chemo—her head as smooth and shiny as a new egg, her eyes lashless and browless, but her smile makes up for it all because it's the kindest, homeliest thing I've ever seen, crinkling nearly up to her ears. As I walk towards her, she comes forward and takes me by the shoulders, as if inspecting me, and then she hugs me hard before kissing me on both cheeks.

"I am *so* glad to meet you," she says, and I know she means it utterly. I don't know what Mike has told her about me—not about Dylan, obviously—but whatever it is, I've already become important to her, and instead of making me more anxious, it makes me feel relieved.

Mike's sister, Kerry, comes out to say hello almost as warmly, followed by her two children, eight- and ten-year-old girls, who hang back, smiling shyly.

"Come in, come in, it's freezing out here," Deb says, and we all head into the house, which is full of lovely, family kind of smells—roast turkey and cranberry sauce, pumpkin pie and cinnamon.

In retrospect, the afternoon passes in a blur of good will. Deb asks me about my family, my job, everything, and I find myself telling her more than I expected. I hint at where Dylan is, not wanting to put it into stark words, and she nods in understanding and doesn't press. I don't see any judgment in her face, and that feels like a miracle.

I find myself watching Kerry, a single mom with two seemingly happy, well-adjusted kids. I watch her give them quick, careless hugs, and then how they run off to play and she doesn't track them with her anxious gaze; she just lets them go. I have absolutely no doubt that she loves them as much as I love Dylan, but from my vantage point now, I can see how that love looks very different. I don't know what to make of it, and I don't want to think about it too closely today, so I file it away for another day and try to stay in the moment.

After Thanksgiving dinner, the table groaning with food, Deb shoos Mike and me out for a walk around Windsor. We end up driving to Windsor Meadows State Park, and walking along the steel-gray ribbon of the Connecticut River. It's bitterly cold, but the sky is clear and there is something starkly beautiful in the barrenness, something I don't think I was able to see before. A flock of Canadian geese take flight from the river, arcing up into the sky in a perfect V, with the accompanying honking and flapping of wings. Mike and I both stand still to watch, and then he turns to smile at me.

"I'm glad you came today," he says, and then, fumbling a bit, he reaches for my hand.

We walk hand in hand along the river like two teenagers, but it doesn't feel as weird or forced as I might have once feared. It's nice, and I feel happy, although it's a happiness that's tangled up with sorrow and regret and a fearful what-if I can't even name yet, and choose not to.

For today, Mike is holding my hand, and his family has been kind, and the sky is blue and I am happy—and amazingly, that is enough.

CHAPTER TWENTY-TWO

ALLY

The Saturday morning before Thanksgiving, having barely slept, I wake up and stare at the ceiling, feeling as if the rest of my life has started and I don't want any of it. I don't even want to get out of bed.

Nick is already up; I can hear him talking to Dylan downstairs with the same cheerful running patter that I use. When I finally rouse myself and peek in Josh's room, my heart swells with both love and pain at the sight of him sprawled on the bed, innocent in his sleep.

How could he hurt us like this? How could the family I'd done my utmost to nurture and protect fail so spectacularly? I could cry out with the pain of it, doubled over as if someone had punched me in the stomach. In the end, I just go back to bed, pulling the duvet back over me, wanting only to block out the world.

I don't know how long I lie there, huddled and heartsore, but at some point, I realize I am being watched. I roll over and see Dylan staring at me unblinkingly from the doorway.

"Oh, Dylan…" I can't summon a smile for him, never mind the reassurance that I am okay, or that he is. We all are. So I just roll back over so I'm not facing him, and after a few minutes, I feel rather than hear him leave.

I must fall into a doze, because it is mid-morning when I wake again, and my throat constricts to speechless tightness when I see what Dylan had left on the pillow next to mine—his precious bunny. The only way he knows to help me feel better.

That night, I head over to Julie's for a wine and cheese evening with a bunch of neighbors—a good old gossip, except there is absolutely nothing less I would like to do. The only reason I decided to go was so they couldn't gossip about *me*.

Halfway through the evening, Julie corners me in the kitchen, topping up my glass of Pinot Noir and giving me a concerned smile. "Is everything all right, Ally? You seem distracted, and as one of your best friends, I think I can be honest and say you look exhausted."

"There's a lot going on," I half-mumble as I sink my nose into my glass. I'm too tired to dissemble more than that, or put on some airy attitude that everything is actually okay when it feels like nothing is.

"Is it your foster child?" she asks, and I try not to sound annoyed as I answer.

"Actually Dylan is the one thing that seems to be going okay. He's doing really well, coming out of his shell a bit." If humming in the bedroom and screaming less can be called that, which I think it can.

"Then what? It's not Nick, is it?"

I think of how, after our conversation with Josh last night, we lay in bed with our arms around each other, unable either to speak or sleep.

"No, Nick's fine. It's just… teenagers." I try for a wry smile, but it wobbles. "They can be hard."

"Oh, tell me about it," Julie says as she puts her arm around my shoulders. "Their attitude is incredible. Unutterable. Who's giving you grief now? Josh or Emma?"

Both. This afternoon, just three days before she was due to come home for Thanksgiving, Emma called to say she wasn't. I gaped like a fish on the phone as she told me, quite matter-of-factly, that she was going to spend Thanksgiving with a friend.

"A friend? What friend?"

"Someone from here. You obviously don't know them, Mom."

I couldn't help but notice the gender-ambiguous pronoun. Was this romantic? Should I be worried? I was. "Still, I'd like to know who you're spending the holiday with," I said rather stiffly. "Especially as you were meant to spend it with us." Her first time home since going to college. Even in my dazed, grief-stricken state, I'd still managed to buy a twenty-pound free-range turkey. Only that morning I'd gone to the pumpkin patch in Avon with Dylan and we'd picked several beauties.

Emma gave a drawn-out sigh, as if I was being too tiresome for words. "Her name is Sasha, okay? I'm going home with her to Rhode Island."

"Did we meet her at the parents' weekend—"

"I don't think so."

"But…" I couldn't keep the hurt from my voice as I said as reasonably as I could, "sweetheart, we were expecting you home. It's *Thanksgiving*…"

"Mom, I'm eighteen." As if that meant that she had no more ties to us, no more reason to care about us all. I tried to absorb the sting of her words, her tone, without letting it show.

"It's only that it's important to us, Emma, to be together as a family."

"I'll be home for Christmas." This was said with the same sort of slight sneer Josh had had last night, and as I finished the call, promising to call her on Thanksgiving Day at least, I wondered when—and more importantly, why—my children had developed this complete disdain of our family life, of their parents, and particularly of me.

I've done everything right. It was a smug, pointless refrain, yet I couldn't keep myself from thinking it, just as I had with Josh. I read the parenting books, I breastfed for a year, I set boundaries and gave them healthy snacks and lots of hugs, I created baby books for *both* kids, I helped with homework, I gave positive reinforcement, I made sure to schedule quality time. I took Emma to New York when she was thirteen for a big birthday trip—we watched *Wicked* and had tea at the Plaza. Just last summer, we had a spa weekend in the Hamptons, before she went to Harvard, facials and manicures and girly time together.

And now this?

Parents aren't supposed to want payback, a return on their investment, yet that was what I felt. I deserved better. We both did. But more than that—so much more than that—it felt as if the overwhelming love that had motivated everything I'd done, every single bit, was being summarily rejected. Of course, I couldn't explain any of that to Julie. I didn't even like admitting it to myself.

"Emma decided not to come home for Thanksgiving," I say briefly, and her face collapses with sympathy.

"What? Oh no…" Julie gives my shoulders a squeeze. "Full of college attitude and airs. I remember when Brad was the same. Came home from his first semester at Middlebury and acted as if he knew it all, and we knew nothing."

"Yes, but he came home." I try to smile, but I can't quite manage it.

"Sometimes I wished he hadn't! He made it seem as if he was in prison the whole time, he was *so* unpleasant, and we found a half-drunk bottle of Johnnie Walker in his bedroom, and he refused to apologize for it." She shudders theatrically at the memory, and I can't help but be surprised.

"You never told me that, Julie."

"I didn't tell anyone. I was mortified. But I'm telling you now, because we've all been there. Emma will get over this, Ally. Of course she will. It's just a phase."

I nod, smiling my thanks. I know Julie is trying to make me feel better, but I only end up feeling worse. I *wish* I was dealing with a contraband bottle of whiskey. That sounds like child's play right now.

Another neighbor, Anita, comes into the kitchen for more wine, and Julie beckons her over. "Come cheer up poor Ally. Emma's just told her she's not coming home for her first Thanksgiving."

I school my expression into something more rueful and even nonchalant as I try to suppress a surge of annoyance that Julie decided to announce my news to another friend. I know she means well, everyone always does, but now they *are* going to gossip about me.

"Oh, Ally!" Anita gives me a quick hug, and with Julie's arm still around me, it feels like I am being suffocated. "It's so hard, isn't it?" she says, pulling a face as she releases me. "You absolutely adore them and you give your very *soul* for them… and then they break your heart." Her sympathetic smile threatens to slip off her face, and for a second she looks like the one who needs a hug. I wonder what is going on with her sixteen-year-old twins, Freya and Lindsey. Josh took Freya to the eighth-grade dance what feels like a lifetime ago.

"I'll drink to that," Julie announces, and she pours us all more wine. We toast each other rather grimly, and then we stand and sip our wine, thinking about our wayward teens.

But are any as wayward as mine?

Last night, at about two o'clock in the morning, when Nick had finally dropped off but I still couldn't sleep, I crept downstairs to my laptop and looked on the foster care message boards about problems with your own children while fostering. All I found were empathetic arguments and warnings to make sure you look after your own children while caring for a foster child, and how sometimes they can feel a little bit left out. But that wasn't Josh's problem, because, according to him, he'd started dealing drugs back in spring.

Full of despair, I typed *when your child is a drug dealer* into the search engine and then let out a groan when I saw the results—some terrifying, some depressing, all of them awful. I didn't click on any of them; I couldn't.

Now, gritty-eyed from lack of sleep and feeling twice as fragile from Emma's defection as from Josh's sins, I can't summon the emotional energy, or even the interest, to ask Anita about Freya and Lindsey. I know I should, clearly something must be going on, but instead I simply sip my wine and stew in my misery.

"Let me know if there's anything I can do," Julie says a little while later, when I make my excuses an hour earlier than is expected or even polite. "Really."

"Thanks, Julie." But there's nothing she can do, of course, and I think we both know it.

Back at home, the house is quiet—Dylan asleep, Josh shut up in his room. He handed his laptop and phone over to Nick last night and Nick spent a frustrating few hours trying to find incriminating evidence on them as if he were some CSI expert before he gave both back, exasperated and humbled. Josh smirked and said nothing. I can't help but feel we've somehow made everything worse, yet what else could we have done? Where's the parenting manual for this situation? *How to Discipline Your Drug-Dealing Kids*. Wouldn't exactly be a bestseller, would it?

"Did you have fun?" Nick asks without much enthusiasm when I find him in the family room, listlessly flicking through channels.

I sit on the edge of the sofa with a sigh. "Not really."

We're both silent, staring at the TV screen and the montage of commercials as Nick continues to scroll through Saturday night's unappealing offerings.

"It's not going to feel like Thanksgiving without Emma," I say after a moment, because it's easier to talk about her than Josh.

"No. We could invite someone else, I guess."

"Who?"

He shrugs. "Beth?"

I actually brighten at this thought, even though Beth makes me uncomfortable and I have a strong feeling she seriously dislikes me. Still, it would be a nice thing to do, and I feel like helping someone, since I don't seem to be able to help myself or my family. "That's a good idea. But I don't have her phone number or any contact information."

"Call Monica?"

"I suppose I could."

But when I call Monica on Monday, it flips over to voicemail; she's taken the week off. Even DCF employees get vacations. I don't have Susan's number, and the DCF number is only for emergencies. I leave it, because the truth is I'm too weary to make more of an effort for Beth's sake.

"We could go to your parents'," Nick suggests on Monday night, as we're undressing for bed. Tomorrow is Josh and Dylan's last day of school before the break; usually I'd be flying around, making pies, decorating, feeling festive and homely and happy.

Instead, I spent the morning trying to work, and the afternoon taking Dylan to get the last two of his fillings. The dentist kindly decided to use a general anesthetic to reduce his anxiety, and the result was that Dylan was sleepy all afternoon, and went to bed promptly at seven, with a mouth full of healthy teeth.

"We can't," I tell Nick dully. "We need permission to take Dylan across state lines."

"Oh, for…" Nick shakes his head. "Would they even have to know?"

"I think that's a big one, Nick. Anyway, my mom would just worry about Emma not being there." My parents are lovely and well-meaning, and they've been supportive, if a bit skeptical, about the whole foster care thing, but I feel too fragile to endure any concerned barbs about anything related to my parenting choices right now, even if they're deserved. "Let's just stay here," I tell him dispiritedly. "Anything else is too much trouble. I've bought the turkey already."

"If you're sure." Nick gets into bed and reaches for his phone to scroll through the news.

I pull on my pajamas and climb into my side before I say, "I think we might have to tell Monica about Josh."

Nick lowers his phone before turning to me with a direct, almost challenging look. "Why?"

"Why? Because he's been dealing—"

"I looked online, Ally. DCF only has to be informed if someone in the foster family has been convicted of a felony, and from what I've read, they usually don't care unless it's child-related."

I stare at him for a moment, trying to gauge his tone, what he's actually saying. "But if we *know*, Nick—"

"What? You want to ruin Josh's life? If DCF knows, Ally, everybody knows."

"That didn't seem to bother you too much last night, when you were telling Josh how he had broken the law." I try to speak levelly, lowering my voice because of Josh and Dylan nearby, and also because I don't actually want to accuse him of anything. Still, I can't help but point out his about-face.

"I've been thinking," Nick says after a moment, his gaze back on his phone although I don't think he's actually looking at it, "it's not like Josh has been dealing meth or crack or something like that."

I recoil slightly, more of a twitch than anything else. "That's what he said." And what I thought. And yet it all feels so wrong.

"I know, I know, but really, Ally, the drugs he's been selling... you or I could get them online with a couple of clicks. They're not actually illegal substances."

"They're not M&M's, Nick. If anyone found out—"

"But they're not *drug* drugs," Nick insists. "We're not talking hardcore here."

I simply stare at him until he looks away. I don't know what to think. Part of me is desperate to agree with him; another part is repulsed by his pathetic justifications. Surely we have a moral obligation to Monica, to *Dylan*, and also to Beth, to report what we know.

"All I'm saying," he resumes after a few seconds, "is that we don't need to ruin Josh's life just because of this one… episode."

"It's an episode that's lasted for six months."

"But it's over."

Is it? I can't make myself voice that doubt. It isn't even the drugs, such as they are, that bother me the most. It's Josh's attitude, that slight curling of his lip, the sneering tone, the defiant stance. He isn't sorry at all about anything except being caught. But I don't want to voice that, either.

"So what?" I ask eventually, weary now as I lean back against the pillows. "We just leave it all? Move on and hope for the best?"

"We give Josh some space to get his act together. He's got prospects, Ally. A future. This is nothing more than a blip."

"It's a pretty big blip."

"Still."

We're both silent again, and I feel too tired to press for one outcome over another. I don't really want to tell Monica, or anyone, about Josh. And it isn't as if Josh has the drugs in the house. When he was at school, I did a complete sweep of the room and found nothing. It's not as if Dylan is at risk from him, either. But now I am the one justifying, and it feels as pathetic as Nick's attempts did.

"Fine," I say as I reach for the book-club novel I really don't want to read. "Why don't we give it until next semester? There are only three weeks left in this one, anyway, before Christmas. Then we'll see."

"Okay." Nick nods, a man given a reprieve. "That sounds like a plan."

*

I am expecting Thanksgiving to be nothing more than a gritting of teeth with the way things are—Emma gone, Josh sullen and distant, although I suppose he is no more than before, but now it has a different, darker flavor—touched with arrogance, steeped in deceit.

Surprisingly, the holiday isn't a complete washout—and that's because of Dylan. He is filled with wonder at the smallest things we do—picking pumpkins, swirling whipped cream on top of a golden-crusted pie. I do the things with him that I've done with Emma and Josh years ago—those precious, childhood traditions that seem so sorrowfully sweet now my own children have no interest in them.

We make handprint turkeys, painstakingly writing out what we are thankful for on each finger. Dylan's writing is a barely legible, phonetic disaster, but I make out *food*, *Lego*, *puzzles*, and *Ally*. The pinkie finger is left blank, and Beth is conspicuously absent from his list of blessings, which I note but don't mention. I am so touched he's written my name, and when I hug him after I read it, he wraps his arms around my middle and I close my eyes, savoring the moment. I don't get many like it these days.

Although the holiday isn't what I had planned or hoped, I find it incredibly soothing, to stand in the kitchen with Dylan the morning of Thanksgiving, sunlight slanting through the windows, and help him sprinkle cinnamon sugar over an apple pie. Josh is still asleep, Nick in his study, the house quiet and seeming very un-Thanksgiving-like, and yet right now, with Dylan, I find peace.

His head is bent over the pie, his dark lashes fanning his cheeks as he sprinkles the sugar with painstaking concentration. Every few seconds, he looks up at me, a shadow of anxiety in his eyes, to check that he is doing it correctly, and I lavish him with praise—he soaks it up like a sponge, basking in it like a cat sleeping in the sunshine.

As he finishes the pie, I take the risk of doing the unexpected and dot a bit of cinnamon sugar on his nose. He blinks in surprise, and then shyly touches his nose, catching the sparkling grains of sugar, before licking them off his finger. I smile, and he laughs—the first time I've heard him laugh—the sound as pure and crystalline as a ringing bell.

"Again," he says, and I am so shocked that for a second I simply stare. Is he even aware that he spoke?

He waits expectantly, and some deep instinct tells me not to make too much of this moment.

"Okay, Dylan," I say casually, and I dot another bit of sugar on his nose. He wipes it off again and licks his finger, giving another little laugh, and then I smile and cover the pies for later, trying to act as if this moment is normal and expected, and not unbearably poignant and wonderfully sweet.

The rest of the day passes in a blur of sorrow punctuated by moments of fragile happiness—Josh comes to the table and hurls himself in a chair as if he can think of nothing worse than eating a meal that has taken me four hours to prepare. Even Nick seems preoccupied, unable to summon the same level of genial bonhomie he usually has on these occasions, when we're all together and he is at the head of the table, carving knife and wine glass to hand. Now he puts his phone by his plate. I cut Dylan's turkey for him, and he smiles at me.

It's always been our tradition to say one thing—just one thing—that we are thankful for as we are eating the meal, and with aching effort, I summon the energy to remind my family of this. Josh looks blank and Nick looks trapped.

"Come on," I say firmly, trying for cheer. "There has to be something."

"I'm thankful for this wonderful meal," Nick says, giving me a shamefaced smile. He knows he should make more of an effort.

"Thank you." I steel myself as I turn to my son. "Josh?" He shrugs. "One thing." I'm not looking for a showdown, but if it comes to that, fine.

"The meal, I guess," he half-mumbles, and I feel like pounding the table in frustration. *Is that all you can manage?* I don't say it.

"Dylan?" I say, smiling at him, and after a few seconds' pause, he points to me. My heart, battered thing that it is, heals just a little. I smile back at him.

"And I'm thankful for you," I say, meaning it more than I ever thought possible.

We smile at each other, Josh exhales under his breath, a sort of non-verbal mutter, and after Nick says grace, we begin to eat.

I am just bringing out the pies that Dylan so proudly helped me with when the house phone rings. It's so unusual for it to ring, everything goes to our cells, that Nick and I exchange a surprised look.

"It's probably my parents," I say. "I'll call them back later."

The phone switches to voicemail, and we hear the automated voice's annoying staccato echo through the kitchen, followed by a beep, a pause, and then a message I never expected or wanted to hear:

"I'm calling for Ally Fielding, the mother of Emma Fielding? This is the Emergency department of Massachusetts General Hospital."

CHAPTER TWENTY-THREE

BETH

The Tuesday after Thanksgiving I show up for my regular visit with Dylan and, to my surprise, Nick answers the door. He's haggard, unshaven, his shirt untucked. I stare.

"Sorry," he says. "It's been…" He shakes his head and lets me in.

I come cautiously, as if he's dangerous. This is not at all what I expected. Panic is icing my insides, everything in me tense with a nameless dread.

"Where's Dylan?"

Nick jerks his head back towards the kitchen. Dylan is where he has been the last two times I've come here, curled up on the sofa watching PBS Kids. But this time, the house is a mess—dirty dishes piled in the sink, a fetid smell of trash needing to be taken out in the air. An upturned box of cereal leaves a trail of stale Cheerios across the smeared counter. I look at Nick, who shrugs apologetically, and then I go to Dylan.

"Hey, Dyl." I wrap my arms around him and he comes willingly, holding me tightly. My heart expands with relief—and anger. I turn to Nick and say as mildly as I can, "What's going on?"

He rubs his jaw. "Ally's not here."

That much is all too obvious. "Where is she?"

"She's…" He stops, shaking his head. "Emma…" he starts again, and his voice cracks. He covers his face with his hands while

I watch, holding Dylan, struggling between a natural concern and a growing fury. If there was a problem, they should have told me. How has Dylan been affected by this—whatever this is?

"What about Emma?" I ask, and my voice comes out hard.

Nick drops his hands from his face, and half-walks, half-staggers over to the coffeemaker and pours himself a cup. "She's having a hard time at college," he says, his back to me. "Ally went up to see her. Sorry about the mess." He lapses into silence, as if that is enough explanation.

I look around the dirty kitchen, and then I look down into my boy's face. "Are you okay?" I ask softly and he nods against my chest.

"If you were having a problem managing Dylan's care," I tell Nick in a steady voice, "you should have been in contact with Susan."

Nick turns to look at me blankly. "Who's Susan?"

"Dylan's caseworker?" I can't believe I'm actually having this conversation. I'm the one whose child was taken away. "You have a social worker too." I search my memory and come up with a name. "Monica."

"Monica doesn't need to know anything. It's just a messy kitchen."

Except it feels like so much more than that. The house has an empty, lonely, unloved feeling. How long has Ally been gone for? What's really happened? Since Dylan doesn't do well with change, he can't have coped with this very well. "How's Dylan been?" I ask.

Nick shrugs, seeming indifferent. "Fine."

"He must miss Ally." I hate saying that, but it's basically a fact. "When did she leave?"

"Thursday night."

Thursday? Thanksgiving? That was five days ago and nobody told me. But, of course, no one needed to tell me. Foster carers don't need to explain about visits or interruptions, as long as one carer is present. The knowledge burns.

"And when is she getting back?"

"Tonight, hopefully. With Emma." He sags against the counter, the cup of coffee in his hand forgotten.

"I'm taking Dylan out," I say stiffly. "For two hours. I'll bring him back after dinner." Yesterday, Susan called me to say two visits a week, for two hours, had been approved—Tuesdays evenings and Saturday afternoons.

Nick shrugs again. "Okay."

I feel like I could take Dylan away and never bring him back, and he wouldn't care. Not trusting myself to say anything else, I ask Nick to get Dylan's coat and then we leave.

It's a cold, dark evening, more winter than autumn, as if the passing of Thanksgiving was the true changing of the seasons. I didn't want to spend another afternoon with Dylan wandering around town, and so I tell him we're going back home. He looks up at me with an anxious frown, but he doesn't say anything, and holding his hand, we walk towards home.

I spent the morning cleaning the apartment, even though it didn't need it; I even bought the same kind of lemon cleaning spray I saw at Ally's house. I've made chocolate chip cookies, and there is a lasagna in the oven. I want to show Dylan that our home can be as warm and welcoming as Ally's, even more so, but it feels like a competition I'll never be able to win.

And yet I'm his mother. His mama, the woman who birthed and nursed and loved him since the second I knew I was pregnant. Shouldn't that count for something? Shouldn't it count for everything?

Back at the apartment, Dylan looks around cautiously, and I can't tell what he's feeling, which is so disconcerting. Normally I'd know.

"Look, Dyl, I got some craft stuff, and a new puzzle." All bought new at the boutique little toy store in town, an expense

I can't really afford, but one I hope is well worth it. And yes, it's all a bribe. So what?

Dylan goes to the puzzle on the coffee table and opens the box. I sit next to him and watch as he sorts pieces, but it all feels a bit rote. Every few seconds, he glances up at me and I smile, but he doesn't.

I tell myself not to feel hurt, that I can't put my own emotions before Dylan's. Of course he's bound to be confused, uncertain, his loyalties divided. Ally's showered him with possessions and attention, and I've been absent. Maybe he thinks I'm angry with him. Maybe he's afraid I don't care.

"Soon, Dylan, you'll be home with me again," I say as he starts putting the edges of the puzzle together. "Just you and me. Won't that be nice? I can't wait."

Dylan's head is bent over the puzzle and he doesn't look at me as I keep talking.

"I know it's been hard, having you live with Ally. I miss you so much, and I know you must miss me." He tenses, just a tiny bit, but I notice. "Do you miss me, Dylan?" I ask, and then curse myself. What a question to ask.

He looks up slowly, his hair—unbrushed today—sliding into his eyes. Slowly, he nods, but I can't tell if he means it.

I force myself to keep talking.

"It's okay if you haven't missed me all the time, or even all that much. I know it must be really nice at Ally's house. Your room is so nice there." I wait, but he simply lowers his head and keeps on with the puzzle.

I decide to stop trying to orchestrate the conversation, and just watch him instead.

The moments pass slowly, sweetly, like trickling syrup. Outside, the streetlamps come on and I can smell the lasagna bubbling away in the oven. Dylan slots another puzzle piece in and the picture begins to emerge—an antique car in a field.

I want to hold onto this moment, I want to take it in like a well-worn photograph, its edges smoothed away by time and love. I want it never to end.

But it does, of course. Dylan finishes the puzzle and I get out the lasagna, and we eat in the kitchen in a silence that feels fragile, the drip of the leaky faucet punctuating the clink of our cutlery. I wonder if Ally has come back, if she will be checking the clock for when Dylan returns. Maybe they'd rather he was out of the house for a little while, so they can deal with their own problems.

But as the minutes slip past, I can see that Dylan is getting anxious; he looks at me expectantly and I realize he wants to go back. I don't want to keep him out longer, anyway; I can't afford to break or even bend any rules.

And so, hand in hand, we head out into the frigid night, the breath-stealing cold freezing in our lungs.

Back at the Fieldings' house, nothing has changed. Nick answers the door, unshaven, his hair rumpled, his expression blank, as if he didn't expect me to return, and I suppress a stab of irritation.

"Ally isn't home yet?"

"No…"

I shoulder past him towards the kitchen, which is just as messy, if not more so, as before.

Dylan tugs my hand and then nods towards the TV.

"I don't think PBS Kids is on anymore, Dyl," I say, glancing at Nick, who stares around blearily as if he doesn't know where he is. And where's Josh? I turn back to Dylan. "Why don't you play with some Lego?"

Dylan nods and heads towards a big plastic bin full of Lego.

I look around the kitchen and then start loading the dishwasher, because I feel like I need to do something. I am not about to leave my son in this situation.

"You don't have to…" Nick begins, and then trails off uselessly.

I don't bother replying, instead focusing on putting cups with the muddy dregs of old coffee into the top of the dishwasher. I realize I am furious, so furious my fingers tremble as I load another mug.

Why is it, if Susan came into my home when it was like this, my child would be taken away, while if she came into the Fieldings', she would give him to them? The injustice of it is so overwhelming, it chokes me.

"I'm sorry everything is like this," Nick says after a few minutes. I've turned on the dishwasher and am now wiping down the counters.

"What's going on?" I ask brusquely.

"Emma…" He trails off again, helpless, pitiable, and yet my heart is iron-hard as I stare at him.

"Emma?" I prompt coldly.

"She was in the hospital. Ally went to see her."

"She's hurt?"

"She tried to kill herself," Nick says brokenly, and tears fill his eyes. I am still unmoved.

"You should have told Monica or Susan," I say flatly. "If you have a situation that affects your ability to care for the child entrusted to you, they need to know. *I* need to know."

"Ally's coming back tonight. Soon, in fact—"

"And what about all weekend, while she was gone? Has Dylan been cared for? Has he had regular meals? Baths?"

"We're doing the best we can—"

"*So was I.*" I thrust my chin out, glaring at him so hard, I feel as if I could burn up with it.

Nick looks down, abashed.

"He's been cared for," he says quietly. "Honestly, Beth…" He trails off and I don't reply. I can't. Dylan is right there in the family room, listening to every word. I just keep cleaning the kitchen, and Nick lets me.

"Is Emma all right?" I ask abruptly, when the kitchen is nearly clean. I feel a flicker of guilt for not asking earlier, no more.

"She's coming home with Ally. But..." He shakes his head, looking near tears again. "I'm sorry," he says. "I know what this seems like, but, honestly, Dylan has been cared for."

"He needs to get ready for bed."

Nick nods, humbly. "Do you want to give him a bath, or should—"

"I will," I practically spit, and I walk towards Dylan. He looks up from the tower he's been constructing, his expression wary as he scans my face. I try to smile. "Hey Dylan, guess what? Mommy's going to give you a bath tonight." Dylan frowns and then gives his head a little shake, and it feels like a punch to the gut. "Don't you want me to?"

After another second, he nods, the movement barely detectable, and I reach for his hand.

Dylan is docile in the tub, which is a huge whirlpool one with jets and fancy taps, naturally. I scoop water in my hands and pour it over his back the way I used to, but it doesn't feel the same. Nothing does. It's as if we're out of sync; we've lost that natural, easy rhythm that I realize now I took for granted. Whenever Dylan looks at me, I see a shadow of worry in his eyes, and I am so afraid he's worried not about closed doors or broccoli or strangers, but about *me*. The thought is so intolerable, I simply force myself to stop thinking about it.

I am in his bedroom, drying his hair with a towel, Dylan in a pair of new *Cars* pajamas, when I hear the front door open and close, followed by footsteps, and Ally's weary voice.

"Nick...?"

Dylan tenses and so do I, and then we exchange a taut look before he twists away from me and hurries downstairs. I sink onto his bed, the wet towel in my hands, and listen as my son runs towards his foster mother.

I can't hear their joyful reunion from upstairs, but I can imagine it. I look around Dylan's bedroom, with its big double bed piled high with pillows, the puzzles and games stacked in the bookcase. I rise from the bed and open a drawer in the dresser, surveying all the neatly folded clothes, some new, some clearly secondhand, that Ally got for him. I take a deep breath as I close the drawer, knowing I need to go downstairs.

I do so slowly, sensing already that Ally won't be pleased I'm here. She won't want me to see her kitchen, her family, her life, as anything less than gleaming and perfect, and yet I already have.

As I come into the kitchen, everyone stills to form an unthinking tableau—Ally by the sink, Dylan next to her, Nick by the stairs to the family room, hands in his pockets, shoulders hunched. A young woman, with dark hair like Nick's and Ally's brown eyes, is sitting in a chair at the kitchen table, her blank expression sharpening as she sees me. For a long, strange moment, no one speaks.

"Beth," Ally finally says, and I can't discern her tone. "I'm sorry I wasn't here this afternoon," she says after another moment.

"If you've been having difficulty, you should have spoken to Monica." I speak levelly, trying not to sound accusing, but Ally closes her eyes as if I've said something distressing or even intolerable.

"The situation is under control," she says, opening her eyes. Briefly, she touches Dylan's shoulder. "Dylan has been fine. But I appreciate this afternoon wasn't…" Just like Nick earlier, she can't finish the sentence, and I hate the fact that somehow I'm the bad guy in this scenario.

"All I'm saying is, according to all the guidelines and regulations I've read, if your home situation changes, you need to inform the proper authorities."

From her place at the kitchen table, Emma lets out a disbelieving huff, and that makes me angrier. Who the hell is she to pass judgment? To act as if *I'm* the outrageous one? I have no choice but to entrust them with my child, while one of theirs tried to kill herself. Don't I have a right to be concerned?

"Our home situation has not changed," Ally says. Her hand rests on Dylan's shoulder. "But I appreciate that you might have concerns, and if you do, then by all means speak to Monica or Susan." She presses her lips together and meets my gaze, and in her eyes, I see both exhaustion and a torment of emotion, and I experience a rush of guilt, even though I don't want to. *This is not my fault.* I'm not responsible for her child, yet she is responsible for mine.

I shake my head, because even though I do have concerns, I don't want Dylan to be given to somebody else, passed around like the hot potato nobody wants. And, if I'm painfully honest, I'm not sure I'm ready for him home with me yet, not that DCF would make such an offer. My life still feels like a mess, and whenever I'd imagined getting Dylan back, I always had it all together—emotionally, mentally, physically, financially.

The silence in the room stretches on. Emma picks at the frayed cuff of her oversized cardigan, her head lowered. Nick rocks on his heels. Ally sways where she stands, and Dylan watches me with that wary expression I feel like an accusation, a judgment.

"All I'm saying is, it's good to communicate about these things," I finally say. "It all starts to fall apart if you keep secrets."

"We're not keeping—" Nick begins, but he falls silent at a look from Ally.

"You're right," she tells me. "You're absolutely right. I'm sorry." Her apology has the effect of silencing me, because what can I say to that? Damn straight I'm right?

Nick glances at the clock above the stove, and then quickly looks away. It's nearly eight o'clock at night.

"I should go," I say. "Monica told you that I have two visits a week now, Tuesdays and Saturdays?"

"Yes, she mentioned that," Ally says.

"So I'll come by at one on Saturday."

"All right."

I look at Dylan, and he looks away. Everyone watches as I walk up to him and crouch down so I'm eye level with him, holding him by his skinny shoulders. "Bye, Dyl," I say, and he doesn't respond—doesn't put his arms around me, doesn't meet my gaze. Slowly, I straighten. I don't mean to meet Ally's eye, but I do, and she smiles sympathetically, which makes me grit my teeth. I don't need her pity. She's the one with the suicidal kid, not me.

I turn around and walk out of the kitchen, and no one says goodbye. Ally follows me, though, hurrying to reach the front door before I do. She puts one hand on it and I stop, waiting.

"Beth, I am sorry."

"Fine."

"I know what this must look like, feel like, but I promise you Dylan is being taken care of. He's so sweet—I feel as if we talk together, even when he doesn't say a word." Like I used to with him.

I put my hand on the doorknob and reluctantly she steps back.

"I'm sorry," she says again, and I don't say anything as I open the door and walk out of the house.

CHAPTER TWENTY-FOUR

ALLY

I know now I will forever divide my life into before and after—before Emma tried to kill herself, and after. The trouble is, I have no idea what the after looks like yet. What it will hold.

When I answered that call on Thanksgiving, and I spoke to the nurse in Massachusetts' General Hospital, I was dazed and numb, barely aware of what she was saying, only catching every other word. *Incident… critical… emergency room.*

"But she's going to be okay?" I demanded, my tone almost angry. "She's going to be okay."

Nick rose from the table, one arm outstretched. "Ally—"

"I think you should come," the nurse said quietly, so quietly that we both heard my breath catch and tear.

Nick pumped me with questions as soon as I ended the call, but I didn't have any answers. I didn't even know what the nurse had meant by an *incident*. Had she been hit by a car? Assaulted? Suicide didn't even occur to me then.

I left maybe ten minutes later, after throwing some clothes in a bag and giving Dylan a quick hug. Nick wanted to come too, but we couldn't leave Dylan or Josh alone, not considering everything.

"I'll call you," I said. "As soon as I can. And if… if you need to come…"

"I will," Nick said. "Of course I will."

The two-hour drive to Boston passed in a numb blur. I focused on the road, which was empty, since it was Thanksgiving—everyone had already gone where they needed to go. Every few minutes, my mind would veer towards the terrible unknown—what had happened, why, how bad it was. I couldn't let myself go down those despairing alleys, and so I'd make myself stop thinking about it, and focus once more on the empty expanse of highway, the occasional eighteen-wheeler rumbling on the other side of the road, its lights flickering over me.

At the hospital, Emma had been moved off ICU into one of the general wards, which was a huge relief, but when the doctor spoke to me in one of those horrible little rooms, it was to tell me she'd overdosed on Xanax.

"Overdosed." I stared at him stupidly, unable to comprehend what he was so obviously implying.

"Her friend called 911 when she found her unresponsive. We believe she took Xanax, as well as a great deal of alcohol, which is a particularly toxic combination. Fortunately, the paramedics gave her activated charcoal at the scene, and we were able to pump her stomach as soon as she came into the ER."

I shook my head slowly, as if to deny what he was saying. "But…"

"Her friend wanted us to call you. She found your contact on Emma's phone."

I swallow dryly, trying to assemble my scattered, spinning thoughts. "And now…? Is Emma…?"

"She's stable now, and our hope is she'll regain consciousness in the next twelve hours." The doctor paused, looking dutifully sympathetic; he couldn't have been more than thirty. No doubt he'd drawn the short straw when it came to being on call over the holiday. "In these situations, we require the patient to see a mental health worker for an assessment before she is discharged."

"And when would that be…?"

"Depending on when she regains consciousness, in the next day or two."

"And then she can be discharged?"

"Hopefully, depending on the assessment."

I stared at him, his bland face, his ruffled hair. He was trim and attractive, like he'd walked off the set of *Grey's Anatomy*. I couldn't quite believe he was a real doctor, that I was really here. "May I see her?" I asked after a moment where we'd simply stared at each other.

"Of course."

A slight, young Asian woman was sitting by Emma's bed as I came into the room. Startled, she rose when I opened the door. I stared at her blankly.

"I'm Sasha," she said.

"Oh, of course." I nodded, still feeling as if I was catching up, as if there was a three-second lag to every thought. "Thank you for…" I paused, took a breath. "Calling 911."

Sasha nodded hurriedly, already sidling to the door. "I'll leave you alone…"

"Did you know Emma was… depressed?" I asked, my tone a bit too urgent, and she shrugged unhappily, one hand on the doorknob.

"Sort of? She seemed stressed. But everyone does. It's practically like a competition." She nodded towards my daughter lying so still in the hospital bed. "I didn't know she was like this. Thinking about it seriously. I mean… everyone talks about it."

"About killing themselves?" My words were laced with pointed disbelief.

"Joking, like. Because of the stress. It's just how it is."

I shook my head, and Sasha opened the door.

"You'll want to be alone," she said, and then she was gone.

I sank into the chair next to Emma's bed. Even in sleep she didn't look peaceful. Her arms were pale and scrawny, against the hospital sheet, and as I looked closer, I saw hatching marks on the inner side of her elbow—self-harm marks. Lots of them.

I let out a shuddering sigh and closed my eyes. I didn't feel strong enough for this, and yet I had to be.

I spent the night in that chair, half-dozing, jerking awake every few minutes to look down at my daughter. In my mind, a montage of bittersweet moments played relentlessly—Emma as a baby, born three weeks premature, yellowed, wrinkled, and tiny. As a toddler, determined to walk, pushing my hands away, the look of almost grim focus on her little face cute and yet perhaps telling. Emma in sixth grade, spending hours on a science fair project, winning second place. We were so proud, but she shoved the whole project— a model of a space station—in the basement and never looked at it again. She won first place the next year. Emma in eighth grade, with her beauty emerging from awkwardness, self-conscious about her braces, going to a father-daughter dance with Nick. The photo of them dancing together is on our living room mantelpiece.

Then, more recent images—Emma in tenth grade, on a ski trip, all rosy cheeks and long, dark hair; the eleventh-grade prom, absolutely gorgeous in a strapless red ballgown, her date, Rory, doting on her arm, even though Emma insisted he was just a friend. Emma the day we dropped her off at Harvard, a poignant mixture of confidence and nerves. She'd worn a bright green corduroy jacket that was her new college look, and she kept adjusting the lapels, unsure if it was really her or not.

When we'd driven away from her dorm, Nick and I had both struggled not to cry. "It's just that I'm so *proud*," he kept saying, and then sniffing.

That was only three months ago, and now she was here, wan and scarred, a ghost of herself. How did this happen? How did I not see?

I looked back at that lamentable parents' weekend and thought how stupidly self-centered and insecure I was, hurt by Emma's reticence, not thinking for a moment that it could have been a cry for help. A desperate one.

Morning dawned, bright sunlight streaming through the windows, the sky a hard, bright blue. On the TV at the nurses' station there were reports about all the ridiculous Black Friday deals—people storming Walmart for a hundred bucks off a flat-screen TV. I felt exhausted and looked worse; a kindly nurse gave me a toothbrush and a tiny tube of toothpaste, which was just about enough to make me feel mostly human. Emma didn't stir.

The doctor came, checked her vitals, and went away again. I texted Nick for the third time, to tell him nothing had changed, but I thought Emma was going to be okay. It felt like an empty promise, and yet one I clutched at. What was "okay" in this situation?

I waited and waited, my mind too fogged from fatigue to dwell even on memories. And then, towards lunchtime, *finally*, my baby girl woke up.

Her eyelids fluttered once, twice, and I leaned forward, my heart pounding. "*Emma…*"

Another flutter, and another, and then she turned her head to look at me, her dazed gaze sharpening as I came into focus.

"Oh, Emma." I reached for her hand, my voice full of tears, but Emma drew her hand away from mine. She turned her head so she couldn't see me, and my heart dropped like a stone in my chest.

Emma is released four days later, on Tuesday, after forty-eight hours of observation and a mental health assessment that I'm not allowed to know about. She has the name of a counselor in Boston and another in West Hartford, and she's coming home.

In the four endless days that I've been in Boston with her, Emma has barely spoken to me. I checked into a hotel, and bought some clothes and toiletries, and basically lived at the hospital, either in her room or the cafeteria. I've tried patience, and smiling silence, and keeping conversation simply about the basics, but whatever I do feels wrong. The most innocent question serves only to annoy her. When I asked her if there was anyone she wanted me to contact for her, she snapped, "Just *don't*, Mom."

I did contact Harvard, since she was due back there on Monday, and told them she was taking a leave of absence. They said she had to be back for her finals in mid-December for her semester to count, and I didn't know whether to care about that or not. Part of me did, desperately. Another part of me was just so very glad she was alive.

As we drive back home, I have no idea what to expect. I've been so consumed with Emma, I haven't even thought Nick or Josh or Dylan. It's not until Beth comes down to the kitchen, just a few minutes after we've come home, that I realize I forgot about her visit with Dylan today. I can't handle her cold fury, not on top of everything else, and I do my best to appease her. I'm not sure if it works.

After Beth has gone, I return to the kitchen, and gaze at the remnants of my family. Emma, silent and hunched over, at the table. Nick standing in the center of the kitchen, looking lost. Dylan by the sink, his eyes so wide and watchful. And Josh upstairs, barricaded in his room. He couldn't even come downstairs to welcome his sister home.

"Let's get you to bed, mister," I say with a smile for Dylan, and he comes towards me quickly, wrapping his arms around my waist and holding on tight. I rest my hand on top of his head as I stroke his back. "It's okay, Dylan. Don't worry. Everything's okay." His body shudders, and my heart aches. The injustice of subjecting this poor little boy to more anxiety and uncertainty burns within me. I hate that I may have made things worse for him, just when they were starting to get better.

I spend longer than usual putting Dylan to bed, both to reassure him and avoid whatever is happening downstairs. Maybe

Nick will have better luck with Emma than I have. I never considered her a Daddy's girl before, but she's certainly not a Mommy's one now.

By the time Dylan is asleep, the downstairs is empty and dark. It's nearly ten o'clock; I must have dozed off without realizing it. I go upstairs and knock on Josh's door; at his grunt, I open it and see he is on his bed, looking at something on his laptop.

"Hey." He simply stares at me. "Emma's home."

"I know."

I swallow the pointless question *don't you want to see her?* "Have you done your homework?"

"Yeah."

I wait, longing to bridge this chasm, but having no idea how. It's become far, far too wide. "Don't stay up late," I finally say, and Josh doesn't respond. Just as I am opening the door to leave, he speaks.

"Was it drugs?"

I freeze, my hand on the doorknob. I don't know what to say.

"Was it?" he asks, and there is a ragged note in his voice that tears at me.

"Yes." I pause, not meaning it unkindly, but needing him to know. "Prescription drugs."

Josh lets out a choking sound, his head bowed, and I take a step towards him.

"Josh…"

"I'm sorry." The words are barely audible, but I know what he means. Finally, my son is sorry for what he's done. And yet it took this? It took almost losing his sister?

I take a deep breath, needing the moment to weigh my words. "I know you are, Josh." I pause, and Josh remains as he is, head lowered, shoulders slumped. My poor little boy. "Thank you," I say softly. And then, because I can see that he's worried, "She's going to be okay."

After a few endless seconds, Josh moves his head in the barest semblance of a nod. I want to go to him, I want to enfold him in a bone-crushing and life-giving hug, but I know he'll resist. The truth is, I can't remember the last time I've hugged him.

"Sleep well," I say, and I slip out of the door, closing it behind me.

Nick is in our bedroom, already in his pajamas. He gives me a questioning look, and I mouth "Josh."

"He's okay?" He speaks in a whisper, conscious of all the fragile children around us.

"Yes. He's… feeling it, I think."

Nick nods. "It's been a long couple of days," he says. "I think we all need some sleep."

"Emma…?" I ask, and he shrugs.

"She didn't say much. She seems tired too." Nick pulls back the duvet on our bed. "There will be time to work through everything tomorrow."

"Yes." I pull off my sweater, running a hand through my rumpled hair. I am exhausted, and despite everything, I am looking forward to going to sleep in my own bed.

"Ally," Nick says as I come out of the bathroom, teeth brushed. I tense at his tone, which is faintly parental. "We can't keep taking care of Dylan now." He makes it a statement, one I can't deal with right now.

I get into bed, my body and mind both aching. "I thought we were going to talk about things tomorrow."

"Yes, with Emma. But Dylan… we don't have the emotional resources to help him, Ally. Surely you can see that. Beth was pissed off today when she came over, and I could hardly blame her."

"If we don't take care of him, who will?"

"DCF can get another foster family. It's not like we're the only ones out there."

"But Dylan is just starting to make positive steps. To change everything on him now… it's not as if he's any trouble, Nick."

"He woke up every night you were gone. Screaming his head off."

Anxiety tightens my stomach. "Were you able to settle him?"

"Eventually. But it took hours."

"It will be different now that I'm here."

"I'm not sure that's a good thing."

I stare at him, trying to discern his flat tone. "What do you mean?"

"The point of foster care isn't for him to bond with you, Ally. It's for him to get back with Beth. And, frankly, she seems completely capable to me, so I don't know why DCF doesn't just give him back now. The whole thing has gotten out of hand, if you ask me."

"There are other issues…"

"Yeah, *ours*. We can't deal with it anymore, Ally. I think that's obvious. Our daughter tried—"

"I know what she tried, Nick." I don't want him to say it out loud. I don't want Nick to say any of this; I can't bear the thought of Dylan being passed around like a hot potato, and selfishly, I know, I also don't want him to go. He is the one child in this house who actually acts as if he both needs and wants me.

"I'm not sure your relationship with him is helping Beth," Nick says quietly, and my hackles rise instinctively.

"What is *that* supposed to mean?"

"You're not her replacement."

"I'm not trying to be."

"Sometimes it feels like you are. Or you're trying to outdo her in some way."

"What!" I stare at him, full of outrage. "You've never said anything like this before." I can't believe he's leveling these accusations at me now. They feel so unfair.

"I suppose I saw it more, while you were gone."

"How, since I wasn't here?" I can't keep the acid from my tone, or from feeling that Nick is playing this card because he thinks it might guilt me into giving Dylan up. "Maybe we should include Beth more," I say a bit recklessly. Nick doesn't respond. "Invite her to things. Have her over. She has two visitations a week now, and you're right, the goal is to be supportive of her. So we should be doing that, not just passing him along."

Nick stays silent. I know that was not what he was hoping to achieve with his remarks, and I'm not sure I want to spend that much more time with Beth, but it makes sense. I can't take her place. The court hearing is in six weeks.

"What about Emma? And Josh, for that matter?" he asks finally as he switches out the light.

"Why shouldn't it be good for them too? They might stop dwelling on their own problems so much."

"We don't even know what their problems *are*."

And at the moment neither child seems likely to tell us.

I sigh heavily in the darkness, the oppressive reality settling on my chest like a thousand-pound weight. Even though I'm exhausted, sleep feels impossible.

"Do you think Emma will be okay tonight, on her own?" I ask, my voice small and disembodied in the darkness.

"You said the assessment came back saying there wasn't a risk."

"Yes, but it's just an assessment. And Emma's clever enough to know how to answer those things, I'm sure."

Nick is silent for a moment as we lie on our backs, staring at the ceiling. "Do you think she still wants to kill herself?" he asks, and he sounds so sad, I have an urge to comfort him, along with everyone else. Why are we all hurting so much? Why is our world so broken, when we've been so blessed?

"I don't know. I don't think so." I consider my answer, as if testing its weight, and then decide it will hold. "She seems more tired than sad now."

"Still."

"Do you want me to sleep in her room with her?"

"No. She wouldn't like that." He sighs. "Tomorrow we'll all talk."

He says it like a promise, but I already worry it's one we won't be able to keep.

CHAPTER TWENTY-FIVE

BETH

I am furious as I walk away from the Fieldings' house—furious that their lives are such a mess, and furious that I have to leave my son with them. I am full of righteous intentions to call Susan and rat them out, but I don't even reach for my phone before I know I won't do that. I can't.

Because one thing I know after rattling around in the social care system for the last six weeks is that kids don't just get magicked back to their mothers. If Susan decides the Fieldings can't take care of Dylan, she'll just shunt him to somebody else. At least now I know where he is, and I believe he's safe, no matter what problems the family is facing. He's also only a ten-minute walk from my apartment. Who knows how far away the next foster family might be?

But I'm still frustrated and angry, and I can't keep from feeling that something is inherently wrong with the way things are, with the whole world, that Ally Fielding's daughter can try to kill herself and DCF doesn't get involved, but my son has a tantrum in CVS and my whole world falls apart.

Still, there's nothing I can do about any of it, and being angry doesn't help. I have six more weeks before the court hearing, or around that. The date hasn't been set yet, but Susan said it would be in the next few weeks. And meanwhile I need to keep doing everything right, no matter who else does wrong. I can't let my focus slip.

And lots of things are going right, or nearly—the Triple P course isn't terrible, now that we've moved onto potential challenges. This week's class is on setting boundaries, something I realize I have both done too much and not nearly enough of. Margaret must sense my disquiet because in the middle of the class, when Angelica is sneaking glances at her phone and Diane has started with her restless fidgeting, she asks me what I'm thinking about.

"What I'm thinking…" I'm startled and a bit alarmed by the open-ended question. I open my mouth to say "nothing much," but then I decide to be honest. This class has become less about ticking boxes and more about actually learning stuff, funnily enough. "I was thinking about how I've set Dylan too many boundaries but also not enough of them." I let out an apologetic huff of laughter. "I know that doesn't make sense."

Margaret props her chin on her hand, giving me her undivided focus. "Tell me more. What do you mean about too many boundaries?"

I pause, feeling my way through my tangle of thoughts, emerging with words. "From the moment—the very second—he was born, I loved him so much. I'd just stare at him, watch him breathe." Margaret smiles faintly and nods, and encouraged, I continue. "But I guess I was scared, too. There are so many possibilities. So many dangers."

"You were worried something might happen to him?"

"Yes." I swallow hard, remembering the fear that could keep me lying awake at night, eyes straining in the darkness, listening to Dylan breathe, always afraid that in the next moment he wouldn't be. But every new mother feels that to some extent, surely? "Anything could happen, you know," I tell Margaret. I glance at Angelica, who looks bored, and then at Diane, who is frowning as if she can't relate to what I'm saying at all. "You hear things… read stories…" I shrug and spread my hands. "I felt as if I was always scared, even as I was so happy to have him. And then, when he was older, and he started having behavior issues…"

"Anxiety, you mentioned?"

"Yes. And then it felt like I had to make so many boundaries, because he couldn't handle stuff. Crowds. Stores. School." Margaret frowns, nodding for me to continue. "But at the same time maybe I didn't give him *enough* boundaries—I allowed him to have these tantrums, and I shaped our lives around them, creating this routine that felt like it worked—but maybe it didn't." I shake my head. I'm pretty sure I'm not making sense. I'm not even sure what I'm saying.

"Boundaries are important for children," Margaret says, looking around to include all three of us. "Because they give them a sense of safety and security children need to be able to explore their world and venture outside of their comfort zones. So you're right, Beth, in that boundaries can be about too much and not enough. You want your child to be safe, but also to explore."

I'm not sure if I was saying that or not, but I smile and nod as if I was. Does Dylan feel safe with me? Does he want to explore in a way I've never let him? Have I been holding him back?

Margaret has moved the conversation on, trying to engage Angelica, and that is fine by me. These questions feel necessary to ask, but I still don't know if I'm strong enough to answer them. Admitting as much as I did feels like enough for today.

"So when do you think you'll get Dylan back?" Diane asks as she drives me home. It's the beginning of December, and everything is gray. I long for snow—big downy flakes covering everything, softening the hard edges, blanketing the world in white.

"I have a court hearing sometime in January. I'm really hoping it's then." She nods slowly, her expression rather grim as she stares out at the highway. "What about you?" I ask, even though I know it's a loaded question.

"It was a voluntary placement, and they can last no longer than thirty days."

I am surprised; it's been over a month since we've started the course. "So…"

"He's with my parents, in Canton. He's been there for the last ten days, but they're coming to the end of their rope." She exhales heavily. "I don't know what to do. I know I should have him back, of course I should. I *adopted* him. He's as good as my biological child, and yet…" She bites her lip. "You just have no idea. No idea."

No, I don't, and yet I do, because my whole life revolved around Dylan and his needs, for years. I know about tantrums, and kicking and screaming, and sleepless nights and endless days.

"So what do you think you'll do?"

"I've thought about terminating my parental rights," she admits in a low voice, the words drawn from her with reluctance. "But it's not a simple process. You have to go to court, and the court has to determine that it would be in Peter's best interests to be adopted again. And the truth is, I don't think it would."

I am both repulsed and fascinated by her admission; it seems crazy to me that while I am fighting so hard to get Dylan back, Diane is desperate to give her son away. But then I remember that moment of weakness, when Susan was offering me the option of voluntary placement, and how tempted I was, just for a little bit of *relief*.

Parenting is hard. Parenting a challenging child solo can feel near impossible. And since I've never met Diane's son, and I don't know what she faces every day, I don't feel I can pass any sort of judgment.

"You hate me," she says flatly. "Don't you? You think I'm a horrible person. I *am* a horrible person."

"No, no, I don't," I say quickly, and I mean it. "I think you must be going through something very, very tough, to be thinking that way."

She blinks rapidly and then drags a hand across her eyes before refocusing on the road. "I do love him, you know. At times. That sounds awful, but…" She expels a shaky breath that sounds like a sob. "I can't relinquish rights. They probably won't let me, and I don't think I could live with the stigma. I mean, what would I tell people? Everyone at work knows him. And school… and neighbors… what would I say?" She swings her head to face me, as if demanding an answer.

"Umm…" My mind spins and blanks.

"'Oh, yeah, he was too much work, so I got rid of him'? People judge you if you do that to a *dog*. You can't do it to a person. To your only child. Not unless you're a monster."

She sounds so despairing and wild, I can't help but pity her. There is no obvious solution, no easy answer… except one. "You're not a monster, Diane."

She nods slowly. Grimly. "I know," she says. "Which is why he's coming home next week."

The Thursday after Thanksgiving, Susan meets with me to go over Dylan's psychiatric evaluation, except when I see her, I find out that's not what she's doing at all.

"The psychiatrist would like to do some further observations before sharing his evaluation," she says, and I stare at her blankly.

"What sort of observations?"

"He'd like you and Dylan to spend some time together, while he observes your interactions."

I recoil instinctively. Is this what it has come to? My every exchange with Dylan will be put under the microscope, to be examined and dissected, while Ally, with her troubled children, gets a free pass? "Why?"

"He thinks it will help."

"How?" I ask, but then I shake my head, because I don't need an answer. All I can do is comply. Everything else is a risk I can't afford to take. "Whatever. I'll do it. When?"

"I really appreciate your willingness, Beth," Susan says with a sympathetic look, as if she knows how hard this is for me. "And it's not something you need to stress about—he just wants you to play with Dylan, be natural with him. That's all."

Sure. As if I can be natural with some psychiatrist watching and scribbling notes the whole time. "Just tell me when," I repeat wearily.

The observations are set to start next week, for every Friday afternoon up to Christmas, and I think how busy my schedule has become, what with visits with Dylan, the Triple P course, counseling, and now this. There's barely any time to get my jewelry work done, and yet there always feels as if there is too much time—empty hours spent just waiting for real life with my son to resume... if it ever will.

Time spent with Mike is a bright spot on the otherwise bleak landscape, at least. After Thanksgiving, things shifted a little between us, settled into something serious without either of us having said anything, or even kissed—other than on the cheek that one time. I'm not ready for anything else, and I don't think I'd even call my few evenings with Mike dates, and yet he's already become important to me, something that is both scary and profound. I think he feels the same way, but I've never asked, and I'm not ready to.

"When will you get a court date?" Mike asks on Saturday night, when we're eating burgers at a place in Blue Back Square, near the town center.

"Susan says in the next couple of weeks. Hopefully before Christmas." I brighten a bit as I tell him, "I asked her if I could spend Christmas with Dylan, and she said she thought that was a good idea."

"That's great, Beth."

"I just hope he likes it." I glance down at my burger, my appetite disappearing as I recall my visit with Dylan that afternoon—two awkward hours spent at the library and then Whole Foods, our usual haunts that felt a bit empty and unexciting now. I'd thought about taking him to the Science Center, with all of its kid-friendly displays, a whole room devoted to Lego, but I was afraid of the unknowns, a potential meltdown. I wanted to stay safe.

Yet as Dylan walked ghostlike beside me, I wondered if that has been at least part of my problem all along.

"Of course he'll like it," Mike says, reaching for my hand and patting it a bit awkwardly before he picks up his burger again. "Why wouldn't he?"

"You should see his foster family's house. His bedroom is bigger than my kitchen and living room combined."

"So?"

"And they've bought him all this stuff. Clothes. Toys."

"Kids don't care about all that."

"I know, but…" I can't say the real fear that's licking at my insides like some poisonous acid, corroding me. The fear that Dylan might prefer the Fieldings—might prefer *Ally*—to me, not because of the things they give him, but the security they offer. The love.

I love him, more than they ever could, of course. Way, way more. But now I wonder—*maybe too much*. Maybe in a way he doesn't like, even if he couldn't articulate it, in a way that's not good for him. Is that even possible? Or am I just being paranoid?

I'm not ready to say any of that to Mike, though, so I just smile and nod. "Maybe you're right."

"Look, Beth." Mike leans forward, endearingly earnest. There is ketchup on his fingers. "Maybe it seems a little awkward between you and Dylan right now, because he's not living with you, but once you're together, everything will go back to the way it was. It'll just take a little time."

"But things can't go back to the way they were," I remind him. "That's the whole point. They've got to change. *I've* got to."

"Well, yeah, but not too much," Mike says as he wipes his fingers on a napkin, getting most but not all of the ketchup off. "I mean, DCF's been jerking you around."

"The system definitely sucks, but I don't think they've been as bad as I thought they were. I know Susan means well. She's trying to help me."

"Well, still." Mike doesn't look convinced, but more and more, I am.

"They haven't been jerking me around, Mike," I say slowly. "I'm not saying the way things happened was good or even fair, but on some level, I needed this. I couldn't go on the way I was. The way Dylan was. He needs to go to school, we both need to get out more, and I don't think that ever would have happened unless…" I swallow hard. "Unless they intervened." I hate saying that. I hate admitting I've been such a screw-up as a mother that I needed someone to take away my child.

But Mike doesn't see it like that. His face softens and he reaches for my hand, ketchupy fingers and all. I don't mind. "You can change, Beth," he says, sincerity blazing in his face, out of every pore. "You already are. You want to be a good mom, that's the main thing."

And I try to smile even as I think, *is it?*

Another week passes—two more unsatisfactory visits with Dylan, where we go to our usual places and feel adrift. Things seem a bit better in the Fieldings' household, although I never stay long enough to see how they all are. I don't really want to know. The kitchen is clean, at least, and Emma drifts around sometimes, giving me a vague smile when she sees me.

Ally seems hassled, though, and her face looks older, the lines from nose to mouth deeper than they were even two months ago, when Dylan first came to her, but she tries.

"How are you doing, Beth?" she asks me on a Tuesday in mid-December. It's well below freezing outside and her house smells of cinnamon. "It can't be long until the court hearing, can it?"

"January twelfth." The letter came in the mail yesterday, and the date writ in stark, black letters terrified and excited me in just about equal measures.

To my surprise, Ally grasps my hand. It's a brief touch, no more than a few seconds, and she looks as surprised as I feel, removing her hand with a little apologetic smile. "I'm sure it will go well for you."

I nod, not knowing how else to respond. This whole conversation feels weird, almost inappropriate.

"What about you?" I ask. "How is Emma?"

"Oh." Her smile wobbles and then slides off her face. "She's okay. She's not going back to Harvard for the rest of the semester." I'd already figured that much, but Ally says it as if it's a death sentence. "She'll have to redo the whole semester," she explains at my blank look. "Because she won't have taken her exams." Based on what happened, I wonder if Emma should go back to Harvard at all, but I don't say as much. "And how's Josh?" I ask, thinking I'm lobbing her a softball, but Ally tenses right up, stiff as a poker.

"He's fine."

"Good." Judging by her response, I think he's probably not, and I wonder if one day I'll have concerns and conversations like this about Dylan—a normal teen, struggling through high school and college, adolescence and then adulthood. Will I worry about what friends he makes, what grades he gets? Such concerns feel like a luxury, and yet, for the first time, not entirely out of reach.

"I meant to tell you—I've written it in the log I keep. Dylan has started speaking a little. Has he been speaking with you?"

I stare at her, trying to gauge her innocently interested expression, unsure if this is a parry-and-thrust for daring to ask about her children, or if she genuinely thinks he must have.

"Not really," I say when what I mean is *not at all*. "What do you mean, he's been speaking?"

"Oh, just words here and there. He said 'again' when I was playing with him, and he's said a few other words since—yes, goodnight, things like that. His teacher has said the same." She smiles at me, looking so genuine I have to believe she thinks this isn't hurting me. "He's made some other noises, as well—laughing, humming, that sort of thing. Isn't that good news?"

My throat is so tight and aching it hurts to swallow. "Really good news." I have to force the words out. It feels wrong of me to be angry and hurt, and yet I am. *Why is he speaking with other people, and not with me?*

"Also…" Ally hesitates, looking a little shy, and now I am the one tensing. What else is she going to ask me? "We're planning to go to a farm out near Granby to get our Christmas tree this weekend—it's one of those old-fashioned farms where you can cut it down yourself. I thought Dylan would enjoy that."

"I'm sure he would." Is she just tormenting me now, telling me all the stuff she can do with my son, that I can't? That I *wouldn't*?

"And I was wondering if you'd like to join us? We could go on Sunday, so you could still have your Saturday with Dylan." Ally pauses. "With the court hearing a month away, you know, I thought it would be good for you to have more time with him. And from what I've read on the foster care message boards, it's not something you have to have approved by DCF, or anything like that. We can just go."

"That…" I hesitate, my mind whirling from all she'd said. Christmas trees. More time with Dylan. Foster care message boards… what has she been posting on *those*? "That would be nice," I say, because of course I am going to accept. There's absolutely no question about that.

At this point, whether well-meaning Ally realizes it or not, I am in a battle with her for the love of my son.

CHAPTER TWENTY-SIX

ALLY

The morning after Emma comes home, I wake up groggy and heavy-hearted, to the sound of music and laughter from downstairs. It's so incongruous to how I'm feeling, as well as to how the evening ended yesterday, with Nick and I in silent disagreement and despair, that at first I think it must be coming from the TV.

I check the clock and see that it's half past eight, and my heart lurches with alarm as I scramble out of bed. I usually take Dylan to school at eight fifteen, and Josh should have caught the bus an hour ago. I set my alarm for six forty-five. What's going on?

I grab my bathrobe and thrust my arms into the sleeves, already heading downstairs as I knot the sash. I come into the kitchen and blink in surprise, fighting blank incomprehension. I feel like I've stumbled onto the set of a sitcom, or the alternate reality fashioned from my wistful, woebegone dreams.

Nick is at the stove, flipping pancakes. He's swathed in his "Kiss the Cook" apron, which he wears for the rare occasions when he makes a meal—Saturday breakfast, or the occasional multi-ingredient stir fry. Josh is setting the table, a bit sullenly, but *still*, and Emma and Dylan are curled up on the sofa watching *Arthur* on PBS Kids. Dylan's head is on Emma's shoulder, her arm around him, even though they must have only met this morning. All of it, every single bit, fills me with a sense of unreality, along with a fragile unfurling of hope, so I could burst into tears right there.

"What…" I shake my head, unable even to finish that question.

"I turned off your alarm," Nick explains. "I thought you needed the sleep."

"But it's after eight-thirty." I try not to sound panicked. "Dylan and Josh should be at school."

"I thought we'd all take the day off," Nick says easily. "And don't worry, I've already called the school and explained we were having a family day. They were fine with it."

"Were they?" The principal, along with Monica, have drilled into my head the importance of routine for Dylan, and this is decidedly off-piste, but how can I possibly complain when everyone seems so… *happy*?

"There's coffee," Nick says with a nod towards the coffeemaker. "Fresh."

"Thanks." I reach for a mug, trying to untangle the unsettling jumble of my thoughts. I'm happy and hopeful, of course, but there is also a little nettle-sting of resentment buried in the gratitude. I've been trying so hard, and the second I'm asleep, everyone decides to become easy?

Of course I know that thought is utterly unreasonable, shamefully petty, and I banish it immediately. I don't want to think things like that, even for a second, and so I choose not to. I turn around, leaning against the counter as I take my first much-needed sip of coffee.

"So what brought all this on?" I ask Nick.

He shrugs and flips another perfectly round and golden pancake. "I just thought we could all use a reset."

"Definitely." I glance at Josh, and then Emma and Dylan snuggled on the sofa. "How was Emma this morning?" I ask, lowering my voice.

"She seemed okay."

"She and Dylan seem to be getting along."

"You know, I can actually hear you, Mom," Emma calls.

I give Nick a shame-faced smile as I call back to her. "Sorry."

"I love *Arthur*," she continues. "Although someone else is doing his voice now. Weird."

"Someone else?" Josh calls from the table. "No way."

I struggle not to do a double-take. My children are actually bantering. If someone walked in on this scene, they'd think we were a happy, harmonious family. Yet I can't keep from feeling a sense of unreality, an expectation that someone will shout "cut" and we'll all go back to our usual morose places.

But that doesn't happen. Nick brings the pancakes to the table, and I take out the orange juice, and then Emma is leading Dylan to the table by the hand. They seem to have bonded in the space of a single morning. Soon, we are all sitting down in a wintry spill of sunshine, spreading butter and pouring maple syrup.

"It's a beautiful day," Nick says as he digs into his pancakes. "I thought we could hike up Avon Mountain. We haven't done that in a few years, have we?"

To my ever-increasing surprise, both Josh and Emma give their shrugging assent. We haven't done a hike all together since Emma was about twelve, when both kids still liked walking in the woods and spending time with their parents.

An hour later, we are piling into the car in our parkas and hiking boots—I dug out an old pair of Josh's for Dylan. Emma made hot chocolate to put in a thermos, and Nick did his Bear Grylls thing of packing a backpack with a first-aid kit, flashlight, matches, and an emergency blanket.

"You do remember that hiking to Heublein Tower only takes about an hour?" I remind him as he starts the car.

Nick gives me a glinting grin, the way he hasn't in a long time. "Yes, but you never know what could happen."

*That much is certainly tr*ue, I think as I stare out the window. I want to be buoyed by optimism, the way Nick and even Emma and Josh seem to be, but something is keeping me down. Maybe it's that I don't trust this sudden new cheeriness, or maybe it's that it happened without me. Whatever it is, I do my best to push it away and enjoy the day—a bright blue sky, stark, leafless trees, and brown mountains undulating to a hazy horizon.

As we head up the mountain, the first part of the trail the most difficult, we fall into natural groupings. Emma takes Dylan's hand, and Josh, full of energy, forges ahead, a trailblazer. Nick hangs back to fall in step with me, and we walk in silence for a few moments over the steep terrain until it levels out a little and I can talk without panting.

"Thanks for all of this," I say to Nick. "I think you're right. We did need a reset."

"Well, it's not as if a hike is going to solve all our problems," Nick answers with a huff of rueful, sorrow-tinged laughter. "I know that, Ally, even if you think I don't."

"I never—".

"You didn't need to. I knew exactly what you were thinking when you walked into the kitchen this morning. 'Here goes Nick, thinking he can solve this crisis with some pancakes and a walk through the woods.' I don't, you know."

I am silent, struggling with the truth that I was thinking that, and that Nick knows me so well. "I'm sorry," I say at last.

Nick nods, accepting my apology, his mind already seeming to have moved on. I stumble over a tree root and he grabs my elbow to steady me.

"Look," he says. "About last night. The whole Dylan thing." He lowers his voice, even though Emma and Dylan are at least thirty feet in front of us. "I didn't mean to sound unfeeling. I know I haven't been as into the foster thing as you are."

"You said Dylan was too weird," I remind him before I can stop myself, and Nick flinches.

"I didn't really mean it like that."

"You didn't?"

"No." He pauses, and we keep walking, the crunch of dry, brown leaves under our boots the only sound—along with my ragged breathing. I forgot how steep this seemingly short hike could be. "I've found it all hard," he says quietly, and I almost stumble again as I turn to look at him.

"What do you mean?"

Nick is silent for a long moment, long enough for Emma to look back and check we're following behind. She's still holding Dylan's hand, and the sight fills me with both love and gratitude. Josh has found a big stick and is whacking everything he can with it, the way he did when he was Dylan's age.

"You asked me if it was all a bit too close to home a while back," he says slowly. "And I told you it wasn't."

"Yes…"

"Well, I lied," I he says flatly. "I don't think I even realized I was lying. I tend not to think about my childhood at all, and I mean at *all*."

I nod, because that is how he has always seemed to me—like an entirely different person to the son of that sad, decrepit woman in Albany I only met once.

"And I wasn't like Dylan when I was growing up, that much is true. But seeing him—seeing Beth, who is nothing like my mother was, by the way—it just… *prodded* something inside me. And I started to remember how it felt to be the kid with raggedy clothes, or whose mother didn't show up to the school play or field day or whatever."

"Oh, Nick." I want to reach out to him, hold his hand, but his own are jammed in the pockets of his parka, his head lowered. A display of affection might tip him over the edge, and he'll clam up again. I know my husband well enough to realize that, at least.

"I've kept those memories back for over thirty years. I think some part of me thought I could keep them back forever, if I stayed away from Dylan. If I didn't get too close."

"So what has changed your mind?"

Nick releases a long, low breath. "The realization that we're not invulnerable. You can do everything right, you can make good money, live in a nice house, tuck your kids up into bed every single night and something still goes wrong." He turns to look at me, his face full of a bleakness I have been struggling with since I first found that wad of money. "Josh… Emma… I never thought that would happen to them. To us."

"I know," I whisper.

"We were meant to be the ones who had it all under control. We're supposed to be helping Beth, right? And yet she was the one cleaning our kitchen. It's all… humbled me. To the dust."

I nod, unable to speak. I feel exactly the same.

"I'm sorry, Ally," Nick says. "For letting you down."

"You haven't…"

"I have. With Dylan. And maybe with Emma and Josh. I don't know. I don't know anything anymore, except that I feel like a failure."

"So do I." I hate to admit it so starkly, but it's a truth that radiates from my deepest self. *I'm a failure*. I must have failed as a parent, as a *mother*, for my children to do the things they have. For my son to turn to drugs, my daughter to suicide. I must be a complete and abysmal failure, and the worst thing is, I thought I was okay. I was actually *smug*.

Nick takes his hands out of his parka and reaches for mine. "At least we're failing together," he says with a wobbly smile, and I nod, my throat still too tight to manage words, as we walk hand in hand up the mountain. For the first time in a long while I feel a sense of possibility, of hope.

By the time the two of us reach the summit, with the elegant Heublein Tower shuttered up for winter, Emma, Josh, and Dylan have all been there for a few minutes. Dylan runs towards me as I crest the mountain, and I hold my arms out to him. He doesn't run into them, but he stops right before me and gives me a lovely, shy smile. I smile back.

"Hey, Dylan. You've done such a good job on this walk. I bet you're tired."

"Hot chocolate," Emma sings out, brandishing the thermos, and I marvel at the change in her. Gone is the silent, morose patient from the four days in the hospital. She still seems fragile, her skin almost translucent, but there is a lightness to her that wasn't there before. And Josh… I'm so happy to see him outside, interacting, without his phone or his laptop or the endless sulky silence. I feel as if I've stepped from a stuffy, stale existence into fresh air; I feel as if I can finally breathe.

We find a flat rock to sit on while we drink our hot chocolate from tin mugs; the vista of the Farmington River Valley is a muted yet breathtaking patchwork of browns on this wintry day, the Hartford skyline visible in the other direction, hazy in the distance.

We sip our hot chocolate, quiet and content, when Emma suddenly speaks.

"I'm not going back to Harvard."

Nick jolts, nearly spilling his hot chocolate, and I feel myself tense right back up. "You don't need to make any decisions right now."

"I sort of do," Emma responds. Her tone is matter-of-fact. "Finals start next week."

So soon? It hasn't even been a full week since Thanksgiving. "Even so," I say, a bit feebly, because Emma is already shaking her head.

"I don't want to take my finals."

"That's fine, Em," Nick jumps in quickly. "Of course it is. There's no rush. Harvard will hold your place, and repeating the semester isn't such a big deal."

It kind of is, I think, especially for an overachiever like Emma. She'll be behind all her friends, and I know she'll hate that.

Emma stares out at the view for a moment, her lips set, before she replies. "I don't want to repeat the semester."

Nick and I exchange uneasy glances. "This is too soon to be talking about this," he says in his firm, fatherly voice. "Or making decisions. Let's just take it easy for the next few days, all right?"

Emma shakes her head, but she drops the subject, and Nick attempts a change of conversation that is so glaringly obvious, Josh actually winces.

"I was thinking we should get our Christmas tree soon. Head out to the farm."

Every year we have cut our own tree at a farm in the northwest corner of the state. It is a bit of a trek, but it's truly magical—snowy fields of fir and spruce, clean pine-scented air, and a barn with a Christmas shop and café. It's one tradition we've never broken; the kids have always been up for it.

Emma presses her lips together, seeming to resent the change in subject, but then she nods. Josh shrugs his agreement, but even that feels like a win, considering what life has been like lately.

"And I thought we could invite Beth," Nick continues, surprising me. He glances at Dylan. "Would that be fun, buddy? If your mom came with us?"

Slowly, warily, Dylan nods. And then he smiles, and Nick nods back, pleased. We'd talked last night about having Beth over more as we head towards reunification, but I'm not entirely sure how I feel about her accompanying us on a sacred family tradition.

But then, as I look at my children finishing their hot chocolate, and then the view of fields and farms that stretch on forever, I realize that nothing is sacred. All the rules, all the promises, have already been broken, for Beth—and for me.

I never thought I'd be here, with a suicidal daughter considering dropping out of college, and a son who might still be dealing the kind of drugs she took in her attempt to kill herself. It's all so horrible, and yet it's real, and I'm staring out at fields and sky and beauty and I want to both cry and laugh and shake my head in wonder.

Nothing is sacred, and yet everything is.

As we head back down the mountain, I feel as if we're re-entering reality. We'll need to talk with Emma about her future, and we really should have a follow-up conversation with Josh about what he's been up to, confirming that he is done with the drugs for good, keeping the communication open. Dylan has a CBT session tomorrow, and Beth is coming over on Saturday for her second visit, which for some reason feels like it takes out the whole weekend. Julie has texted me twice, asking me if I'm okay, since Nick saw her when he was taking out the garbage and alluded to our situation, although with no concrete details.

All of life presses down on me, heavier and heavier with each step that I take. Part of me wishes that I could have stayed on top of the mountain, simply staring out at the view, breathing that clean air.

As we reach the bottom of the mountain and head towards the car, Nick takes my hand.

"Okay?" he asks quietly, and I manage to nod.

"It just feels like a lot."

"I know. But we're in this together, Ally. Really."

I nod again, and he squeezes my hand. I'm grateful for all he's done and shared today, *so* grateful, but some small, cynical seed in me has already taken root.

Nick can be a man of grand gestures rather than small, everyday actions. I just hope he means what he says, and we'll be in this together tomorrow, and the day after, and then the day after that. Because I really don't think I can do all—or any—of this alone.

CHAPTER TWENTY-SEVEN

BETH

Sunday, the day when I'm meant to accompany the Fieldings and Dylan to cut down a Christmas tree, is as bright and perfect as a postcard, tailor-made for this kind of family activity—blue skies, a hard frost that almost looks like snow, and the air is as crisp as an apple, as clear as a drink of water.

I show up at their house feeling more nervous than usual, both because I don't know what to expect from today, and also because of yesterday, when I had the wretched therapy observation with Dylan. Ally drove us both to the psychiatrist's office in Simsbury, which awkwardly made her feel like my mom, and James, the psychiatrist, a friendly but studious-looking guy with glasses and a beard, sat in the corner of the room, jotting notes on a pad of paper as I desperately tried to be normal with Dylan and wasn't. I'm not sure I even know what normal is now, if I ever did.

It certainly wasn't what was happening between us then, with my voice high and wavering and Dylan seeming to deliberately ignore me. He was concentrating on building a tower of blocks, and I tried to help, afraid that if it fell over, he might have a meltdown, and guess what? It did, and so did he. I tried to keep the tower from falling, lunging forward to catch the blocks in my hands, and that's when Dylan started screaming.

"I'll fix it, Dyl," I said desperately. "Don't worry I'll fix it, I promise."

Eventually he calmed down, but I was a shaky mess and James kept scribbling. I didn't like to think about what he might be writing, and it was nothing but a relief when the hour finally ended, tempered by the awful acknowledgement that I'll have do it again next week, and then the week after that.

Now I try not to fidget as Nick opens the door and welcomes me in. He's dressed like an ad for Eastern Mountain Sports, with matching waterproof parka, hat, and gloves, and a pair of hiking boots that probably cost at least two hundred bucks. I feel inadequate in my winter jacket straight from Walmart, my beat-up sneakers. How can I possibly compete with these people?

"Hey, Beth," Nick greets me easily as he opens the door wide and steps aside to let me in. His smiling gaze takes in my pathetic winter gear before he adds, "Great to see you. I think it's probably snowing up at the farm, so do you want to borrow a pair of Ally's boots? What size are you?"

"Um, six and a half."

"Ally's a seven, but I think with an extra pair of socks it should be fine." He gives me a paternal smile that manages to feel both genuine and patronizing. I mutter my thanks.

Everyone is milling around downstairs, getting coats and hats, scarves and mittens, and I find Dylan in the family room, dressed in all his new winter gear, looking like a magazine ad as well, with his hair brushed back and his matching hat and mittens in navy blue.

"Hey, Dylan." I decide to ruffle his hair instead of going in for a hug, but he ducks his head away and I withdraw my hand, telling myself not to feel stung. He's seven; he's growing up. That's all it has to be.

Ally comes downstairs, looking as magazine-perfect as everybody else but me, if a little tired.

"Hey, Beth. We should all be ready in a minute."

I wait with Dylan while they rush around, trying not to feel surplus to requirements, and then it's time to head into their car, a big six-seater SUV that's built like a tank. Ally orders Emma and Josh into the backseat, and Dylan and I take the middle. I smile at him, and he looks away. Why do I feel like he hates me? I don't know if I'm being paranoid, analyzing every microsecond of our interaction, or if I'm not being fearful enough. What if he always resents me? What if these three months away change everything?

It's an hour's drive to the Christmas tree farm, and at first Nick chivvies everyone along with quizzes and games, but after half an hour, Josh takes out his phone and Emma looks out the window like she's lost in her own world, and Nick lapses into silence.

I'm grateful; I wasn't any good at the games and Dylan, of course, didn't say a word, although now that Ally has said he is speaking part of me is determined to hear him talk, even though I know pushing him is hardly going to help matters between us.

About fifteen minutes from the farm, we start to see snow, a soft, fleecy blanket draped over the fields and frosting the trees like a birthday cake. It's so beautiful, compared to the cold, barren grayness of West Hartford, and I lean closer to Dylan to point out the sights—branches bowed down with the soft weight of the snow, drifts all the way up the fence posts.

"There must be eight inches here," Nick says, sounding both impressed and benevolent, almost as if he had something to do with it.

Ally murmurs something in reply, but I can't hear what it is. She's been pretty quiet for the whole journey, her expression preoccupied, her fingers tapping against her thigh, and I wonder what's going on. Is she worried about Emma and her Harvard plans? Or is there something else?

At the farm, we troop into a barn that has been festooned with Christmas decorations right up to its beams, and are given a saw and a map.

"We always get a blue spruce," Nick tells me, and I nod and smile even though Christmas trees look all the same to me.

Soon we are setting off in the snow, which sinks up past the edge of my boots and soaks my socks. I look for Dylan, but I see he has run ahead and is now walking hand in hand with Emma. I swallow my hurt and tell myself it's fine. I'm not going to force anything. We don't have to spend the entire afternoon in each other's pockets.

"They've really bonded," Ally says as she falls in step with me, a dozen feet behind everyone else. "Watching children's shows on PBS Kids, of all things. I think Emma enjoys the simplicity."

"How is Emma?" I'd rather talk about her with Ally than about Dylan.

Ally sighs. "She's okay. She doesn't talk to me about anything. She's been home for over two weeks and we've barely had a conversation. I'm trying not to push, but… it's hard." She shoots me a quick, furtive sort of look. "Sorry. You don't want to hear all this."

"I don't mind."

"I don't think it's affecting Dylan's care—"

I wave my hand. "Don't worry about that." It's all too obvious Dylan is settled and happy with the Fieldings. Any protest I make now would be petty, and I don't want to, anyway.

"I think it's nice they've struck up this friendship," Ally resumes quietly. "It feels… uncomplicated. And maybe that's what they both needed." She shoots me another one of those glances. "Sorry, I didn't mean—"

"It's okay." I dig my hands into the pockets of my jacket, which feels too thin now that the New England wind is cutting through it. "My relationship with Dylan is complicated. I do realize that."

"I think every mother's relationships with her children is complicated," Ally says with a raggedy laugh. "I thought mine weren't, but I'm discovering they are, very much so."

"Because of Emma?" I ask cautiously. I appreciate her honesty, but it startles me.

"And Josh." She presses her lips together as if she wished she didn't say that much, but now I'm curious.

"What's going on with Josh?"

"Oh…" Ally lets out a wavery laugh. "He's made some bad choices. I suppose all teenagers do."

"I certainly did." I wonder what Josh is up to—alcohol? Drugs? Porn? Or maybe he just got a B in chemistry. I tell myself that's not fair; Ally has one suicidal daughter already. Josh's problems could be pretty serious.

"Did you?" Ally glances at me uncertainly. "If you don't mind me asking, what were they? I mean… how…" She trails off and I grimace.

"How did I end up like this?"

"No, I don't mean that," she says quickly. "I just wondered… you don't seem to have much support. Susan said something about it. Are your parents…"

"My dad lives in Bloomfield, but we're basically estranged. My mother walked out in the spring of my senior year of high school, married someone else, and moved to New Hampshire." I smile wryly as I do my best to relate this without bitterness. "It screwed me up, to be honest."

"Oh Beth, I'm sorry." Ally looks genuinely aggrieved on my behalf, and that comforts me.

"It was a long time ago now, and I wouldn't have had Dylan if she hadn't left."

"Why…"

Briefly I give her the highlights of my misbegotten youth—the DUI, the withdrawal of my college offer, Dad kicking me out and Mom not wanting to know. And Marco.

"That all sounds so tough," Ally says when I finish with what I hope passes for a wry shrug. She looks quietly appalled, and

I'm wondering what she's thinking. Has all I've said changed her opinion of me for better—or for worse? "Are you still in touch with your dad?" she asks. "Your mom?"

"Not really. I talk to my dad maybe once a year. My mom…" I blow out a breath. "A bit more. My therapist suggested I contact them, actually. Work to reconcile, or at least for some closure." I don't know why I'm telling her this, but it actually feels kind of good to talk to another woman, someone who has some wisdom and experience.

"And do you think you'll do that?"

"I don't know if I can bear to, with my dad. It was all pretty awful before I left. But my mom…" My voice trails off as something tugs at my heart, like the string of a kite. *I miss my mom.* It's something I haven't let myself think, never mind feel, for a long time.

"You should contact her, Beth," Ally says quietly. "For your sake, as well as hers. I can't believe a mother wouldn't want to hear from her child."

"You'd be surprised," I say, but I know that's a bit unfair. My mom hasn't been displeased whenever I called, more just unenthused, a bit uncertain, almost as if I'm a grenade that might go off over the phone. "Anyway." I give Ally a direct look. "You might be worried about your kids, Ally, and how complicated the relationships feel, but speaking from the other side, I know that all you really need to do is *be* there for them." I hear the throb of emotion in my voice, but I don't care. "Just be there. Show up—again and again, even when they mess up big time. And they will."

"Yes." Ally brushes at her eyes as she tries for a smile. "Yes." She lets out a shaky laugh. "Thank you, Beth."

I don't know how to respond, because it seems so odd that I of all people am giving parenting advice to the woman who is taking care of my son, but so much about this situation hasn't been what I expected. How can I be surprised by yet another bend in the road?

"I think we've found a tree!" Josh calls, and Ally gives me a quick, warm smile before starting towards her family.

The rest of the day passes easily enough, but I don't spend much time with Dylan. In the bosom of the Fieldings, there isn't really room for me, and I understand that even as I chafe against it. If it were just Dylan and me, it would be different, although maybe not in a good way. Not anymore.

I try to enter into the spirit of the occasion, more for Ally's sake than my own. She seems to take the weight of everyone's else emotions on herself, working hard without trying to seem to, to make sure everyone is happy.

We all take turns with the saw, lying flat on our backs on the snow, under the fragrant spruce branches, hacking away at the trunk. It's a lot harder than I expected, and I barely make a dent in the wood before I give up.

"Come on, Beth," Nick jollies me along. "You've got to put your whole shoulder into it. Really give it your all."

And so, with all the Fieldings watching me, I do my best to saw at the trunk, and manage a bit more. They all cheer, which is kind, and part of me warms to it all while another part shrinks back. I don't belong here, not really, yet more and more it seems as if Dylan does.

Josh helps him saw the trunk; no one even asks if I'd like to be the one to do it. On the way back, with Nick dragging the tree, Dylan runs ahead with Emma and Josh. No matter what problems Ally's children might be facing, they look like happy-go-lucky kids right now, as does Dylan, all of them frolicking through the snow. The sight gives me a rush of joy, a flash of pain, the emotions tangled together.

Back at the barn, one of the staff members binds the tree in wire while we have hot chocolate in the little café.

"We have a tradition," Ally tells me a bit shyly, "everyone picks out an ornament in their shop. I'd like you to, as well. And Dylan too, of course."

"That's very kind. Thank you." I turn to Dylan, determined that we at least spend this part of the day together. "Shall we have a look at them together, Dyl?"

Am I imagining the trapped look on his face as he holds his mug of hot chocolate with both hands? I smile, waiting for a response, willing for him to say a word. Yes. Mama. Anything. After what feels like an endless few seconds, he nods, and then buries his face in his mug, so when he lifts his head, there is whipped cream on his nose.

We finish our hot chocolates a few minutes later, and I take Dylan's hand as we wander through the aisles of different Christmas ornaments—some tasteful, some tacky, some ornate, others simple.

"What do you think, Dyl?" I ask my son. "Is there one you like in particular?" I check the price of a smiling Santa carved out of wood—sixteen bucks. These are not cheap.

Dylan shakes his head and we keep walking—past shiny baubles and carved sleds and skies, frosted snowflakes and glittering ballerinas. There is every ornament imaginable here.

I decide on a simple silver bell, and when we come to an aisle of ornaments aimed at children, Dylan rushes towards a basket full of ones made of Lego. The big, sloppy grin on his face makes me both smile and ache. He picks out a Christmas tree decorated with little dots of red and yellow, and turns to me with a question in his eyes.

"That looks like a good one," I tell him.

Ally appears at the end of the aisle, her step faltering as she sees us, clearly not wanting to interrupt the moment, but then Dylan runs to her, waving his little Christmas tree.

"That's a great choice, Dylan," she says, ruffling his hair with an easy affection that feels beyond me now.

My hands clench into fists and I force myself to uncurl them and relax. This doesn't have to be a competition, even if it feels like one I'm always losing.

Dylan is still my son.

Back at my apartment a couple of hours later, I drift around, unable to settle to anything. The Fieldings invited me for to stay for dinner, a Chinese takeout, but Dylan had already raced inside with Emma and Josh, and I'd felt left out and out of sorts, so I declined, telling Ally I'd see Dylan on Tuesday as usual.

It's five o'clock on a Saturday evening and I have nowhere to go, no one to talk to. Mike is out with some high-school buddies, not that we spend every weekend together anyway. I thought about going up to see Angela, as I have a couple of times before to write letters, but her combination of sweetness and confusion feels too tiring to deal with right now. I want to be with someone who *knows* me.

Which is why I end up calling my mom. It's not that unusual an occurrence, although it always feels as if it is. I talk to her maybe once every three or four months, short, stilted conversations that never really get anywhere. I don't know why tonight will be any different, yet as my mother answers my call, I realize I want it to be. I need things to change—even this.

"Beth…" As usual, she sounds both happy and alarmed to hear from me. I imagine her checking her watch, a slight frown on her face.

"Hey, Mom." I take a deep breath and will myself on. "Can we talk? I mean… really talk?"

CHAPTER TWENTY-EIGHT

ALLY

The week of Emma's exams slides by with no one saying a word about them. Besides the one abbreviated conversation on top of Avon Mountain, we haven't spoken to Emma about it, which feels wrong, but Nick said there were worse things than missing a semester of college, and I *know* that. Of course I know that. We've experienced several worse things in the last few weeks alone.

And yet… Harvard. Emma's future. Everything she's worked for all these years. Everything *we've* worked for. Is it wrong to feel that way? The trouble with owning my children's successes, I realize, is I have to own their failures, as well.

As it turns out, I don't have to talk to Emma about her exams, because she comes to me first. It's the Wednesday after we went to cut down the Christmas tree, an outing I think went reasonably well, although Beth seemed to hurry off at the end, refusing to stay to eat with us while we decorated the tree. Still, I choose to call it a success.

Now I am in my office, trying to get several boutiques' books done before the Christmas holidays, and Emma comes to stand in my doorway, her hair loose about her face, an oversized sweater dwarfing her petite frame. She looks both wan and gorgeous, and I turn to her with the approximation of a smile.

"Hey."

"Hey," she returns quietly. The cuffs of her sweater hide her hands and she fidgets a bit as she watches me.

"What's up?" I ask as lightly as I can. "Do you want to talk?" She hasn't wanted to talk in the three weeks since Thanksgiving, but I keep trying.

"Actually, yeah," she says, not looking at me. "If you don't mind…?"

"Of course I don't mind." I close my laptop immediately, my heart starting to hammer. "Do you want to go in the family room?" I ask. "It's more comfortable there."

Emma shrugs, and then drifts out of my study, and I follow her to the family room, trying to act natural, as if this isn't a big deal. I'm thrilled she's talking to me, but I'm also scared. Terrified, in fact.

"So." I perch on the edge of the sofa, just as I once did with Josh, and Emma is standing in the same place as Josh, next to the steps into the kitchen, as if she doesn't want to commit to the conversation. I wait, eyebrows raised, a faint smile on my face, trying to look engaging and interested and sympathetic all at once. Lord, but it can be hard to be a mother.

"So." Emma comes further into the room and curls up on the opposite side of the sofa, all sweater and tumbled hair. "I'm not going back to Harvard."

I blink, keeping the smile on my face, trying to process her simply stated words. "Not for exams," I say, and Emma's face tightens. I realize I've said the wrong thing, but I can't take it back. "Not for exams, of course not," I say, and that is even more wrong. I am scrabbling for more words, better ones, but then Emma shakes her head.

"Not ever." She sounds firm but also sad, yet not for herself. For me. And somehow that stings, because this is about her life, not mine. I know that, at least.

"But why… Emma…"

"I hated it, Mom. I hated every minute of it." She speaks matter-of-factly, without rancor, and somehow that makes it worse.

"Why didn't you say anything?"

"I knew you didn't want to hear it. You'd have been disappointed in me, and you would have told me to keep trying, and weather it out for my freshman year at *least*, and all the rest."

"I wouldn't have," I say, feebly, because I know I would have. Of course I would have. Every parent I know would have done the same. You don't let your child just *quit*. It was a parenting rule we'd followed from the beginning, whether it was Little League, ballet lessons, chess club, whatever. They had to give it a good try, and if they still wanted to quit after three sessions or lessons, they could, but they had to tell the teacher or coach themselves, *after* the class, not before.

Yet how can I apply that maxim for childhood to this?

"Why did you hate it?" I ask Emma, and she hunches her shoulders.

"The pressure. The posing. The smugness of everyone—professors *and* students. The feeling that it never ends. I thought AP Physics was bad enough—Introduction to Law was a thousand times worse."

"But you didn't breathe a word," I say, even as I acknowledge to myself that she didn't say anything good, either. She basically stopped talking to me, and I told myself it was because she was having such a fabulous time. I felt hurt, which was far better than what I feel now, which is guilt. Endless, crippling mother-guilt.

"I told you, I couldn't. I knew you didn't want to hear it, and I couldn't stand for you to tell me to just give it a semester or whatever." She rolls her eyes, as if that advice is too ridiculous for words, and I think, *is it?*

"If I'd known you were having such a hard time…"

"I didn't want to disappoint you." Emma's voice has lowered, and I hear a tinge of despair that only adds to my guilt. "You and Dad were so thrilled when I got into Harvard. I think you were more excited than I was."

"Of course we were thrilled. For *you*."

"And for you," Emma says shrewdly. "I get that. I'd probably be the same, if I were a parent. But it felt like even more pressure, and I already had more than I could deal with. I felt like I was going to explode—or maybe implode. Just… collapse inside."

I shake my head slowly. "If it was really that awful for you, I wouldn't have told you to stick it out." I want—I need—to believe that.

"You would have, Mom. You always would have."

"Emma—"

"You told me to take the extra AP class because it would look good on my college application. To run for yearbook editor because that was another fricking feather in my cap. To play JV tennis even though I was still the worst member on the team my *senior* year."

I goggle at her, as gape-mouthed and gormless as a fish. "Emma, *you* wanted those things."

"Not as much as you did. And sometimes I think I only wanted them because it made you so happy and proud. Sometimes I think I would have been just as happy—no, *happier*—to mess around for four years and go to Conn State."

Conn State, like Beth had been planning to. Her sad story had left me feeling heartbroken for her, but also a little bit relieved, knowing I wouldn't make the kinds of mistakes her mother had.

And yet it seems I've made a boatload of other ones.

I sink back against the sofa cushions, my mind reeling. I can't process everything Emma has said. I don't want to. I already felt like a failure, but it was in a way that I could talk myself out of, as I reminded myself of all my successes with my children. Now I can't. I failed without even knowing it, all along, all the time.

"I never meant to make you feel that way," I say faintly. I feel as if I can hardly form the words. "I never wanted you to feel pressured. I thought... I thought you were pressuring yourself."

"Even if I was, you didn't mind," Emma returns in that same matter-of-fact voice. "I think you liked it."

I look away, not wanting to show her the naked hurt I know must be visible on my face. She makes me sound like some sort of maternal monster, and yet there is more than a grain of truth in her words.

Yes, I'd felt pride in the way Emma was, and all she'd achieved. What parent *doesn't* want their child to be successful and driven? Is that so wrong? Yet if it had been a clear choice between success and happiness, *of course* I would have chosen the latter for her.

But, I realize, choices are so rarely that clear.

"I'm sorry," I say at last, because what else can I say? "I'm sorry I made you feel that way. I'm sorry you felt that you couldn't tell me. I'm sorry—"

"Oh come on, Mom." Emma stops my self-pitying litany, sounding a little bit irritable. "Don't make yourself into a martyr. I'm not saying it was all your fault. It was Dad, too. And it was me. I'm not abdicating all my responsibility. I'm just trying to explain."

From monster to martyr. I inhale deeply, trying to sound rational instead of devastated. "So it was this pressure that led you to... to..."

"To OD'ing on Xanax? Yeah, I guess." Emma sounds, to my incredulity, almost amused. I think of what Josh said—*they're like Skittles were in your day*, and I wonder if he was actually right. But Skittles don't kill you. "I didn't mean it," Emma continues, and I can only stare. "If I'd meant it, I would have done it seriously—you know, razor blade in the bathtub or maybe hanging myself. There are YouTube videos you can watch to make sure you do it properly."

"*Don't*, Emma." I can't keep a visceral shudder from rippling through me. The thought of those videos, of young women or men watching them, suicide as commonplace, something merely tedious or practical... I shake my head. "Please don't."

Emma sighs. "Sorry. All I'm saying is, I think I knew I wouldn't actually *die*. I was sharing a bedroom with Sasha. I knew she'd find me before too long."

I think of Sasha's frightened face at the hospital, the doctor's serious expression. "That wasn't a very nice thing to do to your friend," I say, and then wish I hadn't. Emma looks wounded.

"It wasn't like I was playing a *prank*."

"I know—"

"It felt like a way out. To be able to leave Harvard that wasn't just slinking away, another deadbeat dropout who couldn't hack it."

Slinking away would have been a hell of a lot easier. I close my eyes briefly as I try to summon yet more strength.

"Now you're even more disappointed in me," Emma says flatly.

"No, I'm not—"

"For trying to kill myself as well as quitting Harvard." She shakes her head disbelievingly, as if I am meeting all her incredibly low expectations of me, and a sudden, surprising spark of anger fires through me.

"Don't put words in my mouth, or thoughts in my head," I snap. "You've just offloaded a ton of information on me, Emma, and I'm trying to process it. I'm trying to understand it. And I'm *trying* to figure out the best way to support you. But I am not disappointed in you, okay?" My voice has risen to something close to a shriek, which I recognize is not a good thing.

Emma gives me a level look. "You sure sound it," she says, and with a groan of frustration I rise from the sofa. I have a sudden, frantic need to move, like there is an itch all over my body and I have to scratch it, but I can't. I'm not allowed to.

Emma twists around to look at me as I pace the kitchen. "What are you doing?"

"I'm unloading the dishwasher," I tell her, and I start to do just that.

She lets out a huff of breath, as if she can't believe I think a clean kitchen is more important than a healthy daughter, and I know she doesn't understand this need of mine to move, and not to think, because if I do, I will break down right there, sobbing and shrieking, and that won't be good for either of us.

After several minutes of stacking plates, I feel calm enough to ask, "So if you're not going back to Harvard, what are you thinking of doing instead?"

Emma shrugs. "Get a job, maybe, for the rest of the year? Then see what I want to do. Maybe travel. I'd like to go to Thailand."

I nod slowly, as if this idea doesn't appall me. She's nineteen. She needs to make her own choices. I know that, and yet... dear God. *Harvard*, and now this. Some minimum-wage job and following a hippie trail through Thailand.

"Okay," I say, and start taking out the cups.

"You think that's awful, don't you?" Emma says, rising onto her knees on the sofa so she can see me better. "You'd be embarrassed if I had a job at McDonald's or something, and I served your friends their McSalads."

"My friends wouldn't go to McDonald's," I retort before I can think better of it, and Emma smirks. Is she baiting me on purpose? *Why?*

"You know what I mean."

"I would never be embarrassed by honest work," I tell her, which sounds like something Nick would say.

"Even if I was serving up Big Macs to Julie and Anita and everyone else?" Her eyes spark defiance.

"I wouldn't."

"You *so* would."

I slam the dishwasher shut, which does not make nearly as satisfying a noise as slamming a door does. "Do you *want* me to be disappointed in you, Emma?" I demand. "Is that what you're going for here?"

"I want you to be honest."

"You've already decided what that looks like."

"I know what it always has been before," she fires back, and we stare at each other—me drained and weary, Emma defiant and more energized than I've seen her since she's come home. She looks beautiful, with her dark hair and rosy cheeks and bright eyes. Is being angry with me so worthwhile, so *enjoyable*, an activity for her?

"I don't know what to say," I finally tell her, because I honestly have nothing left. "I don't feel like there's an answer I can give you that you'd be happy with."

"I just want you to admit it."

"Fine. I'd be disappointed. With your intelligence and ambition, as well as the opportunities you've had, I'd feel like you were wasting your life asking if people want fries with that." I give her a flat look; I feel empty inside. "Happy now?" I say, and Emma just glares at me and huffs out of the room. Perfect.

I recount the conversation, as painful as it is, to Nick that night as we get ready for bed, our voices hushed because Emma is just across the hall. She gave me the cold shoulder for the rest of the day, and I pretended not to notice. I was busy enough, anyway, catching up on work, running errands, and then coming home to make dinner and clean the kitchen, which looked like a bomb site after I'd been gone for several hours. No one seems to know how to load the dishwasher except me.

"I know I didn't handle it well," I tell Nick as I slip into bed, everything in me aching. "But I don't know how I should have."

"She's just trying to push your buttons." Nick sounds irritatingly unfazed. I know he likes to be calm in a crisis, but right now I would be happy to see him emote a little, the way he did when we were walking up Avon Mountain.

"But why?" I demand, my voice rising before I remember to lower it. "Why is she so angry with me?"

"She has to be angry at someone."

"*Why?*"

Nick shrugs. "That's human nature, Ally. Imagine if everything she said to you, she was really saying to herself."

"So you're a psychiatrist now?"

"No, but I think I saw a meme that said something like that on Facebook." He smiles wryly and reaches for me. I go, even though I'm a little bit annoyed by his laidback manner, because I need to be held and part of me at least knows he is right. "I'm sorry. I know it's hard to hear all that from her. This whole thing is hard." He exhales wearily. "Just when I feel like we're making progress, there's another setback. But it's definitely two steps forward, one step back, and not the other way around."

"And if she doesn't go back to Harvard? Or college at all?"

His arms tighten around me. "Then she doesn't."

I twist up to look at him. "Do you really believe that?"

"I'm trying to. Like I said, it's hard. But dropping out of college is not the end of the world."

"I know it's a first-world problem," I say a bit grumpily. "I *am* aware. But it's different when it's us, our child."

"I know."

I close my eyes as I rest my cheek against his chest, his heart thudding under my jawbone. "She might have been saying it to herself, but she was saying it to me, too. Maybe I have been too pushy."

"Maybe," Nick agrees, which stings, "but so what? Lots of parents are pushy, especially in this part of the country. Everyone wants their kid in an Ivy League. It wasn't like you were actually cracking the whip, and Emma could never doubt that we both love her."

"So you think she should have just got over it?"

"No." Nick sighs. "I don't know what I think. Only that we all love each other, and we're all trying to help each other, and that should count for something."

"Yes." Except right now it feels like it doesn't.

"There isn't an instant fix," Nick says gently.

"I know." Even if I want one. I tell myself to take things in my stride, not to get so hurt when Emma is deliberately trying to wound me. To understand the disappointment that she's so desperately trying to hide. On an intellectual level, I can absolutely appreciate all of that. But on an emotional level, it's a kick to the gut every time. "I'm trying," I say, and Nick kisses my hair.

"I know."

"I've been so consumed with thinking about Emma, I forget to think about Josh," I say on a sigh. Today has been an Emma day; yesterday was a Josh one, when he came home more monosyllabic than usual, if such a thing was possible. I tried to engage him, as I have been trying since this whole thing blew up, and he told me to leave him alone before slamming up to his room.

"You can't take the whole world on your shoulders," Nick says, which feels just a little bit too trite in this moment.

"I'm not, just two children."

"Three," he reminds me, and I close my eyes. Dylan, at least, has been easy.

The next morning, I wake up feeling weary but determined to do better today. I get Josh and Dylan off to school, and Nick to work, and Emma still hasn't come downstairs. I clean the kitchen and do a load of laundry, check my work emails, and try not to feel anxious. Should I check on her? What if…? But it's only a little after nine.

Then, as I am making a shopping list, she comes into the kitchen. She's still in her pajamas, sporting a case of bedhead, looking sleepy and warm. She reminds me of when she was three or four, and she'd come downstairs with her arms out and I'd scoop her up and take her to the sofa. We'd cuddle quietly for twenty minutes or so before the day had to start. Those days passed in a blur of exhaustion and yet right now they seem so easy. So sweet.

"Good morning," I say as cheerfully as I can, but the words sound stilted.

Then Emma comes over, her arms held out just like when she was a child. And she puts them around me, burying her head in my shoulder, and all my hurt and fear crumbles to nothing, absolutely nothing. I wrap my arms around her and we stay like that for a minute or more, a silent hug that we both desperately needed.

It's broken when my cell phone rings, and Emma straightens, even though I don't want her to. I'm happy to ignore the call, but Emma has already moved away and I see it's Josh's high school.

I am in an emotional limbo between the sweetness of the hug and the worry of the call as I answer. "Hello?"

"Mrs. Fielding?"

"Yes—"

"You need to come to school right away, please."

CHAPTER TWENTY-NINE

BETH

There is snow in New Hampshire, lots of it—pillowy drifts and houses frosted like birthday cakes, drooping boughs and buried fence posts edging the pure sweep of white fields. It's like something out of a made-for-TV Christmas movie. All we need is the jingling soundtrack. So far, however, the trip up to my mother's place has been silent.

I was frankly amazed when Susan agreed to my request that I be allowed to take Dylan to my mother's house in New Hampshire for four entire days over Christmas. As surprised as when my mother made the invitation, when I called her and asked to talk.

We didn't talk over the phone, not properly, but I told her, haltingly, about what had happened since October, and she expressed her sympathy and maybe even her regret—if "I wish you'd told me" can be construed as that—and then she ended the call by asking if I would come there for Christmas.

"It would be good to have you here, Beth," she said. "And Dylan, if he's allowed to come."

She's made these invitations before, but they've felt so half-hearted that usually I don't even make a response; it's a passing comment that goes by, ignored and unpursued. But this time felt different. This time I wanted to go, even if it meant missing Christmas with Mike and his family, as he'd already invited me over to his mom's for Christmas Day. This felt more fundamental, more important. And so I said yes, and I asked Susan's permission, and here we are, on December twenty-third, driving north.

I glance back at Dylan, who is staring out the window of the rental car I can't really afford, his expression thoughtful and a little sad, but maybe that's simply the way his eyes droop. I can't read my little boy anymore, and it both saddens and terrifies me. But I am hoping and praying that these four days together provide us with a much-needed reset, because I know we can't just go back to the way we were, yet I still don't know what the future can look like for us.

The day didn't start well—when I picked Dylan up this morning with the car already packed, explaining we were going away for a few days, he resisted. He ran to Ally and wrapped his arms around her waist, and for a second I felt like screaming the way he used to; I had to stop myself from marching over and pulling him away from her.

Ally tried to pry him off her, gently, telling him how much fun he was going to have, but she sounded like the mom and I felt like the mean babysitter. I should have told him before, prepared him for the change, but I was reluctant to because I knew I'd get the reaction I did, and it hurt so much I couldn't breathe.

He was silent as we pulled away in the car, refusing to look at me, his face set in discontented lines. Already I felt frazzled and teary, and I had to pull myself back from the edge, never mind Dylan. This wasn't the way it was supposed to be. And yet I could understand his anxiety, because we'd never done anything like this before, at least not in his memory. The last time I'd taken Dylan to my mother's, he'd been three.

And so we drove, three hours north through barren brown fields and then through snow, to the small town on the Vermont border where my mother now lived with her husband Ron, a jovial man who has always seemed nervous around me, and whom I barely knew.

My mother comes to the door as I pull into the drive of the barn-red house with a wide front porch that stands at the edge of a wood, now under a canopy of snow.

I turn back to Dylan.

"It's Grandma, Dylan. My mommy. Isn't that funny?" I smile at him, and he stares at me with wide eyes. "Shall we go say hello?"

After a few silent seconds of staring, he nods.

I get out of the driver's seat, giving my mother an uncertain wave before I open the back door for Dylan. Everything about this feels strange, like clothes that don't fit. When did I last see my mother? Several years, at least. She came to visit after Marco left, but I don't remember much about it. I can't remember if I've seen her since then.

My mother takes a step forward, everything about her hesitant, the look on her face one of sudden, surprising yearning. I help Dylan out of the car.

"Hello, Dylan," my mom calls out, her voice wavering a little. "It's so good to see you."

Dylan leans into me, which feels good, and I rest my hand on top of his head. The snow crunches under my feet.

My mother's face crumples and then she collects her composure and manages a smile.

"Hi, Mom."

"Hello, Beth." She strides towards me and then I am enveloped in her arms, and so is Dylan, and he doesn't protest and neither do I; even though it feels so strange, something about it is incredibly right.

Of course, a hug doesn't solve everything. In fact, it doesn't solve anything. The moment my mother releases me, the tension is back—twanging between us, tightening in my chest. *Why did you leave me?* Of course I don't ask that desperate question out loud. I never have. Yet while there might not be a solution, there is a beginning, and the three of us walk inside.

*

It isn't until much later that my mother and I are able to talk, just the two of us—a conversation I've been both dreading and longing for since she first invited me here, or really, since she left nine years ago.

Dylan has finally settled to sleep after a restless hour, although since we've arrived he hasn't screamed once, just been very quiet, a silence that feels deeper than usual, because I can't read his emotions the way I used to be able to. I can't keep from feeling he's here on sufferance, but I tell myself that will change. It has to.

Ron has made himself scarce after an uneasy dinner where he kept jumping up to get things, his smile too wide, the look in his eyes a little panicked. I don't think he knows what to do with me or Dylan, although he tries.

I find my mom in the kitchen, wiping down already clean counters, as if she is simply waiting for something. She turns as I come in, a smile popping onto her face like a button has been pushed.

"Dylan went down okay?"

"He's asleep."

"Great." Her smile starts to fade as she nods, and I stare at her, waiting, although I'm not sure for what. "I'm so glad you came," she finally says.

"I felt like I should."

She keeps nodding, a bit uncertainly, not sure what to make of my words. I'm not sure, either. My relationship with my mom was never super close; we didn't do girly days together, or share our secrets, but I still thought it had been solid. She worked as a nurse throughout my childhood, and her erratic shifts meant she wasn't always home, but when she was, she was there, dinner on the table, laundry folded, a kind of old-fashioned motherhood that didn't involve quality time so much as basic, competent provision. I suppose that was in part because my father is a very old-fashioned man—a plumber by trade, expecting a dinner every night at six, his evenings in front of the TV with a beer or three all sacrosanct. He still made time for family—barbecues, occasional trips to the park, his attention rare and yet wonderful when I got it. I thought most fathers were like him; even now I think most probably are. Until my mother left, and I got in trouble, and my father turned into someone who didn't seem to like me at all.

Now, nine years later, my mother and I have never really talked through the why or how, and I'm not sure how to start.

"I'm seeing a counselor," I say abruptly, and my mother blinks.

"Oh. Okay. That's good, I think?" She raises her eyebrows, her smile skirting off her face and then creeping back, like some shy animal that wants to be petted.

"Yes, it has been. It's brought up a lot of issues for me—the way Dad was, the way you were." The words lie there, heavy, immovable. I realize they sound accusing, but I didn't mean them to be, at least not entirely. "How it all affected me, I mean."

My mother keeps nodding, but more slowly now. "Yes. Yes. Of course it affected you."

I draw a breath and force myself to continue. "And I guess what it's made me realize, what I really want to know after all these years is why?"

My mother stares at me uncertainly. "Why?"

"Why did you leave the spring of my senior year? I mean, I get that you weren't happy with Dad. I do understand that, and I can see why, in a way. But why then? Why couldn't you have waited until I was at college? It would have made so much difference. You had to have known that, right?" My voice rises with each question, throbs with pain. My mother looks away without answering, her body seeming to sag and deflate. "And why," I continue, louder now, "did you have to move to New Hampshire right away? Why did you have to cut yourself off so completely, like you didn't even care anymore? Maybe you didn't."

"Of course I cared, Beth." The words are quiet and intense.

"It didn't look that way from where I was standing."

"You were angry with me."

"Of course I was—"

"You didn't *want* to come with me," my mother continues, her voice sharpening and then rising like mine. "I'm not saying I wasn't to blame, I know I was. If I could have waited, I would have."

"Could have?" I scoff. "You make it sound as if you had a gun to your head."

"Not a gun, no," she says quietly, and for a second it's as if everything has tilted and slid, as if the very ground beneath me has trembled.

"What is that supposed to mean?"

My mother looks away. "It was a complicated, difficult situation."

"That doesn't tell me anything."

"I know."

"So?" She doesn't reply and I blow out an impatient breath. "What's the point of keeping secrets now? You know I haven't talked to Dad in years."

"What?" My mom looks shaken. "I didn't know that."

"How could you not know that?"

"You never told me. I assumed… I assumed you were still in touch. Quite regularly, in fact."

I shake my head in disbelief. "Mom, he threw me out of the house after the DUI."

"What?" My mother looks even more troubled, and I stare at her, trying to figure out why our narratives seem so different. "I thought you left of your own accord. To live with Dylan's father."

"Well, yes, but that was a couple of months later."

She shakes her head slowly. "Beth, you never told me that. If you had…" She draws a quick breath. "Well, there is no point in thinking that way now. What happened? What do you mean, he threw you out of the house?"

"All right, he didn't *throw* me out," I relent. "Like, onto the street. But he made it clear he wanted me gone, and if I stayed, it would have been difficult. Really difficult. So I left." Looking back, it was probably more childish pique than anything else; I wanted him to ask me to come back. He never did.

"I didn't know," my mom says quietly. "You didn't even tell me about the DUI until six months later."

"Didn't I?"

"You were very angry with me, Beth."

"You *left*."

"I know."

I pull out one of the chairs at the kitchen table and sink down onto it. Sometimes I forget just how angry I acted with my mother, because the truth was all I felt was hurt. Yet now I remember that I refused to talk to her; I didn't tell her anything about my life until after it had happened, and I didn't care about it anymore. *That* wasn't childish pique, though. That was self-protection. I knew it would hurt too much if she didn't care about something I did. I'd already found that out the hard way.

"I'm sorry," she says, coming to sit down in the chair next to mine. "You have no idea how much."

I give her a look of blatant disbelief, because really? Nine years of barely being involved in my life, my son's life, and she's going to come out all apologetic now?

"I don't believe you."

"I'm not surprised."

"Why didn't you wait until I was at college?" That's the question that's bothered me the most. To tell me out of the blue just a month before my final exams? What kind of mother does that?

She sighs and looks down at her lap. "I had to. Your father made me."

"What…"

"He found out I wanted to leave. I was planning to do it after you were settled in college. Ron was willing to wait. Then your father said if I didn't leave then, he'd make me leave. And I knew he would."

"How could he make you leave?"

"He owned the house, Beth. His name was on the mortgage. But more than that, he could make my life miserable when he chose to. He never hit me, but he knew how to hurt me all the same."

I struggle to process that, because while I've always known my dad wasn't Mr. Sensitive—how could I not—I hadn't considered anything like this. "And you thought it was okay to leave me with an emotionally abusive man?" I ask after a few moments.

"He loved you. I know he didn't always show it, but he really did love you. He used to take you to call-outs in his trucks when you were just a baby, show you off to all his customers. It was me he hated—he told me that every day, did his best to make my life as miserable as he could, and I took it, for your sake, but…" She lets out a shuddering breath. "It was hard, Beth. It was so hard."

I don't know what to say to any of that, and so I just shake my head. Considering how my dad treated me, maybe I shouldn't be surprised that he acted similarly towards my mom. And yet it doesn't explain everything; it doesn't fix anything.

My mother sighs wearily. "I didn't want to leave you. I asked you to come with me. Maybe you don't remember that."

Vaguely, I do. In the heat of an argument, and I'd tossed it back in her face because of course I wasn't going to move to New Hampshire two months before graduation. "Why couldn't you have stayed in the area, at least? I could have stayed with you then." Although I probably wouldn't have.

"I had no money."

"You had a *job*, Mom—"

My mother sighs and shades her eyes with a trembling hand. "My paychecks went into your father's bank account. He gave me housekeeping money."

"What?" That is so ridiculously old-fashioned and sexist I can't believe my mother put up with it for years. Decades.

"It made sense at the beginning," she says wearily. "Your father had a way of making things seem reasonable. Of course we should keep all our money in one account. We were *married*. It was only later that I started to question it, why he had access and I didn't, and by then it felt too late."

"Couldn't you have told your boss you wanted your paychecks moved into a different account?"

"Yes, I suppose I could have." My mother drops her hand from her eyes and for the first time she looks almost angry. "If I'd been thinking sensibly. If I hadn't been so worn down. If you hadn't been so angry, and had seemed as if you wanted to stay with me. But I didn't, and you weren't, and Ron had this lovely house and open arms and I *needed* that." Her voice trembles.

"I don't even know how you met him," I remark, and she gives me a watery, wobbly smile.

"At the hospital, actually. He was visiting his grandmother. I gave him change for the coffee machine, and we got to talking…" She shrugs. "He was so nice, Beth, and I needed that. I *still* need it."

"Don't we all?" I say a bit sourly, and she nods, as if expecting this.

"I know I let you down. I told myself it was for only a few months, that soon you'd be in college, and you wouldn't be so angry with me, and you could spend holidays with us here. I had a vision of how good it would be—you could have stayed with us during your breaks—but then you met Marco and you didn't seem to want to have anything to do with me…"

"You never really tried."

"No, not hard enough. I know." My mother bows her head, as if accepting my judgment, and yet suddenly I find I don't have it in me to condemn her anymore. I almost wish I did, but I don't.

My throat aches and I have to look away, caught between sympathy and an anger I am still trying to hold onto, even as I yearn to let it go. I know she means what she says, but surely you can't wipe away nine years of hard history with a couple of heartfelt sentences. And yet perhaps that would be easier… for both of us. "And in all the time since then?" I finally ask.

"What do you mean?"

"You hardly ever call. Barely visit."

"You haven't wanted me to." She sounds surprised, even disbelieving. "When I came after Dylan was born, you basically told me to go home. The same thing happened after Marco left. You said me being there made Dylan anxious."

"It did, but—"

"I invited you for Christmas when Dylan was a baby, and at the end of the visit you said it didn't work and you wouldn't be back. Yes, I could call more, Beth. I know that. I could ask you to visit more. I should. But I feel like I put myself out there again and again only to be rebuffed every time, and after a while I stopped wanting to do it. You're a grown woman now, and you have been for a while. If you didn't want a relationship with me, I wasn't going to push it."

I don't reply, because I can't. My throat is tight and my head is spinning and I can't quite reconcile her version of the last nine years with mine, even as part of me *can*. Yes, I told her to leave. Yes, I said it didn't work. Because she seemed so unenthused to be there, because life was hard enough, and yes, because I was still angry. But I needed her to be my mom, to push through my crap and love me anyway. Isn't that what moms *do*?

Or, I wonder bleakly, is it sometimes better for a mother to walk away? Better for her, and maybe even better for the child?

I know I can't blame my mother for every hard or bad thing that happened to me. Maybe it was actually better that things happened the way they did. Who knows how life would have turned out for either of us otherwise?

"I'm sorry I didn't have the resources to help you more," she says quietly, a throb in her voice. "The emotional and the financial ones. I really am."

I nod, accepting, unable to reply, because the emotions are skating far too close to the surface, and on this point I know exactly how she feels.

CHAPTER THIRTY

ALLY

It's Christmas Eve. Outside, snow has started to fall, blanketing the street in softness, as the streetlights begin to blink on, creating warm pools of light. It is a scene worthy of a photograph, a snapshot for my memory.

Even though the house is decorated with evergreen and holly, with candles and red velvet ribbon and a big, jolly wreath on the door, the tree laden with ornaments and presents, a smell of shortbread in the air, I can't feel festive. My heart is like a stone within me, and I press one hand on the cool glass of the living-room window, as if the shock of it will somehow jolt me out of this leaden feeling.

It's been eight days since Josh was suspended, kicked off both varsity teams, his name whispered throughout the school and up and down our street, my phone lighting up with texts and voicemails I choose to ignore. Apparently the mother of a girl in his class found drugs in her bedroom; the girl ratted out Josh as a way to exonerate herself, and it worked because no parent wants to believe the worst of their child.

The hardest part of it, perhaps, is the fact that Josh *had* stopped dealing. He insisted he had, anyway, and he'd told us the girl must have been keeping the drugs for a couple of weeks, at least. He was so angry, so *hurt*, that I felt a powerless sympathy for him; it's not as if I could tell the principal it was okay, because my son wasn't dealing drugs *now*. We were lucky they decided not to expel him, because of his "stellar academic and athletic record." Suspension for the rest of the term was light in comparison, even if it didn't feel that way in the moment.

I did feel I had to tell Monica about his suspension, although Nick insisted I wasn't required to legally; she wasn't pleased, of course, but she said that since Dylan was most likely only going to be with us for a few more weeks it was "not a significant enough issue to warrant his removal."

"There are no drugs in the house," I told her, hating that I had to say it. "I've made absolutely sure of that, and Josh isn't involved in any of that any longer."

Monica didn't reply; whether she didn't believe me or didn't care, I wasn't sure.

It's been nine days since Emma said she wasn't returning to Harvard and officially withdrew from the university; she filled out an application for a job at Subway, mostly, I think, just to annoy me. That one heartfelt hug aside, my daughter has continued to ignore or be angry with me. I don't know which is worse.

It's been almost as long since the whole idea of who I was as a mother, as a *person,* imploded on me. I still haven't found the strength to reconstruct my identity. I don't know how to begin. For the last eight days I've been going through the motions of this busy time of year—writing Christmas cards, wrapping presents, existing in a fog, trying to figure out where any of us go from here even as I struggle to think at all.

Yesterday morning, Beth picked up Dylan, and as much as I'd been determined to look forward to it just being the four of us again—hoping somehow this might help to heal us—I hated to see him go. He clung to me, and I struggled not to cling to him. Somehow, in the midst of all this wreckage, Dylan, in his uncomplicated need for affection and his easy giving of it, has become the glue that holds us together.

Now it is Christmas Eve, and I haven't seen my children all day. They're both skulking in their rooms, and I wonder if they will for the whole vacation. Perhaps the presents under the tree that I bought in an online frenzy will remain unopened; the turkey taking up half the fridge won't be cooked. I feel suspended between the past and the future, and the present isn't a place I want to be.

"Ally?" I turn to see Nick standing in the doorway, a slight frown on his face. "What are you doing?"

"Just watching the snow. Isn't it beautiful?" My voice sounds a bit monotone. It's so hard to know how to be normal now, even as I recognize that maybe, just maybe, I am overreacting. The prospect causes a sense of an out-of-reach relief. Still, I remind myself, both my children are healthy and here. That's more than many people have. This isn't the end of the world, but it is the end of *a* world, a fantasy one I had been happy to inhabit.

Nick comes over and puts his arm around me and I lean into him, taking comfort from his solid strength. This has hit me harder than him, perhaps because I have always responded more emotionally to the children than he has. He loves them, is proud of them, but he hasn't bound up his whole sense of self in them the way I have. Considering how I feel now, surely that is only a good thing.

"The Christmas Eve service is in an hour," he says, his mouth against my hair. "We'll need to leave soon if we want to get a seat."

"I don't know if we should go this year."

"Ally." Nick straightens, easing back so he can look at me, although I don't particularly want to meet his eye. "We always go to church on Christmas Eve. It's a tradition."

"I know."

"There's no reason not to this year," he says quietly.

"I'm just not in the mood."

"If Josh or Emma said that, you'd tell them to get in the mood by going."

I try to smile at that, but I can't quite manage it. "I'm not even dressed."

"That would take five minutes."

I sigh, and Nick looks at me seriously, importantly, in a way I can't avoid. "What is upsetting you the most?" he asks, and I shrug. I don't know where to begin. "Is it Josh being suspended? Emma's situation? Or something else?"

"You know, I don't actually care whether she goes to Harvard or not," I say suddenly. Savagely. The strength of my feeling surprises me. "I don't care about Josh playing baseball or running 10k. None of that is what is important."

"I know—"

"It's the *relationships* I care about, Nick." The love. "They act as if they either hate me, or they couldn't care less about me. They blame me for everything. They won't talk to me, and I don't know what to do. I don't know how to *be*, because all the things I was doing right have turned out to be wrong."

Nick is silent for a moment. "They're teenagers. They're not known for acting warm and fuzzy. You can't make decisions based on what they're feeling in the moment. You have to have a bigger picture than that."

"I know, but…" I think of all the photo Christmas cards currently residing on our mantelpiece, all the snapshots of joy and togetherness that every friend and relative and even minor acquaintance has felt compelled to send me, along with the humble-brag updates detailing all their accomplishments, from report cards to charity runs to vacations skiing in Vail or sunning in the Caribbean. All of it feels like an indictment of my life, my choices, my parenting.

"This feels like more than a stage or a phase," I say. "More… fundamental."

"Are you sure that's not just in your mind?"

"Nick, our daughter tried to kill herself."

"That's not your fault."

Isn't it? I just shake my head, tight-lipped, despairing.

Nick pulls me towards him. "Let's go to the service," he murmurs against my hair. "Candlelight on Christmas Eve. Carols. It will lift your spirits."

I still don't want to go, but I nod, reluctantly, because it feels too selfish and mean to refuse.

Nick gives my shoulders a quick squeeze before he steps away. "Great. I'll get the kids ready."

Ten minutes later, we're all walking towards the Episcopal church in the center of town, with its stained-glass windows and arched red doors. It's still snowing, which makes everything magical, and there is a festive spirit in the air, with people smiling and nodding at each other, the occasional "Merry Christmas!" ringing out.

It's hard not to be affected by it, at least a little, and even though I'm still dragging inside, I summon a smile for both Emma and Josh. They don't smile back, not exactly, and I see a flicker of uncertainty in their eyes—or am I imagining it? Hoping for anything other than the unyielding hardness I've felt from them for the last few months?

We walk in silence into the church, slipping inside the candle and evergreen-scented interior, an organ playing "What Child is This" as we take our place in one of the pews. The place fills up quickly, the mood both hushed and happy.

I think of all the Christmas Eves we've come to this church, from when Emma and Josh were babies, to toddlers running through the aisles and then a bit older, bouncing off the walls with excitement over Christmas. Even as teenagers, they got into the spirit of the thing, happy to hold their candles as the congregation sang "Silent Night." Nothing has to change now.

As the service begins, I tell myself to count my blessings, because I know that I still have so many, even if it's hard to remember what they are. Then, as we stand to sing "Once in Royal David's City," a sudden, surprising thought occurs to me: *Could even this be a blessing?*

Next to me, Nick sings out lustily, as he always does. "*Where a mother laid her baby, in a manger for his bed. Mary was that mother mild, Jesus Christ her little child.*"

I think of Mary, gently laying her son in his makeshift cradle, having no idea what sorrows and grief were ahead of her. Yet would she have had regrets? Would she have chosen not to have him, if she'd been given the choice? Did she find joy in the sorrow, blessing within the curse? *Would I?*

Of course, I can hardly compare myself to Mary, yet I think of mothers everywhere—mothers who loved so hard, whose hearts were broken, who gave themselves again and again and sometimes—often—got nothing back. Would they regret loving their children, giving them all that they could, when they could? I don't think so.

Nick glances at me, and I realize I've stopped singing as the thoughts unfurl inside me. Could Emma dropping out of Harvard actually be a blessing? Could Josh's suspension? Could hard things get us to a good place, one where we didn't even know we needed to be?

"Ally…" Nick whispers, concerned, and I do my best to smile at him and then I start to sing.

Christmas has neither breakthroughs nor breakdowns, and I count that as a blessing. There are no heartfelt conversations, no terrible arguments. Josh smiles and says thanks when he opens the hoodie I got him for Christmas; while making dinner, Emma offers to do the gravy. Small things, but I treasure them in a way I wouldn't have before. I feel fragile, but I also feel strong. I have no idea what the next few weeks or months or years will bring.

By the time Beth brings Dylan back the day after Christmas, I have at least edged back from the brink. I open the door as soon as I see their car pull into the drive. Beth gets out slowly, but when she opens the back door, Dylan clambers out and barrels towards me.

I let out a startled but happy "oof" as his arms come around my waist. Then I look up at Beth and see how stricken she looks, before she clears her expression, and gently I pry Dylan off me.

"It's good to see you, Dylan."

"Good," he says, smiling at me. "Good."

Beth draws a hitched breath before turning to get Dylan's bag out of the car.

"Did you have a nice time?" I ask Dylan, and he hunches his shoulders before trying to hug me again.

"We did," Beth says as she comes towards me with his bag. She doesn't sound very convincing, though, and her face is drawn and pale, violet shadows under her eyes. I wonder what happened; or maybe it's what didn't happen.

I step out of the doorway and, seeing Emma, Dylan runs into the house without a backward glance for Beth.

"Do you want to come in?" I ask. "Stay for dinner?"

She peers into the hallway beyond me; Dylan has already disappeared. "No. Thanks though, but I should unpack. Do laundry."

They sound like flimsy excuses to me, but I can hardly force her. "Okay… if you're sure…" She nods. "Not too long till the court hearing, right?" I've already submitted my written statement about Dylan and his care, and so has Nick.

"A couple of weeks." Already she's edging back towards the car. "Not long at all."

She nods again, and then she waves, and she's back in her car before I can even say goodbye.

*

When Beth shows up the following Tuesday for her usual visit, Dylan and Josh are in the midst of building a Lego empire all over the family-room floor. I feel guilty, because I should have gotten him ready to go out, but he was enjoying himself so much and, amazingly, Josh was, too. The result, though, is that when Beth tells him they have to go, he has a meltdown of the kind I haven't seen in weeks.

"Dylan." She puts one hand on his arm and he shrugs it off almost violently, a look of fury on his face that makes Beth bite her lip.

"No," he says, and the firmness of the word surprises us both. "*No.*"

"You can do the Lego when you get back," I suggest. "Josh will wait for you."

Beth shoots me a savage look and I fall silent. She rises from where she was kneeling. "You can stay and finish, Dylan," she says quietly. "I'll watch."

She spends the entire two hours sitting on the sofa in silence, watching Dylan with a distant look on her face while he pays absolutely no attention to her. I'm not sure what to make of any of it, and I end up hovering in a way I'm sure annoys Beth, before I finally retreat to my office.

"It feels as if she's withdrawing from him," I tell Nick later, as we settle on the sofa after dinner. Dylan is in bed, Emma and Josh in their rooms. "Because he's withdrawing from her."

Nick shrugs and sips his wine. "I suppose that's a natural consequence of the situation. It will be better once he's back with her full-time."

"Yes…"

He turns to look at me. "You do think she'll be given back custody, don't you?"

"I hope so." As much as I've come to love having Dylan with us, I know it's best for him and for us—and of course for

Beth—for him to go back home. It's just over a week now till the court hearing, and I feel both anxious and eager for it. I want Dylan to be settled, and I want us to be able to move on as a family. I want Beth to have her son back, but I will miss him. Everything is a tangle of emotions, the feelings too close together to separate.

"Hey, I wanted to tell you something."

Both of us turn to see Emma standing in the kitchen, her hands deep in the pockets of her holey jeans. Nick puts down his wine glass as we both adopt that friendly, hyper-alert expression common to all parents when their teen announces they want to tell them something.

"Yes?" Nick says with raised eyebrows and a smile. "What's up, Emma?"

"I'm applying for a job at the music store on Park Avenue."

"Okay…"

"I didn't get the job at Subway, and I like this better. Also… I'm thinking of taking some music classes at Hart Music School. Piano and voice."

"Okay," Nick says again, looking a little flummoxed. Emma stopped piano lessons when she was twelve.

"It's just something I've been wanting to do," Emma says. "It might not come to anything."

"Not everything has to have a result," Nick says in his easy way. "You can just do something for the fun of it, Emma." She nods slowly, and I wonder if, in our ambition to get her into an Ivy League, she somehow forgot this. If we all did.

"That sounds great, Emma," I say, and she narrows her eyes, instantly suspicious.

"Because it's not McDonald's?" she jeers, and I try not to flinch.

"Because you're following an interest and you seem excited about it." I do my utmost to keep any edge from my voice, and after a second, seemingly appeased, Emma nods and slopes out of the room.

It's only when we hear the click of her bedroom door shutting that Nick turns to me. "Progress," he says, and I nod.

Yes, progress, even if in the smallest of weary increments. It still counts.

The next week passes in a flurry—Josh back to school, Emma getting an interview at the music store, Dylan's last CBT session, and Beth's visits, both of which go better than before, if only just. I can't keep from feeling that Beth has somehow mentally checked out; there is a distance to her demeanor and expression that makes me uneasy even as I do my best to dismiss it. I've become paranoid about everything; I know I need to relax.

The Tuesday of her last visit, the day before her court hearing, I ask if she wants a cup of tea after she brings Dylan back. It's a little after five, and dinner is in the slow-cooker; shadows are gathering outside and there's a crust of hard, icy snow on the ground, typical January weather.

Dylan has run off to find Josh, who has humored him more than usual lately, doing puzzles or playing with Lego, and Beth stands in the middle of the kitchen, seeming isolated and adrift.

"A cup of tea would be nice," she says, surprising me.

I put the kettle on the stove and take two cups out, while Beth simply stands there.

"Are you nervous about tomorrow?" I ask sympathetically, because of course she has to be. Mother on trial. I feel, in a way, as if I've been on trial, at least in my mind, these last few months, but Beth's situation is so much more nerve-wracking and real. "I'm sure it's going to go well, Beth. You've done everything you've been meant to, haven't you? The parenting course…"

"Triple P." She gives me a twisted sort of smile. "I'm the only one who completed it, actually."

"Are you?"

I frown, and she explains, "Angelica dropped out before Christmas. She's got a two-year-old and was pregnant—she must have had her baby by now. She's only sixteen, but she's decided to surrender both children to the state."

"Oh…"

"And the other parent in the course was Diane, who is in her forties, a single mom with an adopted son. She missed the last session and she's considering terminating her parental rights, too, although maybe not." She gives me a wry look. "Some company I'm keeping, eh?"

I'm not sure what to say, so I focus on making the tea. "I'm sure they had good reasons."

"Yes," Beth agrees after a moment. "They would have to, wouldn't they? Anyone would."

"What about the other things you've done?" I ask, deciding a change in subject might be best. "You were having counseling…?"

"Yes, that has been helpful." She looks away, and I decide it's too invasive to ask any more about that.

"And the observation sessions with Dylan? Those went okay?"

"They did what they were meant to, I think," she says after a pause, her voice flat.

I decide to drop my line of questioning. "Tea's ready," I say as cheerfully as I can, and I bring the cups to the table.

We sip in silence for a few minutes as shadows gather outside. From upstairs, I hear Josh say something and then Dylan laugh, and I smile at Beth, but she's not looking at me. I'm trying not to feel unduly concerned, but she seems incredibly preoccupied—but then she would, wouldn't she? The court hearing is tomorrow, after all.

"You love him," she says abruptly. "Don't you?"

Startled, it takes me a second to respond. "You mean Dylan? Yes. I mean… yes, we've all grown fond of him. Very fond." She nods slowly, and I can't tell if that was the answer she was looking for, but what else could I have said? Besides, I do love him. He's quirky and shy and wonderfully sweet. "We'll all miss him, of course," I add, but she doesn't seem to hear me.

"I should go," she says abruptly, standing up even though her tea is only half-drunk. "It's getting late."

"Oh… all right." I stand up, as well. "Do you want to say goodbye to Dylan?"

She glances up towards the ceiling, as if she can picture him in his room, playing with Josh, and then she shakes her head. "No, it's okay. He's busy. Happy."

"Anyway, you'll see him tomorrow," I say with conviction. "This time tomorrow he'll be back with you." Which gives me a pang of bittersweet sorrow. I really will miss him. We all will.

"Yes," Beth says, but she sounds unconvinced.

"Look, Beth…" I say as I see her to the door, "if you want me to… if it would help… I could come to the court hearing?" I'm not sure what makes me suggest it, only that she seems so alone. "Only if you want me to."

To my surprise, Beth nods rather vigorously. "Actually, Ally, that would be really great. If you don't mind."

"Of course I don't."

"Thanks." She smiles at me, and then, again to my surprise, she gives me a quick, clumsy hug. "Bye," she says, her voice choking a little, and she walks quickly out of the house, swallowed up by the wintry darkness.

That night as I'm tucking Dylan into bed, I wonder if I should say something to him about tomorrow. I haven't, because I don't want to make him anxious and nothing is certain, but it feels wrong to not say a word and have it all kick off so suddenly, so he's yanked from one home to another.

Yet as I've seen so often on the message boards, that's how it often works with foster care.

I don't say anything, but maybe he senses something anyway, or maybe Beth said something earlier, because it takes a lot longer for him to fall asleep. Finally, after about an hour of lullabies, he drops off, and I kiss his forehead before I creep out of the room. It feels so strange to think this is most likely the last night he will be in our home.

As we're getting ready for bed, I tell Nick about going to the hearing.

"That's nice of you, to offer the support." He smiles wryly. "I'm really going to miss the little guy, but it will be good to focus on our family again."

"I think Dylan has been good for our family," I protest as gently as I can. "I think he's helped both Emma and Josh." That evening, Josh gave Dylan a hug before he went to bed. It was just an arm quickly slung about his shoulders, but it made me smile. "Josh has played more Lego in the last few weeks than he ever did as a kid."

"I know Dylan has helped," Nick says. "I didn't mean it like that."

"I know." I sigh, not wanting to be prickly.

Nick pulls me into a hug. "I know you'll miss him," he says, and I nod, my throat suddenly tight with emotion. I really will.

The next morning, I wake up suddenly, as if someone has poked me. Nick is in the shower and, outside, the light looks pale and gray. It's a little before seven, but I have a sense of being late, of missing something.

And that's when it hits me. Beth isn't going to show up at the court hearing. The thought falls into my head as if from the sky, and lands with the solid thud of total certainty. Her distant demeanor, the way she hugged me goodbye, how she asked me if I loved him, even the mention of those other mothers who gave up their parental rights. It all makes sense now. Too much sense.

I scramble out of bed and race into the bathroom.

"She's not coming," I tell Nick and he pokes his head out of the shower.

"What?"

"Beth's not going to show up to the court hearing!"

He frowns. "She told you that?"

"No. I just know."

"Ally…"

"I *know*," I say, and then I rush back into the bedroom to get dressed.

CHAPTER THIRTY-ONE

BETH

So how do I get from a hopeful there to a dead-end here? From fighting tooth and nail, heart and soul, for my child, to being willing to give him up completely, without looking back, like the most heartless of mothers? I'm no better than Diane or Angelica or even the worst bleary-eyed, skinny-wristed druggie of a mother that I saw skulking around the Juvenile Court back in October.

It happened by increments, but it also happened all at once. A realization that crept in so slowly, and yet then seemed to emerge fully formed in both my head and heart, carved into my consciousness with painful letters. *He's better off without me.*

It hurts more than I can bear to think that, to *know* it, but it's an idea that started when Susan first took him away, and it is fully borne now, as I sit on my sofa, clutching a pillow to my chest, and watch the clock tick its minutes towards the court hearing I'm not going to show up for. Again. But this time I mean it.

So many things have led to this moment—Dylan's brushed hair, the sewn-up ear on his rabbit, the way he hugged Ally or held Emma's hand. The pure sound of his laughter as he played with Josh. All of them together presented a picture I couldn't ignore, an achingly beautiful picture that hurt me like no other and led me to realize with an inevitable sense of certainty: *He's better off without me.*

But more than any of that, so much more, was the realization I had when I received the psychiatrist's observations in the mail a week ago. I unfolded those typewritten sheets and realized that not only was Dylan better with Ally, but he was *worse* with me. Much worse than I'd ever even feared to think.

> *Dylan is a quiet child who is friendly but shy. However, when in the presence of his mother, he sometimes demonstrates serious signs of anxiety that I believe could stem in part from the intense and possibly unhelpful nature of their relationship.*

That one summing-up sentence felt like a fist to my gut, a knife to my heart.

I read on, dazed and reeling, as James the psychiatrist seemed to point the finger at me for just about everything Dylan had ever suffered from. His selective mutism was, according to James's theory, because I filled in his sentences, and I never let him talk. His fears emerged from my own, born, James seemed to think, from my lack of stability and abandonment by my parents, for his safety and well-being. His shyness was because I hovered incessantly. On and on it went, connecting the dots relentlessly. Everything was my fault, although he never said that in so many words. He certainly implied it.

And the worst thing about it was, as I read the evaluation, part of me wasn't even surprised. Part of me had been coming to this realization myself for the last three months, and having it so starkly there in black and white just confirmed what I'd been starting to both feel and fear. Dylan was better off without me. Better off with the Fieldings.

Every time I went over there, I saw it. Ally clearly loved him, Nick too. Emma and Josh would love a little brother, and Dylan would do so much better with siblings—a whole family, a beautiful house, a room of his own, toys, clothes, opportunities. Security and safety in a way I'd never been able to give him. It made so much sense, I knew I couldn't possibly resist it.

I also knew Ally wouldn't accept him like some sort of birthday present or consolation prize. I couldn't ask her to adopt my child, just like that. But if I didn't show up at the court hearing, she'd have him for at least another three months—three months where I wouldn't jump through any more damned hoops. By that time, I thought, all the Fieldings would be ready to consider adoption, and Dylan would be happy. So happy. He was already forgetting me; I saw it in the wary look on his face every time I went there. Even when we were together in New Hampshire, he seemed distant, as if he would have rather been somewhere else. He would have rather been with Ally. This was the best way for everyone… except me.

Sitting on the sofa in my pajamas as it turns eight o'clock the morning of the hearing—I'm meant to meet my attorney in half an hour—feels cowardly, like the worst kind of defeat, but I don't know what else to do. I want to call Susan and tell her I'm not just being a deadbeat, but that would defeat the purpose. If I tell her I want to give up my parental rights, Dylan would find out one day, and I can't stand the thought. Besides, I'm not brave enough to make that complete cut. This—a deliberate no-show—is about as much as I can take, and even it feels like too much.

It's been devastating, coming to this decision, and since Christmas, when I started to think properly about it, I've been walking around in a fog, as if I'm only half in this world. I've even been avoiding Mike, because I can't see the relationship—if that's even what we have—going anywhere now. What will he think of me, when he knows I've given away my own child? So I haven't answered his calls or responded to his texts since New Year's Eve, when he asked me to go some party and I said no, I was having an early night. He's stopped trying to be in touch in the last week, so I suppose he got the message.

Once again I'm completely alone, but I'm not going to feel sorry for myself. I chose this. It's no more than what I deserve. It's what Dylan deserves.

I clutch the pillow more tightly to my chest, just as someone hammers on the front door.

"Beth! Beth! I know you're in there."

I stiffen in shock, because it sounds like Ally, but it can't be. She's meant to be at court, and she doesn't even know where I live.

"*Beth!*" She's shrieking my name, and I hear Angela's door open upstairs.

"Is everything all right?" she calls down in her wavery voice, and I get up from the sofa.

When I open my door, Ally is on the landing, explaining to Angela that she needs to talk to me. Angela is, predictably, looking confused, but she brightens when she sees me.

"Beth! I was going to come see you today. You'll never guess what happened." I can't summon so much as a look of interest, but Angela continues on blithely regardless. "I received a letter from my daughter yesterday! She wants to see me again. Isn't that wonderful?"

For a second, Angela's obvious joy pierces my own numb despair. "That's great, Angela." I do my best to smile. "Really great."

Angela smiles and waves before going back inside, and I turn to Ally, my voice full of accusation.

"You're meant to be in court."

Her mouth drops open as she goggles at me. "*You're* the one meant to be in court."

I shake my head, both frustrated and furious that she's deviating from my plan. Since when has she ever thought to check up on me? "Why are you here? How do you even know where I live?"

"Dylan showed me."

"Dylan?" I crane my neck to see past her, hoping for one more glimpse of my boy. "Is he here?"

"Nick took him to school."

I deflate, and then I turn around and head back inside. Ally follows me.

"You don't have much time," she says briskly. "You're due at court at nine—"

"Eight-thirty," I say flatly. "It's too late, Ally."

"It's not," she retorts. "If you get dressed right now. I'll drive you, Beth. You can do this."

I shake my head slowly. "No."

Ally looks at me in bewildered exasperation. I know she doesn't understand at all; she thinks I'm just being the kind of deadbeat she suspected I was all along. "Why not?" she demands. "Beth, why on earth not?"

I didn't want to have this conversation, forced and difficult. I wanted Ally to take Dylan on naturally, to realize slowly and rightly that he belonged with her and her family. I never expected her to hunt me down.

"Beth." She sounds like a school teacher.

"He's better off with you."

She stares at me, blankly, as if I was speaking a foreign language. "What?" she finally says, shaking her head. "No."

"He's happier there. He loves you and your whole family—"

"Beth, this was only ever meant to be temporary."

"So you'd refuse to take him?" This was what I was afraid of. "You wouldn't adopt him?"

Ally sinks onto the sofa next to me, still shaking her head. "That's not the point."

"It is. You can't deny he's better with you, Ally. You're able to give him so much more than I can. Sometimes I think he already loves you more than he ever loved me."

"That is *not* true."

"Isn't it?"

"Where is this coming from?" Ally asks after a moment, still sounding bewildered. "Because all along you've been so determined to get him back, and that's the right choice, Beth. I know it is."

I don't want to explain about the psychiatric evaluation, and so I simply reach for the sheets of paper and hand them to her silently.

Ally scans them for a few seconds, her breath coming out in a quick, disbelieving exhale, before she shakes her head yet again. "This is—"

"The professional's opinion."

"Why," Ally asks as she puts the papers down, "do we so often blame mothers for their children's choices?"

"Dylan's behavior wasn't his choice."

"I know, but..." Ally sighs and then turns to me. "Look, Beth, we don't have a lot of time to hash this out. We needed to be leaving five minutes ago, so I'll just say this. Every mother in the world makes mistakes. And most mothers—you most definitely included—do the best they can. And that is all a child ever needs."

"Dylan's anxiety—"

"I don't care what some psychiatrist says. Were you responsible for some of Dylan's anxiety—"

"All of it—"

"He didn't even say all, but maybe you were. So what? That's the past. This is the present. You've changed. So has he."

"I haven't changed enough." I realize I am crying, tears trickling down my cheeks unchecked, a river of regret.

Ally grasps my hand. "You've changed enough to realize you needed to change. That's the important thing. All of this is a process. Things aren't going to fall into place the second you get Dylan back, and that's okay. You love him, and he loves you. I *know* he does."

"Still—"

"Let me remind you my daughter tried to kill herself. And my son got suspended from school for dealing drugs." I stare at her in surprise, because she neglected to mention that. "Sorry," Ally says, realizing her slip, "I should have told—"

"It doesn't matter now," I tell her, and I realize it doesn't. "I've seen how Josh is with Dylan. He loves him."

"Even so, I'm not exactly going to win Mother of the Year Award, am I?" She gives me a smile that tries to be wry but just looks sad. "But I'm *trying*. Trying to love and accept and not blame myself all the time. You should do the same. You *can* do the same. You need to, Beth."

I shake my head, the tears still trickling down my cheeks, my voice clogged. "I can't." I'm so scared that I can't. It's like a fog shrouding my mind, clouding any hope or determination I might have once felt. I *know* I can't. I'll fail. Again.

"You can," Ally insists. "And I'll help you. You don't have to do this alone anymore, Beth. We're friends, aren't we?" She looks at me determinedly as I simply stare. *Friends*? Really?

"Yes," I say after a few seconds. "I suppose."

"So let me help you, and you can help me. You already have, by telling me how important it is for a mother just to be there." She glances at her watch. "But if you don't show up to this court hearing, you risk losing any chance at trying, and I know you can't want that. Please, Beth, for Dylan's sake. For your sake. *Do* this."

I stare at her, her face full of compassion and determination and strength, her hand still holding mine, and a sudden terror jolts through me, as if I've stuck my finger in an electric socket and gotten the mother of all shocks. It's eight-fifteen.

"It's too late," I gasp the words out.

"No, it isn't. Get dressed, and I'll get the car. We can be there in ten minutes."

"Traffic—"

"Get *dressed*!" Ally barks, and I lurch up from the sofa, already at a loss.

Gently but firmly she steers me to the bedroom.

Three minutes later, I am in the passenger seat of Ally's car, wearing the same black shirt and white blouse I did for the first court hearing I missed. They're both crumpled, my hair is a mess, and I'm carrying my shoes, a brush, and a lipstick. My whole body is shaking.

I've barely shut the door before Ally zooms off, racing down my street at forty miles an hour. "Ally—"

"We are *not* going to be late."

"I'm so stupid," I mutter, because I can't believe I might have lost it all, and for what? I was feeling sorry for myself while pretending I wasn't. But despair is an invisible, insidious enemy; it clouds your thinking and obscures your judgment until the most ridiculous thing feels rational. I'd talked myself into a terrible corner, and I know now I want out. I'm so thankful Ally came to find me. *What if she hadn't?*

Because now that we're speeding towards Hartford, I know one thing. I want my son back.

"You're not stupid," Ally tells me fiercely. "You're strong and independent and you've *got* this. Now brush your hair."

I let out a hiccup of tremulous laughter and do as she says.

We pull up in front of the courtroom at eight thirty-two. Ally lets me out while she goes to park. There are three people in the security line, and my attorney, Lisa, is waiting on the other side as I practically stumble towards her. She smiles when she sees me; it's now eight-forty.

"I'm sorry I'm late," I half-mumble, trying to flatten my hair down in the back.

"It's fine," she says briskly. "We've got plenty of time."

I start to relax for what feels like the first time in weeks. Months. There are damp patches on the underarms of my blouse and my hair is still a little wild, but I'm here. I made it.

"So we'll be hearing from Dylan's caseworker as well as the Fieldings' written statements," Lisa explains. "And the judge will also look at the reports that have been filed from Dylan's teacher, his therapist, and his psychiatrist who did the evaluation."

"I'm not sure he liked me," I say, trying for some sort of smile, but I sound and feel near tears, especially when I think of that damned evaluation, of having any part of it read aloud.

Lisa puts a comforting hand on my arm. "This isn't about being liked or disliked. Everyone involved in this case wants to see you and Dylan reunited, Beth. Everyone."

"It hasn't always felt that way," I mumble, ducking my head, and Lisa squeezes my arm.

"I know."

As we head into the courtroom, I fight a sickening wave of terror that threatens to completely undo me. I feel like fainting, or throwing up, or running away. Maybe all three. I'm afraid of everything that is going to be said and heard, the judgments that need to be made as a *necessity*. The way people will look at me, and also the way they won't. I am, quite literally, on trial.

I'm afraid of getting Dylan back and having him hate me; I'm afraid of not getting him back and maybe even losing him forever. I'm afraid, so afraid, but I'm *here*, and as we take our seats, I see Ally hurry in and sit in the back. As I glance at her, she gives me a wide smile and a thumbs up. I smile back as hope—faint, fragile, precious—unfurls within me. Whoever would have thought it would be Ally, of all people, who got me here, who stayed by my side?

A few seconds later, the door opens for the judge to enter. Another wave of terror rolls through me as I stiffen my spine. I'm here to fight for my son, and I'm going to do it. I know it won't end here in this courtroom, that there will be many battles ahead of me. Battles for Dylan, battles with Dylan. Battles fought for love, to be the best mother I can, just as Ally is trying to be. I straighten my shoulders as the bailiff intones, "All rise."

EPILOGUE

BETH

Eighteen months later

"What about this one?" Mike calls, and holding Dylan's hand, I stroll towards him. It's a beautiful June day, warm but not hot, the sky a robin's-egg blue, the air sweet and drowsy.

"Maybe," I tell him as I peer in the dusty window. I glance down at Dylan with a smile. "What do you think, Dyl?"

He shrugs and looks at the empty storefront. "Maybe," he parrots me.

It's been a long, hard year and a half, since the judge listened to all my flaws and strengths, her face impassive, and then decided in my favor. Susan hugged me, and so did Ally. I cried, and tried not to, and then realized it didn't matter anymore. I wasn't on trial any longer.

That day in court, Dylan was returned to me. According to the law, I could have picked him up from school that afternoon and that would have been that. He never had to see the Fieldings again if I didn't want him to. We could have simply walked away from them all. Once, that is exactly what I would have wanted.

Fortunately, though, that's not the way it happened. Ally and I agreed to have a more gradual approach, for all our sakes. Dylan came home with me that night, but he spent many afternoons at the Fieldings', and he still does. Josh has been his Cubs leader since March.

As idyllic as all that sounds, it hasn't been easy. That first night, Dylan flailed and screamed for hours, and I could hardly blame him. I lay next to him as he hit his head against the floor and did my best to speak calmly, although I was in tears too. I was trying to be less emotional, less panicked, but it was so hard. I still felt alone, even though I knew I wasn't. Not anymore.

Slowly, so slowly, as the weeks and months passed, we began to find a new normal. Dylan continued at school, and with therapy, and so did I. We saw the Fieldings regularly, and I began dating Mike for real. I made friends in unexpected places; Diane got in touch with me. She decided to keep custody of Peter, and we've met up a few times, with the boys. I never heard from Angelica again. I've seen my mother a few times. I even wrote my father a letter, and he didn't respond, and that was okay. All of it has been progress, of one kind or another.

Dylan has started speaking more—not much, not yet, but enough. He has a friend in school named Jenna. She is autistic, and Larissa tells me they're pretty much inseparable.

And now we're here, on this beautiful June day in the center of Bloomfield, to look at potential retail spaces for Crafty Kids, the shop I'm hoping to open, with the help of a business loan—in part thanks to Nick—and also Ally's offer of doing my accounts for free. I can hardly believe it's even a glimmer of possibility, but it is.

"What do you think?" Ally calls as she, Nick, Josh, and Emma come down the street. We've agreed to meet in Bloomfield to look at possible spaces and then go out for a pizza.

"I'm not sure. It might be too small."

"But it might not," Ally says cheerfully. She's had her challenges this last year and a half, as well. About a year ago, Josh was suspended again, this time for drinking at school. Emma quit the job at the music shop and drifted for a while, depressed and aimless.

They've worked it out, though, as much as any of us can. Josh got his act together along with an afterschool job and Emma started counseling and has applied to Connecticut State, to study education. She starts in September.

All of it has made me realize that life isn't easy—not for me, not for Dylan, not for any of the Fieldings. No matter how charmed someone's life looks on the outside, on the inside everyone is messy and uncertain and afraid. Everyone needs help. Everyone holds possibility.

Ally brandishes the key she picked up from the real estate agent. "Shall we have a look?" she asks, her eyes alight, and with a smile for Mike, for Dylan, for everyone, I nod.

Ally unlocks the door of the empty shop and I breathe in dust and hope.

Still smiling, holding Dylan's hand, I step inside.

A LETTER FROM KATE

I want to say a huge thank you for choosing to read *When You Were Mine*. If you did enjoy it, and want to keep up to date with all my latest releases, just sign up at the following link. Your email address will never be shared and you can unsubscribe at any time.

www.bookouture.com/kate-hewitt

I have always loved exploring ideas around motherhood, and this is an especially rich and complicated issue when it comes to foster care. As I explored both Ally and Beth's lives and stories, I realized I could identify with them both—and I think most mothers probably can. Perhaps the most important part of this story for me is the hope at the ending. I really do believe even the most difficult and complicated situations can be redeemed.

I hope you loved *When You Were Mine* and if you did I would be very grateful if you could write a review. I'd love to hear what you think, and it makes such a difference helping new readers to discover one of my books for the first time.

I love hearing from my readers—you can get in touch on my Facebook page, through Goodreads or my website.

Thanks,
Kate Hewitt

 katehewittauthor

 @katehewitt1

 www.kate-hewitt.com

ACKNOWLEDGEMENTS

I needed a lot of research help with this book, in particular to make sure all the details about foster care and the laws surrounding it were as accurate as I could make them, and for that I am very thankful to my sister, Susie, and her experience as a foster mother. She fielded my many random questions, and also spoke freely of her own experience. Thanks, Suse!

I'm also grateful to the many sources of information and encouragement for both birth and foster families there are on the internet, as well as for the authors of the memoirs I read of foster parents, children, and birth parents. All of it helped to inform my experience and allowed me to write from both sides of the story.

As always, I am thankful to the fantastic team at Bookouture who work so hard for both me and my books. Thanks to Isobel, my lovely editor, and also Kim, Noelle, and Sarah in marketing and publicity; Alex H, Alex C, Leodora, Peta, Radhika, and many others whose time and talents invested in this book I'm not even aware of! You are all unfailingly great!

Thank you also to my readers who enjoy my books and let me know it! I love hearing from you, and you're the reason I keep writing. Thank you!

Lastly, thanks to my family, who are patient with my preoccupation with another world—the lives of Beth and Ally took over my mind for a good two months while my real family patiently waited. Thanks guys!